1

Ancient Lights

First published in the UK by STAR Distribution 2008

STAR Distribution,
Celestine,
Trendle Lane,
Bere Alston,
Devon,
PL20 7HT.

Printed and bound in Great Britain by
York Publishing Services.

FORWARD.

Patrick Moore is without question the most well known and well respected of amateur Astronomers within the United Kingdom. Patrick Moore has personally inspired countless numbers of people to take Astronomy as both a hobby and pastime, not to mention being the inspiration for people who have chosen to make Astronomy and many related sciences their life's work.

When Patrick made his first appearance on the BBC back in 1957 I doubt he could ever have imagined the profound influence he would have on so many people throughout his long career, though career is probably the wrong word because as Patrick would be the first to remind us, he has "not held one days employment in his life", this is because he has always worked for himself and been fortunate to have spent his all his life doing what he enjoys most, writing books and working within Astronomy.

During Patrick's earlier days he wrote many science fiction novels, including "Crater of fear" and "Destination Luna", these two books alone are now reaching in excess of £300.00 as collectors items.

In all Patrick has written over twenty four science fiction novels all of which are highly prized by collectors today.

This book "Ancient Lights" was written by Patrick Moore in 1947 but never saw the light of day, until now. Patrick says "The Moon came along" so it remained unpublished, resigned to the bottom draw of his desk.

When we visited him a while ago we asked why he had not had it published, he said "No one would be interested because there was no sex, violence or swearing in it". Well I beg to differ. We have read it and it is our personal privileged to see this book, so long overdue for reading by his admirers now in print.

It is our hope that the people reading this book, as we have, which was written so long ago, enjoy it as much as we have.

Thank you Patrick.
Jeremy, Simon, Stephen and David Rundle.

AUTHOR'S FOREWORD

This book is a period piece – and has absolutely nothing to do with astronomy! It was written in 1947, not long after the end of the war and I had taken off my R.A.F. uniform for the last time. It was my one attempt at a farce novel. I meant to submit it, but at that stage my life was taken over by the Moon, and everything else was wiped from my mind. "Ancient Lights" was put away in a drawer, and totally forgotten.

The typescript - the only one - somehow survived. Over sixty years later a friend who was staying with me stumbled across it, read it, laughed, and told me to submit it. I gently pointed out that it belonged to a bygone era; no f-words, no political message, no steamy sex scenes not a gay in sight, outdated 1947 expressions; also £100 was a veritable fortune in those days. Nobody would want to read it.

Or – would they? I don't know, but make up your own mind. It means going back to a world you almost certainly never knew, and by Page 2 you will know whether or not you want to go on. I will fully understand if you don't!

Patrick Moore.   June 2008

ANCIENT LIGHTS

Chapter 1

Charles, the waiter, rubbed his chin thoughtfully. In his forty years' service at that fashionable restaurant, the New Westminster, he had seen many harassed fancies ranging from the slightly worried countenance of the wretch unable to pay his bill to the bucolic despair of the elderly Anglo-Indian colonel served with an underdone chop: but never had he ever seen such a hunted-looking individual as the bulbous-eyed, fair-haired youth who was sitting at the far table, fiddling with his spectacles and crumbling bread in an overwrought manner. His resemblance to a worried goldfish was so marked that the waiter would not have been surprised had he ordered some poached ant's eggs. Still rubbing his own chin, Charles sought enlightenment from one of his fellow workers, a senile old buster named 'Erbert.

"Oo's the cod-faced geezer with the Hadam's apple, goggling at the door?", he demanded, jerking his thumb with the refinement of a delicacy natural to him.

'Erbert squinted.

"Table ten?"

"Yes."

"I know 'im," admitted 'Erbert grudgingly. "Davenhill, 'e calls 'imself – one of them nobs. Lives on the whacking' great hestate down in Sussex. Only comes 'ere once in a blue moon. Why?".

Charles shrugged. "Oh, I dunno. Looks like a proper stew, don't 'e? Bet you 'e'e on 's beam-ends. That sort always is."

"You've said it," agreed 'Erbert, who was a member of the Communist Party and believed in giving no quarter. "The time will come, me lad, when you and me will see the likes of 'im a-runnin' down Mayfair with an bowling mob at 'is 'eels. Meantime, get busy on the boiled crab at table seven – 'e 's getting' impatient."

It is doubtful whether Mr. Spencer ("Spennie") Davenhill that he had caught the eyes of Charles and 'Erbert, but he certainly would not have cared. As a matter of fact he was more or less past caring about anything except the non appearance of his friend, Mr. Roy Whittle, who had promised to join him at 1.15 and was already ten minutes late. Mr. Davenhill was by nature a tolerant person, and he knew that punctuality was not one of Mr. Whittle's virtues, but his train back to Wollingham Hall was due out of Victoria at two o'clock, and he had no desire to miss it. The next train – a slow - did not depart until five past six, and Mr. Davenhill had a special reason for wanting to be home before dark.

Frowning, he re-polished his glasses and stared intently out into the street. Then he gave a sudden jump, as though he had been poked with the sharp end of a bradawl, and uttered a soft exclamation of surprise.

"Fredl, "he muttered. "Dr. Fredl, of all the people. What the devil is he doing here?".

Anxiously he ducked his head, and opened a copy of the "Evening News" that he had just bought a few minutes earlier. When he looked up once more he was relieved to see that the doorway was clear except for a big, husky-looking young man with dark hair and shoulders like a prizefighter's, who was peering round the restaurant in a baffled manner.

Mr. Davenhill waved his hand and uttered a horse croak. The young man, having stared in all possible wrong directions, finally managed to locate the source of the noise, and threaded his way between the tables, a welcoming grin on his pleasantly ugly face.

"Wotcher, Spennie old lad," he began cheerfully. "You look like a corpse. What's the trouble?".

Mr. Davenhill looked at his watch.

"You're late," he said reproachfully.

"I know I am," admitted Mr. Whittle, without showing any obvious signs of contrition. "Actually, my dear old lad, you're damned lucky to get hold of me at all. I'm leaving for France tomorrow morning, and I haven't even started packing yet."

Mr. Davenhill repeated his imitation of a bullfrog calling to its mate, and clutched his friend by the arm.

"Good Lord, why?"

"Lightweight Championship of Europe. Marcel Popinot v. Gustav Leblocq. I've wangled myself a ringside ticket."

12

Mr. Davenhill heaved a sigh of relief.

"Thank goodness,", he said, passing a clammy hand across his brow and signalling to the nearest waiter. "I was afraid it might have been something important. Sit down, Roy, and let's have some lunch, I've only got half an hour, and there are several things I must tell you before you come down tomorrow."

Mr. Whittle did as he was bid, but he gave his friend an austere look in the process. He was fond of Spencer Davenhill, but even his friendship had its limits.

"Spennie, " he said coldly, "You're talking pure bread-sauce. I work here like nobody's business for fifty weeks in the year, and I'm damned if I'll miss seeing a perfectly good fight merely to come down and spend a social weekend at your infernal village. So you can put that in your pipe and – well, do what you like with it."

Mr. Davenhill gave vent to a hollow laugh. It was a horrid sound, and caused an elderly, white-bearded old coot at the next table to start so violently that he dropped half a rissole into his lap.

"Social weekend, eh? Roy, you don't understand. You can't leave me in the lurch now." Mr. Davenhill reached out and pawed his friend's cuff imploringly. "Ever since we were at school we've seen a lot of each other, and I've always felt you were the one person I could always turn to. When we were at St. Cuthbert's - "

Mr. Whittle made a terse, pithy remark about St Cuthbert's, and removed Mr. Davenhill's hand from his cuff. He then requested his friend to come to the point.

"It's all very well, " said Spennie unhappily. He paused while Charles the waiter placed two places of anaemic-looking soup on the table, and then continued: "I don't know what the devil you think. Look here, Roy, do you believe in black magic?.

"Eh?"

"Black magic. You know – spells, and witch-doctors, and things. Because I believe I've got a Roman curse on me."

Mr. Whittle looked alarmed.

"Take it easy, Spennie old lad," he said soothingly. "Don't worry about it. I expect you've got a touch of the sun."

"I have not got a touch of the sun." Mr. Davenhill rapped impatiently on the table, and upset a salt-cellar. "Don't look at me like that – I'm neither drunk or mad. Anyhow," he added inconsequently, "I don't see how I could have got a touch of the sun. It's been cloudy for weeks."

"I know," admitted Mr. Whittle. "Only a suggestion. What is all this guff about Romans and curses? Have you been -"

"I haven't been anything. If you you'll stop yapping for a couple of minutes, I'll tell you what's wrong." Mr. Davenhill adjusted his spectacles, and paused in order to marshal his facts. "You know Aunt Violet and Aunt Clara?"

"I do," said Mr. Whittle regretfully.

"Quite. Aunt Clara, as you know, is an archaeologist, and spends most of her time grubbing for fossils in various remote places like Egypt and Mesopotamia. Well -"

"Do archaeologists grub for fossils ?" murmured Mr. Whittle softly. "Strange, I thought they rooted about in old cities, and that sort of thing."

"Fossils or cities, it's all the same." Mr. Davenhill looked impatiently at his watch. "Damn it, I shall have to rush. As I was saying, Aunt Clara came back from Egypt about six weeks ago, and promptly happened upon an ancient Roman camp being underneath the waste land at the back of our old cricket field."

"Your land?" interrupted Mr. Whittle, keenly.

"Yes. I didn't see any harm in digging it up, so I gave her a free hand, and was jolly glad to have her fully occupied. She got a couple of her weird friends down from London – Professor Weatherill and an Austrian named Fredl – and the three of 'em kept at it from morn till night, as happy as sandboys. Aunt Violet didn't cotton on to the idea at first, but she soon came round, and things seemed to settle down quite nicely."

Mr. Whittle raised his eyebrows.

"Strikes me you're pretty lucky." he observed. "You've got hold of something to keep Aunt Clare quiet until she trots off on he travels again, and from what I know about her that's a damn good thing. Do you remember the salmon incident ?"

A spasm of pain contorted Mr. Davenhill's cod-like countenance.

"Don't. I'm trying to forget it. If the magistrate hadn't been old General Heron we should have been landed in the most frightful scandal, and Aunt Violet would never have let us hear the last of it. It was bad enough as it was. That wasn't all, though – did you hear what happened when the Bishop of Bexhill came down to confirm a batch of the local kids?"

Mr. Whittle looked interested.

"No. What?"

"Aunt Clara – oh, damn it, never mind that now." Mr. Davenhill mopped his forehead. "I wish you wouldn't keep going off on at tangents, Roy. About a fortnight after Aunt Clare and her precious cronies started excavating, they came across some very interesting things. The first that cropped up was a piece of parchment covered with what is evidently a code, joined on to a map that seams to be of the Old Hall - "

"Treasure Trove? The legendary Wollingham black pearls?".

"Might be. The story has been handed down in our family for generations, but I can't say I've ever put much faith in it. I'll tell you more about it tomorrow, though as a matter of fact you're probably as wise as I am. Aunt Clara's next discoveries were an inscribed tombstone and a particularly grisly skeleton. Have you ever heard of Quintus Maximus ?".

"I've never met him." admitted Mr. Whittle. "Still, I've got a shocking memory for names. Is he one of the locals?".

Mr. Davenhill tapped his foot on the floor.

"Don't be a doddle-pate. Quintus Maximus died close on two thousand years ago. He was one of the Roman generals who served under Claudius in the invasion of Britain, and is supposed to have been killed in the battle somewhere near Arundel. From what she can gather from the tombstone, and from various other things found near by, Aunt Clara seems pretty sure that the skeleton belongs to Quintus himself."

"Interesting," conceded Mr. Whittle. "Any clothes ?"

"Of course not. They'd have crumbled away centuries ago. Aunt Clara carted the beastly skeleton up to the house – she's turned the old armoury at the back of the East Wing into a regular museum – and put it with her old specimens. Well, I don't mind that particularly, but almost at once all sorts of peculiar things began to happen."

"Such as -?"

Mr. Davenhill pondered.

"The first," he said, "was that Lily, one of the housemaids, tripped over a mat and fractured her wrist,. Then something went wrong with the central heating, and when Stoker went to investigate, the big radiator in the lounge started squirting water and wouldn't stop – it completely ruined the carpet. Then all the bells started to ring – not only the indoor bells, but even the telephones. I disconnected the one in my study after a bit. Then Terry -"

"Terry?" Mr. Whittle looked surprised. "I thought he'd been called up. He's eighteen, isn't he?"

"He's nineteen, I do wish you wouldn't butt in," said Mr. Davenhill plaintively. "As I was saying, Terry had the most fearsome row with old Dr. Fredl, and the atmosphere has been unbearable ever since. We've all been on edge except Aunt Clara, who wouldn't care anyway. All that wasn't so bad, but then odd things stared happening to me. Twice I woke up feeling certain that there was somebody prowling about my room – in fact I know there was, because the second time I found a Roman coin on the floor, and it certainly hadn't been there when I went to bed. The whole house seems creepy. I can't explain properly, but you're bound to see what I mean as soon as you arrive. There's another thing too. I went for a stroll late yesterday evening, and on my way back I passed the cricket field - and saw a ball of light floating about just where the excavations are going on. It wasn't a bit like a torch – more like a lantern, but fainter. It gave me the loo-loos." Mr. Davenhill shivered. "I ran towards it, and it promptly went out. When I go to the camp there was absolutely nothing to be seen – I'd got my own torch, of course and I was just going to get back to the house when I heard the most awful laugh." Mr. Davenhill broke off, and gulped at his soup. "I can't possibly describe it. It seamed to go through and through me. It was like – like"

"Like somebody laughing?" suggested Mr. Whittle helpfully.

"It didn't sound like a human being." Mr. Davenhill again mopped his brow. "I don't mind telling you I bolted for it. I can

16

face most things if you can see them, but this was different."

Mr. Whittle frowned thoughtfully.

"You're sure it wasn't a bird?"

"Of course I'm sure it wasn't a bird. It was nothing like a bird.

"A bat then?"

"Certainly not."

"In which case, " said Mr. Whittle slowly, "there are only two possible explanations. Either you imagined the whole thing, or someone is trying to scare the pants off you. Are these archaeological ducks likely to indulge in practical jokes?"

In spite of himself, a wan smile crossed Mr. Davenhill's careworn face.

"I should say not! Weatherill must be at least seventy in the shade – a dried up old beaver who never smiles, let alone laughs. As for Fredl – well, you can judge for yourself when you meet him, but I tell you here and now he simply isn't the type. Of course, there are Strudwick and the two girls, not to mention young Terry, but I can't see any of them playing fool tricks of this kind."

"Girls?" echoed Mr. Whittle, with a sudden show of interest. "What girls ?"

"Pauline Wrightman, old Weatherill's secretary, and some relation of Fredl's who calls herself Carole Czernak. Still, as I say, they don't come into it. This wasn't a girl's laugh." Mr. Davenhill started as a nearby clock chimed a quarter to two. "Good Lord, Roy, I must be making a move, or I'll miss my train. What time will you arrive tomorrow?"

Mr. Whittle felt that it was time to clear the air.

"I'm not coming tomorrow, " he said gently. "Spennie, my lad, I love you like a brother, but neither you nor I nor all the spooks in the home counties are going to do me out of that fight. I'm due back at work on Monday week, and this is my only chance."

Mr. Davenhill blanched, and allowed his jaw to sag foolishly.

"You don't mean you're letting me down?"

"I do."

17

"But you can't", wailed Mr. Davenhill piteously. "Roy, there's something badly wrong at Wollingham, and I don't know what to do about it. I never was a practical man," he added, unnecessarily. "You've always been a tough sort of person, and this is just your line."

"Sorry, no." Mr. Whittle shook his head firmly.

There was a brief pause, during which Mr. Davenhill revved up the wheels of his brain and thought furiously.

"Roy" he said at length.

"Yes, old lad?"

"Carole's a damned attractive girl."

"Oh?" said Mr. Whittle casually, doing his best to look bored.

"Yes. Young, too – can't be more than twenty." A dreamy look came into Mr. Davenhill's eyes. "Auburn hair – brown eyes – lovely figure – accommodating nature -"

"Are you trying to dangle this wench in front of my eyes?" demanded Mr. Whittle resentfully, with an inward feeling that his iron resolution was being subtly undermined.

"I don't have to," retorted Mr. Davenhill blandly. "From what I know of Carole, she'll do all the dangling that is necessary." He rose. "Well, Roy, what about it? Are you on, or are you going to leave me flat?"

"Blast you" said Mr Whittle with some vehemence." "I'm on."

"Good. Telephone when to expect you, and I'll see there's a car to meet you – otherwise you'll have to walk. And now," said Mr. Davenhill, "I really must rush. Good-bye, old lad – see you tomorrow." With which he opened his throttle, let in his clutch, and made a hasty exit.

Left to himself, Mr. Whittle lit a cigarette and allowed his eyes to wander idly around the restaurant. Spennie, he reflected, was really something pre-eminent in the way of doddle-pates; good type though he was, he was fundamentally incapable of handling any situation that had got even remotely out of control. At the same time he was not in any way imaginative, and Mr. Whittle felt that there was a good chance of the next few days being mildly exciting. He hoped so. Four years in the R.A.F had

18

not fitted him for a solicitor's office, and nowadays he found life very dull.

Besides, Carole Czernak sounded interesting, and Mr. Whittle himself could hardly have been described as a modest violet.

Chapter 2

Mr. Whittle grunted, and opened his eyes. He had been asleep for some time, and the train carriage seemed hot and oppressive; fortunately it was not crowded – in fact there was only one other occupant, a swarthy, black bearded duck with pince-nez spectacles and a sinister scar upon his forehead. Mr. Whittle decided that a cigarette would be in order. He therefore produced his case, and selected one.

"Nein." said the black bearded gentleman, suddenly.

Mr. Whittle lit up, and exhaled a cloud of smoke. It was only then that he realised he was being addressed, and looked up in surprise.

"Hello?" he inquired.

The black bearded gentleman adjusted his pince-nez, and spoke in a thick voice that indicated his Teutonic origin as clearly as if he had written the word "Hun" on a placard and strung it around his neck.

"It is vorboten," he said pompously, "in the train the cigarette to smoke. On the window he is write." He gestured towards the 'No smoking' sign. I to you demand that you put-out, nein?".

"Nein," agreed Mr. Whittle, eyeing his fellow passenger with dislike.

Blackbeard waved his fists, and and showed every symptom on an imminent explosion. He coughed, and uttered a string of rude sounding words in German.

"Take it easy, old cock," urged Mr. Whittle soothingly. "Count ten before you speak. Remember your blood-pressure."

Blackbeard snorted.

"Young man -" he began.

"One moment," interrupted Mr. Whittle. "For your future reference, My name is Whittle – Roy Stanford Alistair St. John Whittle – and not 'young man'. Being addressed as 'young man' makes me annoyed, and if I get really annoyed I am very apt to hand out pokes on the snoddle. Savvy?."

There was a short pause. Mr. Whittle yawned and lay back

in his seat, wondering vaguely what time he would arrive at Wollingham. The train was scheduled to get in at 3:30, but it was now ten to four and they had not even reached Upper Spottlebury; that meant another twenty minutes' journey at least. Still, even if Spennie's car did not wait, he ought to be at the Hall in time for tea.

"You this cigarette to extinguish decline, yes?" demanded the black-bearded gentleman abruptly.

Mr. Whittle opened one eye.

"Go fly a kite," he requested, aware that he was being thoroughly ill mannered, and revealing in the fact. He was not naturally a boor, but he had no love for Central Europeans of any kind.

"Very well. You of this will hear more." Blackbeard fumbled in his waist coat pocket, and produced a notebook and pencil. "Herr Whittle, it is not?"

Mr. Whittle left forward, and tapped his companion meaningly on the knee.

"I cannot tell a lie," he said virtuously. "My name is not Whittle. It is – he paused - "William Shakespeare."

Blackbeard made a quick note of this in his book.

"The address?" he inquired.

Mr. Whittle thought hard.

"Hathaway Cottage, Stratford-on-Avon," he said solemnly, wishing that he could remember the right county and wondering whether to take a sporting chance on Worcestershire. "My telephone number, in case you want it, is Stratford 999. Anything else I can do for you ?"

Blackbeard made no reply, but shut his notebook with a snap and retreated to the far corner of the compartment, glaring at Roy with unconcealed malevolence. A minute or so later the train shuddered and came to an untidy halt; whistles sounded nearby, and a raucous voice proclaimed "Spottlebury! Upper Spottlebury!" Blackbeard jumped up, grabbed his suitcase and made for the door as though he had just discovered that the coach was on fire. Pausing only to direct a final glance at Roy as he leaped agilely on to the platform, his voice could be heard shouting for a porter.

Mr. Whittle thought quickly. It seemed probable that

21

Blackbeard was out to create trouble, and the delay now would be irritating in the extreme; on the other hand it would be even more irritating to leave the train – Mr. Whittle had bitter experience of the Sussex railway service, and he had no desire to spend an indefinite number of hours kicking up his heels in Upper Spottlebury. Peering out of the window he saw Blackbeard was talking in an animated fashion to a porter, waving his arms and pointing in the direction of the carriage; presently the two started to march purposefully down the platform, and Mr. Whittle hesitated no longer. Short of making a graceful exit through the opposite window, there was only one possible course of action. Thrusting his case under one seat he crawled rapidly under the other, repressing an overwhelming desire to sneeze as he inhaled a lungful of pure Essex dust. After what seemed centuries the door opened, and Blackbeards voice was heard.

"... and he to me tell I am to go and fly a kite," he was saying. "I am – Blitzen, he is gone!".

"Was this the right carriage, sir?" demanded a slow country voice.

Blackbeard wrapped the floor with his stick.

"But yes. With no doubt, he is the carriage. The man he has perhaps up the platform gone?"

"Nobody's a-got off exceptin' you, sir," replied the country voice. "Are you sure there really was another gentleman? Seems funny, like."

"Dummkopf!" Blackbeard's feet sailed in to Mr. Whittle's view, executing some complicated dance-steps that would have made Fred Astaire green with envy. "You think that I to him imagine?"

The country voice made no immediate reply. Mr. Whittle extracted a dead spider from his left nostril, and silently consigned both Blackbeard and the porter to the deepest recesses of hell.

"Well, there's nobody 'ere now," observed the porter finally. "Are you getting' off, sir? We can't hold up the train any longer – we're behind time as it is."

Blackbeard gave an ungracious grunt.

"It is the outrage," he commented, replacing his case in the rack and sitting down once more. "Very well. I to Wollingham go.

It is that you may depart."

Silence ensued, and after a further pause the train jerked into motion once more. Mr. Whittle waited a moment or two and then emerged, brushing himself ruefully. Then he cleared his throat. Blackbeard, who had been staring fixedly out of the window, uttered a sharp bark and spun round.

"Donner and blitzen!" he spat. "It is you, nein?"

Mr. Whittle assumed a pious expression.

"I do not think we have met," he said primly. "I joined the train at Upper Spottlebury. My name" he added, "is Shelmerdine – The Reverend Matthew Shelmerdine. I am present on holiday, hence the absence of ecclesiastical attire. Perhaps you are confusing me with someone else?"

Blackbeard chewed his moustache, and thought this one over. At length he seemed to decide upon a watching brief, and relapsed in to moody silence, still gnawing his face-fungus and eyeing Roy as though looking at a particularly offensive drain. No further conversation took place until the train halted once more. Mr. Whittle collected his case, and alighted.

"One moment, sir," he said in his carefully-cultivated clerical accent, seeing that Blackbeard was about to follow. "Did I understand you to say you were destined for Wollingham?"

Blackbeard grunted. "That is so."

"This," Mr. Whittle informed him untruthfully, "is Much-Binding-in-the-Marsh. Wollingham is the next station. Good afternoon!"

He went on his way, hoping for the best. Luckily his judgement was not at fault. Wollingham station consisted of one shaky platform, not named in any way; and the only porter was far too sleepy and decrepit to have announced the identity of the station in a reasonably audible voice, even if he had wanted to. With inward satisfaction Mr. Whittle watched the train move out, Blackbeard still on board, and gave vent to a sharp bark of laughter. If memory served him correctly the next station was Chipwood Magna – a matter of six miles or so along the line.

Evidently the taxi had called it a day and gone home, for the station yard was empty; and Mr. Whittle was resigning himself to a three mile walk when there was the welcome sound of an engine, and a trim Austin saloon appeared round the bend. The driver, a youngish man with a receding chin and a small but vaguely offensive moustache, leant out of the window and gave tongue in a reedy treble.

"Mr. Whittle?"

"That's me," agreed Roy, reflecting that the Wollingham taxi agency had been reduced to employing some pretty feeble-looking specimens. "Can I put the case in the back?"

"By all means," assented the driver pleasantly. "Stick it on the seat. You'd better come in front with me, I think – the back springs aren't too good."

Mr. Whittle obeyed the instructions, and climbed in. The driver looked at his watch, and nodded with satisfaction.

"We'll be in time for tea," he said briskly, engaging the gears with a shuddering crash and letting the clutch out with a jerk. "Davenhill said he'd wait for us. These country trains are the deuce, aren't they? By the way, I expect you know who I am – Strudwick, Raymond Strudwick. I'm the local M.P."

"Of course," said Mr. Whittle hastily, thanking his lucky stars that his earlier mistake had not caused him to drop any major bricks.

"Conservative, of course," amplified Mr. Strudwick. "Don't go thinking I'm one of those Socialist agitators – ha, ha! Not that idealistic Socialism is fundamentally bad," he continued, "but in this country we have not yet the machinery for even attempting a drastic reformation of social life. By the end of the next decade, of course-"

Mr. Whittle sighed. He had already formed a low opinion of his companion, and it was obvious that unless he took prompt action he was in for a lengthy political lecture.

"Have there been any more of those accidents up at the Hall?" he demanded, ruthlessly cutting across Mr. Strudwick's speech.

"Accidents?" The M.P looked puzzled. "Oh, the housemaid and the butler, you mean? Oddly enough, I myself experienced a painful fall this morning, and gave my knee a severe graze. This continual run of bad luck is most annoying. Poor Davenhill is most disturbed- unnecessarily so, in my opinion."

"Do you think it is entirely luck?" Mr. Whittle lit a cigarette and passed over the case. "Spennie seems to have other ideas."

Mr. Strudwick laughed easily, showing a row of teeth that were rather too white and regular to be genuine.

"Oh you mean Weatherill's story about the curse?" he said, twisting the wheel in order to skirt around a solitary sheep that was standing helplessly by the roadside. "Poor old fellow, this mystical business has got a thorough hold on him. He's brilliant in his own line, of course, but he must be past his prime now, and I strongly suspect him of socialistic tendencies. In fact -"

"What is the story?" asked Mr. Whittle firmly.

The M.P blinked

"Oh, it's a lot of far fetched rigmarole," he said vaguely. "Can't remember the details – something about this fellow Quintus Maximus laying a solemn curse upon anybody who disturbed his bones. Quite ridiculous, of course, and I don't suppose for a moment that this skeleton Mrs. Debenham dug up has anything to do with Maximus. My own knowledge of archaeology is slight, but I find it hard to believe that anybody that has been buried for close on two thousand years can be identified with certainty."

Mr. Whittle looked thoughtful. It was not his habit to jump to conclusions, but he was the reverse of credulous, and to him the whole affair had a strong odour of bad fish. He decided to find out what he could about the other occupants of the house.

"Did somebody tell me that young Terry's finished his time in the Army?" he asked casually.

Mr. Strudwick gave vent to an annoyed grunt.

"He has, the impertinent young cub. I am a tolerant man," he went on, with a palpable lack of accuracy, "but there are limits to broad-mindedness, and that boy oversteps them. He calls himself a Communist, of all things."

"A Communist?" repeated Mr. Whittle, with some amusement.

"Yes." The M.P nodded moodily. "Mind you, I believe in young people forming their own opinions – that's where the Conservative party differ so markedly from the Socialists – but nothing can excuse pure bad manners. You will hardly credit this

– but yesterday evening, after I had reproved him for his rudeness, he actually threatened me with physical violence."

Mr. Whittle stifled a bark of laughter.

"Did he, by Jove? What did he threaten to do?"

"A poke on the snoddle was the actual expression he used. Of course, I merely turned on my heel and left him." Mr. Strudwick looked down his nose, and compressed his lips in to a thin line. "I had no intention of allowing myself to be drawn in to an undignified scuffle, and in any case brute force is not the correct way of dealing with adolescents."

Mr. Whittle nodded sympathetically.

"Young Terry's a hefty kid, too," he observed. "Boxed for his school, didn't he?"

Rightly or wrongly Mr. Strudwick appeared to take exception to this well-meant remark, and for some minutes there was silence apart from the usual rending crash as he changed down in order to negotiate the steep hill separating Wollingham village from Weeple Wimbhurst. Mr. Whittle pulled at his cigarette, and thought hard. It was east to tell that there were some strong undercurrents at the Hall, and as yet he had not even broached the subject of Aunt Clara. He decided to do so without delay.

"How is Miss Debenham?" he asked.

Mr. Strudwick gave his companion a glance.

"Very well, I believe. I see little of her."

"Still causing chaos and destruction wherever she goes?" persisted Mr. Whittle, chattily. "Whenever she comes to England she seems to take a fiendish delight in collecting all the most weird and wonderful people in the home counties, and dumping them on poor old Spennie. Aunt Violet's collection of senile wrecks is almost worse. I'm damned if I know how Spennie puts up with the two of them."

"I myself," said Mr. Strudwick icily, "came to Wollingham Hall at the invitation of Mrs. Violet Fane."

Mr. Whittle retired into his shell, conscious the he and the M.P were by no means kindred spirits. For the time being he made no further effort at polite conversation, and as his companion had lapsed into wounded silence he had plenty of opportunity to take stock of his surroundings.

It was some time now since he had been to Wollingham – his work had taken him north, and his office was situated in the middle of Manchester – and he gazed out at the pleasant Sussex countryside with marked anticipation. Wollingham and it's neighbour, Weeple Wimbhurst, were typical Home Counties villages, sleepy, picturesque, and apparently unaffected by the passage of time. In the distance Mr. Whittle could see the silhouette of Weeple Keep, a ruined castle reputed to have been built by the Romans, while Wollingham Hall itself, perched high upon the hill, was coming into view ahead. Suddenly he sat up, and peered intensely. Either the fading light was playing him false, or there was definite activity going on between the main road and the Hall.

His first reaction was to seek enlightenment from Mr. Strudwick, but a wary glance showed him that the M.P was still in no amiable mood; his lips were tightly pursed, while his eyes were cold and hard like those of a dead halibut. Mr. Whittle shuddered slightly and turned back to the window. No doubt about it; something unusual was happening, and a few moments' concentration gave him a probable solution. The whole area was covered with little ditches and mounds, while ant-like figures pottered about carrying loads of earth from place to place; wheelbarrows were much in evidence, while to one side was a rough shed, near which three people were engaged in earnest conversation. Mr. Whittle's thoughts turned automatically to Aunt Clara. Everything indicated that the old trout had got the bit firmly between her teeth and was hard at work, doubtless accompanied by Dr. Fredl, Professor Weatherill and the rest of the archaeological gang.

Mr. Whittle gave a suppressed snort of mirth. He was essentially a practical man, and it was his opinion that a woman who spent all her days and most of her nights grovelling about unearthing bits of pottery and rusted coins could only be classed as a pre- eminent doddle-pate. However, he supposed that there was no accounting for tastes. He closed his eyes and lay back in his seat, content to let matters take their course; and in due time Mr. Strudwick pulled up the Austin with a final jerk outside the door of Wollingham Hall.

27

Chapter 3

Mr. Whittle collected his case, and leaving the M.P, to garage the Austin, pottered up the stone steps and rang the bell. While waiting for the appearance of Stoker, the aged butler, he let his eyes rove idly around. The general scene was by no means unpleasing. Wollingham Hall itself was built on massive lines; part of it dated from good old Elizabethan days when no wall was considered adequate unless a full yard thick and bathrooms were looked upon as unnecessary luxuries, but most of it had been modernised and reconstructed by Spennie"s great grandfather – a bearded old buffer whose portrait now disfigured one complete panel of the billiard room. This in itself was all very well, but, carried away by his enthusiasm he had gone too far, and thrown in a series of hideous glass conservatories that protruded from one side of the house like unsightly growths. Mr. Whittle winced slightly as his eye slighted on them. He remembered them well, but he had never wholly conquered his desire to fall upon them with a mallet and start smashing.

After a long interval the front door swung open, and Stoker stood in the entrance, staid and dignified as ever, but with a large bandage bound across his forehead, Mr. Whittle blinked owlishly.

"What-ho, old lad," he said in cordial tones, for the butler was an old acquaintance. "How's the arthritis?"

Stoker stared balefully with his one visible eye.

"Arthritis, sir, is the last of my troubles," he admitted, collecting the suitcase and ushering Mr. Whittle into the hall. "Very pleased to see you once more, sir, if I may take the liberty of saying so. I only hope that you will come to no harm during your visit."

"Harm?" echoed Mr. Whittle, wondering whether the strain of recent events had unhinged the old butler's mind. "I don't follow your drift."

"You will, Mr. Roy," Stoker assured him in a tone of sombre satisfaction. "A curse has been placed upon us. We walk in fear and dread, never knowing who will be next to suffer."

Mr. Whittle suppressed a bark of mirth.

"Stoker, old lad," he said kindly, "you're talking pure, unadulterated, bread-sauce. What you want is a good tonic. Your liver's out of order, I expect."

The butler looked offended.

"I am not subject to internal disorders, sir," he said in an austere tone, "except, of course, if I am unwise enough to consume starchy foods. In any case, I do not consider my liver capable of ringing bells or deranging hot water systems."

Mr. Whittle was somewhat baffled by this remark, but before he could question Stoker further a newcomer appeared at the far end of the hall – a trim, competent – looking girl, with black hair and shrewd grey eyes. Mr. Whittle pricked up his ears. This, he reasoned, must be either Pauline Wrightman or Carole Czernak, and he was prepared to bet heavily upon the former. He decided to take a chance.

"Lo there, Paul," he said brightly.

The girl looked puzzled.

"Paul?" she echoed, while Mr. Whittle chuckled softly. "I – I'm afraid you must be making a mistake."

"I never make mistakes" Mr. Whittle informed her modestly. "You're Pauline Wrightman, aren't you?"

"Yes, but -"

"No buts about it. Remember you're talking to a budding solicitor." Mr. Whittle offered his hand. "My name, as you probably already know, is Whittle – Roy Stanford Alistair St. John Whittle. Stoker here will back me up. Won't you, old lad?" he added to the aged retainer, who was standing nearby radiating disapproval.

"Whittle," repeated the girl thoughtfully. "Yes, I remember Mr. Davenhill saying that somebody of that name was coming down. Are you another archaeologist?"

Mr. Whittle snorted.

"I am not, my dear Paul. Don't say that sort of thing, even in fun. I may not be a genius, but at least I've too much common sense to waste my life grubbing about in holes looking for mummies. I can think of better things to do, can't you?"

"Plenty," Agreed Miss Wrightman placidly. "One of them, Mr. Whittle, is to stop calling me 'Paul'. For some reason, it jars

29

me. Do you mind?"

"I do," admitted Roy, "but I'll grin and bear it. Does that mean you've taken one of those instant dislikes to me?"

"Not at all. I'm far too busy to waste my time taking dislikes to anybody."

Mr. Whittle raised his eyebrows. He decided he liked this girl.

"You are, are you?"

"I am."

"We must do something about that. Can't have you working your fingers to the bone, you know." He turned to Stoker, who had coughed. "Swallowed a fly, old lad?"

"No, Mr. Roy. I was merely endeavouring to attract your attention," replied the butler frigidly. "You will be in the Green Room, sir. I will go and inform Mr. Spencer of your arrival".

"Do. Note that", said Mr. Whittle, over his shoulder. "Stoker says I'm sleeping in the Green Room. File that for future reference."

"I've quite enough to file, thank you, without bothering about information that doesn't concern me," Pauline said dangerously. "Moreover, Mr. Whittle, I'm busy. Good afternoon."

"Toodle-oo," murmured Roy, as the trim figure disappeared through the library door. "Damned nice girl that, Stoker. And when I say 'nice' ."

"So I gathered sir," agreed the aged butler, letting in his clutch with extreme caution and moving off in the direction of the stairs. "No doubt Mr. Spencer will be with you immediately."

Left to himself, Mr. Whittle pottered about examining things. The main hall at Wollingham was more in the nature of a long room; occasional tables and ornamental vases littered the place up, as well as two immense grandfather clocks, a stuffed stag, and the inevitable ancestor. Mr. Whittle peered at the latter closely, although he had seen it many times before. Most of the dead and gone Davenhills bore a strong family likeness to Medusa, but this particular one was a welcome exception; a woman's face smiled down from the wall – a face of quite remarkable beauty, painted with superlative skill. Mr. Whittle was conscious of feeling regret that he had been born three and a half centuries too late.

"Thank God you've arrived at last." said a voice, and Spencer Davenhill limped downstairs, looking thoroughly used-up and with his left wrist encased in plaster. "I was beginning to think something frightful had happened to you on the way. This situation is getting completely out of control."

"So I gather. The place looks more like and ancient depot than a country house. What have you been doing – indulging in a free fight ?"

Mr. Davenhill passed a hand over his brow.

"I wish it was as easy as that," he said. "Honestly, I feel all in. Things were bad enough yesterday, but today has been a long nightmare, ever since this morning."

"Rather Irish, but I see what you mean" murmured Mr. Whittle. "Pull yourself together, old lad, and explain. To begin with, how did you get that wrist ?"

"I fell downstairs. One of the rods was loose."

"Didn't you see it?"

"Would I have fallen over it, if I'd seen it?"

"Depends on when you saw it."

"Well, I didn't see it until it was too late. Damn!: Listen to that!"

Mr. Whittle obliged. "Sounds like the telephone," he ventured, cautiously.

"It is."

"Well, what of it?" Mr. Whittle asked, in a baffled tone. "It sounds like a perfectly ordinary ring to me. Do you expect it to play the Blue Danube?"

"Of course I don't, but if we go and answer it the exchange will say they don't want us. If I've answered the 'phone once today I've answered it a dozen times, and it's always the same."

"Do you think the wires are faulting somewhere?"

"It isn't only the telephone, "retorted Mr. Davenhill despondently. "All the bells have been going off at intervals ever since Aunt Clara dug up that infernal skeleton. Weatherill keeps on babbling about disturbed vibrations, whatever they may be."

"Does he? To me." said Mr. Whittle frankly, it sounds brimming dish full of bread-sauce. In fact, it positively reeks.

Incidentally, where are the grub-hunters?"

"Weatherill and Aunt Clara are down on the camp. They spend all day there, and half the night as well. Fredl's up in London again – I expect him back to tea, but something must have held him up." Mr. Davenhill led the way in to the dining-room. "It's the wrong time really, but would you like a drink?"

"Have you ever known me to refuse a drink ?"

"No." Spennie produced a bottle of fine old whisky, and poured out two generous bracers. "I've always thought one of your ancestors must have had illicit relations with a sponge. Well, cheers!"

"Cheers," echoed Mr. Whittle, tossing off his whisky at a single gulp and passing over the glass for a refill. "Now then, Spennie, tell me the worst, omitting no detail, however trivial. As a start, have you seen any more of your pet spook ?".

Mr. Davenhill shuddered.

"No, but only because I've taken damn good care to keep away from the camp after dark. I still go prickly all over when I think about it. When I got home yesterday I found the fire engine here; one of the sheds at the back of the house had gone up in smoke for no apparent reason, and very nearly set fire to the kitchen quarters. Soon after we'd finished with that the gardener's boy fell off a ladder- or, rather, it gave way under him – and we had to send for the doctor in a hurry. This was about five thirty. Then we had a short interval of calm before dinner, apart of course for the incessant bell ringing."

"Peace, perfect peace," murmured Mr. Whittle.

"Quite. Damn it, there's the 'phone again. I expect Stoker'll see to it, but there won't be anybody calling." Mr. Davenhill refilled the glasses with a shaking hand. "After dinner there was a frightful row between Strudwick and young Terry, and Terry threatened to bash him in the clock."

"Poke him in the snoddle," Mr. Whittle corrected him.

Spennie looked surprised.

"How do you know? Have you seen Terry, then?"

"No. My informant was Strudwick himself. Candidly he strikes me as being a Grade A wet lettuce, and my sympathies are with our lusty young soldier. Going off at a tangent for a moment, where exactly does this Strudwick bird come in ?"

Mr. Davenhill shrugged.

"One of Aunt Violet's friends. She's been elected to the Rural District Council, and talks Politics, Politics, Politics from morning till night – we all get sick to death of it, even Terry. I don't want to say anything against her, of course, but I'm bound to admit it was a relief to get her out of the way for a bit."

"Where is she, then ? Dead ?"

"No," Spennie informed him, a trace of regret in his voice. "She's in hospital with mumps."

"You don't really mean she's got mumps ?"

"Yes. Why not ?"

"I don't really know why not, " admitted Mr. Whittle, "except that it isn't the sort of disease you'd imagine her catching. Too undignified. If it had been cardo-enteritis, or anything like that, I could have understood it. How long is she likely to be in dock ?"

"Some weeks yet, I hope. Getting back to last night, Strudwick and Terry argued solidly for half an hour at least, getting angrier all the time -"

"In Heaven's name, why? What was it all about?"

"Communism."

Mr. Whittle rubbed his chin. "I thought Strudwick was a Conservative. In fact, he definitely told me he was. Has he changed parties overnight ?.

"Of course not, you doddle-pate. Strudwick's a Tory as they make 'em – in fact, he regards me with deep suspicion merely because I voted Liberal in the last election but one; From the way he talks anybody would think I was accustomed to go about in a square beard and a conical hat, juggling with time-bombs and distributing Red propaganda. Terry's the trouble. He's turned Bolshie."

Mr. Whittle chuckled.

"Pure adolescence," he said tolerantly. "We all go through it. Even I did. It's a normal disease – like growing pains, or, for the matter of that, Aunt Violet's mumps. He'll recover. I suppose he's got hold of all the stock expressions? Bloated capitalist, martyred proletariat, and all that?.

33

"Every blessed one. In fact, it was his calling Strudwick a bloated capitalist that started all the rumpus last night. Aunt Clara didn't help matters by swigging nearly a whole bottle of whisky and providing musical accompaniment in the form of Egyptian chants. Eventually I got fed up with the lot of 'em, and went to bed."

"Awkward," conceded Mr. Whittle. "Where were the two girls all this time?"

"I fail to see the connection," retorted Mr. Davenhill, with justifiable annoyance, "but if you must know Pauline Wrightman was typing out some of Weatherill's notes, and Carole – well, I don't know where she was, but she certainly wasn't anywhere near my bed, if that's what you are insinuating."

"What a mind you've got," Said Mr. Whittle primly. "Guilty conscience, I suppose. Er – is this Carole woman really as hot as you made out yesterday, or were you merely using her as the bait ?"

"Judge for yourself when you see her. To continue. The night went off reasonably well on the whole, but at one stage, in the early hours, I could have sworn somebody was prowling about my room. I turned on the light, but there was no one there – and I left the light on after that. Nothing else happened."

"I see." Mr. Whittle helped himself to another tot of whisky, and knocked it back with practised skill. "And this morning?"

"The usual series of breakages and bells and disturbances. Shortly after breakfast all the electricity failed, and Dr Fredl got his beard jammed in a packing case."

"Eh?"

Spennie repeated his remark. Mr. Whittle looked puzzled.

"When you first said that," he said, after a short pause, "It didn't make sense – and it still doesn't. How the devil could the old coot get his beard jammed in a packing case ?"

"I'm trying to tell you, confound it. Weatherill and Fredl and Aunt Clara had unearthed another fossil, or something, and brought it up here in a packing case – they've turned the old armoury into a kind of museum, as I believe I told you. They were hauling the wretched case up the stairs when it slipped, and Fredl got the end of his beard squashed between the crate and the wall. You'd hardly credit the row he made. It was like a steam-siren, only about ten times more powerful. We'd only just got him out of that when Stoker fell into the cellar and cracked his head on the floor, which meant sending for the doctor again – for the third time in twenty four hours. I believe he thinks we've all gone raving mad."

This was so exactly Mr. Whittle's own opinion that he had nothing to say, but the ensuing pause was broken abruptly by a thunderous crash which caused the walls to quiver and the bottles and glasses on the sideboard to vibrate like harp strings. Both Mr. Whittle and |Mr. Davenhill uttered evil words, and rose several inches into the air.

"Oh well," said Spennie resignedly, upon returning to his terra firma, "it was about time something happened. There's been a sort of unearthly quiet since lunch. I suppose we'd better go and investigate."

He made for the door, and Mr. Whittle, pausing only to fill his pipe, followed. The cause of the disturbance was not far to seek. A large picture was laying face-down in the middle of the hall, while a small table lay in ruins nearby and the surrounding area was littered with pieces of broken china. Mr. Davenhill blinked helplessly.

"Oh, dash it all!" he said plaintively, "this is the last straw. Where's Stoker? We'd better get this put back up before we tackle anything else."

"Put what back up where?"

"The picture back up on the wall, you doddle-plate. What did you think I meant?"

Mr. Whittle evaded the question. "It'll take two or three people to lift it, I should think," he observed, poking the gilt frame with his toe. "It must weigh a ton at least. What is it? One of your gargoyle-like ancestors?"

"Great-Aunt Caroline," admitted Mr. Davenhill gloomily. "Curious. We were talking about here only the other night."

"What the hell's going on now?" broke in a voice from behind them, and Mr. Whittle turned to see a tall, good looking boy dressed in khaki whom he recognized as Terry Fane, the expert in snoddle-poking. "How did it happen?"

"It fell," Mr. Whittle explained patiently. Terry was not one of his favourites; he was generally sullen and something in his manner made Roy long to kick him in the pants. In fact on the occasion of their last meeting, some two years before, he had actually done so. "The force of gravity, you know. It acts that way."

Terry grunted. "Very funny. You ought to be on the stage."

"I can't help making witty remarks," said Mr. Whittle modestly. "It's my Irish blood." He smiled amiably as Pauline Wrightman, who had emerged from the library carrying a sheaf of papers and wearing a pair of large horn-rimmed spectacles. "Come and join the milling throng – the more the merrier. Great-Aunt Caroline's fallen bottom upwards."

Miss. Wrightman treated him to a cutting look, but before she could reply there was a disapproving noise from the back of the hall and Stoker joined the little group. The aged retainer looked profoundly displeased with life in general, and eyed the fallen picture the same way as he would have eyed an eel that had strayed into his bath.

"Devil's work, sir," he muttered, casting his eyes upwards. "The forces of evil -"

"The forces of evil my left eyebrow," grunted Mr. Whittle. "I can smell a strong smell of bad fish."

"Well," said Mr. Davenhill bitterly, "I don't know what to make of it, but if this bird Quintus Maximus is responsible I hope his guts rot."

"Has a skeleton got guts ?"

"I neither know nor care," Mr. Davenhill gave a hog-like snort. "Do something about this thing, Stoker – it clutters the place up where it is, and if we leave it there someone's bound to fall over it. We don't want any more broken limbs than are absolutely necessary. Hallo, Strudwick," he added. "Nothing to worry about."

"I thought I heard a noise," began the M.P doubtfully, from the staircase. "What was it?"

"A little birdie calling to its mate," Terry informed him briefly.

Mr. Davenhill hastily interrupted. "Only a picture," he said. "I expect the string had frayed. We'd better check up on the others; we don't want this happening again. Someone may be underneath next time. Pity about the table – it was rather a nice one." He peered thoughtfully at the shattered remains. " I wonder if the picture itself is damaged? Curious that it should be Great-Aunt Caroline, of all people".

"Curious nothing," said Mr. Whittle energetically, bending down to examine the frayed cord. "Look at this, Spennie."

"What about it?"

"It was cut. To be more exact, it was cut at, and left hanging on by a few strands." Mr. Whittle straightened out the kinks in his spine, and handed over the cord for inspection. "That settles it, old lad. Ghosts don't cut cords – not even Roman ghosts.

"You mean the chord was deliberately tampered with?"

"I do. It was."

"Seems a queer thing to do, "observed Mr. Strudwick suspiciously, craning his neck forward. "Yet it certainly looks like a cut. Whoever can have done it?"

"The same person who rang the bells and played Old Harry with the hot water system," said Mr. Whittle, with decision. "It gives us a line, anyhow. It must have been done pretty recently – within the last couple of hours, I should think."

"Not necessarily. It may have been hanging by a thread all day."

"I doubt it. Stoker, have you seen anybody lurking about in the hall recently?"

The butler looked pained. "I cannot say that I have sir. Not that I really understand what you mean by 'lurking'"

"Well, I mean -" Mr. Whittle paused, rather at a loss. "Slinking, loitering, creeping along in a sinister fashion, like one of those late lamented Gestapo."

"I am a butler, sir, not a professional sleuth," the butler informed him, in a marked manner. "Should I encounter any person behaving in such a way, I should pay little or no attention. I trust I know my place".

"Personally," said Mr. Strudwick, "I am not yet convinced that the string was deliberately cut at all. It doesn't seam logical."

"Do you the moth got into it?" retorted Terry scornfully. "Use your loaf, for God's sake!"

The M.P pursed his lips, but before he could think out a satisfactory answer footsteps were heard, and a tall, dark girl entered the hall, causing Mr. Whittle to catch his breath and make a rather unpleasant gulping noise. He was a fair judge of feminine beauty, but a single glance told him that this girl was something new in his experience; so far from exaggerating, Mr. Davenhill had certainly been guilty of grave understatement. In addition to her raven hair and straight features she had a figure that would have compared favourably with Venus de Milo's – plus arms, of course, though it was not her arms that caught Mr. Whittles attention. He became dimply aware that Spennie was talking to him.

"... nothing much," he was saying. "I hope the bang didn't startle you. It was only my great-aunt falling off the wall."

"Your great-aunt?" The girl's voice, low and husky with the barest trace of a foreign accent, caused Mr. Whittle's heart to bound, wildly, and then start fluttering like a captive canary. "She is hurt?"

"I expect her glass is broken," said Mr. Davenhill gloomily.

"Pardon?"

"Her glass."

"Her – ah, I comprehend." A dazzling smile crossed the girl's face. "A picture, yes?"

"You haven't introduced us, Spennie old lad," murmured Mr. Whittle gently.

Mr. Davenhill, reminded of his duties as a host, rectified the omission. Mr. Whittle took Miss Czernak's outstretched hand, and held it a little longer than was strictly necessary.

"I've been looking forward to this meeting," he admitted, "and I am bound to say that it was worth waiting for. You aren't on the films, by any chance?"

Miss Czernak gave a wry smile. "The films? But no. I am – how do you say? - a secretary. I help my Uncle Felix in his work.

Mr. Whittle was about to make a gallant reply when he happened to glance at Pauline, and stopped short, feeling – rather

38

unaccountably – annoyed with himself. Before he could regain his mental balance Mr. Davenhill broke in.

"That reminds me," he said "where is Dr. Fredl? He ought to have been back ages ago if he caught the 2:30, and there isn't another through train tonight."

A horrid thought struck Mr. Whittle. "Spennie, old lad," he began diffidently, "did I hear somebody say that this Dr. Fredl has a black beard?"

Mr. Davenhill look puzzled. "I don't know if anybody said so, but he has. Very black."

"Oh," said Mr. Whittle. "This puts a new complexion on things. I'm sorry to disappoint you all, but I'm am afraid you won't see him just yet – unless the connections between here and Chipwood Magna are a lot better than they used to be. With the best intentions in the world, I think I rather misled him."

"Misled him?" repeated Miss Czernak. "But I do not understand. You know my Uncle Felix?"

"By sight only," Mr. Whittle explained hurriedly. "I had a short talk with him earlier on, and he seemed to be under the impression that my name was either William Shakespeare or Shelmerdine. That's why I directed him on to to Chipwood Magna."

"What the devil do you mean?" asked Mr. Davenhill testily. Just because he mixed you up with somebody else I don't see why you wanted to send him off to a God-forsaken village like Chipwood Magna. Besides, you didn't tell me you'd come across him."

"I didn't know."

"Eh?"

"I mean, I didn't know who he was. He doesn't wear a placard round his neck, you know – not that it would be much use if he did, unless he pruned that fungus."

"Strikes me you're talking a lot of rot, "growled Terry, stubbing out one cigarette and lighting another. "Fredl's a pretty easy person to recognise."

"Mr. Whittle's reply was drowned by a sudden clamour from the front door bell. Mr. Davenhill shrugged. "Damn the thing," he said. Another false alarm, I suppose. What do you think

39

we ought to do with Great-Aunt Caroline? No point in trying to re-hang her until the glass has been mended."

"We don't know for certain yet if it's been smashed," pointed out Mr. Strudwick sagely. "Suppose we roll her over on her back?"

This suggestion met with general approval, and the whole party bent to the task, straining and heaving at Great-Aunt Caroline's massive frame. After what seemed like hours of patient labour they succeeded in standing her upright, revealing her for what she was – a gimlet-eyed, square jawed old trout with a pointed nose and protruding teeth. Mr. Whittle shuddered slightly.

"I liked her better on her front," he admitted.

"You would," grunted Mr. Davenhill. "Was there anybody at the door just then, Stoker?"

"No, sir." The butler closed his throttle and came slowly to rest, wheezing as though he had just returned from a five-mile sprint.

"Interesting," murmured Mr. Whittle. "You're sure of that?"

"Perfectly, Mr. Roy. My eyesight is in no way defective."

"Nor are my ears, old lad, and nobody's going to tell me that bell didn't ring. Inference – somebody rang it. Hello, " he added, there goes the 'phone. May I take it, Spennie?"

"Do what you like with it", grunted Mr. Davenhill, whose temper had not been improved by the struggle with Great-Aunt Caroline, "but I tell you here and now you're wasting your time."

Mr. Whittle shrugged and made for the telephone cabinet, which was situated at the far end of the hall. After an interval he returned, rubbing his chin thoughtfully and looking decidedly perplexed.

"Well?" asked Mr. Strudwick. "Any result?"

"Nothing tangible. I've told the exchange to check the lines and ring us back, so answer the next call." He sucked viciously at his pipe. "All this talk about skeletons and curses is a load of old bread-sauce, but there's certainly some monkey business going on. Any ideas, Spennie?"

"Yes," said Mr. Davenhill, with decision. "Whisky."

"He disappeared into the dining-room, followed by the rest

40

of the group, apart from Miss. Wrightman, who collected her sheaf of documents and faded away, and Stoker, who, with a last reproachful glance at Great-Aunt Caroline, pottered off in the direction of the kitchen and quarters.

Whisky, as Mr. Whittle had often observed, is an almost certain cure for everything except (possibly) the Black Death, and Spennie, negligible though he was in many ways, preserved enough common sense to keep a generous supply of it. After sinking four tots in record time Mr. Whittle began to feel distinctly better, and even the persistent ringing of the front door bell, did not disturb him. Not so Spennie, who was quivering like a bullrush in the wind, and wincing visibly at each fresh clang.

"Say what you like." muttered Mr. Strudwick, after a few minutes' pause, "it is an odd thing that all this should start as soon as Miss Debenham dug up that skeleton. I am not a credulous man – indeed, I flatter myself that I am of a practical turn of mind – but I do seriously wonder whether it would be advisable to call in the Psychical Research Society."

Mr. Whittle uttered a bark of laughter. "And ask them to exorcise a Roman spook that damages hot water systems and hacks picture cords? They'd soon tell you where to get off. There's nothing psychic about this business."

"Weatherill thinks there is." volunteered Terry, thrusting his hands deep into his pockets and blowing out a cloud of cigarette smoke. "So does Fredl, and they ought to know what they are talking about."

"Nuts." Mr. Whittle took out his ancient brier, and stuffed it carefully. "I'm no expert on spooks, but the best way to deal with the average ghost is with hot lead – and if I ever so much as smell our pal Quintus, I'll put a couple of bullets up his spine. Damn that bell! It's getting on my nerves." He paused, and listened intently. "Moreover, Spennie old lad, I can distinctly hear someone banging on the door."

"So can I, "agreed Mr. Davenhill. "I believe there is somebody there, after all. I'd better go and see."

Mr. Whittle, fearing the worst, turned back to the sideboard and dealt speedily with another tot of whisky. He had barely finished when voices were heard outside, and a familiar figure burst into the room – a figure with a black beard, pince-nez spectacles and a battered suitcase. Upon seeing Mr. Whittle, it raised its fists and gave tongue in a tone that was anything but cordial.

"Schweindhundt!" it began, ejecting two distinct sheets of flame from it's nostrils and pawing the carpet with one foot. "So, Herr Shakespeare, with you once more encountered have. It is good. You to make me insulting – it is true, ja? Ver' well. To the police I shall go -"

"Have a drink," suggested Mr. Whittle, holding out a glass filled with inviting-looking liquid. "Then count to ten and start all over again."

"So?" Dr. Fredl glared angrily at the glass, snatched it, drained it, and passed it back as though it had been a rattlesnake. "Herr Shakespeare, I like not what you call the practical jokings. Donner and blitzen! Well for you it is that I a good-tempered man am. First you to me with smoke suffocate -"

"I can explain all that," Protested Mr. Whittle, tactfully refilling the old coot's glass and handing it back. "Merely a misunderstanding, If I'd know who you were, it would never have happened, I'm more than willing to apologise."

"Apologise?" Dr. Fredl thought deeply, and then shook his head. "No! It is not good enough. To the police I go."

"For Heaven's sake -" began Mr. Davenhill disparately.

Mr. Whittle thought quickly. Quite obviously the old buster regarded being sent to Chipwood Magna as a major insult, and unless he could be corked up quickly there was bound to be a good deal of unpleasantness. Revving up the wheels of his brain he concentrated grimly, and was rewarded by an idea – a forlorn hope, but the only one he could see.

"I am deeply hurt," he said with as much dignity as he could muster, taking another surreptitious pull at the whisky. "Dr. Fredl, I had looked forward to our meeting. After all, I think you have some reason to be grateful to me."

"Grateful?" Blackbeard stared. "Hein? Young man, you talk the – how you say? - the bread-sauce. Alone I was, in a small village where even the drinkings impossible to obtain is – I to return a taxicab hire to have, and you say I grateful am to be?

42

Dumnkopf!" He stepped forward, waving his fists threateningly. "It would to me great pleasure give to you a dot in the kisser to present!"

Mr. Whittle backed away, and held out yet another glassful of whisky. Dr. Fredl paused briefly in order to drain it, and then resumed his fist-waving dangerously close to Roy's nose.

"Considering that I save your niece's life only an hour or so ago," said Mr. Whittle slowly and distinctly, "I think you're behaving very badly."

The effect of this speech on his audience was considerable. Spennie, Terry and Mr. Strudwick stared mutely at one another, while Miss Czernak's shapely mouth dropped open and the fist-waving Hun stopped short, glaring suspiciously.

"Hein?" he inquired. "What is this? You say that you have my niece the life of saved, ja?"

"Most certainly." Mr. Whittle drew himself up to his full height. "I don't want to boast, of course – anybody else would have done the same – but if I hadn't been so quick when the lorry ran on to the pavement Miss Czernak would have been badly injured, if not killed outright".

Dr. Fredl hesitated. Then he rounded on Carole, pointing an accusing finger in Roy's direction.

"Carole !" he thundered. "This man, is it that he speaks the truthfulness?"

Mr. Whittle held his breath. Should the glamorous Carole fail him there was nothing for it but to bop the old archaeologist right on the snout before he had time to take the offensive, and he clenched his left hand in readiness. For what seemed minutes there was a deathly pause, and then Miss Czernak's husky tones broke the silence.

"But yes," she said uncertainly. "It is so, Uncle Felix. Mr. Whittle saved me. He was magnificent," she went on, warming to the theme. "Like a flash of lightning. The lorry, it charged – I screamed in terror! Then I find I am lifted from the path by strong arms, and I swoon with fear -"

"Damn it all!" - began Terry, and then he checked himself.

"Herr Shakespeare!" Dr. Fredl dropped his fists, took a rapid step forward and grasped Mr. Whittle round the waist, kissing him firmly on both cheeks. "Herr Shakespeare, it is that I never to you reward can. Of the truth!" Having apparently tired of kissing Mr. Whittle's cheeks he had a go at his forehead, and broke into sobs that echoed round the room as though they were being wrenched out of him by a stomach-pump. "My dearest little Carole ! To think that but for you she beneath a lorry at this moment laying squashed might be!"

Mr. Whittle choked. His mouth and eyes were full of beard, and for once in a way he felt wholly unequal to the satisfaction – in fact, he would infinitely have preferred the dot on the kisser that had been mooted a few moments earlier. Fortunately Dr. Fredl relaxed his grip in order to deal with another tot of whisky, and Mr. Whittle subsided weakly against the sideboard, gasping and panting as he exhaled fluff and whiskers.

When he recovered sufficiently to take an intelligent interest in what was going on he saw that Terry and Mr. Strudwick were no longer among those present, while Dr. Fredl was crying like a child on Carole's shoulder and Spennie gaping at them like a stranded hake. Feeling limp and spineless Mr. Whittle gave Carole an eloquent look in which admiration and gratitude were nicely blended and, pausing briefly in order to tackle a final whisky, faded from the scene. He was conscious of an urgent desire for solitude, and the only place he was likely to get it was in the sanctuary of his own bedroom.

Still removing traces of black hair from his nose and mouth, he made his way upstairs.

Chapter 4

The Green Room, as Mr. Whittle remembered, lay in rather an isolated position at the end of a long passage. He had often slept in it before, and recalled that the thick ivy outside was quite strong enough for climbing purposes, which might be useful if he had to make any nocturnal excursions. When he entered he found Stoker in residence, doddering about straightening things, and decided to see whether he could get any useful information.

"What-ho, old lad," he began cheerily. "Still hard at work buttling?"

The old retainer uncorked another of his prodigious sighs.

"I fear that my days of service are nearly over, sir," he confessed, folding back the bedspread as though expecting to find a rotting corpse underneath it. "Never did I expect to be caught in the toils of the occult, but if people will go poking about into things that don't concern them – well, sir, what can one do?"

"It isn't a question of poking." Mr. Whittle sat down on the bed and swung his legs idly. "Do you seriously and honestly believe that Aunt Clara and her gang have unleashed the phantom of old Quinnie? Damn it, They've only dug up a skeleton, and we've no proof that it's even his."

The have disturbed the rest of the dead, sir," retorted the aged butler vehemently. "I don't wonder that the late Mr. Maximus is showing his annoyance in this way, particularly being Italian."

"Roman," Mr. Whittle corrected him gently.

Stoker shrugged his shoulders.

"Roman or Italian sir, he is a foreigner, and all foreigners are touchy – with no disrespect to Dr. Fredl, sir, you understand."

"Don't mind me, " murmured Mr. Whittle. "Come down to earth, old lad. Tell me what you really think of this business in general, and Aunt Clara's fossil-hunters in particular."

The butler raised his eyebrows.

"Really, Mr. Roy, I could not dream of taking such a liberty. It is not my place to criticise Mr. Spencer's friends".

"Tomato juice. In the first place, they aren't Spennie's friends – they're Aunt Clara's and Aunt Violet's; and secondly I swear I won't let out anything you say. After all, we've know each other for years, haven't we? Remember the times Spennie and I used to slip down to your pantry behind Aunt Violet's back, " he went on reminiscently, "and you used to slip us ginger pop and cream biscuits from the larder? Lord, it seams a long time ago!"

"It is a long time ago, sir."

"Quite. That's probably why it seems like it." Mr. Whittle pushed the butler into a chair and, producing a bottle of whisky from his suitcase, rinsed out a couple of tooth-glasses and started pouring. "Have a quick snifter, and then tell me just what you know."

The old retainer looked uncertain. Such behaviour was normally outside his code, but – he reasoned to himself – Mr. Whittle was not an ordinary young gentleman, and in any case the glass of whisky was really too tempting to be refused. With a quick gulp, therefore he knocked it back, and cleared his throat importantly.

"Just as you say, Mr. Roy. What do you want me to tell you?"

"I want your candid opinion about these three fossil-experts," replied Mr. Whittle, refilling both glasses. "First of all, Professor Weatherill. What's he like?"

Stoker considered.

"Like a corpse, sir, that has been lying in water for some time," he replied at length. "I wish to say nothing against him, Mr. Roy, but I must in all honesty describe him as a slimy old bastard – very slimy. He creeps, and he looms. Also I should be most surprised to learn that he ever washed."

"Fair enough." Mr. Whittle grinned. "That's the kind of stuff I want to hear. Is he good at his job?"

"I am hardly in a position to judge, Mr. Roy," the butler pointed out, sipping his second bracer with an air of contentment, "but he appears to be a recognised authority, and I hardly think Mrs. Debenham would be deceived by an impostor."

"No, I suppose she wouldn't. I hold no particular brief for Aunt Clara, but at least she knows her fossils. How about Fredl?"

"Very touchy, sir, and very hard to please – most offensive he was when I thoughtlessly brought him some shaving water –

and altogether a most suspicious character. I lock my door at nights nowadays," admitted Stoker gloomily. "He prowls."

"He what?"

"He prowls, Mr. Roy, and I have a morbid dread of him coming in to my room and slitting my throat while I sleep."

"This," said Mr. Whittle, "is interesting." He leaned forward. "How do you know he prowls, old lad? Don't you think I doubt you for a moment, but I merely want to collect all the facts I can."

The old retainer paused in order to marshal his ideas in their correct sequence.

"About four nights ago, Mr. Roy," he began, "my arthritis was exceptionally bad – really terrible; not a wink of sleep could I get." Mr. Whittle made sympathetic clucking noises. "I bore it until the early hours, and then it became so painful that I decided to go down to my pantry and imbibe a glass of whisky – that being the one thing I have so far found capable of alleviating my arthritis, even at its worst." He nodded gratefully as Mr. Whittle tactfully filled up his glass. "It was a moonlit night, and knowing the house as well as I do there was no need for me to carry a torch or turn on any lights. Well, sir, I had my whisky, and was about to return when I heard footsteps coming from the direction of the hall." He paused.

"Go on," prompted Mr. Whittle.

"I considered it my duty to investigate, Mr. Roy – quite a lot of burglaries there have been around these parts lately. I crept cautiously into the hall, and there, plain as brass, was Dr. Fredl, crawling about on all fours sniffing like a bloodhound and carrying a bit of paper that I took to be a plan or a map."

Mr. Whittle looked puzzled.

"Do you mean he was actually, sniffing like a bloodhound?"

"I do, sir. At least, he was certainly on all fours, though whether or not he was sniffing was impossible to ascertain owing to the dim light."

"Strange," murmured Mr. Whittle. "What the devil can he have been up to? Do you think the sanitation can be out of order, or anything like that?"

"Certainly not, sir. The entire sanitary system was overhauled only a few years ago, and has not given the slightest trouble since. Besides, had there been any unpleasant smell I should most certainly have detected it. I have a very keen nose." admitted the old butler modestly, "which is partly why I dislike going too close to Professor Weatherill. No, Mr. Roy, I have little doubt that Dr. Fredl was in search of the legendary Wollingham Black Pearls."

"Eh?"

"The Wollingham Black Pearls, Mr. Roy. Surely you have heard of them?"

"Of course I've heard of them, but every Davenhill for the past two centuries has had a go at tracking them down without any success. Why should Fredl be interested?."

"Because of the map, sir." Stoker prodded Mr. Whittle meaningfully in the chest. "Mark my words, that map has some deep significance, and Dr. Fredl is doing his best to find the key."

Mr. Whittle thought this one out.

"Pretty reasonable," he agreed. "You've got something there, old lad. I must tackle Spennie about that map as soon as I can get hold of him. What did you do next?"

"What could I do, Mr. Roy? It was obviously not my place to interfere. If Mr. Spencer's guests wish to crawl about the hall sniffing, even at three o'clock in the morning, that's their own affair, not mine. I accordingly withdrew unobserved."

"I see. Did you tell Spennie?"

"Certainly not, sir,. To do so would have been most unethical. I believe in keeping my own counsel."

"Wise of you," conceded Mr. Whittle. "Leaving Fredl on ice for the moment, we come to Strudwick. Is he a regular visitor these days?"

"He spends a great deal of time here," admitted the butler. I understand that he and Mrs. Fane have common political views, and are even now drafting out a scheme to standardise all the sewage in the country." He lowered his voice confidentially. "I may say, Mr. Roy, that there is some talk of her contesting the next election as Conservative candidate for the Chipwood and Wortlebury division."

"So that's it," muttered Mr. Whittle. "Aunt Violet, M.P! As a matter of fact she'd probably do it very well; God knows she can talk the hind leg off the proverbial camel. What about Struddy himself? He strikes me as being a wet lettuce."

"He is, sir," the butler assured him. "I have frequently experienced an almost overwhelming desire to drop heavy articles upon him from a great height."

"More power to your elbow. Young Terry?"

The old retainer pursed his lips.

"I hardly know what to say, Mr. Roy. He can be most irritating, but there's no vice in him, though he has been very strange lately."

"In what way strange?"

"Moody, Mr. Roy. Depressed. Acting as though there was something on his mind."

"I see. How long has he been here?"

"Only a week or so, sir. I believe he is endeavouring to obtain an executive position in a shipping office. I do not wish to jump to conclusions," added Stroker cautiously, "but I have a feeling that he may perhaps have been unlucky in his – er – investments."

"Horses?" asked Mr. Whittle, going straight to the root of the matter.

"Precisely, sir. You will hardly credit it, but only yesterday he asked whether I could lend him fifty pounds." Stroker chuckled gently at the recollection. "I can well understand that his mother would not approve of these investments, considering that she is vice president of the Anti-Gambling Society and will certainly introduce an anti-betting bill as soon as she takes her seat in the House."

"I can hardly imagine Aunt Violet at a race meeting," agreed Mr. Whittle. "Come to think of it, though, Aunt Clara would be perfectly at home – in fact she used to get hold of some pretty hot inside information. I wonder if she still does?"

"I doubt it sir. Nowadays Miss Debenham takes little or no interest in anything less than a thousand years old."

"What an existence!" Mr. Whittle held up the bottle. "I think we might treat ourselves to a final snifter, don't you?"

49

"By all means, Mr. Roy," assented the butler readily, handing over his glass. "Excellent whisky, this – far superior to our own. I am sure it will keep my arthritis at bay for a week at least."

"I never travel without it. Let me see, who comes next? What about the girls?"

Stoker wrinkled his nose doubtfully, thereby achieving a really startling resemblance to a senile rabbit. "I find myself somewhat at a loss, Mr. Roy. I really know very little about Miss Wrightman, though she strikes me as a very quiet, respectable young lady. I confess that I am rather surprised at he attachment to Mr. Strudwick."

Mr. Whittle gave vent to a loud bark, causing Stoker to wince as though he had been prodded with the business end of a screwdriver.

"What? What's that?"

"I was merely indicating, sir, that I really can not understand how Miss Wrightman can bring herself to form a match with Mr. Strudwick." The butler coughed. "I trust you will treat this as highly confidential -"

"Of course."

" - but their engagement will be announced almost at once. I overheard their discussing the matter only last night – quite by chance, I may add."

"Well I'm damned," Said Mr. Whittle frankly. "She's too good for him by half, and I'm not at all sure I shan't stick my oar in."

"I hardly follow you, sir."

"No matter. How about the gorgeous Carole? Don't tell me she's carrying on a great romance with Spennie or Terry?"

Stoker thought carefully before voicing an opinion.

"I should consider such a thing only too probable, sir, especially in the case of Master Terry," he observed at length. "Miss Czernak is a viper, a snake in the grass, a serpent, and a scheming vixen."

"All at once?"

"I was not speaking literally, sir," retorted the aged retainer stiffly. Miss Czernak is even less trustworthy than her uncle. I have little doubt that she, too, is capable of prowling round the house at night."

Mr. Whittle licked his lips.

"I wonder! Loads of 'it' there, old lad. Doesn't your old heart bound when you see her?"

"The only thing that can make my heart bound nowadays sir," admitted the butler, "is indigestion. In my younger days, I might possibly have felt different. Miss Czernak is certainly not devoid of physical attraction."

"Attraction isn't the word."

"No, sir."

"Anyway, she pulled me out of a most ticklish situation a few moments ago, and I shall have to seek her out and thank her in the approved manner. Don't look so staid and Victorian, old horse. I'm not falling for her, and you needn't think it. As a matter of fact I'd far rather have Pauline Wrightman.

"I applaud your choice, sir, though it is possible that Mr. Strudwick might raise certain objections." The butler set down his glass. "Is there anything else you want to ask me, Mr. Roy?"

"Yes. Stoker, old lad, we've beating about the bush. Frankly, do you or do you not believe that Aunt Clara's let loose a ghost?"

"I do, sir," confessed the aged retainer, without a shadow of hesitation. "In fact, I should say there was no possible doubt about it. Moreover, I believe it's in league with Dr. Fredl."

"Eh?"

"In other words, sir, I believe Dr. Fredl to be a black magician."

Mr. Whittle passed a hand feverishly across his brow.

"Good God," he said weakly. "My dear old lad, have you come completely unhinged? You'll be telling me next that he rides about on a broomstick, and sacrifices white cocks at the crack of dawn."

"Time will tell, Mr. Roy," predicted the butler, in sombre tones. "I hope I am wrong, but I see certain signs that cause me grave misgivings. Were I a cock, I should most certainly give Dr. Fredl a wide berth." He rose. "And now sir, I must return to my duties. Dinner is due in less than half an hour, and the kitchen is still in a state of chaos. I trust that I will have been to some extent helpful?."

"You've given me something to go on, anyhow."

"That is very gratifying, sir."

"Mind you, I think this Black Magician idea of yours is pure tinned spaghetti. Keep your eyes open, and let me know if you come across anything suspicious."

"I will spare no effort, sir."

"Good. One last question – where's this museum of Aunt Clara's? I'd like to have a dekko at it before she comes in."

"It is next to the smaller larder, sir, at the extreme far end of the hall. You doubtless recall that during the war it was used for storing Home Guard equipment. I never go near it nowadays," admitted Stoker, shuddering slightly. "Hoarding dead bodies and bones and fossils – gives me the creeps. Brrrrrrrr! I really must go, Mr. Roy. Dinner will be served at eight o'clock precisely, God willing." With which he bowed himself out, leaving Mr. Whittle to complete his unpacking and – incidentally – knock back two or three more generous tots of whisky.

Chapter 5

The museum proved to be much as Mr. Whittle had expected. The last time he had been there, some five years earlier, the whole room had been piled high with rifles, grenades, and ammunition of every size and calibre – things that he really understood; but all these things had long since been cleared out and parked somewhere in readiness for the next war, and the room looked very different. The main feature was a lank, grim-looking skeleton, standing on a pedestal near the window, and Mr. Whittle eyed it with interest. Evidently this was Quintus Maximus in person, and the old buster looked anything but amiable. The atmosphere was clammy and depressing, and the whole room smelt musty, as though the windows had not been opened for a month at least.

"No accounting for tastes," mused Mr. Whittle, pottering idly about and examining the various bones and remains. "I don't like old Quinnie one little bit. God!" he added aloud, "what in the hell was that?"

He paused, the hair rising on his neck and his ears strained to their utmost. Either he was losing his grip completely, or somebody had groaned.

Mr. Whittle shook himself irritably. He realised only too well that once his imagination started to run away with him, he was a spent force. Resolutely he prodded Quintus Maximus' left rib, and stood still, pointing like a retriever. He had not long to wait. A low, quavering moan broke the silence, as though someone had been horribly tortured.

"Come out of it," said Mr. Whittle, sharply and distinctly. "That sort of onion soup doesn't scare me."

There was no response to this cordial invitation, and Mr. Whittle was conscious of a momentary feeling of panic. Having successfully fought it down he started to make a systematic examination of the room – no difficult matter, since it was small and compact. He had about finished when the sound of approaching footsteps fell upon his ears, and he paused, undecided. There was no reason at all why he should not be found in the museum, but some inner feelings prompted him to see without being seen, and he accordingly retired behind a large packing case to await events. Presently the door opened, and Mr Whittle, peering round the suitcase, muffled an instinctive snort. The newcomer was Pauline Wrightman, businesslike and efficient as usual, and with her immense horn-rims perched upon her nose.

Mr. Whittle watched closely as Pauline went to the table, drew out a wad of papers, and then checked them carefully against a list in her hand. He was wondering whether to open a conversation when the question was settled for him by providence – suitably disguised as a small flying insect that charged up his nostril and caused him to give vent to a thunderous sneeze.

"What -" began Pauline, spinning round.

"Me," said Mr. Whittle meekly, emerging from his hiding place and brushing himself down. "Thought I'd have a look round."

"Do you generally creep behind cases and jump out on people?" inquired Miss Wrightman hotly. " I should have thought you were too old to play hide-and-seek."

"A moot point, Paul," replied Mr. Whittle. "Do you mind if I gouge out my left nostril? Some species of insect has gone up it on a tour of exploration." He did so, and snorted with relief. "Did I startle you, by the way?"

"Oddly enough, you did. It was a fool trick, particularly just now." Miss Wrightman replaced the papers, shut the drawer with a bang. "What was the idea?"

"There," admitted Mr. Whittle, " you have me. I really don't know. All I do know is that there's some dirty work going on, because a minute or two ago I distinctly heard a groan coming from thin air."

"What!"

"Fact. It got under my skin for a moment."

Quite evidently it had got under Miss Wrightman's skin, too. She caught her breath, and steadied herself against the desk.

"You're sure?"

"Perfectly sure. I'm not a bird who imagines things."

"What sort of a groan was it?"

"I don't know how you'd classify it. It was just a groan,"

54

said Mr. Whittle dubiously, "and I couldn't find out where it came from – in fact I still can't. i say, you do look dicky. Shall I go and rustle you some brandy?" "In a minute . Let's get this clear. You're absolutely sure it wasn't a mouse, or anything?"

"Mice don't groan. I merely prodded old Quintus with my finger – like this -and then ... Good lord! There it is again!"

A soft wail echoed through the room. It was far a from pleasant sound, and Pauline uttered a snort of dismay, after which she flung herself into Mr. Whittle's arms and remained here, with her eyes closed and her body vibrating like a turning-fork. Roy, holding her tightly, decided that – spook or no spook – he was rather enjoying himself. After what seemed hours the sound ceased.

"Come out of this," said Mr. Whittle swiftly. "I've got some whisky in my room. Feel fit?"

"No, but I'll do."

"Right. On your way."

Still with his arm round her, Mr. Whittle led her up the back stairs and into his bedroom, where he sat her down in the armchair and went to work upon a fresh bottle of whisky. Miss Wrightman was still breathing in short gusts as though having trouble with her wind-pipe, but she seemed to be recovering. Roy gazed at here thoughtfully. She really was pretty, he decided – not in the same way as Carole Czernak, but definitely pretty. He felt an irrational desire to wring Mr. Strudwick's neck.

"I wish you'd take those glasses off, " he said suddenly.

Pauline looked surprised.

"Why?"

"Because they hide your eyes, and I want to have a good look at them. Are they bluey grey or greyish blue?"

"Neither – green ." Miss Wrightman removed her horn-rims and smiled shakily. "Mr. Whittle -"

"Call the Roy. It would do my heart good."

"Roy, I'm sorry I made such a fool of myself. I felt sort of knocked over." She hesitated. "It sounds silly, and you'll probably laugh at me, but I simply talk to somebody and I don't think Raymond – Mr. Strudwick – would understand."

"He isn't an understanding sort of bird. In fact, he's a

doddle-pated wet cucumber." Mr. Whittle snorted. "Come on, tell Uncle Roy all about it."

"You won't tell anyone else?"

"My middle name is Discretion."

"And you won't laugh?"

"No. Well?"

"It was like this," began Pauline diffidently. "About a week ago I went up to London for Professor Weatherill, to study some documents at the British Museum. I stayed later than I'd meant, and it was past ten before I got back to Wollingham; the last bus had gone, of course, so I thought I'd walk back by the path near the camp. As I came up the path I saw a light flashing about near the excavations, and thinking it might be either be Miss Debenham or the professor I went over to it."

"And it went out," murmured Mr. Whittle.

"It didn't. It was there, all right - a sort of hard blue glitter." Miss Wrightman paused. "When I got   near I realised there wasn't anybody holding it – it was just floating about – and then I saw something else."

"What?"

"It's difficult to describe," admitted Miss Wrightman in a low voice. "It looked like something straight out of hell – a luminous skeleton with staring green eyes that shone like a cat's. Then I saw Dr. Fredl."

Mr. Whittle could not repress a sharp snort, and dropped his cigarette.

"He seemed to be prancing about," went on Miss Wrightman in a half-choked whisper. "Going round in circles, with that awful thing following him. It was ghastly."

She stopped short, and Mr. Whittle considered the affair from every angle. If Dr. Fred, in addition to sniffing the floor at three a.m, was addicted to holding nocturnal open-air dancing classes, it seemed to him the sooner the old coot was properly certified and stored in a home the better.

"You're sure it was Fredl? I mean , it wasn't some trick of the light?"

"It couldn't have been, because there wasn't any. It was Fredl, without a doubt. The moment I saw him I bolted, because I knew then that all the stories I'd heard about him were true."

This time Mr. Whittle was really shaken.

"Stories?" he said roughly. "Come on, Paul, brace up. What stories?"

"Lots of stories, mostly unpleasant." Pauline shuddered, and raised no objection as Mr. . Whittle eased himself into the spacious armchair and slipped one arm round her. "When I was out in Egypt with Professor Weatherill, working on the tombs of the Tutankhamen dynasty, we heard a lot about him. People said he was some sort of bogey man, and most of the Egyptians themselves were perfectly convinced he was a genuine Black Magician."

"Stoker!"

"What?"

"Nothing," said Mr. Whittle soberly. "Just an idle thought. You're making too much this, old girl. Can you see a comic old buffer like Fredl getting up to any really sinister tricks?:

"He isn't comic. I used to think so, but I don't know now. He's slimy – like a poisonous reptile, waiting to strike. He looks at me sometimes as though he'd like to – oh, I don't know."

"I can guess," grunted Mr. Whittle "Let me catch at it, the whiskery old – er- archaeologist. I'll stuff his beard down his throat and wrap it round his tonsils. Not that I blame him for looking at you," he added handsomely. "Did anyone ever tell you you were worth looking at?"

"When you're secretary to a busy man," said Miss Wrightman dryly, "you don't have time to bother about that sort of thing. I've always tried to be efficient, but at the moment I fell like jelly. I know it's stupid of me, Roy, but I'm scared stiff"

Mr. Whittle looked thoughtful. Quite obviously the girl needed comforting, since Mr. Strudwick was palpably useless in such an emergency – in addition to not being present, anyway – it seemed his duty to take the appropriate action. He did so.

"I hope you don't mind being kissed?" he asked casually, pausing for breath.

Miss Wrightman sat up and untwined herself.

"I ought to," she admitted, "but somehow I don't. I doubt if Raymond would like it, though. Did you know I'm more or less engaged to him?"

"I'd heard rumours to that effect, but frankly I took them with several cartloads of salt. You can't possibly be in love with that lop-eared bacillus."

"He is not a bacillus!"

"Pardon me, he is – and a disease, to boot. Your honeymoon will probably be spent discussing the Anglo-Peruvian Trade Treaties and listening to dear Raymond rehearsing his speech to the Grandmothers Guild. Also, I'm prepared to bet that he talks in his sleep."

"He doesn't."

"What?"

"He doesn't. At least," amplified Miss. Wrightman, "he's often gone to sleep when we've come down from London in the train, and I've never heard him so much as mutter."

"Hardly a parallel case," said Mr. Whittle coldly. "Still, I suppose even Struddy must give him jaws a rest sometimes. Take my advice and break it off."

"It isn't even on," pointed out Miss Wrightman.

"Good. Long may it stay that way. In a few weeks' time -" Mr. Whittle paused. "I say, old girl, there's somebody coming. I don't want to cause alarm and despondency, but if you were found here it's just possible that certain people might get hold of the wrong end of the stick, if you see want I mean."

"Judging from you efforts just now," commented Pauline, "they wouldn't be far out, either. Strangely enough I feel much better for it, unless the whisky's responsible. Is there there room for me under the bed?"

"There is. Down you go. If you go. If you find anything in the way shift it."

Fortunately the bed was massive four-poster that might have been made specially for an emergency of this kind, and Miss Wrightman crawled rapidly out of view. She was none too soon. Hardly had she disappeared when the door-handle turned and Carole Czernak entered, wearing a low-backed a dress that showed up her natural advantages to an amazing extent. Mr. Whittle gulped. Under any other circumstances he would have been far from displeased, but as it was something told him that this

58

interview was going to be hard going.

"What-ho," he began, in what he hoped was a conventional tone. "Nice evening, what? Looks as though we're in for a fine spell."

Miss Czernak closed thee door quietly behind her.

"I have come," she announced, in husky tones that at once banished Mr. Whittle's hopes of keeping conservation on a strictly meteorological level, "to thank you for saving my life. You English are so brave, is it not?"

Mr. Whittle felt slightly embarrassed. "I'm most frightfully sorry about that," he said sincerely, "but I didn't see what else I could do, short of coshing your uncle one on the beezer. He was after my blood."

"After what you did – do you blame him"

"I don't," admitted Mr. Whittle frankly, "but when I led him up the garden I had no idea he was staying here."

"Up the garden?" Miss Czernak looked puzzled. "But he said he was sent to – to Chipwood Magnus , was it? I know nothing of any gardens."

"I didn't mean a real garden. It's just a saying, you know – to lead one up the garden."

"A saying". Ah, I comprehend." Miss Czernak sat down on the bed and lay back comfortably. "You English, you are full of sayings. You talk, talk, talk, but never act. If you were of my country, now, you would at this moment be thanking me for – how how is it you say? Pulling you out of the hole."

Mr. Whittle, having nothing to say, kept silent.

"Talk – talk," repeated Miss Czernak softly. "How well do we speak of the cold Englishman. You are a little afraid of me, yes?"

"Afraid of you? Why?"

"I know not, yet you seem distant – strange." Miss Czernak sighed. "In Austria, how different would it be: come and sit beside me, Roy. And tell me why you are distant."

"You'd never guess," said Mr. Whittle desperately, wincing as the bed creaked beneath his weight. "Er – it's not dinner-time yet, is it? I haven't finished changing, and it always takes me the deuce of time to change into dress clothes."

"We have yet some minutes," Miss Czernak assured him. "I like you, Roy. You are ugly, yes, but you are so big and strong." Mr. Whittle made no comment. "Kiss me."

Mr. Whittle closed his eyes and, praying that Pauline was listening, dealt out a parrot-like peck on Miss Czernak's cheek. When he opened his eyes again he saw that the glamorous Carole was eyeing him with a sort of hopeless despair.

"But no!" she said vehemently. "No, no,no! Oh Roy never have you kissed, is it not? You have no fire, no – how is it you say – no umph!"

"Oomph," Mr. Whittle corrected her weakly.

"As I say, umph. I show you how to use the umph. Like this ..."

"I see what you mean," said Mr. Whittle breathlessly, a minute or so later. How old are you, Carole?"

"Twenty. Why?"

"I only wondered." Mr. Whittle started as one of the chiming clocks in the hall went ion the air. "Lord, it;'s nearly dinner-time. We'll be late if we're not careful."

Miss Czernak sighed, and rose reluctantly.

"You are so practical," she complained. "You will learn, yes, but I see you were still afraid of me."

Mr. Whittle snorted under his breath. This continual harping on his on his timidity was, to say the least, annoying, and he resolved that as soon as he could manage an interview without an audience he would banish such an illusion once and for all.

"I've lived a sheltered life," he said shamelessly, hoping that such a statement would not bring the roof crashing about his ears.

"So? It is sad, that, but I will soon teach you not to be afraid. Until dinner, Roy," said Miss Czernak gently, and floated from the room without seeming to touch the ground at all.

Mr. Whittle wiped the sweat from his brow and, tottering over to the whisky bottle – which was fortunately tucked out of sight behind a jug – downed two generous bracers without pausing for breath. "Phew," he said feebly "What a shock? It's all right, Paul!"

"I don't know what you mean by "all right," said Miss

Wrightman testily, poking her head out fro beneath the bed like a tortoise examining the landscape. "I've swallowed about a hundredweight of dust, and nearly knocked my brains out into the bargain."

"What on?"

"Never mind."

"Have a snifter," suggested Mr. Whittle tactfully.

"I need it." Pauline emerged, and dusted herself down. "Incidentally, what exactly were you two up to?"

"I wasn't up to anything. It's a long time since I had such a sticky five minutes."

"What?"

"Well, damn it all," said Mr. Whittle defensively, "it was emphatically the sort of conversation that should have taken place in private. Afraid of her – isch!"

"Especially when you're so big and strong, even if you are ugly," said Pauline maliciously.

Mr. Whittle grimaced. "That remark, young Paul, was in the worst of taste. I may not be an Adonis, but at least I'm not in the Strudwick class."

"True enough," concerned Miss Wrightman, who was basically a fair-minded girl. "Besides, it cuts both ways. I haven't got much what she calls "umph", and I don't want it, but neither have I got a mind like a drain. Anyway, my spell under the bed seems to have pulled me together. I feel ready for anything now."

"Good."

"Within reason," added Pauline, glaring. "On second thoughts I don't see why you and the Carole witch shouldn't make an ideal couple – you both think along the same lines. I must go and change."

"Want me to come with you ?"

"Oddly enough, I think I can change without any assistance from you. Thanks for the whisky," said Miss Wrightman, and pushed off, leaving Mr. Whittle to start cramming his massive frame into dress clothes.

Chapter 6

Mr. Whittle came downstairs in a preoccupied mood. So far he had to admit that he was baffled, and it seemed a sound scheme to buttonhole Aunt Clara and Professor Weatherill to see what he could get out of them; but unfortunately neither of them were among those present – they were, it seemed, still working at the camp – and dinner was a silent meal, interrupted only by a few brave efforts at light conservation by Mr. Davenhill and a number of acrimonious exchanges between Terry and Mr. Strudwick, plus persistent bells. The one blessing, from Mr. Whittle's point of view, was the absence of Dr. Fredl. Carole explained that he felt tired, and he asked for dinner in his room.

"He is so upset," he said, with lowered eyes. "Poor Uncle Felix, the thought of my escape has thrown him into a consternation."

Mr. Whittle made no reply, and he was not sorry when the meal petered out and he was liberty to escape to the billiard-room. He wanted time to think things over and map out his plan of campaign, but after he spent ten minutes or so practising cannons Terry Fane joined him, sullen as usual and with the inevitable cigarette drooping out of the corner of his mouth.

"Looking for a game?" he asked, without much enthusiasm.

Mr. Whittle struggled.

"If you like. I warn that my record break is eight, inclusive of two flukes and a push-shot, and I have no scruples about potting my opponent's white."

"I don't suppose you're any worse than I am ," grunted Terry, setting up the balls. "Billiards is all right, but is not active enough for me." He shot, and, more by luck than judgement, achieved a brilliant in-off. "How's the detecting going?"

"What detecting?"

"Well, that's why you came, isn't it? To find out what's going on?"

"More or less," admitted Mr. Whittle, "but there's no need to broadcast it, if you don't mind. I don't pretend to have got far yet, but one thing I do know, and that's that all this talk about black magic and Roman curses is so much tinned spaghetti. It doesn't make sense. Stories about spooks and curses are as old as the hills, and they smell."

"I wouldn't be to sure," muttered Terry.

Mr. Whittle blinked. "Come again?" he said incredulously. "Don't tell me you've seen a prancing skeleton, too?"

"Too?" echoed Terry. "What do you mean?"

"Nothing," said Mr. Whittle hastily. "I was thinking of something else."

"All the same," commented Terry slowly, "it is queer, you know. Bells don't ring themselves."

"Anyone with a bit of gumption could rig up an electrical circuit of some sort and make them ring till the cows come home," pointed out Mr. Whittle. "That reminds me. When will Aunt Clara and the rest of her gang be back? I want to have a squint at that map they've unearthed."

Terry bent over his cue. "Wish you luck. I've tried to get a dekko at it myself, but old Weatherill always says he hasn't got it handy. Truth is, he's keeping it under his hat."

"Even when he's indoors?"

"No need to be so bloody funny," snarled Terry. "Damn, that's three to you. Can you lend me fifty quid?".

Mr. Whittle, concentrating grimly on his shot, jerked his cue viciously and made a complete hash of an easy cannon. "Don't say that kind of thing when I'm trying to aim," he said, as soon has he had made sure that the cloth was undamaged. "My dear, good kid, what makes you think I've got fifty quid to spare? And even if I had, what the devil would you want it for?"

"Debts," muttered Terry sullenly.

"Horses?"

"None of your business."

"Well I'm damned," said Mr. Whittle. "For sheer cheek, you just about take the biscuit. Why not ask Spennie? He might help."

"I have. He won't."

"I don't blame him. Hoe about Strudwick?"

Terry flushed. "I may be in a hole, but I've more sense to go to that weak-kneed jellyfish. He's one of the class who do there damnedest to grind down the workers of this world until they've got no rights or liberties left-"

"Bloated capitalists," murmured Mr. Whittle. "Sweated labour."

Terry looked up. "What do you mean? I didn't know you were interested in politics."

"I'm not. I -"

"Of course, I've only been in the movement a couple of months," explained Terry, "but I've done a lot of reading – that is, when I've had the chance; training in my unit didn't leave much spare time." Mr. Whittle nobly repressed a bark of laughter. "A man I know took me to one of the Party meetings a little while ago -"

Mr. Whittle felt bound to make his own attitude clear.

"Don't go so fast," he said peaceably. "Personally I've no use for communism. I've seen ii in action."

"Where?"

"Russia – Romania – Czechoslovakia. Not so long back, either." Mr. Whittle cursed briefly as he absent-mindedly chalked his cigarette instead of his cue. "Believe me, it's not pretty, and anyone who has any fool ideas about Russia being working man's paradise had a better go and see. I take It that you're not on the best of terms with dear Raymond?"

"No. we had a bit of a set-to last night, and I threatened to carve him up. I would have done, too, if he hadn't taken himself off."

"Young blood," murmured Mr. Whittle, in a patronising tone. "Well, you've had your fifty quid so far as I'm concerned. I'll give you a bit of advice, though – chuck backing horses until you really know something about it; it's a mug's game at the best of times, unless you get first-class hot tips."

"You couldn't put in a word with Spennie?"

"I could not."

"Oh, hell!" said Terry savagely, jabbing at his cue-ball venomously, as though it had been Mr. Strudwick's snoddle. "This house gets me down. Look at it!" he gave a grand gesture. "Twenty rooms – only about ten of em used regularly, while in Glasgow and Liverpool families are sleeping five or six to a bed. Doesn't it make you sick?"

"Not really," admitted Mr. Whittle. "Mind you, I've no desire to sleep five I a bed – it'd be three too many – but if you like I suppose you can always spend the rest of your demob leave in Liverpool or Glasgow. Incidentally, I don't see what all this has got to do with my lending you fifty pounds."

Terry said no more, and for some time conservation languished. Eventually Mr. Whittle broke the silence. "Going off at the tangent," he said, "what do you make of this Fredl duck? Is he as crazy as he looks?"

"Search me." Terry shrugged. "I wouldn't trust him an inch, if that's what you mean, but I'd rather have ten of him than one of Weatherill."

Mr. Whittle found this interesting.

"Why?"

"Weatherill makes me squirm," said Terry. "Ouf! I'm sure he's crawling with maggots. I'm damned if I know how my Aunt Clara puts up with him – or Fredl either, for that matter. "He slashed at the white and sent it spinning into a pocket. "Sorry, your ball. How many for a game?"

"Two," said Mr. Whittle sadly, looking at his own marker which registered a paltry six. "What-ho, Spennie old lad. What's the latest?"

"Jules," said Mr. Davenhill wearily limping into the room and sinking down into a chair. "He's developed an attack of the vapours and retired the bed, which means the joint tomorrow will be like wet leather. The boiler's gone wrong too. I only hope doesn't go up into smoke – it looks dangerously volcanic to me. Have you two finished?"

"We're through," said Terry ungraciously. "Don't let me hold you up."

"We won't," Mr. Whittle assured him. "Thanks for the game. Surly young brute, he added as Terry went out, banging the door behind him. "What he needs is a good kicking. What awful secret am I going to learn now, old lad? The skeleton in the Davenhill family cupboard?"

Spennie shuddered.

"I wish you wouldn't talk about skeletons. I'm trying to

forget they exist."

"Why? You'd look pretty silly without one. We've all got em, yo know."

"Not ones like Aunt Clara's."

Mr. Whittle considered this. "I suppose not. Anatomical differences, thank God."

"I didn't mean that, you doddle-pate. I was thinking about Quintus."

"I'm getting tired of hearing about this Quintus duck," said Mr. Whittle frankly. "Don't ramble, old lad. Come to the point."

"Once you let me get a word in, instead of doddering on about skeletons," said Mr. Davenhill unreasonably, "I will. You know that passage that leads from the cellar out into the rose garden?"

"The one we used to call the Smugglers' Way, you mean? I've been through it often enough when we were kids. Why?"

"Because someone's been poking about there. I went down to the cellars just now to haul up some more whisky – Stoker didn't seem to be about, and I don't like the other servants messing about down there – and I saw a cigarette-stub near the entrance to the way, so I investigated."

"Doesn't seem much to go on," Mr. Whittle protested. "It's probably been there for years."

"It looked new. Stoker and I are the only the people who ever go down, and neither of us smoke. Then I found that the panel had been oiled. It was absolutely dripping with three-in-one. So,"concluded Mr. Davenhill lamely, "I thought I'd better come and tell you about it."

"You haven't been through the Way?"

"Not yet. It struck me that you might want to be there, in case we came across something, you know."

"You aren't suggesting that Quinnie clanked down and put oil on the door?"

"I'm not suggesting anything. I'm merely telling you what I found out."

"Well," said Mr. Whittle judicially, "evening kit isn't the best get-up for crawling about underground, but from what I remember the way is pretty roomy. I can't imagine why the devil our archaeologist pals should be interested, but I suppose I can't do any harm to have a look around. Let's go."

Frowning thoughtfully, and ramming some more tobacco into his pipe, he followed Spennie through the kitchen quarters. He remembered the Smuggler's Way perfectly, but it had never, so far, lived up to its romantic name; indeed, it was nothing more than a built-in passage connecting the cellar to the grounds, and there was nothing even remotely secret about it.

"Careful," said Mr. Davenhill warningly, unlocking the cellar door and shining his torch down the steps. "Stoker took the devil of the toss here yesterday. I think the stone must be slippery, though I've never noticed it before." He led the way into the main cellar, a large, irregularly-shaped apartment containing a vast number of inviting bottles and barrels, but very little else. "Look at this, Roy. See what I mean?"

"I do," muttered Mr. Whittle, dropping on his knees and examining the panel critically. "Phew! It reeks of machine oil. How does it open? Isn't there a knob, or something?"

"There's a spring of sorts, but if you undo the catch you can pull the whole thing back with your hand." Mr. Davenhill did so, revealing the entrance to a tunnel about four feet high and three broad. "The place has been disused for years - nobody's been through it since we were kids, so far as I know."

"Looks like it," commented Mr. Whittle, flashing his torch and revealing several large, black spiders that yawned at him and blinked in an offended manner. "I suppose we may as well search it while we're here, though I don't expect for a moment that we'll come across anything worth finding."

Bending himself down he started through the tunnel, straining his eyes for any sign of life and collecting a great quantity of dust and cobwebs in his hair. Spennie followed, and for minute or so they groped along a silence.

"It's not more than a couple of hundred feet from end to end, is it?" asked Mr. Whittle presently, pausing to gouge some dirt out of his eyes. "We come out near the - " he broke off, and paused. "I say, old lad, what was that?"

"I don't know. It sounded like a door slamming."

"Door?" barked Mr. Whittle. "Damn it, someone's shut the

panel on us. Back, old lad, and don't spare the horses!"

"All very well," Mr. Davenhill panted, making valiant efforts to turn in his own width. "Curse it; I believe I've swallowed a spider-"

Stopping only to call Spennie and his spider an evil name, Mr. Whittle managed to push by, and , opening his throttle to its fullest extent, charged back towards the panel. As he had expected, he found it immovable.

"Won't it open?" Mr. Davenhill asked.

"Does it look as if it will?"

"I don't know. I can't see through you."

"For your information,: Mr. Whittle informed him patiently, "it won't, which is why I'm sweating my guts out heaving at the confounded thing. We can get out the other end, and I suppose, but when I find out who's playing the fool with us I'll scoop out his liver and ram it down his gullet."

Mr. Davenhill opened his mouth to reply, and then stopped short as a low moaning sound came from somewhere close at hand. It was at least an hour since Quintus Maximus has last been on the air, and the old coot evidently decided to make up for lost time, producing a series of long, choking howls that got right into Mr. Davenhill's innards and churned them up in the manner of an egg-whisk.

"Yuk," Spennie said, in a strangled voice. "What is it?"

"Mice," Mr. Whittle informed him, as the first moan died away in a sort of death-rattle.

"Mice my left eyebrow." Spennie winced as Quinnie, adjusting his frequency and turning up the volume, uncorked another howl. "I don't like it. I say, suppose the garden end's blocked, too?"

Mr. Whittle had already thought of this unpleasant possibility, and without delay groped back along the tunnel, muttering lurid curses and threats under his breath. Three or four minutes brought to what seemed to be a dead end.

"This the door?" asked Mr. Whittle.

"Yes. That's the handle, on your right. Pull it downwards."

Mr. Whittle did so, and was relived to feel it give beneath his weight. Evidently this too had been oiled, for it swung smoothly back and the pair emerged thankfully it's into God's clean air, snorting with relief and brushing themselves down. It was dusk now, and in spite of a crescent moon difficult to see far; the dim outlines of the Hall showed up against the sky, while from the direction of the camp flickering lights could be seen.

"Let's get in," said Mr. Davenhill abruptly.

"Not so fast, old lad. I may be wrong, but I believe I can see some duck slinking about over there. Get down, and keep quiet."

"What of it? It's probably somebody taking a stroll. Fredl, for instance, or Strudwick."

"Quite so. It might also be someone on there way to wall us up," said Mr. Whittle dryly. "He obviously doesn't want to be seen. Get under that bush, and stop breathing."

"It's prickly," Mr. Davenhill protested weakly.

"Don't make such a fuss. Quick!" with which Mr. Whittle thrust his long-suffering friend into the heart of the bush and followed suit, winching as a thorn made it's presence felt in particularly vulnerable part of his anatomy.

It was at this point that the moon, with typical cussedness, retired behind a large cloud and went out as though it had been switched of at the main. Mr. Whittle swore softly, and tensed.

"Shift over, can't you?" spluttered Mr. Davenhill, in a frantic whisper. "You're -"

"Pipe down!" hissed Mr. Whittle. "I'm going to jump on his gizzard. He's going straight to the Way entrance."

Spennie was in no fit state to argue; playing hide-and-seek with skeletons, being blocked up in a passages and rammed into spiny bushes did not agree with him, and he had now reached the stage of being past caring what happened. Lying back in what seemed to be the least uncomfortable position, he awaited developments. For what seemed hours silence reigned, broken only by stealthy footsteps; the came a startled grunt, a scuffle, and a flash of light.

"Got him," said Mr. Whittle breathlessly, fumbling with his torch. "Give me a – my God, it's Stoker!"

"Stoker?"

"None other. Do you think we ought to help him up?"

"You can't sit on him all night, if you wan't to," grunted Mr. Davenhill, "but don't expect me to stay here and hold your hand. Have you killed him, or merely laid him out?"

"Neither. He's as right as rain." Mr. Whittle rose, and assisted the old butler to his feet. "Sorry if I gave you a fright, old lad, but you've only yourself to blame. Feeling all right?"

Stoker wheezed painfully, and gave a perfect imitation of a calf calling to it's mother.

"Indeed I am not, Mr. Roy," he gasped, when he had recovered sufficiently to speak. "I doubt whether I shall ever feel all right again. I'm sure my spine is dislocated -"

"You're lucky I haven't kicked it through your hat," Mr. Whittle assured him brutally. "What's the big idea, trying to block us up in that infernal passage?"

Stoker removed a beetle from his ear, and glared balefully. "I have never consciously attempted to block any passage, sir, infernal or otherwise. To do so would be to exceed my duties. I trust you will not be offended if I speak freely, Mr. Roy?"

"Of course not. Go right ahead."

"Thank you, Mr. Roy. In that case," said Stoker, "I am bound to express the opinion that hiding in the bushes and playing leapfrog is fully as bad as sniffing about the hall at midnight. In fact, sir, I can only describe you as a ham-handed young doddle-pate. Grrrr!" - with which he made a dignified withdrawal into the darkness, leaving Mr. Whittle and Mr. Davenhill gaping at one another.

"Odd," said Mr. Whittle at last.

"Most odd," agreed Spennie." Being ticked off by my own butler is just about the last ruddy straw". I suppose he really did shut us in?"

"I'm damned if I know. It doesn't Stokerish to me. Much more like young Terry."

"It – it could have shut itself," said Spennie in a low tone.

"And latched itself?"

"Stranger things than that have happened within the last day or two. Besides how about the howls?"

"Well," said Mr. Whittle, "first thing tomorrow I'm coming here with a hammer and chisel, and I'm going to have the locks of these panels. If anybody really did get walled up, they might not be found for days. As soon as you get indoors, go down to the cellar and see if you can spot anything."

"Aren't you coming in, then?"

"Not for a bit. While I'm out here I'll potter down to camp and have a word with Aunt Clara and her gang. Feel like a stroll?"

"No," admitted Mr. Davenhill cravenly, "I don't. Wild horses wouldn't drag me down there tonight."

"They're not likely to try," Mr. Whittle assured him. "How long will it take to walk?"

"Not more than five minutes."

Spennie shivered. "I'm off. Keep to the left, and carry straight on – you can't miss the camp, but you won't be able to see much in this light."

"I have a feeling," said Mr. Whittle morosely, "that the darker it is, the better these ducks will look. See you later." With which he removed a lingering ant from his chin, re lit his pipe, and marched purposefully off in the direction of the flickering lamps in the distance.

Chapter 7

The moon was still bashfully hiding her face, and Mr. Whittle's torch was not a powerful one; but he remembered the layout of the hall grounds pretty well even though he had not been there for some time, and he walked along at a good pace, thinking things over as he did so. He was still fogged. That Stoker had deliberately to look them up he frankly did not believe; the old retainer may have had his peculiarities, but he would certainly have considered it unethical to wall an old friend in the damp tunnel – apart altogether from the fact that he could have no conceivable motive for doing so. Mr. Whittle had no desire at all to spend a week or so shut up in the dark with only Spennie for a companion. Had it been Miss. Wrightman, now ... Mr. Whittle's thoughts turned automatically into a different channel. Pauline was not so breath-taking as Miss Czernak, but on the whole she was perhaps preferable (though Roy was honest enough with himself admit that he would have liked to have had the chance to cultivate both).

By this time he had crossed the old cricket-field, and could see various lights twinkling among the mounds only a hundred yards or so away. He could also hear voices – a bleating masculine buzz, and strident feminine tones that he recognised at once as Aunt Clara's. He was about to give a cheerful "view halloo!" when the ground suddenly failed beneath his feet and he fell into what appeared to be a bottomless pit. After what seemed to be minutes he landed with a depressing squelch in some slimy, evil-smelling substance, and gave vent to a cry in which rage, bewilderment and despair were nicely blended.

"Ouf!" he spluttered, fumbling frantically for his torch. "What the merry hell – God, I'm in booby-trap, or something like it!"

The feeble light revealed that he had fallen headlong into a circular pit about ten feet deep (not ten miles, as he had at first supposed), with vertical walls. He also realised that he was knee-deep in mud, and that his only suit of evening dress would have to be written off, temporarily at least, as a dead loss.

After a few seconds a lantern appeared over the top of the hole, and a head poked over the side.

"Is anybody there?" it inquired.

"Yuk," replied Mr. Whittle, thrashing about.

"Dear me," said the voice. "How very odd. Miss Debenham, I fancy that" a sheep has fallen into our refuse pit"

"A sheep ha, echoed the female voice. "Nonsense. What would a sheep be doing at this time of night?"

"Falling into our pit, apparently," reported the head. "Most inconvenient. What do you think we ought to do about It?"

Mr. Whittle, having scarped some of the mud of his vocal chords, made a violent suggestion. There was a brief pause, and then the head spoke again.

"Do you know," it said, "I don't believe it is a sheep, after all. I distinctly heard it say something."

"Then what the devil is it?" asked the female voice testily. "Shine the light down, and we might be able to see."

"You doddle-pated, dim-witted old coot -" yelled Mr. Whittle, at the top of his voice. "Will you -"

"Language," said the head reprovingly, and a second lantern appeared over the shaft. "Really, there is no need to get so excited. I take it you are not a sheep, but a man?"

"I was a man once," grated Mr. Whittle, "But now I believe I'm a mud fountain. For God's sake let down a rope, or something, and haul me up!"

"But who are you?" persisted the head, helplessly.

"Whittle – Roy Whittle. I'm staying at the Hall." Roy spat mad, and cursed luridly.

"Indeed?" said the head, mildly. "Most interesting. My name is Augustus Weatherill. How do you do?"

Mr. Whittle made an effort to control himself.

"I shall be extremely well," he said patiently, "once I manage to get out of this infernal death-trap. I'm a little wet, if you see what I mean."

"I do, I do," agreed Professor Weatherill cheerfully. "It must be extremely damp down there. Smelly, too. However did you get there?"

"For Rameses sake," broke Aunt Clara impatiently, "fish

73

him out with a hook, or something, and lets get back to work. We haven't nearly finished excavating that moment yet, and once the moon sets it'll be too dark to carry on."

"Hallo, there," called out Mr. Whittle. "Is that Aunt Clara? I'm Roy."

Aunt Clara peered into the pit, and shone her torch directly in Mr. Whittle's eyes. "So you are," she said. "You look wet – and muddy. I thought you were still in the Navy."

"Not only am I not in the Navy," Mr. Whittle assured her, "but I never was in the Navy. In the days of my youth I was in the R.A.F., but at the moment I'm working in the solicitor's office."

"But you aren't, my dear fellow," bleated Professor Weatherill infuriatingly. "You're sitting in a muddy hole. Can't you get out?"

"Not having suction-pads on my feet," said Mr. Whittle scathingly, "I can't. A rope, please – or, failing that, a ladder."

"There's a ladder near the East Wall," said Aunt Clara brusquely. "Go and get it, for Pharaoh's sake, and lets get on with our work."

"I suppose you haven't got a snifter of whisky on you?" Mr. Whittle asked hopefully, as the professor plodded off. "I'm soaked, and my feet are frozen."

"Naturally," agreed Aunt Clara. "If you will sit waist-high in the mud you must be prepared that sort of thing. I remember that mud was always did have a strange fascination for you, even as a child. Sorry, but I've left my damned flask up at the house, so you'll have to wait." She gave vent to a bark of mirth. "Your trousers must be in what state!"

"They are," Mr. Whittle assured her "What kind if stuff is this? It hasn't rained lately, so far as I know, but this hole is absolutely swamped."

"As a matter of fact," said Aunt Clara, "we use it as a general waste-pit, and tip all sorts of things down it – in fact anything we don't want; we spend most of our time here these days." Mr. Whittle gave a subdued groan. "The whole camp is a magnificent find," she went on enthusiastically, "and right on my own doorstep! The headquarters of Quintus Maximus, who was second-in-command to Claudius himself -"

"What sort of stuff do you tip down here?"

"Anything. Waste tea, and the like." Aunt Clara lit a cigarette, and peered down. "I suppose we really ought to put a lid over it, but there never seems to be time – we have so much to do. Where the hell is that ladder? You're holding us up."

Roy expressed his regret.

"Oh, it really doesn't matter, I suppose," said Aunt Clara handsomely. "There's always tomorrow. By the way, I really must show you that superb engraving we found last week. So far as I can judge it was done by a local artist to celebrate the opening of a new swimming-bath about the time of the Emperor Hadrian – in splendid condition, too." She broke off. "Thank God, here's the ladder."

Mr. Whittle echoed the sentiment, and climbed wearily out of the pit, shaking himself like a dog and showering mud in all directions. In the lantern light he could clearly see both of the rescuers, and paid a mental tribute to Stoker's descriptive powers; for once the aged retainer had hit the nail squarely on the head. He had described Professor Weatherill as slimy, and slimy he was; a thin, scraggy man with a hooked nose and sunken eyes, combined with a general aspect of griminess. As regards age, he might have a youngish eighty or a somewhat senile seventy. Aunt Clara herself did not appear to have changed much; her leathery face was perhaps more lined, but taking everything into account she had stood the assault of years remarkably well.

"Ouf!" Mr. Whittle snorted with relief as he stepped off the ladder on to a firm ground once more. "God, what a place!"

"It certainly isn't the kind of spot to lounge about in," agreed Aunt Clara, truthfully if ungrammatically. "If I were you, young Roy, I'd go and wash. You stink like a polecat."

"I'm going to," Mr. Whittle said ruefully, looking at the wreck of his trousers. "You haven't sprayed any more death-traps around, have you?"

"One's quite enough for all we want," Aunt Clara assured him. "Incidentally, why were you prowling around? Of course, if you want to come and help us with the excavations."

"Excavations," said Mr. Whittle politely, "leave me cold, and mummies and skeletons give me the loo-loos. All I was doing was taking a casual stroll. I suppose I'd better go and take a look for some disinfectant. See you later."

"By the way," interrupted Professor Weatherill, "it occurs to me, Miss Debenham, that we have not yet partaken of dinner. Perhaps if we returned to the house now, and finished the monument in the morning"!

"Not on your life," said Aunt Clara positively. "I'm going to finish that monument if it takes me all night."

"But it's dark," bleated the old trout, in a plaintive tone.

"Considering that it's past ten o'clock," retorted Aunt Clara, "I see nothing odd about that. Go and feed your face if you like, but I'm going on digging." She sniffed . I can't waste any more time on you, Roy – besides, I prefer you at a distance just now. You smell worse than seven crocodiles of Amhop-Tarkus, and that's saying something."

Mr. Whittle snorted and, repressing the urge to say something pithy about crocodiles, turned on his heel and squelched dismally back to the house. As he made his way up the steps and rang the bell it was borne upon him that he would hate either Miss Czernak or Miss Wrightman to see him in this condition, and prepared to make a quick dash up to his room.

After the usual five-minute interval Stoker opened the door and peered out – after which he shied like startled horse and chocked violently, clutching at the wall for support.

"Only me, old lad," said Mr. Whittle cheerfully. "Nice evening, what?"

Stoker gave him a fishy stare, and wrinkled his nose delicately like a rabbit who has found a slug in the lettuce. "You look wet, sir. I trust you have not had a mishap?"

"Oh, not at all," Mr. Whittle assured him. "I felt rather hot, so went for a dip in the lake."

"In your clothes, sir?"

"Of course. Why not?" Mr. Whittle grinned acidly. "I never bother to change into a bathing-costume – I can never get one to fit me."

The aged butler looked thoroughly baffled, and thought this one over, chewing his lip dubiously. Before he could think of a suitable reply Mr. Strudwick emerged from the drawing room, carrying a pile of books and sniffing offensively.

"Dear me," he began. "Is anything the matter? I can detect an unpleasant aroma -"

"You mean I pong?" asked Mr. Whittle cheerfully. "Quite right. I do. Considering where I've been I'm not surprised, either. Stoker, old lad, is the water in the bathroom hot?"

"There is no water available, sir, hot or otherwise," Stoker informed him gloomily. "Only a few moments ago the boiler exploded with considerable violence, and Mr. Spencer ordered me to turn off all the mains."

Mr. Whittle gave a growl of annoyance.

"Damn. What do you suggest? I mean, I can't go about like this."

"I say, you're all wet," pointed out Mr. Strudwick cleverly. "Is it raining?"

Mr. Whittle bared his teeth in an animal snarl.

"No. I've been for a swim. Any ideas yet, Stoker?"

"I hardly know what to suggest, Mr. Roy," muttered the old butler, rubbing his chin. "The vacuum-cleaner would be unsuitable, I fear ... ah! The well!"

"What well?"

"The well near the North Tower, sir. It still contains a certain amount of water."

"No," said Mr. Whittle firmly, "I draw the line at that. I've been swimming in a well. It's probably full of frogs."

"Almost certainly, sir,: agreed Stoker, "but you misunderstand me. I was about to propose that a quantity of well-water be raised by means of a bucket, heated over the gas, and conveyed to your room. I fear it may be somewhat impure, but I see no alternative."

"It couldn't be worse than the stuff I fell in," muttered Mr. Whittle "God! It's awful, isn't it?"

"It is, Mr. Roy." Stoker nodded his head decisively. "In fact, you remind me of a very old drain that has not been cleansed for many years. If you care to proceed to your room, sir, I will follow you with the necessary water almost immediately."

Mr. Whittle grunted thankfully and plodded wearily upstairs, spraying mud in all directions and leaving little pools of liquid to mark his trail.

Chapter 8

It was nearly an hour before Mr. Whittle had cleaned himself up sufficiently to be fit for circulation once more. Stoker's well-water had proved to be somewhat better than expected; once Mr. whittle had removed a piece of wood, half a matchbox, several pounds of leaves and a parboiled tadpole from the bottom of the bucket he was able to have a tolerable wash, and though he still felt sticky and offensive he decided that there was nothing more to be done at the moment. He accordingly lit his pipe and pottered downstairs, wondering vaguely whether the aged professor had succeeded in dragging Aunt Clara away from the monument.

The first person he met was Pauline Wrightman, and as this was just as he wanted most he uncorked a genial smile. "What – ho, Paul. Where is everyone?"

"In the drawing room," Miss Wrightman informed him, "drinking."

"There's nobody in the conservatory?"

"No. Why should there be?"

"Splendid," said Mr. Whittle heartily. "In that case, that's where we'll go. I have much to say to you, young Paul, that is not for the public ear."

Miss Wrightman raised no objections, and allowed herself to be led into the nearest of the glass conservatories, a large place crowded with potted palms and odd-looking plants of all shapes and sizes. There was also an iron seat, conveniently screened by a palm, and on this the two settled themselves comfortably.

"Well?" said Pauline, after a pause. "What do you want?"

"Do you really want to know?" murmured Mr. Whittle.

"Be serious, Roy. I take it that you didn't bring me here to talk about the weather?"

Mr. Whittle sighed. "No," he said truthfully, "I didn't. I've several points to make, but let's get the dull part over first. How long have you been secretary to this duck Weatherill?"

"About four years. Why?"

"I just wondered. How the devil have you stood him for four years?"

"He's always been very pleasant. Besides, I'm, interested in archaeology. I like travelling, too."

"And he really does know his fossils?"

"Of course he does. He's written a dozen books at least."

"I see." Mr. Whittle pondered. "Point number 2, what's all this about a map?"

Miss Wrightman laughed lightly. It was a musical sound, and made Mr. Whittles heart do a brief gavotte inside his diaphragm.

"Goodness only knows. It's obviously a fake. Someone must have given it to Dr. Fredl as a joke."

"Given it to Dr. Fredl?"

"Well, it was Dr. Fredl who found it. The professor happened to see it among his papers, quite by accident, and as Fredl had gone to London he showed it to me."

"What makes you so sure it's a phoney?"

"Everything about it. The writing isn't in the old style, for one thing, and the paper looks new – oh, it just shrieks at you. I thought Mr. Fane might have planted it."

"Not a chance. Young Terry takes himself and his Bolshevism far too seriously to go about playing kid's larks of that sort. I haven't any faith in the thing, but I must say I should like to have a brief look at it. Has Weatherill still got it?"

"I suppose so, if he hasn't thrown it away. Shall I ask him?"

"Don't bother. I'll see him when he comes in."

"He's bound to be along shortly. Anything else you want to talk about?"

"Yes. How do you stand with the Strudwick bacillus?"

"He's not a bacillus!"

"Pardon me, he is a bacillus. He reminds me of one of those things you find in cheese."

Miss Wrightman coloured. "I don't see what you have to do with it. Anyhow, Raymond is a clever and charming person."

"I can think of several adjectives to describe him," admitted Mr. Whittle, "but I'm bound to say that those weren't the two I would have selected. He hasn't got a chin, for one thing, and his eyes are like a dead cod's."

Miss Wrightman looked up.

"You're being rather beastly," she said slowly. He can't help not being good looking or strong, and it isn't fare to hold it against him."

Mr. Whittle, for once, felt faintly ashamed.

"I didn't mean to be unfair. I know he can't help looking like he does – if he could he'd obviously do something about it. Are you in love with him?"

"I thought I was," Pauline admitted, "but now I'm not so sure. He loves me, I know, and that means a lot ... I don't know. I wish he wasn't so wrapped up in his career."

"Anyone who could wrap himself up in a career while you were around must me a Group A doddle-pate," Mr. Whittle assured her. "I couldn't. Don't be so distant, confound you." Anybody would think I had the mumps too, like Aunt Violet."

"I'm only a few inches away."

"That's several inches too far." Mr. Whittle rectified matters, and silence reigned for perhaps fifteen seconds. "I'll bet Struddy never told you that you have eyes like twin stars?"

Miss Wrightman disentangled herself, and stood up.

"One fine day" she said dryly, "somebody will take you down a peg, Roy, and it'll do you good. Have you quite finished?"

"For the moment," Mr. Whittle informed her reluctantly, "but only for the moment. Damn," he added, "that's torn it. I wonder if he's got hold of the wrong end of the stick?"

"Who?"

"Terry, blast his eyebrows. Prying at us through the glass door. No matter – we're no concern of his, and in any case I don't care."

"I do. Roy, please!" said Miss Wrightman urgently. "I should hate Raymond to find out you kissed me. He'd be terribly hurt. After all, I am half-engaged to him."

"Grrr," growled Mr. Whittle. "All right. I'll shut Terry up – not that I suppose he's interested one way or another. Come and have a drink. I need one myself, and besides, I want to have a word with your grimy-faced employer."

Chapter 9

Professor Weatherill was easily run to earth. As Pauline and Mr. Whittle entered the drawing-room they were greeted by the sight of the old trout polishing off a whisky-and-soda. As his method of drinking was to hook his false teeth over the edge of the glass and then suck, the effect was – to say the least – unedifying, and Mr. Whittle, with a slight shudder, turned his attention elsewhere. Most of the local population seemed to be present. Dr. Fredl, Mr. Strudwick and Mr. Davenhill were chatting amiably together, while Carole and Terry occupied the settee, Stoker hovering around like a senile butterfly. Aunt Clara, holding a glass of fine old port in one hand and a book in the other, was leaning nonchalantly against the piano puffing a pipe. Mr. Whittle gave a short snort of mirth. He had quite forgotten the old aunt's fondness for smoking a pipe – a habit of which her sister Violet strongly disapproved.

Mr. Whittle bade the company good-evening and made for the sideboard like a homing pigeon. Having fought his way successfully through the seething mob he downed two stiff bracers in quick succession, and felt a great deal better for it.

"I've been washing," he explained, in response to a casual inquiry from Mr. Davenhill."

"Oh?, why?"

"I smelt. For the matter of that, I expect I still do. Where does that wall lead to, old lad – a farm?"

"I've no idea. This water business," Said Mr. Davenhill moodily, "is the outside limit. The boiler went off like a gun."

"Evil forces," muttered Professor Weatherill gloomily.

"Evil forces my left nostril." said Mr. Whittle frankly. "Much more likely to be due to a couple of fuses in mercuric fulminate, or something of the sort. Trouble is, we can't prove it." He turned to Stoker. "What do you think it was about, old lad? Have you viewed the mangled wreck?"

"I have not been near it, sir," admitted the aged butler. "In my opinion the article in question is possessed of the Devil. Such an explosion, coming at such a time, is far from natural."

"Agreed, but my point is that it's much more likely to be caused by a fuse than a spook." Mr. Whittle grinned. "If you're all so certain that Quinnie's spirit is pottering about, why not call in a psychic research expert and persuade the old coot to come and discuss it over a whisky? Once he got thoroughly sozzled -"

"It is hardly my place to criticise, Mr. Roy," said Stoker in an offended tone, "but I fear that light-hearted jesting on such a subject may have serious consequences. Will you require me any further, Mr. Spencer?"

"Spennie shook his head wearily, and the aged retainer, casting a marked look at Mr. Whittle, withdrew. When the gash in the atmosphere caused by his departure had closed up Roy shook his head, and sighed.

"Poor old trout," he observed. "Senile decay. Wonder how old Quinnie would cope with brandy? I don't suppose it had been invented in his day."

"A tight spook ought to be easier to handle than a sober one, I suppose," admitted Mr. Davenhill absently, "but they haven't got any bodies to drink with, so the argument strikes me as futile."

"Astral bodies, old lad. Composed mainly of ecto – something, I believe."

Dr. Fredl revved up his engine, and cleared his throat importantly.

"Herr Shakespeare," he began, "you the affair with much jokings treat, yet of a gravity utmost it is. A phantom most certainly awakened we have, and one thing only to be done there can be. We the skeleton to it's grave return must, and this hauntingness at once stopped will become."

"What, bury the thing again?" said Mr. Davenhill thoughtfully. "That's an idea."

"But, ja. I, Felix Fredl, I know!" The old archaeologist leaned forward, and prodded his host meaningly in the stomach. "A case before encountered I have, and finished it was only the return of the body to its resting-place by. The only method disaster to avert this is."

"What's that?" asked Aunt Clara suddenly, putting her book down with a bang. "Get rid of the skeleton? I'll see you damned first. It may prove to be a vital clue in my investigations."

"All very well. Spooks or no spooks, there's something funny going on. Fires and bangs and bells -"

"Bells to you," snorted the old aunt. "I'll not do it. Ridiculous!"

"I agree," Mr. Whittle put in. "The spook theory's pure onion soup. It won't make the slightest difference whether the skeleton's in the museum, under the ground, or – or in your bed."

"Well, I certainly don't mean to take it to bed with me," conceded Aunt Clara, "but until my researches are finished it's staying right where it is, and that's flat. Damn, I'm out of tobacco. "What kind do you smoke, Roy?"

"Navy Cut. Here you are."

"Wishy-washy stuff," commented the old aunt, eyeing the proffered pouch with contempt. "Not like the brand we get out East – I know it's mostly camel dung, but it smokes well." She filled her pipe energetically, and lit up. "Augustus, you're not saying much. What do you make of it all?"

The professor chewed his straggly moustache.

"It's hard to tell," he admitted. "I quite agree that there are evil forces around us, but I fear it may prove a difficult matter to placate them." He turned to Dr. Fredl. "This case you spoke about – how many deaths were there before it was settled?"

"Two," the whiskered doctor informed him briefly. "A man and his daughter. In their bath, they had their throats cut."

"Must have been a big bath," commented Mr. Whittle.

"You miscomprehend, Herr Shakespeare. Two baths they were in – not one, you follow?"

"More or less," said Mr. Whittle, "but just because a couple of probably neurotic people slit their gizzards about ten years ago it doesn't follow that we're dealing with a ghost now."

"The facts -" began Mr. Strudwick.

"Yes," said Mr. Whittle, "the facts. Tell me this, old lad. Have you, or anybody else, come across anything that can't be explained without dragging in Quinnie and Co.? I don't mean the routine tapping and voices. Those stunts are as old as the hills, and they smell of decaying fish. I mean real, tangible proof."

"Most certainly," Professor Weatherill informed him

blandly. "I understand that both Mr. Fane and Miss Wrightman have witnessed perfect materializations."

"Pauline!" ejaculated the M.P "When was this?"

"I've heard about that," Mr. Whittle broke in before Miss Wrightman had time to reply, "but I'm not convinced. She didn't get near it, and it was pretty dark at the time. How about you, Terry?"

Terry grunted, but showed no desire to go on the air and explain.

"Out with it," Aunt Clara rapped impatiently. "Don't gape like a stranded fish. What have you seen?"

"Never you mind."

"I do mind. Come on, come on, come on."

"Nuts. It's my own business."

"Youthful imagination," murdered Mr. Strudwick in a stage whisper to Mr. Davenhill.

He had said the wrong thing. Terry, crimson in the face, made one dive at him, grabbed him by the collar and waved a fist threateningly in front of his snoddle, while a babble of voices broke out on all sides and Mr. Whittle watched curiously, wondering how long it would take before the luckless M.P's eyes dropped out of their sockets.

"You young ruffian -" choked Mr. Strudwick, writhing disparately.

"I've wanted to do this for days," grated Terry, shaking the M.P's neck like a dog worrying a bone. "If you'd ever -"

Pauline jumped forward, but Mr. Whittle was before her. It seemed unless he took prompt action Wollingham Hall would shortly contain two inert skeletons instead of one, so – rather reluctantly – he caught Terry in a neat ju-jujitsu grip and spun him back, leaving Mr. Strudwick clutching his collar and making repulsive noises like a seal with croup.

"You bone-headed doddle-pate," said Mr. Whittle cheerfully, "do you want to be jugged for manslaughter?"

"Never you mind. Let me go, damn you," breathed Terry, straining against Mr. Whittle's scientific hold.

"Please, Roy." This, rather unexpectedly, from Miss Czernak. "You are hurting him."

"I'm not. Still, I'll let him go if he behaves himself." Mr. Whittle relaxed his grasp, and Terry staggered away. "Struddy old lad, you really do ask for it. One day you'll get yourself a really good poke right in the clock, and honestly you'll only have yourself to blame."

"Hooliganism," Said Mr. Strudwick thickly. "My neck! I shall be stiff for weeks. It is not my habit to engage in vulgar brawls, or I should -" He paused in order to think this one out.

"Well, what?" Terry asked truculently.

Mr. Strudwick did not appear to be certain, and adopted the wise policy of keeping silent. At this point Professor Weatherill stuck his oar in once more.

"Really," he said mildly, "this violence will do no good. Doubtless Mr. Fane has his own reasons for not wishing to enlighten us-"

"What you'd really like me to say," said Terry belligerently, "is that I've seen a ghastly figure in white, with hollow eye-sockets and blood dripping from it's jowls -"

"It's what?"

"Jowls," Terry repeated, glaring at Mr. Whittle.

"Oh? I don't follow you, old lad. Can ghosts bleed?" Mr. Whittle lit a cigarette thoughtfully. "I mean to say, they haven't got anything to bleed with, apart from this ecto-whatever-it-is."

"What the devil does it matter? Mr. Davenhill asked reasonably. "They can bleed as much as they like, provided they don't do it here. The point is nobody seems to have any definite ideas as to what to do, and honestly I feel inclined to let the psychic society loose. I don't see that they can do any actual harm."

"May I make a suggestion?" asked Professor Weatherill diffidently.

"Do. What?"

"I have been thinking the matter over," went on the mildewed archaeologist, "and while I agree that Dr. Fredl's solution has much to recommend it, I believe that Mr. Whittle's suggestion is by far the best. By a singular coincidence, I have a friend in London – a very well known authority on the subject – who is, I feel sure, the one person capable of clearing up this affair without difficulty."

Spennie rubbed his chin. "What is he? Professionally I mean?"

"A psychic research worker, and, incidentally, and eminent authority upon ancient history. His name is Ratcliffe, Nehemiah Ratcliffe. Doubtless he would give us his opinion for a very moderate fee."

"Fee? Aha, now we're getting down to brass tacks." Mr. Whittle chuckled. "tell me, old horse, does you pal Ratty spend all his time going about the place chasing ghosts, or is he only a part time spooker?"

"The name," Weatherill informed him coldly, "is Ratcliffe, and I doubt whether he would appreciate being described as a spooker. Please consider my suggestion withdrawn. I was only doing my best to help." He moved over to the sideboard in order to grab a fresh whisky-and-soda, radiating umbridge from every pore.

"I don't know," Mr. Davenhill admitted helplessly. "I'd pay a good many pounds to get this business sorted out, and if this Ratcliffe can do any good I'm all for calling him in. Have you known him long?"

"For many years. We were at college together."

"Borstal?" Mr. Whittle inquired delicately.

The professor elected to ignore this one, and a loud whirring noise proclaimed that Dr. Fredl was about to speak.

"I cannot this suggestion agree with," he announced, having engaged his gears with the usual cough. "I, Felix Fredl, of the hauntingnesses know, and of this Ratcliffe never heard have I. Of no use is it these matters to halt until beneath the earth this skeleton once more is."

"And I've already told you," Aunt Clara informed him curtly, "that it's staying right where it is until I've finished excavating the camp, which might take weeks."

"All right," said Mr. Davenhill with decision. "Anything's better than nothing. How soon can you get hold of this Ratcliffe?"

"Tomorrow, if not sooner," the professor assured him,. "I feel sure I have his telephone number in my diary. There may be – er – a slight financial adjustment to be made; I believe that

Nehemiah likes to settle all these trivial matter before getting down to work."

"Cash in advance?" suggested Mr. Whittle.

"Well – yes, I suppose one could call it that," agreed the old buffer, "Of course, we must remember that Nehemiah is a most unworldly man. Sordid matters like money mean little to him."

"Don't give us that guff," Mr. Whittle requested him brutally. "From what I know of spookers they're out for as much as they can get. Incidentally, does your pal charge so much per head, or does he make a reduction for quantity?"

"Again you are joking make," s aid Dr. Fredl reprovingly. "Herr Shakespeare, this is no occasion for laughing is. Donner and blitzen! Many deaths have I known ..." He broke off, looking at Pauline, who had been sitting quietly in a corner taking no part in the merry prattle. "But of such things not to speak better it is, nein?"

A brief silence followed, broken by a groan from Mr. Strudwick; soft, certainly, but so nerve-racking and deathly that it might have well have come from the fleshless lips of Quintus Maximus himself. The general effect was electric. Everybody leaped violently into the air, and a chorus of exclamations broke out.

"Don't do it," said Mr. Whittle testily, making a neat two point landing on his chair. "What's up?, cramp?"

"My neck. I believe a bone is bruised," said Mr. Strudwick, massaging himself gingerly. "It feels most peculiar."

"It looks most peculiar," agreed Terry, "but then it always does."

Aunt Clara uncorked a short bark from mirth.

"Rameses!" she said, "from the way you carry on anyone would think you'd been mauled by the sacred pumas of Ptruthelthoh. Why the deuce did you let him do it?"

"Brawling," said Mr. Strudwick, "is not my way of settling disputes. I consider it not only ill mannered, but childish."

"Pity you don't brawl a bit more," commented the old aunt, puffing at her pipe and exhaling a cloud of acrid smoke. "It might do you good. When I was your age I was always having scraps –

won most of 'em, too" she added modestly.

"I'm sure you did," agreed Mr. Whittle courteously. "Frankly, I shouldn't care to tackle you myself even now."

"What you need," said Terry truculently, glaring at the M.P, "is a few weeks in my regiment. "We'd soon lick you in to shape."

Mr. Whittle looked quickly at Pauline, and was in time to see two tongues of flame shoot from her nostrils. Mr. Strudwick pursed his lips and said nothing, and once more conversation flagged; there was a long and decidedly uncomfortable pause, broken only by the revolting, slushy noise of Professor Weatherill dealing with yet another whisky-and-soda. Eventually Stoker came in, and announced evening coffee in much the same manner as the ancient Athenians must have offered Socrates his bedtime glass of hemlock.

Mr. Whittle, finding himself left behind in the general rush for the door, paused in order to down yet another snifter, musing upon the latest developments. He rather fancied that a certain amount of light was appearing in the murk, but at the moment his ideas were vague and unformed.

He did wish, though, that Terry had broken Mr. Strudwick's neck instead of merely wrenching it.

Chapter 10

Twenty minutes or so later Mr. Davenhill joined Mr. Whittle an the billiard-room, looking even more harasses than usual, and grasping a very large whisky in his paw. "I say," he began, "Weatherill's arranged for his psychic pal to come down here tomorrow. What do you think of the idea?"

"Frankly," Mr. Whittle admitted, "I think it reeks of bad fish. What's he charging?"

"A hundred quid"

"What?"

"On results only. I know it sounds a lot," Said Davenhill defensively, "but he made it quite clear he wouldn't take any money unless he cleared the whole thing up."

Mr. Whittle gulped at his whisky.

"Spennie," he said, as soon as he had recovered his breath, "you ought to be certified, and tucked away in a padded cell with at least two keepers. You doddering, brainless pinhead, how do you know this duck isn't an out-and-out fake? If he's connected with Weatherill, he probably is. Hell," he went on with feeling, "you've got a nerve. You drag me away from a perfectly good fight to come and see you through, and now you drag down some crack-brained fortune teller without so much as asking what I think. I've a damn good mind to go off in the morning and leave you to it."

"You wouldn't do that?"

"The way I'm feeling right now," Mr. Whittle assured him, "nothing would please me more."

"Mr. Davenhill gave a hoarse croak.

"Roy, do be reasonable. After all, what harm can Ratcliffe do?"

"He can separate you from a cool hundred quid, for a start. Pretty good gravy, if you ask me."

"Weatherill says it's the usual fee."

"That's all right what Weatherill says. I wouldn't put any trust in any friend of that unwashed old buster, even if there was a genuine spook to lay – which there isn't."

"You think that Terry and the Wrightman girl are telling lies?"

"I don't, but I'm prepared to bet it was all done with mirrors or something. By the by, what exactly did young Terry see?"

"I don't know. He won't tell me."

"He'll tell me," said Mr. Whittle grimly, "even if I have to beat it out of him. I suppose it hasn't occurred to your fertile brain to check on the Ratcliffe bird's references?"

"I haven't even spoken to him yet." Spennie admitted. "Weatherill did all the talking. I suppose he's on the level, but I don't see how we can find out until he arrives."

Mr. Whittle pulled at his pipe. "I was thinking of Gregory Tallon," he said slowly. "Do you remember him?"

"I do. Damn it, he was mixed up in that frightful business about Aunt Clara and the salmon."

Mr. Whittle chuckled. "So he was – I'd forgotten. Trust old Gregory to get involved in any thoroughly disreputable affair of that sort! Well, shall I ring him?"

"Why? I mean, is he any connection of Ratcliffe's?"

"Gregory," Mr. Whittle informed him dryly, "is on the 'Daily Globe', and I very much doubt if there is any scandal in the whole of Southern England that he doesn't know. In any case, he could easily check up on all we want without anyone being the wiser."

"Might be an idea. Can you get him tonight?"

"He's sure to be at the Press Club." Mr. Whittle polished off his whisky and set down the glass. "Hang on, and I'll see what I can do."

From bitter experience with the Sussex telephone service Roy was prepared to spend a considerable amount of time getting through, but for once in a way the old buster at the Exchange was right on the dot, and after only a quarter of an hour – five minutes waiting for Trunks to answer, and another ten explaining to a cold-voiced lady that he was not, and never had been, the local laundry – Gregory Tallon's voice floated down the line.

"Hallo," it said. "Is that you Julie?"

"No," Mr. Whittle informed him briefly. "Ought it to be?"

"That depends," Mr. Tallon admitted cautiously. "If you

aren't Julie, who are you?"

"Roy. Can you hear me properly? I don't want to shout."

"Unfortunately," said Mr. Tallon, "I can. Not that I've taken a sudden dislike to you," he added, "but I was expecting somebody else, and I am afraid you're rather a poor substitute, if you see what I mean. Are you in town?"

"Wollingham. You know, Spennie Davenhill's place."

"Spennie Davenhill?" repeated Gregory. "Lord, yes. I'd almost forgotten him. Isn't he some relation to that extraordinary old bird who took a salmon -"

"We won't go into that right now." Said Mr. Whittle firmly.

"Better perhaps not," agreed Mr Tallon. "As a matter of fact, I never really managed to get to the bottom of it. How on earth she ever managed to -"

"I wish you wouldn't keep going off at tangents. Listen, Gregory, do you know anything about Mr Nehemiah Ratcliffe?"

"A what?"

"A Nehemiah Ratcliffe."

"The name seems to ring a bell," confessed Mr. Tallon after a short silence, "But I can't connect it up for a minute. Pal of yours?"

"Not exactly a pal. In fact, I've a shrewd suspicion I'm going to hate his guts. I haven't actually met him yet, but he calls himself a psychic research worker. From what I can gather he spends most of his time smoking ghosts out of haunted houses at a hundred quid a head. Also, he's mixed up with two ducks who call themselves Weatherill and Fredl."

"Fredl?" echoed Gregory. "Yes, I know Fredl all right. Drop me a line about it will you? I expect Julie's trying to get through."

Roy paused briefly not in order to curse not only Mr. Tallon, but also his parents. "This is important, you beetle-wit. Let Julie wait for a few moments, and I'll tell you more about Fredl."

"She's been waiting for three weeks already," said Mr. Tallon disconsolately. "I've been over in New York for the elections, and only got back today."

"In that case she won't mind an extra quarter of an hour.

What exactly do you know about Fredl? The one I am talking about is a bearded, pot-bellied old Hun, who talks like something out of a musical comedy and has a distressing habit of kissing people."

"You don't mean he's kissed you?"

"He has."

Mt Tallon uttered a harsh bark of mirth.

"That," said Roy coldly, "was a signally dirty laugh. If you must know, Fredl kissed me because I'd pulled hie niece out from underneath a lorry. It was one of the nastiest experiences I've ever had – like being poked with a wire brush."

"Pulling his niece from under the lorry , you mean?"

"No you addle-head. Being kissed by Fredl."

"I see what you mean," admitted Gregory. "From what I know of him, which isn't really much, Fredl is a duck to avoid. He spends most of his life digging up revolting objects that would be far better off left where they were, and in his spare time he goes in for spells and incantations. Out in Egypt they look on him as a messenger of Serapis."

"Why?"

"Serapis. The Egyptian equivalent of the Devil."

"Sounds faintly indecent to me. Anything else?"

There was a short pause.

"Can't think of anything," said Gregory, "but I'll do some checking up. Look here, what the deuce are you up to, kissing archaeologists and falling down drains? It's not my idea of a summer holiday."

"Nor mine," Mr. Whittle admitted ruefully, "but there are wheels within wheels, old lad." He gave his friend a brief resume of current events at the hall. "How soon can you let me know something about this Ratcliffe disease?"

"As soon as I can track him down," said Mr. Tallon. It's early yet, and there's no point in going to bed at this hour. Incidentally, it doesn't look as though Julie's going to ring me tonight."

"Association of ideas?"

"There is only one thing, though," went on Mr. Tallon, treating this one with the contempt it deserved. "I may be wrong, because it's ages since I saw the old buster, but from what I remember of Fredl's beard it was Vandyke, short and clipped. Is it like that now?"

"Far from it. It's a yard long at least, and bushy. Most unsavoury. I shouldn't think he ever washes it."

"Perhaps he has it dry-cleaned" suggested Mr. Tallon. "Do you think they'd do it for him at a laundry?"

" I doubt it. Beard-cleaning must be a specialised job."

"There might be a future in it," said Gregory pensively. "I've heard of window-cleaners and carper-cleaners, but I can't believe I've ever come across a firm of beard-cleaners. I remember once, an old uncle of mine -"

"The devil take your uncle!"

"He has."

"Good. Greg, do you think this bird really is the genuine Fredl? Or is he a fake ?"

"That's what I wondered," said Mr. Tallon. "I'll do what I can, of course, but it may be a bit difficult to follow up, because the old coot is always liable to wander off into the most peculiar places and disappear for months on end. If I were you, I'd pull his beard."

"What?"

"Pull his beard."

"Why the devil should I pull his beard? I mean, do you expect it to ring a bell, or something?"

"No you doddle-pate," said Gregory impatiently, "but if this duck is phoney he'll be wearing a false beard, won't he? Very well. Tug it, and off it'll come."

"Suppose it isn't false?"

"Well, make some excuse," said Mr. Tallon vaguely. "It shouldn't be hard, particularly if you are on kissing terms."

"Only this afternoon," Roy informed him dryly, "he nearly knifed me merely because I'd directed him to Chipwood Magna instead of Wollingham. No thanks - I'd rather play postman's knock with a rattlesnake. Any more bright ideas?"

"Lots," said Gregory cheerfully, "but obviously my first step is to track down this Ratcliffe bird. Frankly, I think the whole business reeks of bad fish. And now," he added firmly, "I'm going to ring off, just in case Julie's trying to get through. By the way, there's just one point I'd like to clear up. When the old girl first produced the salmon why did the Vicar -"

Mr. Whittle made an indelicate noise like a gas-mask breathing out, and replaced the receiver on the hook. Experience has taught him that Gregory in one of his really inane moods was capable of going off at any one of a number of tangents, and the only course was to sign off.

Chapter 11

Greatly to Mr. Whittle's relief most of the occupants of the Hall seemed to have decided to hit the hay and put up the shutters for the night, since the drawing-room was empty except for the gaunt, scrubby figure of, Professor Weatherill. Mr. Whittle gave a grunt of satisfaction. A chat with the aged grave- digger was just what he wanted at the moment.

"What-ho," he began, making for the sideboard and helping himself to a mild snifter. "Where's Aunt Clara?"

The professor blinked behind his steel-rimmed spectacles.

"In bed, I believe. I intend to follow her example very shortly. We have had a tiring day down at the camp."

"Oh, you have, have you?" muttered Mr. Whittle. Well, before you push off. Do you think you could do something for me?"

"By all means," assented the old coot amiably, stuffing some tobacco into his evil looking pipe. "Some phenomenon you want explained, no doubt? Psychic forces are all around us, and if you have encountered any sort of materialisation -"

"I haven't, and if I did meet any kind of materialisation I should try some hot lead on it. No I want to have a look at that map."

"What map?"

"The map Fredl unearthed. You showed it to Pauline Wrightman."

"Map?" echoed the professor vaguely. "Oh, yes! I remember something about a map, but I'm really not sure what I did with it."

"Think," urged Mr. Whittle.

"The old buffer obliged, and from some moments there was silence apart from the low buzz of his mental machinery. Eventually he gave it up, and shook his head sadly.

"Unless, I fear, "he announced, re-lighting his pipe and puffing a cloud of yellow smoke. "My memory fails me completely. I really can't remember just what I did with it."

"Too bad," said Mr. Whittle regretfully, putting down his

glass and removing a cigarette from his lips. "That means I'll have to prod you in the snout."

"What?"

"Mr. Whittle repeated his remark. The professor looked uncertain.

"You wouldn't really do that?" he asked, without much conviction.

"I would," Mr. Whittle assured him, "like a shot."

Professor Weatherill uncorked what was probably meant to be an airy laugh, but which sounded more like a frog's death-rattle.

"I'm glad to see you taking it in this merry fashion," commented Mr. Whittle, rolling up his sleeves and clenching and clenching his hands to make sure they still worked. "The last fellow I prodded in the snout didn't like it a bit. Ready?"

"Come, come, there's no need to be hasty," protested the professor, backing away and turning several shades paler beneath his layer of grime. "I feel sure that if you gave me a few moments to collect myself I shall be able to remember where the map is. One might think that you imagined that I had no wish for you to see it – ha, ha!"

"Ha!" Said Mr. Whittle. That's just what I do think, old lad, so either produce it or get used to the idea of a prodded snout."

The professor thought this one out.

"In the museum," he said suddenly. "Yes, I feel sure that I left it in the museum. I'll go and get it."

"We'll both go and get it," corrected Mr. Whittle, draining his glass.

If the professor was against this last suggestion he was too wary to say so, and led the way meekly into the museum. Seen under artificial lighting the place looked even more sinister and depressing than before, and Roy wrinkled his nose disdainfully; even the presence of Professor Weatherill was insufficient to drown the strong musty smell.

"Morbid curiosity," he observed, lifting up the white sheet that covered the earthly remains of Quintus Maximus and peering at the bones. "How would you like your joints to be stuck up and stared at like this?"

"Probably no more than Quintus does," admitted the

professor, "though I doubt whether I should show my annoyance in so marked a manner." He fumbled in one of the drawers. "Do you know, I don't believe the chart is in here after all."

"Let me have a squint," said Mr. Whittle, ruthlessly pushing the old archaeologist to one side and going to the draw that he had seen Mrs. Wrightman use earlier on. "What's this? - No you don't!" he added, seizing Weatherill firmly by the scruff of the neck and yanking him back. "Just you stand clear."

The professor gave a bark of pain and rage, and cursed loudly. Roy raised his eyebrows. He had hardly suspected the old coot of possessing such a fluent vocabulary.

"You shock me," he said piously, giving another shake for luck. "I'm not, you know."

"God damn you," sputtered the professor, wrenching his collar away from Roy's affectionate grip and massaging it wildly. "My neck -"

"Much less painful than that prod on the snout you may have got," pointed out Mr. Whittle. "Look on the bright side, old lad. I'll take this chart, if you don't mind – or, for that matter, if you do. You can have it back tomorrow."

"You young bastard," snarled the professor.

"I've already told you that I'm not," Mr. Whittle informed him coldly. "I don't mind being called a bastard, but I do object to being accused of lying, and if you do it again I'll wrap your spectacles round your oesophagus. Savvy?"

Evidently the ancient tomb-hunter did, for he subsided, muttering under his breath and examining his neck for broken ligaments. Mr. Whittle deciding that under the circumstances formal conversation was virtually impossible, left him to it, and retired to his bedroom. Here he unfolded the chart and laid it on the bed, wondering whether it was going to prove worth the trouble he had taken to get it.

He quickly decided that it wasn't. The chart was far too much like something out of "Treasure Island" to ring true, and altogether it simply reeked of decaying fish. It was drawn on yellow, parchment-like material, and was in two parts; one depicted what was eventually meant to be the outline of the house, the other a cross-section of a large room. Underneath were some badly written words. Mr. Whittle rather thought it was Latin, but although his work in a solicitor's office had taught him the rudiments of that language he was no expert at it, and had to confess himself baffled.

"Odd," he murmured, eyeing the chart as though it had been a particularly fat and bloated Colorado beetle. "Nothing old about that. I wonder who the devil planted it?"

For some minutes he poured over the parchment, and even examined it with a pocket magnifying-glass, but to no purpose. At last he folded it up and stowed it in his pocket, feeling annoyed and frustrated, and considered his immediate plan of action.

He wanted to talk to Spennie. He also wanted to talk to Terry, and it occurred to him that he he might also give Pauline and Carole a look in. The only problem was which to tackle first, and on the whole he thought that Terry had prior claim. Business before pleasure.

Chapter 12

Terry's room was on the third floor, well away from the main stream of traffic. Mr. Whittle, having arrived there without incident, banged loudly on the door.

"Anyone there?" he inquired, and went in. Terry laying on the bed smoking a cigarette, looked up and grunted.

"Hello. What's up?"

"Precisely what I am trying to find out, old lad. Mind if I sit down?"

"Does it matter whether I mind or not?"

"Not a bit." Mr. Whittle planted his massive frame on the edge of the bed. "Actually, I want some information."

"What about?"

"Spooks."

"Better go and ask old Bluebeard, not me."

Mr. Whittle lit his pipe.

"When I said 'spooks', I was generalising. What I'm after is one particular spook – yours. I've heard Pauline Wrightman's story, and I've heard something from that old beetle-wit Stoker, but I still think the whole business smells. What can you contribute to the fund?"

Terry made no reply.

"Well," Mr. Whittle persisted.

""Nothing," Terry said sullenly.

"Weatherill seemed to think you could."

"The devil take Weatherill!"

"He undoubtedly will, and I hope soon, but that isn't the point. Come clean, old lad. It's not just idle curiosity on my part. If we don't get to the bottom of this Spennie's going to be a hundred quid down, and that's big money."

"He'd be a fool to pay," muttered Terry.

"Agreed, but common-sense isn't his strong point." Mr. Whittle snorted. "why the deuce are you making a mystery about it?"

"Let me alone, I'm sleepy."

"Look," said Mr. Whittle with studied patience, mastering

an impulse to seise the nearest portable article and break it over his cousin's head, "let's get this straight. If you won't say anything I shall start to believe Strudwick was right about it's being imagination."

"You can believe what you bloody well like. I couldn't care less."

"Incidentally," went on Mr. Whittle, "if you're so touchy about it now, why tell Weatherill in the first place?"

"No business of yours."

"Oh yes it is," Mr. Whittle corrected him. "If Spennie hadn't hauled me down here to have a look round, I'd be in France now."

"I wish to God you were," Terry admitted. "Shut the door after you."

"You seem anxious to get rid of me, old lad," murmured Mr. Whittle, blowing a series of smoke rings and leaning back on the bed. "Expecting anyone?"

"What the devil do you mean?"

"It just crossed my mind," admitted Mr. Whittle. "Force of habit, I suppose."

"Coming from you," said Terry explosively, "that's just too rich. I shouldn't burn me up too far, Roy. Did you know Pauline Wrightman was more or less engaged to Strudwick?"

"I've heard rumours," said Mr. Whittle cautiously.

"Well, then!" Terry tossed off a bark of mirth. "What you choose to do is no affair of mine, but next time you want to go into a huddle with someone else's fiancée take my tip and don't do it in a room with a glass door. Strudwick may be a wet lettuce, but if he'd seen what I did he'd scoop your guts out."

Mr. Whittle growled. His eyes shone, rather as though a powerful electric torch had been switched on inside of his head, and two thin wisps of smoke curled up from his nostrils. "And if I don't make myself scarce, you'll go to Struddy and tell him all – is that it?"

Terry looked uneasy. "I didn't say that"

"I know, and it's darn lucky for you that you didn't, old lad – because if you had, I'd have pulled your arms out of their sockets and stuffed them down your gullet. As a matter of fact it strikes me as being a soundish scheme, even now.

Terry thrust out his jaw, hoping he looked more comfortable than he felt.

"Go fly a kite," he advised briefly.

Mr. Whittle made a movement, and Terry leaped out of bed in the manner of a rocketing pheasant. Indeed, few pheasants would have been sprightly, even with the imminent threat of a load of buckshot up their feathers. There was a whirr and a blur, and the thing was done.

Roy paused, and ground his teeth. His face was never particularly handsome, but Terry had never before realised how unpleasantly tough it was, his cousin reminded him strongly of a gorilla – not a placid, amiable gorilla, full of the milk of human kindness, but a short-tempered gorilla who has just found his wife in compromising circumstances with a lowcast monkey. For some moments there was silence, apart from the harsh grating of Roy's teeth, and then soft footsteps were heard outside.

"Someone's coming," muttered Terry.

"So I can hear, old lad. Lucky for you, what?"

Before Terry had time to think out a reply to this one the door opened, and Carole Czernak entered, wearing a flimsy night dress and an even flimsier wrap. On seeing Mr. Whittle she pulled up short.

"Oh," she said faintly, "I didn't know -"

Mr. Whittle switched off the light in his head, and unleashed a subdued snort of laughter. "Come right in," he said easily. "Come right in."

Miss Czernak accepted the invitation, but it was obvious that she had been put right off her stroke and was misfiring on at least two cylinders. Mr. Whittle decided to make himself pleasant.

"Nice evening for a stroll, what?" he began cheerily, re-lighting his pipe and offering Miss Czernak a cigarette.

There was a somewhat sticky silence, and Mr. Whittle, realising that unless he did some smooth talking the situation was liable to become positively awkward, tried a fresh tack.

"Do sit down," he invited, indicating to the bed. "Sorry we can't offer you a drink – or can we, old lad? You don't by any chance keep a private store?"

"No!" said Terry in a suppressed voice.

"A mistake. Of course, I suppose we could always potter downstairs and collect some."

"Roy," said Miss Czernak suddenly.

"Hello?"

"I know what you are thinking," said the girl, in a low voice. "I see it so plainly!"

"Like hell you do," thought Mr. Whittle guiltily. He sincerely hoped that the glamorous Carole did not practice telepathy, particularly now. Aloud he said: "I don't know that I was thinking about anything special. Should I have been?"

"But you were. You believe Terry expected me, no?"

"Of course. Didn't he?"

"I did not!" breathed Terry.

"All right." Said Mr. Whittle peaceably, "you weren't. It doesn't worry me either way. I don't go about snooping."

Terry made no reply to this thrust, and after a few seconds Carole went on the air again.

"You will not perhaps believe why I have come," she announced, "yet it is the truth. You will listen?"

"I think I'd better be pushing off. There are occasions when three is the very devil of a crowd. Tell me about it tomorrow, what?"

"But no. You must listen." Miss Czernak laid a hand imploringly on his arm. "Terry, I have come for one thing only."

"What?"

"Don't tell me if you'd rather not," Mr. Whittle assured her hastily. "I don't mind a bit."

"I must. I have come to ask you to tell me what you know."

"What I know?" echoed Terry. "I don't get it."

"But you remember. I asked you about Maximus," Carole hesitated. "I will be frank, yes ?" Perhaps there are evil spirits, but I am not certain. You, my Terry you have something that you call – spook, yes? Very well. I have come to ask."

"Well I'm damned," breathed Mr. Whittle.

"My Uncle Felix" continued Miss Czernak, sitting down on the bed and gathering her wrap around her in a way that made Mr.

Whittle's temperature rise a full degree, "he believes in these spirits. Myself, I have doubts. I wish to make sure."

"That goes for me, too." agreed Mr. Whittle, seating himself rather closer to Miss Czernak than was strictly necessary. "Sure you're not cold?"

"A little." Carole admitted.

"I'll put my arm around you, if you like".

"Thank you."

"Like this?"

"So," agreed Miss Czernak.

Terry uttered a low groan, like a dog wrestling with a wishbone.

"Right," said Mr. Whittle, uncorking a genial smile, "we're all set for the ghost story, old lad. Let's have it."

"I'm – oh, course it" said Terry violently. "Will you get the hell out of here if I tell you?"

"I promise," Miss Czernak assured him.

"Not you, damn it. Roy."

"Done. Just as soon as I get the griff, I'll fade away like a beautiful dream. Where did you see that thing? In the museum?"

"No. Near the camp, last Monday night." Terry flushed. "It sounds stupid enough right now, but it wasn't at the time. I couldn't sleep, and about three nights ago I thought I'd go for a stroll – it was a warm night, so I didn't bother to dress. I wandered about a bit, and then I thought I'd go down to the camp. Well, I was nearly there when I saw a light, and – well -"

"Good Lord!" You're sure?"

"Of course I'm sure. It isn't the sort of thing one imagines."

"You didn't see any pink elephants or indigo cows at the same?"

Terry let out an annoyed snort. "I wasn't tight, if that's what you mean. I hadn't had a thing."

"I'll bet you did afterwards. What did you do? Bolt?"

"No, blast your eyebrows. Think I'm scared of things like that?"

"Yes. Go on".

"I ran towards them," continued Terry, glaring malevolently at his relative, "and they gradually disappeared. By

104

the time I got to the camp itself the whole place was absolutely quiet and deserted. I had a good squint around, and then came away. That's all."

Mr. Whittle chewed his pipe stem. "You didn't recognise the bloke with the beard?"

"I didn't get close enough. I only saw him for a moment."

"It didn't look anything like Dr. Fredl, for instance?"

"I tell you, I couldn't see," grunted Terry, with a side glance at Carole. "Well, that's the lot. Are you going?"

"A bargain's a bargain," agreed Mr. Whittle, reluctantly unwinding his arm from Miss Czernak's waist. "I'm dashed if I can fathom this. Spennie, Pauline and you .. My God." he added, "what's going on now?"

A violent uproar had broken out somewhere in the house shrill screams rent the air, mingled with deep male voices and running feet; altogether it sounded as though the hall was being stormed by a perfect battery of spooks, each mounted on horseback and clad in chain-mail. Mr. Whittle, bounded to his feet, let in his clutch with a jerk, paused for a second or so in order to rev his engine, and streaked out of the door at full throttle, leaving Terry and Carole rocking gently in his slipstream.

Chapter 13

Travelling at top speed Mr. Whittle reached the landing in a matter of seconds, and stopped short, drinking in some scene and trying to make some sense out of it.

Mr. Davenhill occupied the centre of the stage. He was clutching the banisters as though trying to wrap himself round them, opening and shutting his mouth and giving vent to a series of fearsome howls that sounded like a steam-siren with croup. His spectacles were missing, and his pale blue eyes, normally protected by a thick layer of plate-glass, looked as they were about to part company with their sockets. Pauline Wrightman was making futile efforts to calm him, while Dr. Fredl, dressed in lemon-coloured pyjamas with a faint green twill, hopped about In the manner of a sparrow on a hot plate, and Professor Weatherill loomed grubbily in the background, his scraggy neck craned forward and his Adam's apple working overtime.

"What -" began Mr. Whittle, but his voice was drowned by another piercing yowl from Spennie.

"Of a truth, he of his senses leave taken has," announced Dr. Fredl in agitated tones, as Spennie collected a fresh supply of breath preparatory to another bellow. "A spirit most evil to him possessed has taken -"

"Eeyowh," roared Spennie with the full force of his lungs, and the whiskered doctor retired baffled, holding one hand over his leeward ear and gnawing at his beard thoughtfully.

"What in the name of Osiris is going on?" inquired a strident voice, and Aunt Clara appeared, wearing a red flannel dressing-gown and brandishing a shotgun. "Burglars?"

"But nein. Madame, he of a devil ensnared has been," Dr. Fredl informed her, raising his hands as though invoking divine assistance. "Blitzen! For days this to come expected have I. Of darkness the powers for us too strong are greatly – danger most horrific to us is near. The skeleton at once we return must, before to us the worst befalls."

"Onion soup," snorted Mr. Whittle, stepping forward and gripping Spennie by the collar. "Pull yourself together, old lad.

What's up?"

Mr. Davenhill gasped and subsided weakly against the banisters, bubbling like a baby seal seemingly incapable of speech. At this moment Miss Czernak joined the little group, and went on the air with a pertinent query. "Is he ill?"

"No – scared," Mr. Whittle told her briefly. "Brandy, someone."

Dr. Fredl produced a bottle with the air of a conjurer taking a rabbit out of a hat, and passed it over. Mr. Davenhill gulped.

"Thanks," he spluttered, after a moment or two. "Sorry to kick up such a shindy. Fact is, I've just had the most frightful shock. Grrr! It makes me feel quite cold."

"What kind of a shock?" Aunt Clara asked keenly. "You look as though you've seen Serapis himself. Rameses! I've not heard any one man make such a noise since old Major Saunderson fell off a pyramid back in 1922."

Mr. Davenhill paused in order to make a few more revolting noises.

"A skeleton," he mouthed. "Quintus – in my bedroom, grinning at me. Ouf!"

"Well, I'm glad he's got a cheerful outlook, at all events," grunted Mr. Whittle. "When did you find it?"

"Just now. It was tucked away behind my door, and just as I was going to get into bed I – I saw it." Spennie shuddered. "I've never had such a turn in my life. I don't want to see anything like it ever again ever."

"Doubtless not," agreed Dr. Fredl mournfully. "From the grave he risen has, to us to inform his intentions so fearful. The worst will shortly arrive."

"Be quiet, you old fool," snarled Mr. Whittle. "Our practical joking pal's up to his games again, that's all. When I get at him I'll wrap his intestines round his windpipe and throttle him. Stoker," he added, seeing the aged butler coming up the stairs in low gear, "more brandy. Quick."

"I don't want any more," protested Mr. Davenhill.

"I do. On you way, Stoker old lad."

"Very well, Mr. Roy. I thought I heard a noise," volunteered the old retainer doubtfully, "but perhaps I was

107

mistaken. Do you desire me to bring large glasses, sir?"

"Tumblers, if you like. Meanwhile," said Roy, "we'll go and look at this room-mate of yours, Spennie. Come on. It won't bite."

Mr. Davenhill did not appear too sure about this, but led the way reluctantly to his room, and pushed open the door. "There you are. Against the wall."

Mr. Whittle strode in, the crowd pressing on his heels, and rubbed his chin thoughtfully. There could be no doubt that the skeleton had an extremely dirty look on its face, and he could well understand Spennie's reluctance to spend the night anywhere near it.

"Nasty sort of critter," he admitted, standing aside to give the others a full view. "I should think old Quinnie was a pretty average stinker in his day. He seems even smaller than he did downstairs – do you think he can have shrunk?"

"That," said Aunt Clara dryly, "is easily explained. Really, Roy, your ignorance is painful. This isn't Quintus Maximus."

"Are you sure?"

"Of course I'm sure, you fool. It;'s nothing like him."

"All skeletons look alike to me," Mr. Whittle admitted frankly. "It is a bit shrivelled, though. No chance of Quinnie having given birth?"

"Don't be more of a doddle-plate than you can help," the old aunt snorted, accosting Stoker as the old butler returned from his errand and getting first cut at the brandy. "If you want to know, this skeleton is a totally unimportant one I brought home some years ago for lecturing purposes. It's stored downstairs, in the museum cupboard."

"In which case," said Mr. Whittle, "we'd better put it back there, what?"

This suggestion met with general approval, and Mr. Whittle and Mr. Strudwick between them picked up Spennie's gruesome visitor and trundled it back to the museum. Here another surprise awaited them. All appeared to be in order, the specimens and the shelves undisturbed, but of Quintus Maximus there was no sign. The old buster had vanished into thin air, leaving now a wrack behind, and even Mr. Whittle felt a crawling sensation at the base

108

of his spine.

"Odd," he muttered, gazing blankly around. "Struddy, old lad, I'm not sure I'm keen on this."

"I'm quite sure I'm not, " confessed the M.P. "I suppose we'd better see what Miss Debenham has to say."

"Roy nodded absently, and the two returned to the landing, which contained nearly the whole population of the Hall and was buzzing like a beehive at the start of the annual honey festival.

"Quinnie's gone for a stroll," Mr. Whittle announced badly. "Anyone seen him tootling around?"

"Gone for a ...," Aunt Clara uttered a broken cry. "You mean, really gone?"

"That's what I said. Vamoosed – hopped it – skedaddled."

"Yuk," said Mr. Davenhill convulsively.

"I don't believe it," breathed Professor Weatherill.

"Come and look for yourself, old lad. I can assure you that the museum's totally devoid of skeletons, apart from the one we've just parked there." Roy lit a cigarette. "Who exactly is the Johnnie – the second one, I mean?" Any relation of Quinnie's?"

"Certainly not," Aunt Clara informed him. "It's of no real interest."

"It isn't exactly ornamental, either," commented Spennie, who was breathing in short gusts and whos face was the colour of damp cement. "Damn it, where can the beastly thing have gone?"

"Back where it belongs. We put it there."

"Not that one, you addle-wit. Quintus."

"I've no idea," admitted Mr. Whittle, "except that wherever he is, someone put him there. I decline to believe he pushed off under his own steam."

Dr. Fredl went on the ether with his usual preliminary whirr. "Without question his own steam under himself removed has," he began. "To his resting-place returned he has gone. It to be feared is that a number of sprites raised he has, his vengeance upon us most horrifically to call down."

"What the blazes are you blathering about ?" demanded Mr. Whittle.

"It most clear is, Herr Shakespeare." The aged tomb-grubber waved both arms violently, catching Mr. Strudwick a

109

glancing blow in the chest and making him emit a whistling sigh. "Most furious will he be his sleep to have been disturbed had. At once we must action take, or a hauntingness most fearful prepare to witness."

"In other words, you believe Quinnie's gone of to collect some of his pals?"

"Completely. No doubt there can be."

Mr. Whittle's fertile imagination conjured up a picture of Quintus Maximus marching upon the hall at the head of a whole gang of skeletons of all shapes and sizes. It was not a pleasant thought.

"I, too, fear the worst," broke in Professor Weatherill in sepulchral tones. "All this reminds me of a very similar case I encountered some years ago, in Iraq. A very dear friend of mine was found dead one morning – strangled, through by no human agency shortly after he had disinterred a High Priest of Ra. Most deplorable,: he went on, more cheerfully. "His face was black, I recall and his eyeballs out of their sockets."

"The High Priest's?"

"No. My friend's."

"I think I'm going to be sick," said Mr. Davenhill helpfully. "I feel all gooey inside."

There was a brief pause whilst he was revived with a further snifter of brandy, and then Mr. Strudwick, seeing that old professor was about to go on with his bed-time story, called the meeting to order with a rasping cough. "You spoke of taking action," he began, addressing Dr. Fredl "What exactly do you propose to do?"

This appeared to baffle the whiskered Austrian, for he chewed his face-fungus for some seconds before replying.

"It most difficult is," he confused at last, still munching. "To me a new experience this has been. The spells of which we need have I remember but a little, though perhaps they to me return will when I attempt make."

"Spells?" barked Aunt Clara. "What in the name of Tutankhamen are you drooling about?"

"You comprehend not." Dr. Fredl prodded her meaningly in the chest. "The position most serious has become, and protection at once we obtain must. A spell most powerful must of a certainly invoked be. I some knowledge of such things have, and to act now the hour arrived is."

"To me," Mr. Whittle admitted frankly, "you seem to be talking a load of pure onion soup, old lad. You don't mean you really believe in spells?"

Professor Weatherill stuck his oar in again.

"I fear that Dr. Fredl is right," he said with decision. "I am no expert in physic matters, but I am told that if my unfortunate friend had taken some elementary precautions he would not have been found as he was -"

"With his face black and his eyeballs staring," said Mr. Whittle wearily. "Nuts!"

"It is not nuts. I, for one, have no desire to be strangled in my bed," the professor retorted shortly.

"I'm not struck on the idea myself," agreed Mr. Whittle.

"In my own bed, I mean. Still, I can't see what conjuring tricks are to do us any good."

"Quite so," said Mr. Strudwick firmly. "I don't believe a word of it."

Nobody seemed to have anything to add to this, and it was left to Aunt Clara to make the first really practical suggestion of the evening. "Well," she said, draining her glass, "whether we're under a curse or not, there's no sense in staying here all night. I'm going to bed. I don't know how in the name of Isis my skeleton has managed to disappear." She looked critically at Spennie. "I'd advise you to go and lie down, Spencer. You appear in imminent danger of being ill on the carpet."

"I am," admitted Mr. Davenhill weakly.

"Incidentally," concluded Aunt Clara, "I sleep with a loaded revolver under my pillow, so anyone who disturbs me is liable to get a bullet I the ribs. Good-night!"

On this cordial note the old aunt pushed of, and shortly afterwards the party broke up in a general atmosphere of gloom. Roy retired to his room, looked himself in, poured out a generous bracer and considered the situation from every angle.

"The plot thickens," he mused with a notable lack of originality, tossing back a mouthful and gargling with it in the approved manner. "No sleep for you yet, Whittle old lad. This is where we go off on a skeleton hunt!"

Chapter 14

It was well over two hours before Mr. Whittle made a further move. Obviously it was essential to give the house ample time to settle down, particularly as it seemed probable that Mr. Davenhill, for one, would not drop rapidly into a dreamless sleep; and accordingly he took out a novel he had brought with him – a well written, profound little work entitled "The Clue of the Twisted Eyeball" - and stretched himself out on a bed. At about five to two the first of the chiming clocks started to announce the hour (Spennie's Aunt Violethad a weakness for chiming clocks, and as none of them synchronised the general effect was rather reminiscent of a cathedral), and Mr. Whittle, yawning slightly, decided it was time to go.

Taking a powerful torch, and keeping a weather eye for bogies, he made his way cautiously down the main stairs and into the hall. Here he stopped, and flashed his light. Nothing startling appeared – no ghouls or revenants of any kind – and he he was about to potter off to the museum when is here caught a rustling sound from above.

Mr. Whittle paused. It seemed to much to expect a skeleton bird, or indeed a bird of any kind, but dirty work of some sort was going on overhead. Warily he raised his torch, and pointed it in the direction of the front door.

"Ouf!" he said convulsively.

"Keep quiet!" hissed a female voice. "Do you want to wake the whole house?"

Mr. Whittle thought this one out.

"What the devil are you doing?" he asked at length. "Roosting?"

"Of course I'm not roosting. Don't make such a noise."

"You look as though you're roosting," persisted Mr. Whittle. "If you don't like beds, why not have a perch built in your own room? It must be draughty up there."

"Who said I didn't like beds?" retorted Miss Wrightman coldly, slipping down to earth and shaking herself. "I wasn't proposing to spend the night up there."

"What were you doing, then? And what the deuce have you – a ladder?"

"The library steps," explained Miss Wrightman. "You gave me a fright, Roy. For a moment I thought you were – well, something you aren't." She shuddered. "If you only knew what an effort it was to make myself come down here, you wouldn't try to be funny. "I lay in bed quaking for hours before I could screw up enough courage."

"I'd have come along to keep you company. If I'd known," said Mr. Whittle handsomely. "Come clean, young Paul. What's the big idea?"

"Bells."

"Eh?"

"Bells," repeated Miss Wrightman impatiently. "Don't you understand?"

"I'm dashed if I do," Mr. Whittle admitted. "How do you mean, bells?"

"Well, the front-door bell kept on ringing, didn't it? If it's someone playing a trick, there ought to be a few extra wires about – connecting up a circuit, or something of the sort. I don't know how much electricity, but I could soon see if anybody had been tampering with the thing."

"Why didn't you consult me?"

"I didn't think you'd be interested."

"I'm a mutt," said Roy in tones of deep disgust. "Ouf! A Grade A mutt. You're right, of course. I wish I'd thought of it sooner." He gave her an admiring glance, forgetting that in the murky gloom the effect was completely lost. "You know, you've got brains, young Paul. In fact you've got everything."

"Do you think so?"

"I do. That's why I'm so against your throwing yourself away on a coot like Struddy. Did you know I could wriggle my ears?"

"I hadn't noticed."

"I can. Also I can dance well, and I'm a responsible performer on the guitar. Not that I want to push myself forward," said Mr. Whittle nobly. "I merely point these things out. Did you find any wires?"

"No. Not a sign."

"Shall I have a look?"

"All right," said Pauline, "but I can assure you there's nothing doing. The dust up there was three inches thick before I disturbed it."

Mr. Whittle ascended the steps, and made a quick inspection. The dust made him sneeze, and he encountered an impressive assortment of the moths and spiders, but as Miss Wrightman had said there was no sign of anything suspicious, and he returned to earth felling faintly disappointed. He was about to a fresh conservation when a distinct creak broke the silence, and he snapped out his torch, pointing like a spaniel that has just a juicy partridge make a crash-landing nearby.

"Where is it?" Pauline breathed

"Upstairs – coming down. Keep still."

Miss Wrightman obeyed,and the two froze where they stood as the creaking grew nearer. Presently a dim light appeared at the top of the stairs, and soft grunts and snorts were heard as a heavy figure plodded downwards. Mr. Whittle peered intently. Unless he was very much mistaken, the Herr Doktor Felix Fredl was about to indulge in another bout of floor-sniffing.

He was right. The figure placed the torch side-down on the nearest table, fortunately with its bean pointing away from the danger zone, and moved obligingly into its rays, revealing himself as a short, square duck with a black beard that could only belong to one person. Next he lowered himself to the ground, giving vent to a series of porcine grunts in the process, and started to crawl about, keeping his nose close to the wainscoting – for all the world as though he had been a hound trying to pick up the trial of the a fox whose smell was not so good.

Mr. Whittle stifled a bark of laughter. He would dearly have liked to creep up and deal the old buster a shrewd kick on the base of the spine, and he was seriously considering this when there came a fresh diversion in the shape – or, rather, sound – of a bump from the far end of the hall. It was difficult to be sure, but he rather fancied that this was followed by a muttered oath. Dr. Fredl heard it too, and with almost incredible quickness he picked himself up, switched off his torch, and melted into the darkness. Mr. Whittle heard him rustling as he made his way back upstairs, and then there was a silence once more.

"Shall we go after him?" whispered Pauline.

"No." Mr. Whittle paused briefly to dry his ear. "I want to see what's happening in the museum. Come on!"

Moving as quietly as he could, and feeling the way with his hands, he led of down the hall, Pauline following with a hand on his shoulder. Hours passed, or so it seemed, and then Mr. Whittle's groping paw encountered something hard and rock like in front of him.

"What ..." breathed Pauline.

Mr. Whittle thought he knew. A strange suspicion had come to him, and, shielding the beam with his hand, he switched on his torch.

"Just as I thought, old girl," he said lightly, stepping back and slipping an arm round Pauline's waist. "Just as I thought. Quinnie's back from his stroll."

Chapter 15

It says much for Miss Wrightman's self-control that she did not let out the high-pitched shriek that Roy had expected. True, she did make a lot of noise like a cat trying to cope with an outsize fishbone, and clutched Roy by the neck as though trying to throttle him, but that was all.

"Is it – moving?"

"Under its own power, you mean? No – and it hasn't, for a thousand years at least." Mr. Whittle grinned. "Quinnie's rambling days are over. Wouldn't win a beauty contest, would he?"

Miss Wrightman made a superb effort, and pulled herself together.

"Too true," she agreed. "He's better than the other one, though. He hasn't got quite the same dirty leer on his face."

"Can't say I much difference," Mr. Whittle admitted. "One thing I do know now, and that is that the spook idea's all washed up. Did you hear anything else besides the bump?"

"When?"

"Just before Fredl pushed off."

"I'm not sure. I thought I heard a voice, but I couldn't be certain."

"I could. I heard it distinctly."

"What did it say?"

"Never mind what it said. It wasn't the sort of thing a serious-minded old coot like Quinnie would say. If he wanted to swear, he'd swear in Latin."

"I suppose he would." Miss Wrightman shivered. "From the look of him, he'd be only to ready to curse us in every language under the sun. What are we going to do with him?"

"What do you want me to do with him?"

"I don't know. Stick him back in the museum, I suppose."

"Frankly," said Mr. Whittle I've no intention of doing anything at all. I've got other business in hand. Someone's carted him as far as this, so for all I can care he can finish the job and return him to store. He's not doing any actual harm where he is."

"Suppose one of the maids finds him in the morning, and

117

has a fit?"

"True. I hadn't thought of that." Mr. Whittle pondered. "We don't want all the servants to give notice on the spot, and that's what might easily happen." A more agreeable thought struck him. "I suppose Struddy doesn't go in for early-morning potters? If he caught sight of Quinnie he might easily be shocked into a decline."

"He would. That's why we'd better do something about him."

"Struddy?"

"No, idiot. Quinnie."

"I suppose so," said Mr. Whittle regretfully. "You're not doing any skeleton-shifting, though, young Paul. You've done enough for one night. Would you like some more whisky?"

"I've got some in my room. I used up most of it trying to pluck enough courage to come down and have a look at the bells, but I think there's some left. I shall be all right."

"You wouldn't like me to come and see you safely tucked up?"

"Don't trouble."

"No trouble," Mr. Whittle assured her gallantly. "Only too pleased."

"I can tuck myself up, thanks," Miss Wrightman informed him, though without heat, "Are you going back to bed yourself?"

"No. I've sundry things to attend to. I'll,look in later, if you like, and tell you if I stumbled on anything."

"You won't get in," Pauline informed him drily. "My door will be locked. I don't fancy sleeping without a good, solid slab of oak between me and the night-life of this precious household."

Mr. Whittle sighed. "You don't imagine a slab of oak will keep out spooks?"

"I wasn't thinking about spooks."

"One might almost think ," said Mr. Whittle in an aggrieved tone, "that you didn't trust me."

"You'd be wrong for once. As a matter of fact, I do trust you. I've met people of your type before. There are – other things I don't trust," said Pauline abruptly. "Good-night."

Rather suddenly she made her departure, leaving Roy rubbing his chin and trying to make out what just what she meant.

At this point the first of the chiming clocks struck two-thirty, and Roy, realizing that there was little time left before dawn, became once more the man of action.

Gingerly he lifted the bony frame of Quintus Maximus and staggered with it down the hall, giving an involuntary shudder as a couple of ribs yielded slightly in his grasp. He was tempted to pitch the gruesome remains bodily into the coal-hole, but his better nature prevailed, and at length he pushed open the door to the museum and switched on the light. Once again his eyes met the unexpected. High up near the picture rail, at the far end of the room, a large section of the wall swung back an a hinge, revealing the entrance to what was evidently another secret passage.

Mr. Whittle lit a cigarette, and considered this new development. At all events, the mystery of groaning heard earlier on was a mystery no longer. Obviously someone as well as Dr. Fredl was on the prowl, and though Mr. Whittle would have liked to explore the passage he had no desire to be walled in; he had no guarantee that there was another exit. On the other hand, it might be possible to put the door out of action. Accordingly, he mounted a chair and examined the hinge closely.

The first thing he noticed was that the lock, like the one in the cellar, was thickly coated with oil; but unlike the door of the Smugglers' Way, the trap was flimsy, and had evident been designed for secrecy rather than strength. Mr. Whittle gave an experimental tug, and felt it yield. Feeling encouraged he bent his whole weight to the task, puffing and blowing and revving his engine to its utmost capacity, and worked steadily for some minutes. At last there was a tearing sound, and the trap sagged limply in his grip.

"So far, so good," murmured Mr. Whittle "That won't be a lot of use until it's repaired."

Cautiously he levered himself through the opening, and found himself in a passage not unlike the Way, though not quite so high. It appeared to be a straightforward, honest-to-God corridor, and though Mr. Whittle kept a sharp look-out he could find no junctions as he made his way forwards. After perhaps twenty years he found himself facing a blank wall, and was about to retire baffled when he trod on something hard.

119

"Odd," he mused, dropping on all-fours. "Another trap, in the floor this time. The whole damn place is worse than a rabbit warren."

Once again the look was well greased, and Mr. Whittle, sliding back a panel in the conventional fashion, lowered himself gently into yet another passage. This time, however, he was not in virgin territory. Unless he was very much mistaken he was back in his old hunting-ground, the Smugglers Way, and he was conscious of feeling of anti-climax. He had hoped for something much better.

Mr. Whittle hesitated. It seemed reasonable to go back and finish his inspection of the museum, but the camp was also in his programme, and it was a pity to waste time unlocking the front door when he could quite well use the way. Accordingly he crawled along to the garden exit and emerged, giving the usual snorts of relief at being in the fresh air once more. Humming lightly, and removing the outer layer of dust from his clothes, he made off in the direction of the camp.

The moon was low, but shed a tolerable light upon the scene, and Mr. Whittle felt he had seldom come across anything more depressing. The entire camp looked as though a colony of giant moles had been holding a jamboree on it (though, naturally, moles would hardly have littered the place up with spades and wheelbarrows), but it was still and silent, and the only sound to be heard was the distant hooting of an owl. Mr. Whittle wondered what it was saying.

Keeping a respectful distance from Aunt Clara's concealed sewage pit he made a close examination of the ruins, but nothing interesting came two light, and after half an hour or so he pottered back in the direction of the Hall. He had reached the edge of the rose-garden when he caught sight of a dim figure ahead, fortunately facing in the opposite direction.

Mr. Whittle ducked down like a billiard-ball dropping into its pocket, and awaited developments. Evidently he was unobserved – he was a light-footed young man – and after a time he began to crawl slowly nearer, doing his best to slither along in the manner of a worm.

Presently he had approached to within a few yards of the prowler, and saw to his surprise, that it was none other than Stoker.

120

Nobody but the old butler had quite that back view; it may not have been handsome, but it was at least distinctive, and there was no possibility of a mistake.

As though to make identification even simpler, the aged retainer bent down and lowered himself on to his hands and knees, wheezing audibly as though something was about to burst under the strain. Mr. Whittle rubbed his eyes. This crawling habit seemed to be catching, and he wondered whether the house had been attacked by some obscure germ of hydrophobia type.

However, Stoker seemed to be following up some definite course of action, for he carefully selected some leaves form a nearby plant, placed them in a china bowl, and set light to them. As leaves flared up with a soft crackle, the butler hauled himself to his feet, raised his arms in the general direction of the moon, and began to whisper strange words even Mr. Whittle had never heard before.

Roy watched, fascinated. Either the butler's aged mind had given way completely or there was a sinister motive behind all this. Roy suspected the latter, and his thoughts turned automatically to Dr. Fredl. With Stoker's peculiar views about black magic and ghouls in general, the bearded Teuton would find him an easy subject ... Mr. Whittle was wondering whether to make his presence known when Fate, giving a dirty chuckle, took a hand, and directed a small insect with innumerable legs up his nose.

"Atchoo!" said Mr. Whittle violently.

Stoker uttered a low, wolf-like owl, and sprang into the air, upsetting the bowl in the process. Mr. Whittle stood up and flashed his light.

"What the devil," he asked tersely, are you up to, old lad? Witchery?"

The old retainer made no reply, but panted as though he had just finished a ten-mile marathon. He was dressed in a bilious green night shirt, an overcoat, and – rather incongruously – a felt pork pie hat, and the effect was grotesque in the extreme.

"Well?" persisted Mr. Whittle.

Stoker, still gulping in large chunks of atmosphere, managed a reply. "I – that is, you startled me, sir. I thought you –

that is to say, I -"

"Don't drivel. Are you off your chump? or merely tight?"

Stoker thought this one out.

"I can assure you, Mr. Roy, that I am entirely sober," he said at last. "Nor an I mentally deranged, despite the serve strain of the past week. I – er- could not sleep, Mr. Roy – my arthritis, you know – so I decided to take a stroll in the grounds."

"At three a.m.?"

"Certainly, Mr. Roy. A very pleasant time." Stoker saw that he would have to do better than this, and revved his mental machinery. "I like to listen to the birds, sir."

"The what?"

"Birds, sir. B for Bustard, I for insecticide -"

"I heard you," snarled Mr. Whittle. "Birds, my left kneecap. Do you seriously mean to tell me that you dressed like that and came out here to listen to birds?"

"Bird songs are very beautiful, Mr. Roy," pointed out the old buster without much hope.

"Never mind about bird songs. You won't hear any birds at this time of the height, apart possibly from bats."

"A bat, sir, is not a bird," the butler corrected him respectfully. "I understand that it is an insect."

Mr. Whittle briefly consigned all bats to the innermost regions of hell.

"Nightjars, then. Which reminds me, old lad, what have you got there? A basin?"

"Of a sort, sir. It was the only one I could find." Stoker looked confused. "I – er – thought I would gather some flowers for my room."

Mr. Whittle, bending down, picked up the bowl by its handle and gave a sharp bark of amusement. Funny sort of thing to collect flowers in," he committed, "especially if you're going to set fire to them. Look here, old lad, stop behaving like a double-pate and come down to earth. Is all witchcraft business one of Fredl's bright ideas?"

"No, sir. I fear I am not at liberty to say."

"Onion soup. Out with it!"

"I am sorry, Mr. Roy. My lips are sealed."

""You'd rather I woke Spennie and told him you were gallivanting round the garden in the early hours, serenading the moon and burning flowers in a pot?"

"You wouldn't do that, Mr. Roy, surely? After all these years?"

"Well, come to think of it, I suppose I wouldn't," admitted Mr. Whittle in a guilty tone. "Damn it, I wish you'd trust me."

"I do trust you, sir, implicitly, but it happens that the position is highly complicated." The old butler sighed. "I have no desire to be found stiff and cold in my bed, with my teeth bared in a ghastly grin, and such a thing might easily happen if I relaxed my vigilance for one moment ."

Mr. Whittle grunted. "I suppose you don't mind my saying I think you're potty?"

"Not at all, Mr. Roy, though I can assure you that I am in full possession of my faculties. Physically. However, I am far from well. All this is extremely bad for my arthritis, sir, and if it so happens that you are in a position to assist me -"

"If you will go crawling about on the damp ground,: said Mr. Whittle severely, "you must expect arthritis. For a minute I thought you were playing at being a dog. I was quite glad there weren't any trees near at hand." he passed over his glass, and the butler gulped gratefully. "Hallo," he added as something flapped by his face, "What was that?"

"A bat, sir," the butler informed him mournfully.

"A bat?"

"Yes, sir, dead, I have no doubt. The forces of Evil are very close."

"Nuts," Mr. Whittle said frankly, flashing his torch and revealing a small bat lying on the ground in a used-up attitude. "How do you know it's dead?"

"I cannot say, sir, owing to my sealed lips," the old butler replied gloomily, "but I fear there can be little doubt." He turned the bat over with one foot, and Mr. Whittle was forced to admit that the creature had definitely decided to call it a day. "Will there be anything further, sir? If you will excuse me, I should like to return to my bed. I fancy that your excellent whisky has some extent relived my arthritis, but the air is somewhat chill."

"If you've quite finished howling at the moon." said Roy nastily, with a suspicious look at the bat, "you'd better go and get some sleep, or you'll feel like corpse in the morning."

"I feel like corpse now, sir."

"No doubt. You don't look so hot, either."

"Possibly, sir, because there is a cool wind," suggested the butler. "The nights are becoming somewhat colder, I fancy."

"If you don't mind," Mr. Whittle said patiently, "don't start giving me a weather forecast just at the moment. I'm not in the mood. Good-night!"

Stoker replied in a similar vein and pushed off slowly towards the house, holding his receptacle in front of him as though it had been the Holy Grail; and Mr. Whittle, having spent an unprofitable ten minutes scouring the grounds to make sure that nobody else was about, crawled back down the Smugglers' Way and returned to the museum. He was hardly moved at the sight of Quintus Maximus back in his old position, leering at him with a particularly dirty expression on the outlines of his face, and came to the conclusion that there was point in staying up any longer; he would have liked to have dropped in on Pauline, or even Carole, but by this time he was so sleepy that he doubted weather he could have done himself justice.

Musing thoughtfully, he went back to bed.

Chapter 16

It was comparatively late when Mr. Whittle awoke the following morning. Apparently the house hold was still too disorganised for the usual routine calls, and when he arrived in the dining-room it was past ten o'clock. Spennie, Terry, Mr. Strudwick and Dr. Fredl were all wading into eggs and bacon, and Mr. Whittle, unleashing a genial smile, lost no time in joining them at the trough.

"What ho," he began, helping himself to a generous portion of the egg and starting work on it. "Lovely morning, What?"

"Apart from the fact that it's raining like the devil," Mr. Davenhill retorted, "it is. Have you seen the museum ?"

"Often, but not this morning. I want some breakfast before I do any skeleton-gazing. Why?"

"Maximus," said Mr. Davenhill tonelessly. "He's back."

"I know. I met him on the way."

"What!"

"I wandered about a bit during the night," explained Mr. Whittle, "and I came face to face with the old coot. He was in the hall then. Later on then I found him back in his old stand. This egg," he went on chattily," is good, old lad. Just what I need."

"Confound the egg!"

"Why? It's a damned good egg – better than you could lay, I'll bet."

"Never mind about the egg! What did you do when you found Quintus in the hall?"

"Lugged him back to the museum. I meant to put him back in the proper place, but when I saw the entrance to that new passage I thought I'd follow it up. By the time I got back Quinnie had put himself to bed, so I didn't have to trouble. Incidentally, I had to wrench that trap off its hinges."

"Why?"

"Because I didn't fancy walled up again. It won't be difficult to repair. What I can't follow is how it hasn't been found long ago."

"I confess," said Mr. Strudwick uneasily, "that I shall be

glad when this Ratcliffe arrives. If we were really dealing with psychic forces, he will know how to cope with them. It does not seem easy to give any normal explanation of the wanderings of the skeleton."

"You'd expect it to curse and swear in the process?"

"Of course not. Did it?"

"It did. When I first heard the noise from the museum, I also heard a voice – and it wasn't speaking in Latin, believe me."

"What did it say?"

There being no ladies present, Mr. Whittle told them , the M.P. raised his eyebrows. "How very odd. Are you sure?"

"Quite sure."

"Funny thing for a skeleton to say," put in Terry, with a splutter of laughter. "Doesn't ring true, what?"

"You couldn't recognise the voice?" asked Mr. Davenhill.

"Well, it was a man, which narrows the field quite a lot."

"Stoker?" suggested Terry. "He's nuts enough."

"I don't think so. This was a younger man's voice. Wish I'd caught him – I'd have scooped out his liver."

Up to this point Dr. Fredl had been far to busy with eggs and bacon to make my active part in discussion, but as the supply of food was now exhausted he cleared his throat, removed a piece of yolk from his eyebrow, and went on the air.

"Most relieved must we be," he began. "Excellent it is that the skeleton to its former position returned has. Of no doubt there can be that a warning to us most solemn been given has, and to such regard it most necessary is, a hauntingness most fearful to avert."

"Come again?" requested Mr. Whittle.

The whiskered doctor repeated his remark, and there was a baffled silence while the others thought it out.

"Do you mean," said Mr. Whittle at last, "that Quinnie went for a stroll just to show us what he could do if he got really marked?"

Dr. Fredl nodded violently. "Of a certainly, Herr Shakespeare. A warning it is that we his wishes obey must. No time to be lost can there be." "Where's Aunt Clara? What does she think about it?"

"I haven't seen her this morning," Spennie informed him, pouring coffee in a preoccupied manner. "By the time I came down she and Weatherill had pushed off to the camp. They'll come in soaked. Well, I'm damned if I know what to think, but we may as well hang on until Ratcliffe arrives."

"When, is he due?"

"Weatherill said he'd be here in time for lunch."

"I'll bet. Trust these spookers to look after their stomachs."

"He won't get much here," said Spennie. with morbid satisfaction. "The water system's all to blazes – the plumbers have managed to get some sort of supply, but from what I can gather it'll take days to get back to normal – and Jules is going about the place tearing his hair and waving his arms. You know what he's like."

Mr. Whittle grinned. Jules, the French chef, was undeniably prone to outbreaks of temperament that would have made a Hollywood star seem like a nun by comparison.

There was a brief silence, during which Mr. Whittle washed down his toast with luke-warm coffee and cogitated. The immediate was to get in touch with Gregory, and he was wondering whether to ring the press club once more when Carole Czernak made an effective entrance. Although she looked as ravishing as usual, and was wearing in a dress that revealed just the right amount of umph, it was obvious that there was something on her mind.

"Has anyone seen Miss Wrightman?" she began abruptly.

"Not down yet," Spennie informed her, pressing the ball. "I'll order some more bacon. This has gone cold, I'm afraid."

"But you don't understand." Carol gestured. "Miss Wrightman, she is vanished – disappeared – gone. Her bed is not slept in -"

Mr. Whittle started. Pauline, when she left him, had undoubtedly set off with a firm intention of hitting the hay, and it was not easy to see what had made her change her mind.

"Are you sure?" he asked incredulously.

"Entirely. I have looked. Her pyjamas, too, they are unused." Miss Czernak sank into a chair. "I was myself coming downstairs, when the maid – Lily, is it? - told me that she had knocked on the door, but with no reply. I knocked too, and then went in. I thought she was perhaps unwell."

"How damned queer," muttered Mr. Davenhill. "She's not down at the camp, by the chance?"

"No go," said Mr. Whittle briefly. "She went off to her room at three o'clock or thereabouts. She was not with me until then."

Mr. Strudwick uttered a strangled croak.

"With you? What do you mean?"

Mr. Whittle saw that he had not made himself clear.

"Downstairs," he explained. "I found her in the hall. She'd had a bright idea that someone might have been monkeying about with the bell."

"What did you do then?"

"Well, talked for a bit. After that she went to bed."

"Is that all?"

"It is."

"You're sure? I mean, you didn't go with her – to see her into her room, I mean?"

"No," snarled Mr. Whittle. "I suppose we'd better go and have a look round the camp, but I don't like this. Stoker," he added, as the aged butler came in with a fresh supply of eggs and bacon, "have you seen Miss Wrightman? She's disappeared."

"Disappeared, sir?"

"Yes. Vanished into thin air."

The effect of this simple observation with startling in the extreme. Stoker dropped the tray with a crash, scattering pieces of egg in all direction, and subsided against the sideboard making curious bubbling noises. Terry, Spennie and Mr. Whittle let out loud barks, and Dr. Fredl chocked violently over a mouthful of coffee.

"What in hell are you playing at , you old fool?" demanded Mr. Whittle, as soon as he could make himself heard. "Are you potty?"

"I would that I were, Mr. Roy," Stoker informed him, raising his hands. "Oh, woe, woe!"

"Whoa!" yelled Mr. Whittle, seeing that the butler was capable of carrying on in the strain almost indefinitely. "Listen to me, you senile old doddle-pate. What are you drooling about? Have you seen Miss Wrightman, or haven't you?"

"The bat, sir. The bat," Stoker quavered, still rolling his eyeballs in a revolting fashion. "To think that I have never realised – oh, this is terrible. Woe, woe!"

"Stark, raving mad," said Mr. Strudwick, with decision. "We'd better ring the doctor, Davenhill. He may try to slit his throat."

"Or one of ours," Terry suggested.

"I'm not so sure," muttered Mr. Whittle. "Stoker, old lad, tell me what you mean by all this mint-sauce about bats. Have you been fooling around with magic?"

The aged retainer shook himself.

"Unfortunately, sir," he replied in more normal tones "yes. I was ill-advised enough attempt certain experiments."

"What kind of experiments?"

"Exorcism, sir, among others. I obtained the necessary procedure from a book at my disposal. I acted for the best, sir, but I see that dreadful little bat – excuse me, Mr. Roy. I must take steps to rectify matters, so far as little lie in my power." Bowing respectfully he pushed off, leaving the breakfast party staring blankly. Mr. Strudwick shrugged.

"Bats? What bats, I wonder? Some delusion, I suppose."

Mr. Whittle decided that he had better make a clean breast of the night's activities. After all, Spennie was not likely to worry whether his butler practised black magic or whether he slept like a normal being; so long as Aunt Violet was mercifully out of the way. Accordingly, he ave the company a detailed account of the episode in the garden. As soon as he came to the untimely death of the little bat, Dr. Fredl gave a sharp snort and flung his arms in the air.

"Ach!" he spluttered. "Donner and blitzen, I the light see, nein? Work of dirtiness going on is. A book from my room have I lost, a book of spells and magic most dreadful. Without doubt it he has, and a spell so potent wrongfully employed. Isch! Was ein dummkopf and schweinhundt -"

"Oy!" bawled Mr. Whittle, banging the table with his fist. "You're not suggesting he's changed Pauline into a bat?

"My God!" said Mt. Strudwick jerkily.

"Herr Shakespeare, I the worst fear," admitted the bearded Hum. "To me a feeling most evil arrived is."

Terry suddenly barked with laughter, and Mr. Strudwick rounded on him like a wounded tiger. " Keep quite, you young cub," he said harshly. "If you see anything amusing in the idea of my fiancée being turned into a bat – not that I believe such ridiculous nonsense for a moment, mind you -"

"Bats my left eyeball," snarled Mr. Whittle. "It was a perfectly ordinary bat, though I don't know why it chose to croak just then."

"Bats don't croak," Terry informed him. "They squeak."

"I don't care if they moo like cows. There was nothing odd about this one."

"Not so, Herr Shakespeare," asserted Dr. Fredl. "Not so, alas. One thing to be done only can there be. Blitzen! I to my room go, and most powerfully incant the affair to correct. It is of necessity that I great haste exhibit."

"Do," said Mr. Whittle cordially. "Push off and get started, old lad."

The bearded doctor nodded violently, drained hid cup in the manner of a suction-pump emptying a puddle, and stormed out, opening his throttle to its fullest extent. Mr. Whittle heaved a snort of relief as he disappeared. "Well," he said, retrieving a piece of bacon from the armchair and munching it thoughtfully, "now that we've got rid of the Crazy Gang, what's the procedure? Are you sure Pauline wasn't in the bathroom, or anything?"

"Quite," Miss Czernak told him. "I looked most particularly."

"In that case, she must be in grounds. Unless .. Struddy, old lad, can you think of any reason why she might take it into her head to do a bunk?"

The M.P. Shook his head. "None whatever. The whole affair is most puzzling. I feel quite disturbed."

"Look here," said Terry suddenly, "what's all this fiancée business? She never told me she was engaged to you."

"I fail to see why she should," Mr. Strudwick retorted, "since the fact does not concern you in any way. The engagement will be officially announced towards the end of the week."

"Always provided Stoker's not rung the bell," murmur Mr. Whittle. "You'd look darned silly trying to sleep upside-down, old lad."

"I beg your pardon?"

"Well, bats always do, you know. They hang from trees. Of course, I suppose we could ring up a perch for the two of you in the oaks by the lake -"

Mr. Strudwick rose.

"I am afraid," he said huffily, "that I am in no mood to appreciate your somewhat crude attempts humour. I have no doubt that Pauline is near at hand, and I propose to go and find her at once. Please don't bother to accompany me."

"I won't. Incidentally, where are you starting?"

"Down at the camp, of course. Probably Miss Debenham knows where she is."

"All right by me. Do you know the way?"

"Of course I know the way. It's perfectly obvious."

"Keep well to the left of the cricket field," advised Mr. Whittle, hoping against hope that M.P would be too preoccupied to notice Aunt Clara's sewage pit. "Cut down past the tennis court, and go through the wicker gate. I'll search the house. Coming, Spennie?"

Mr. Davenhill assented moodily, and the three went their various ways, parting in the main hall without any violent show of affection. As Miss Czernak had said, Pauline's bed certainly not been slept in, and her pyjamas were still folded neatly on the counterpane; her handbag lay on the dressing-table and Mr. Whittle eyed it dubiously. In his experience, women never went far without taking a handbag.

"I say," said Mr. Davenhill suddenly, "I've thought of something. Was Pauline wearing a dress when you last saw here?"

"Of course she was you doddle-pate. What did you expect her to be wearing? Woad?"

"I wouldn't know. I mean, she was, wearing pyjamas and a dressing gown? Because if so, we can check up and see if any of her dresses are missing. She wouldn't have gone out in pyjamas."

"Do you know how many dresses she had with her?"

131

"I hadn't thought of that," Mr. Davenhill admitted. "Strudwick might."

"I don't think it'd be tactful to ask him, but as a matter of fact she was fully dressed when I last saw her, so the idea's washed up. We'd better try the attic, just in case she went up there for something and collapsed, – unlikely, but possible. I suppose. Come on."

Mr. Davenhill obeyed and the two and made a through search of the upper floors, but without result; Miss Wrightman seemed to have made a complete disappearance, and after twenty minutes or also Mr. Whittle began to lose hope. Wollingham Hall was a large house, but he felt sure now that it contained no Paulines, and the thought was depressing in the extreme.

"Damn," he said wearily, as he arrived back on the main landing. "This beats me. If she wanted to shove off, why the devil didn't she say so?"

"She might have not wanted you to know," Mr. Davenhill suggested luminously.

"Onion soup. She said she was going to bed, and that's were she meant to go. No, someone's got at her, and once I find out who it is -" Here Mr. Whittle gave a brief description of a process that would have been embarrassing, to say the least of it, to any victim. "I don't think it's Fredl, fishy customer though he is but Weatherill's the kind of slimy old toad who might do anything, and I've half a mind to go down to the camp and beat the truth out off him."

"Suppose he really doesn't know?"

"I could still beat him up. It wouldn't do any harm."

"True. Well, I'll think it over. I say, what's up with old Fredl? He looks in a stew."

The whiskered doctor did indeed seem far from his usual sunny self. Indeed, little sparks were shooting from his eyes, and he was muttering strange things into his beard. It was plain that something had got right in among his innards and churned him up in no uncertain manner.

"Of an insulting it is," he began, as soon as he was near enough to ensure good reception. "Herr Davenhill, a protest most emphatic to lodge I wish. Robbed I have been."

"Robbed?"

"Ja. A book of importance most terrific from my room removed has been. In English he is write, and to great perils expose us he may. Essential it is possession of him regain at once to."

Spennie blinked. "Who's pinched it? Stoker?"

"Completely. In his bedroom locked he is, and to emerge most energetically he declines." The doctor brooded. "To me he requests that I in the pants a kick to myself to deliver. Donner and blitzen! A great pleasure would it be to him a bop on the snoddle administer!"

"Old fool," grunted Mr. Whittle. "Stoker, I mean. We'd better get and root him out before he burns the house down."

Spennie, with an inward feeling that life was getting a little bit to much for him, nodded dismally, and the trio set course for the servants' quarters. Mr. Whittle raised his fist, and beat a tattoo on the butler's door.

"Stoker," he said loudly. "Are you there, old lad?"

"Yes, Mr. Roy," admitted the butler cautiously.

"Well, then, open up. We want a word."

"I hardly dare, sir," confessed Stoker. "I feel that I might easily be a victim of a personal assault. I may be hasty, but from the general tenor of his remarks I gather that Dr. Fredl is not in an amiable mood."

"That's all right about Dr. Fredl. I'll cosh him in the snout if he starts any funny business. Come on out."

"Intolerable this is," muttered the old archaeologist, gnawing his beard as though it had been an ambrosia. "Without delay the book returned must be. Spells of great power include it does."

"Frankly," admitted Mr. Whittle, "I think this spell business is a can of tinned spaghetti, but we can't have people running about pinching things."

Dr. Fredl made no reply – apart from a porcine grunt – and after a short delay the door opened, and Stoker reappeared in the outside world. The aged retainer was looking careworn and gloomy, and beads of sweat stood out of his furrowed brow.

"Now then," Mr. Whittle began abruptly, "What's all this

133

about a book?"

"Have you pinched anything out of Dr. Fredl's room?" Mr. Davenhill asked weakly.

"Yes, sir." Stoker looked down his nose. "With the utmost regret, I assure you, sir."

"Why?"

"I considered it essential, sir, for the safety of Miss Wrightman."

Mr. Whittle gave a sharp bark. "You don't mean she's in there?"

"No, sir. I can state definitely that such is not the case."

"What the blazes do you mean, then, you old fool?"

Stoker coughed. "I have been engaged in some delicate experiments, sir. I an by no means convinced that they are genuinely potent, but in view of abnormal conditions I consider that full investigations should be made. This particular volume, written fortunately in our language, is an invaluable guide."

"Give!" spluttered Dr. Fredl. "I command that you at once the book produce . Otherwise I to you shall the conk on the beezer present."

"I regret, sir, that I cannot see to do so unless Mr. Spencer so orders me." Stoker drew himself up. "What are your instructions, Mr. Spencer?"

Mr. Davenhill made no immediate reply. Both he and Roy had been distracted by the arrival of Terry and Carole, and before Stoker had time to withdraw from circulation once more Dr. Fredl, barking like a seal, made a panther-like spring in his direction. The aged butler dodged, and then, seeing that the whiskered Hun had really got the bit between his teeth and was preparing for action, took to his heels. It was thirty years since he had last sprinted, but under the circumstances he put up a praiseworthy performance, and snapping into top gear he sped down the passage like a liner under full steam. Dr. Fredl, still barking, followed, and Mr. Whittle brought up the rear, with Spennie panting helplessly behind. Travelling nicely they reached the head of the main landing, to be met with violent knocking and ringing on the front door.

Stoker paused in his headlong flight, and cast a quick

nervous look behind him. In his brain, overtought as it was, Duty fought a brief battle with Self-Preservation. To fail to open the door to a visitor would be a grave blot on his code, but on the other hand he had a shrewd idea that once Dr. Fredl managed to establish contact his (Stoker's) days of buttling would be cut very short. Fortunately, the old archaeologist solved the problem nicely by tripping over a loose stair-rod and taking off in manner of a jet Meteor. For an instant he flew gracefully through the air, fuselage well placed and tail plane extended; but the strain was to great, and he nosedived heavily beard fist, finishing up in the mangled heap at the foot of the stairs.

"Is he hurt?" panted Spennie, when the echoes of the crash had finished rolling round the hall and cannoning off the occasional tables.

"I should think so," Mr. Whittle grunted, plunging down and kneeling by the body. "In fact, it might be a sound scheme to go and ring up the local mortuary. Confound him, the perverse old coot – he's lying flat on his face, and I can't shift him."

"Do you want to?"

"I do. I want to pull his beard."

"Why?"

"To see whether it's false, you doddle-pate. Give me a hand to roll him over."

"Can't you do it yourself?"

"Not being either Hercules or a steam-crane, I can't." Mr. Whittle pulled and heaved. "I believe he's been living on a diet of concrete. Come on, blast your eyebrows!"

Mr. Davenhill was about to obey when a majestic, butleresque sound of throat-clearing told him that Stoker was in full circulation once more, and busy at his old duties, though still wheezing noticeably and looking as though he had paused through a mangle.

"Mr. Ratcliffe, sir," he announced.

Roy looked up sharply, and winced. He did not like what he saw.

Stoker was no oil-painting – even at the best of times he bore a marked resemblance to one of Mr. Epstein's less cheery creations – but compared to the newcomer he was a positive

Apollo. Mr. Ratcliffe, at first sight, was a nauseating spectacle, and when one had had time to get in a long, searching look at him it became clear that his really gruesome points were too numerous to swallow at one go. Pale saffron hair surmounted a yellow, parchment-like face and a thin, tampering snoddle; his mouth hung loosely open, revealing a set of discoloured teeth; he wore blue-tinted spectacles and a scrubby moustache, and had obviously not shaved for some time. The general picture was rounded of by a large, multi-coloured wart on his left nostril, which was about the same size as a threepenny piece. Roy gave vent to a soft snort of distaste. It was his private opinion that Mr. Ratcliffe would be lucky if he got away from Wollingham Hall without collecting a really good poke in the clock.

"Good-morning," began this disease, in a high-pitched, mincing voice. "Mr. Davenhill, I presume? My name is Ratcliffe. Honk!"

"Ratcliffe what?"

"Nehemiah Ratcliffe. I believe you were expecting me for lunch. I hope I am not too early? Honk!"

Spennie looked helplessly at Roy. Evidently the syllable "honk" was not meant to be included in the general context - more likely it was due to adenoid, or a leaky epiglottis – but it was none the less disconcerting, not to say revolting. At this point Mr Whittle, having abandoned his efforts to roll Dr. Fredl into a position suitable for beard-pulling, rose to his feet and went on the ether.

"So you're Weatherill's pal, are you?"

"Precisely." Mr. Ratcliffe extended a lank hand, adorned with an impressive assortment of rings. "This is indeed a pleasure. Honk!"

"It may be a pleasure to you, but I'm darned if it is to me," Mr. Whittle admitted frankly. "You don't mind me telling you, right from the outset, that I think this psychic business is a basinful of onion soup?"

Mr. Ratcliffe thought carefully before replying.

"Not really," he replied, after a pause.

"I mean, you won't take offence, or anything."

"No."

"Quite sure?"

"Good. If people get huffy with me, I'm liable to poke them on the snoddle. And that goes for ducks who try to pull fast ones over me, too. You follow me closely, old lad?"

Mr. Ratcliffe twisted his features into the semblance of a smile, causing his wart to vibrate in a manner that exercised a hypnotic effect upon his audience. Spennie half expected it to change colour in the manner of a traffic light.

"I fully appreciate your scepticism, Mr. Whittle," he admitted blandly. "Honk! You believe, no doubt, that I am an eccentric, a crank, a credulous fool?"

"I haven't made up my mind. I just think the whole business smells bad of fish."

"You will learn," Mr. Ratcliffe assured him. "In my profession, Mr. Whittle, we are used to unbelievers. Laugh, jeer, scoff if you will."

"Honk!" said Roy nastily. "I warn you I'm England's No.1 jeerer, and I can scoff pretty well, too. Incidentally, how did you know my name was Whittle?"

"Isn't it?"

"It is, but that's not the point."

"I should have thought it was very much to the point," the ghost-specialist objected my name. I was christened Nehemiah Horatio, after my paternal grandfather -"

"That's all right about your paternal grandfather, may he rot in his tomb. You haven't answered my question."

"Haven't I?" Mr. Ratcliffe massaged hi wart thoughtfully. "Do you know, I believe I've forgotten what it was."

Spennie, seeing a small puff of smoke issue from Mr. Whittle's nostrils, stepped hastily forward.

"Don't ass about, Roy," he requested shortly. "We don't want any more bloodshed. Stoker will show you to your room, Mr. Ratcliffe, and then perhaps we'd better have a talk about the general situation. Did you bring any more luggage with you?"

"A good deal, but I left most of it at the station. You understand there is certain apparatus I must have ready to hand on theses occasions." Mr. Ratcliffe caressed his wart lovingly. "How ever, there is no immediate hurry. It can wait until after lunch.

Before I can form any definite opinions, I shall have to move about and assimilate the atmosphere."

Mr. Whittle, who was stilled ruffled by the thought that the spook-hunter had had decidedly the best of the preliminary exchanges, muttered something about the atmosphere that caused Stoker to give him an old-fashioned look; but the rather awkward silence that followed was broken by the arrival of Carole Czernak and Terry Fane, and introductions flew to and fro like tennis-balls. Mr. Whittle snorted softly on nothing that as soon as Miss Czernak came fully over the horizon, her umph paraded for all to see, Mr. Ratcliffe's eyes lit up with a strange light, and he twirled his moustache. Evidently the spiritual life he had not completely killed his human feelings. Carole was hardly less affected, though in the opposite way – for a second or two her self-control lopsed but she readjusted it almost at once. Terry was not so polite. He let off a muffled grunt, caught his cousin's eye, and buried his face in his handkerchief.

"Ow do you do?" Miss Czernak inquired. "You are a friend of Professor Weatherill, is it not?"

"Precisely. A very old friend," asserted the spook-specialist warmly. "Honk! Dear Augustus and I have been associate for many years. It will be delightful to meet again." he broke off, and cast a doubtful look at the crumpled body at the foot of the stairs. "Pardon my curiosity, but do I not see an – an earthy shell behind you, Mr. Whittle?"

"Oh, that's only Dr. Fredl," Mr. Whittle explained airily, stepping aside to give the others a clear view. The old tomb-grubber was still sprawled out his face buried in the carpet and the less delicate portions of his anatomy raised up in striking relief. "He's all right."

"All right, you say?" Miss Czernak hiccoughed wildly, like a refine sea-lion, and beat down. "Uncle Felix! Uncle Felix! Roy, he is hurt!"

"I know. I'd forgotten all about him."

"What happened?"

"He took a short cut downstairs. I don't think it'll prove fatal."

"Fatal! "Ow can you be so unfeeling?" Miss Czernak

138

tossed off a reproachful look. "Do something!"

"What?"

"Oh, don't be supine," put in Mr. Davenhill impatiently. "Give him some smelling-salts, or sticks a key down his neck, something. We can't leave him there."

"He certainly clutters the place," agreed Mr. Whittle. "I suppose we could erect a screen or something round him, but it'd be a lot simpler to shift him out of the way. On the other hand, the only key I possess happens to fit my flat, and I'm damned if I'll stick that down his neck – or anywhere else, for that matter."

Stoker cleared his throat, and put his oar in. "If you so desire, sir, I can obtain a key from the kitchen. I understand, however, that such a remedy is efficacious only in the case of a bleeding nose."

"I believe you're right," Mr. Whittle agreed. "Since his nose isn't bleeding, you needn't bother. If you particularly want to practice first-aid I can always tap him on the snoddle for you, but I don't think this is either the time or the place."

"No sir," admitted the old butler regretfully. "If I might make a suggestion, sir, I have always found that there are few ills that cannot be at least alleviated by a judicious quantity of whisky."

Nobody raising any objections to this idea, Terry fetched a bottle from the dining-room, and within a minute or two the bearded Hum was sitting up and taking notice, steering the bottle through his whiskers and chewing the cud with a noise that sounded like a herd of cattle ploughing through a bog. Mr. Ratcliffe, watching the scene with interest and still fondling his rainbow-hued wart, seized the chance to have a private chat with Terry; and Mr. Whittle, reflecting that the old archaeologist would be in no condition to continue his butler-hunt for at least an hour, withdrew. His long-term policy was to continue the search for Miss Wrightman, but his immediate need was a stiff bracer, and Spennie's excellent cellar showed no signs of giving out as yet.

Chapter 17

Having fortified himself by knocking back the three noggins of fine old whisky in quick succession, Mr. Whittle lit his pipe and revved his brain until it was working at full capacity. The situation called for careful study.

Pauline, if still in the neighbourhood, was well hidden - that was definite. Since it was unlikely that she had withdrawn from circulation of her own accord, and still more unlikely that she had pushed off altogether, it stood to reason that someone was keeping her stowed away, and the thought made Roy dilate his nostrils and paw carpet with one foot. He also ground his teeth, desisting only when he felt a front stopping creak under the strain. If he could only track down this dirty work to its fountain-head he was prepared to go through the house like an arctic wind, leaving a trail of poked clocks and prodded snoddles in his wake.

Absently he tossed back another snifter, and came to a decision. Dr. Fredl was well in the running for a prodded snoddle, and since he was temporarily out of action the coast was clear for a quick search of his room. Not that Miss Wrightman was likely to be there, but it might be possible to see definitely whether Dr. Fredl was a genuine article or merely some duck pulling a quick one. Mr. Whittle therefore dragged himself reluctantly away from the decanter and made his way up the back stairs, arriving in fulness of time at the room where the old archaeologist spent that portion of his nights not taken up by wainscote-sniffing expeditions of cupboards and other hiding-places, but no Paulines came to light, and he turned to his attention to the large writing-desk in the window bay. It did not occur to him that should he be discovered in the act of rifling private correspondence his motives might easily be questioned, but he dismissed the objection as trifling, and rummaged cheerfully through the drawers, keeping a weather eye for anything of interest. The letters meant little to him, since they were mainly in German; and since Roy's knowledge of that language was limited to a few swear-words he had picked up in the course of his Service career he found himself baffled. He could, however, satisfy himself that there would be a good number of documents addressed to the Herr Doktor Felix Fredl, and it was evident that if the old coot was an imposting for some years. Presently he made his first real discovery. Tucked away at the bottom of the second drawer was a scrawled map – an exact copy of the one he had screwed out of Professor Weatherill earlier on.

"Odd," mused Mr. Whittle, staring at the grubby piece of paper. "Traced .. Why the blazes should Fredl have a copy of this thing if Weatherill holds the original? Wonder if the two old thugs are trying to double-cross each other?"

At first sight, this seemed a likely theory. Roy's mental machinery was now ticking over nicely, and he reasoned that neither gentlemen would have the slightest hesitation in slitting his partner's gizzard if there was anything to be gained thereby; on the other hand the chart was palpable fake, and therefore worthless. There seemed little point in taking the copy, so he thrust it back into its original position, and turned his attention to the bookshelf.

Here, he saw at once, there was much interesting material, interesting, that is, to anyone fond of magic, witchcraft, Voodoo and general skullduggery. If Fredl was a fraud he was remarkably thorough one, since most of the books were unquestionably genuine. Names like Scheuter, Summers, Home and Aleister Crowley cropped up again and again, and there were also numerous exercise-books filled from cover to cover with spidery German writing. Most of the shelf, however, was taken up by massive archaeolical tomes, including a couple written by Fredl himself and one - "The fascination of the Tomb" - by Augustus Weatherill.

Absently Mr. Whittle picked out one of the Fredl volumes, a slim affair bound in calf, and flicked it open. Then he started violently, as though he had been prodded with an incandescent bradawl. The front piece was heated - in German type - "Der Auteur", and showed a tall, thinnish duck with a trim Vandyck beard and a beaky nose, as unlike Uncle Felix as could possibly be imagined.

Roy breathed hard. Here was proof positive. He examined the book closely, but with his limited knowledge of the Hunnish tongue he could make little of it; and he was wondering whether to risk half-inching it when voices and footsteps were coming down

141

the passage.

Roy cursed, luridly though inaudibly. Fate seemed to be working against him at full throttle, splitting on its hands and mustering all its reserves in an effort to do the dirty on him, but the hectic life at Wollingham Hall had sharpened his wits, and – pausing only to slip the book into his pocket and mutter the five vilest words he could think of – he shot silently behind the curtain, pulling it across behind him and hoping that his curved portions would not show too conspicuously. After a pause the door opened, and a husky, attractive voice went on the ether.

"In here,." it said. "Uncle Felix he puts salts always near to his bed. He says that they alone will - how you say? - pull him out of the faintness."

"These?" Terry Fane asked.

"But yes. We must return."

From tone it did not seem as if it was her dearest wish to race downstairs and ram the smelling-salts up the old tomb-grubber's nostrils, and Terry evidently felt along the same lines, for he closed the door and sat down on the bed. Mr. Whittle felt acutely uncomfortable. His conscience was pricking him at the thought of tuning in to what was evidently going to be a cosy tete-a-tete, but that could have been borne. What really troubled him was the window-sill, which jutted out at a vicious angle and was poking him in a vulnerable spot between the eighth and ninth ribs.

"Let the old trout wait," Terry muttered sullenly. "He's all right – nothing more than a conk on the dome. Carole, we never seem to get the chance to talk together, and I want to like hell."

"To talk only?"

"Well, that'll do to begin with." Terry grinned. "Come and it down. I can't talk to you when you're about half a mile away."

There was a short pause.

"You are worried, is it not?" Miss Czernak asked softly.

"I am. I'm sweating like hell. How did you know?"

"I know much," Miss Czernak admitted calmly.

"I'll bet you do! I wish wish to God I could understand you. Why don't you trust me, Carole? You know I'm – well, that I'll -"

"For the very good reason," said Miss Czernak decisively, "that you don't trust me, my Terry. You think I am a fool, no? Psh!"

she emitted a ladylike snort. "You to me tell the big lie. No, it has – how you call it? - the smell of bad fish."

"I've never told you any lies ..." Terry's voice trailed off. "God, if you only knew what a hole I was in! All right, then – leave me alone. You don't trust me an inch, and you're sick to death of having me hanging around -"

There was yet another pause, and Mr. Whittle, taking his conscience firmly by the scruff of the neck and giving it the bird in no uncertain fashion, risked a quick peep round the curtain. He need not have worried. Neither Terry nor Carole would have noticed had he taken it into his head to dance a hornpipe. In fact, they were so closely entwined that Mr. Whittle wondered whether it would be necessary to get a crowbar and lever them apart.

"Ouf!" said Terry after perhaps half a minute. "Ouf! What a girl! Love me?"

Miss Czernak admitted that she did, and for the next few minutes the conversation became so revoltingly sickly that Mr. Whittle, for once, turned puce in the face and heartily wished himself five miles away. He tried stuffing his fingers into his ears, but with only partial success, and gradually sank into a condition of weak despair. At last, after what seemed eternity, he was jerked back to reality by hearing his name.

"And to think," Terry was saying breathlessly, "that I could've sworn you were hand-in-glove with that oaf Roy!"

Mr. Whittle breathed hard.

"Roy? Him" Miss Czernak uncorked a tinkling, silvery laugh that went though Mr. Whittle like a scimitar. "But my Terry, you make a joke! He is no – so beefy, as you say. Or do I mean hammy?"

"So am I beefy," Terry grunted, "only I don't gas about it. We did some pretty tough training in my unit, you know, and I don't think Roy'd care to tackle me Mr. Whittle, his good-humour more or less restored, stifled a bark of mirth. "Do you like him?"

"I am not sure. I think I do he is what you call the thick-head. He is afraid of me."

"Afraid of you?"

"But yes. Thinks that I and Uncle Felix alone cause these hauntings. Yet he is attracted."

"I'll give him a swipe in the mush," Terry growled. "How much attracted? I mean. Has he -"

"Of course," Miss Czernak replied, in a surprised tone.

"He has?"

"But naturally."

"Often?"

"Twice only. No, three times – or is it four? I forget." Miss Czernak sighed. "He is strong, you know, though he is so ugly. As I lay by him -"

"Here!" Terry gave a sharp bay. "When was this? Last night?"

"Before dinner." Miss Czernak sighed soulfully. "But my Terry, what is a kiss? You are jealous. It is only you I want."

"I know, only I've a pretty good notion what kind of a duck Roy is." Terry uttered a low growl, like a bull-dog who finds a pekingese curled up in his kennel nibbling his favourite bone. "He's got a two-track mind, and other track's booze. He's even after the Wrightman female."

This was news to Miss Czernak.

"Pauline Wrightman?"

"You bet. I saw 'em in the conservatory last night." Terry chuckled gaily. "Love's Young Dream wasn't in it with those two! I don't suppose he means to marry the wench, but if she falls for him properly it'll be rather rough on Strudwick. If he -"

Mr. Whittle drew back the curtain and stepped forward, his jaw working and two thin jets of steam issuing from his ears. Terry broke off sharply, while Miss Czernak gave a falsetto snort and expressed herself in a language that sounded like a sheep gargling. Roy advanced menacingly, still grinding his teeth.

"Don't be a fool -" Terry began, and then, seeing that his relative was intent on murder, put up his hands and prepared for battle. He did not have long to wait. Mr. Whittle, scientifically and impartially, feinted with his left and then hit Terry very hard on the nozzle with his right, causing his organ to bend visibly and gush blood. Terry stumbled against a table, which groaned and collapsed, and then, lunging forward, managed to get close grips and knee Mr. Whittle viciously between the legs. Mr. Whittle retaliated by a venomous left hook on Terry's already damaged

144

snout. Terry fell forward, and the two rolled about in a close but not loving embrace, cursing the while in a manner that caused a perceptible blue haze in the atmosphere. Terry succeeded in getting his teeth to bear upon his cousin's ear, but after a while Mr. Whittle was able to bring his ju-jitsu into play, and Terry found himself lying flat on his stomach, with his legs thrashing the unoffending air and his face buried in the carpet, while Mr. Whittle kneeled on him wondering what to do next.

He had not made up his mind whether to wring Terry's neck or bang his head against the floor, when the matter was taken out of his hands . There was a sharp explosion, and the universe dissolved into a blaze of light; coloured flares shot to and fro with gay abandon, intermingled with shooting-stars, multi-tailed comets and brilliant rockets. These lasted for some time and then gradually faded away, while the world commenced to revolve as high speed, jerking up and down in a baffling manner. Eventually Mr. Whittle came to, to perceive Miss Czernak waving an evil-smelling bottle under his nose, while Terry muttered strange things in the background – apparently in the process of bleeding to death.

"What hit me?" asked Mr. Whittle idiotically, sitting up and massaging his temple. "The Albert Hall?"

"I did," Miss Czernak informed him a strangled voice. "You are the brute, you. Ach! With a jug I gave you what you call a conk on the breezer -"

"The devil you did!" Mr. Whittle grunted, and staggered up. "Gentle things, women. What did you want to butt in for? I was just getting on nicely."

"Next time you want to romp," said Terry darkly, "we'll go into a ring and put some gloves on. If you hadn't taken me by surprise -"

"Taken you by surprise, my left nostril. Is your nose bleeding much?"

"It is, blast your eyebrows. I think it's broken."

"Good. Incidentally, old girl," said Mr. Whittle testily, "Would you mind taking that bottle away? It smells to me like dead skunks pickled in ammonia. What I want is whisky, and lots of it."

"What you nearly got," Miss Czernak informed him

vehemently, "is the broken head." She unleashed a look that reminded Mr. Whittle of a peevish cobra. "I wish you were dead."

"No thanks to you I'm not. Luckily, I've got a tough skull." Mr. Whittle observed the shattered remains of a china jug, and grimaced. "See here, young Carole, it's time we had a real heart-to-heart talk."

"I will not talk with you!"

"You will, and like it. I take it you don't want the police in?"

"And I take it you don't want another scrap?" Terry asked, belligerently. "If you start badgering Carole I'll do my damnedest to scoop your guts out."

Mr. Whittle eyed his cousin with grudging admiration. Terry's snoddle was still gushing blood like the fountains in Trafalgar Square. Also his eye had turned a rich purple, and under the circumstances it was rather surprising that he was ready for more. Incidentally, Mr. Whittle was starting to feel faintly abashed. It was at least ten years since he had lost control of his temper so completely, and he had an uneasy notion that he had rather a fool of himself.

"All right," he said reluctantly. "Go and get some first-aid, and we'll talk later. One thing, though. If you haven't the common decency to keep your mouth shut about things that don't concern you, you'll be asking for trouble in big chunks. Get me?"

"I get you," Terry muttered with an ill grace.

"Good." Mr. Whittle gave his throbbing temple a final-rub, and made for the front door. "By the by, what about Uncle Felix? If he's still waiting for his skunk salts, he's probably had a dozen relapses by now."

"Blast and damn Uncle Felix!" Terry hissed.

"By all means," agreed Mr. Whittle. "I only mentioned it." With which he made as dignified an exit as he could manage.

Chapter 18

Mr. Whittle pottered unsteadily downstairs, musing bitterly. Miss. Czernak may have had bucketfuls of umph, but he knew now that she had also had plenty of physical beef; his head was singing , and the feeling of a tight band above his eyes was only just starting to abate. Fortunately there was a certain remedy near at hand, and after a couple of generous snifter he was conscious of a marked improvement. True, he still felt like a corpse, but not like a corpse that had been drifting in the sea for days on end. He was even able to stand the sudden appearance of Stoker without wincing, though the aged butler was far from being his usual natty self.

"Come in, old lad," Mr. Whittle greeted him. "Have a snifter."

It says much for Stoker's mental state that he accepted without a murmur, and knocked back a glassful of whisky as though drinking in the dining-room was now new experience – instead of being the first time in forty years of butting in that he had even thought of such a very thing. Downing it in two minutes gollups, he ran his tongue round the glass to make sure that nothing had been wasted, and then wiped his mouth delicately with the back of his hand.

"I needed that, Mr. Roy," he confessed. "The strain is fast wearing me down. My days of service are all but over."

"Nuts. Is Fredl recovering?"

"Unfortunately, yes."

"A pity."

"Precisely, sir. I was ordered to fetch him a further supply of brandy, and a temptation to tamper with it was severe."

"How do you mean, tamper? Slip something in it?"

"Yes, sir."

"What? Sulphuric acid?"

"Sulphuric acid would have done very well, sir, it is not a substance that I normally carry upon my person. A certain course of action did present itself to me, but I am proud to say that I rejected it as unethical." Stoker hesitated. "Are you of the opinion,

147

sir, that Dr. Fredl intends to continue his attack upon me?"

"I should think it all depends on whether you return his blessed book. Take my tip, and hand it over."

"No, sir."

"Why not?"

"I cannot say, sir. My lips are sealed."

"Oh, God!" snarled Mr. Whittle. "You're like some damned parrot. Don't blame me if you get knifed."

"I shall hold you in no way responsible, sir." The butler cleared his throat. "I feel that I must have come for some specific purpose, Mr. Roy, but I cannot for the life of me recall what it was"

"Never mind, his Spennie still rallying round old Fredl?"

"I fancy, sir, that Mr. Spencer retired to his room after seeing Mr. Ratcliffe off in the taxi."

"Ratcliffe? Off?"

"Yes, sir."

"You don't mean he's gone?"

"That was the impression I intended the convey, sir."

"But damn it, he's only just come. I wonder if he's given the thing up?"

"No, sir. Mr. Ratcliffe has merely returned to the village to fetch what remains of his luggage." Stoker sniffed. "If I make a personal observation, Mr. Roy I trust that you will treat it a strictly confidential?"

"Of course."

"Thank you sir. In my opinion, then, Mr. Ratcliffe is not a desirable character. I disliked him at first sight."

"We're at one there, old lad," Mr. Whittle agreed cordially. "He stinks."

"Precisely, sir. I am bound in all fairness, to describe him as perfectly bloody. I would infinitely prefer the company of a cockroach."

"Birds of a feather. By the by, old lad, I don't want to seem inquisitive, but you have remembered what you came here for ? I mean, was it important?""

"It has just come back to me, sir. There is a telephone message for you."

148

"A 'phone message? Who from?"

"A Mr. Tallon, sir. Mr. Gregory Tallon."

"Good. What did he say?"

"Nothing, sir. He was holding the line."

"What, now?"

"Yes, sir."

"Then why the hell didn't you say so, you addle-pated old ruin?" asked Mr. Whittle, with justifiable annoyance. "He may have given up all hope by now, merely because you want to stand there and drivel about cockchafers -"

"Not cockchafers, sir. Cockroaches. The insects are entirely dissimilar."

"Cockchafers, cockroaches, or cock-whatever-you-like," snarled Mr. Whittle, "Greg's probably hanging on and cursing like the proverbial trooper." He polished off his whisky, and moved for the door. "If he's given it up as a bad job and rung off, I warn you I'll come back and fillet you."

Fortunately such drastic action proved to be unnecessary. Mr. Tallon was still on the line, though his patience was obviously becoming somewhat frayed round the edges. "Hallo," he said testily, as Mr. Whittle took up the receiver. "Is that you?"

"Yes. Sorry to have been so long. That ass of the butler was drooling on about cockroaches, and never told me you were waiting."

"I don't altogether follow you," said Gregory, "but I haven't time to hammer it out now, because I've got to go and meet Julie as soon as I've finished with you, I said 'about twelve', and it's past that now."

"Damn Julie!"

"Certainly not. She's worth ten off these peroxide Yugoslavs you keep on nattering about. Or do I mean Bulgarians?"

"I suppose," said Mr. Whittle with studied patience, "you'll get round to the point sometime. Incidentally I haven't got any got any Yugoslavs or Bulgarians on tow, peroxide or otherwise."

"Haven't you?" Mr. Tallon inquired vaguely. "I seem to remember you saying something about one. Never mind   I suppose you're too busy with skeletons and poltergeists to notice."

"That's all right about skeletons and poltergeists. Listen,

149

Greg. This Fredl trout's a faker."

"A what?"

"Faker. Spoofer. Welsher. Anything you like. I've come across a photograph of him – but it isn't him at all, if you see what I mean."

"I don't," Mr. Tallon admitted after a baffled pause. "If it isn't him, who is it?"

"Fredl."

"But I thought you said it wasn't."

"Nor is it – not the Fredl I know."

"Then who the hell is it?" asked Mr. Tallon, with some heat. "Donald Duck?"

"No, you doddle-pate. It's genuine. He hasn't got such as a long beard, for one thing."

"Donald Duck?'

"Fool! Listen. It's a front piece of one of Fredl's books, and it's not in the least like the old buster who's passing himself off down here. Now do you get it?"

"Yes. Well," said Gregory, "I've been doing some sleuthing on my own account, but so far a I can gather Fredl's never been mixed up in any really questionable business, apart from messing about with black magic. I don't see what harm that can do."

"What you ought to come down here. Stoker's under the impression that he's turned a girl into a bat."

"What?"

Mr. Whittle repeated his remark. Mr. Tallon chuckled.

"What you ought to do," he said judicially, "is to run a wall round the whole place and certify the lot, not forgetting that extraordinary old trout with the salmon."

"She hasn't got the salmon with her. For the Lord's sake, forget it. I'm fed up with that infernal salmon."

"So was the Vicar," Gregory agreed. "I'll never forget his face when -"

"Stop drooling," Mr. Whittle requested curtly. "What about Ratcliffe? Any gen on him?"

"Quite a bit. Ratcliffe is a bird to steer clear of. He's got quite a reputation as a spook-chaser, but I believe his real game's blackmail – at any rate he's hand-in-glove with that squirmng, crawling snake, Aloysius Peabody."

Mr. Whittle locked thoughtful. He knew something about Mr. Peabody, the Society photographer; not a great deal, but enough to realise that he was on of Mother Nature's gravest lapses. It was an open secret that he made a steady income out of the judicious use of incriminating letters, and his ability to rake up mud in a seemingly clear pool amounted almost to genius.

"Oh," said Mr. Whittle at length. "He is, is he? That opens up a new field. I wonder! Of course, he's all set to get away with a whacking fee, in any case -"

"The hell he is! How?"

"Spennie, the beetle-witted coot, has promised him a hundred quid if he de-ghosts the house. If I'm right, and Fredl's responsible, it ought to be too easy. All he's got to do is square Fredl and Weatherill, even if he's not working with them alread,y. On the other hand, where does the map come in? Why does Fredl sniffing about in wainscoting? Where does Carole come in – and what's happened to Pauline? God damn it," said Mr. Whittle heartily. "I'm fogged. All I know is that I'd like to tie friend Ratcliffe's intestines in a knot."

"Why don't you?"

"I shall, before the week's out. He's a disease. In fact he's in the Peabody class, and I can't say more than that."

"True. Well," said Mr. Tallon, "I can't spend all day chatting to you, much as I like the sound of your voice. I wish I could come down and give you some moral support, but I'm too damned busy with these elections, apart altogether from Julie. Give Spennie my regards. I'll ring again if I come across anything new."

"Right. Chin-chin."

"So long," said Gregory airily, and rang off.

Brooding, Mr. Whittle refilled his pipe and pottered back to the dining-room. Presently Mr. Strudwick joined him, looking hot irritable and with his shoes and trousers liberally caked with mud, and greeted him with a low snort that sounded like a warthog calling to its mate. Rightly or wrongly, Mr. Whittle too umbrage.

"Adenoids?' he inquired.

The M.P. Looked puzzled "I beg your pardon?"

"I asked you if you suffered from adenoids. Form the revolting noise you made just now, I gather that you do."

"I do not suffer form adenoids," Mr. Strudwick informed him stiffly "and I was not aware that I made any sound, revolting or otherwise."

"Well, you did, and if you do it again I shall be compelled to kick you right in the teeth. I don't like people snorting at me as through I stank. Or perhaps you think I do?"

No, no," Mr. Strudwick hastened to inform him, seeing a menacing glint in Roy's eye. "Such a thought never crossed my mind.."

"Good. I was afraid it had."

"Far from it."

"Lucky for you."

Having thus established an atmosphere of calm and good fellowship Mr. Whittle poured himself a bracer and tossed it off with praiseworthy efficiently. It tasted good, and a second, taken rather more slowly, even better.

"By the way," said Mr. Strudwick suddenly, "I suppose you have not yet found any trace of my fiancée?"

"No. No sign of here down at the camp?"

"I was unable to gather any definite information. That place," said Mr. Strudwick moodily, "is a positive madhouse". No sooner did I appear than Miss Debenham fastened upon me and requested my assistance in moving a large, unwieldy statue which – so she said – depicted the god Pan. I make no claim to any great physical strength, but I do feel some of her subsequent comments were in the worst of taste."

"What happened? Did you drop it."

"I missed my footing, and the statue fell with some violence into a pit. Unfortunately part of the head came away, and the base split into three parts."

"And Aunt Clara let rip?"

"She did."

"What did she call you?"

"That is neither here nor there," the M.P. returned with some asperity. "The expressions concerned were both vulgar in applicable. I really can't understand how a women of Miss

152

Debenham's intellect and education can so far forget herself."

"Don't blame the old trout," Mr. Whittle urged charitably. "She's not like other folk."

"She's certainly isn't."

"I mean she lives in a world of her own, if you follow me. Even if you spend all your time surrounded by statues or skeletons. There can be no excuse for calling me a – well, what she did. I feel I am entitled to be seriously annoyed. I seem to remember Mrs. Fane telling me about some very embarrassing episodes last time Miss Debenham visited England – wasn't there something about a salmon?"

"There was."

"What?"

"Never mind. It's best forgotten."

"So Mrs. Fane said. Strange that she had her sister should be so entirely different in their ideas and interests. I only wish Mrs. Fane was here now."

"I'm darned glad she isn't," Mr. Whittle admitted frankly. "Aunt Violet's all very well, but you must admit she's a bit of an old battle-axe."

"I admit nothing of the sort. I have the greatest regard for Mrs. Fane. Did you know that she has consented to stand for the Chipwood and Whortlebury division at the next election?"

"I did, but you're evading the issue. A battle-axe she was born, and a battle-axe she will die. She's one of these people who regard it as their mission in life to disapprove of everything. Damn it, she doesn't even drink."

"Nor do I."

"You don't?"

"No. Drink is a cancer in the body politic."

"Well said Mr. Whittle reasonably, "that strengthens my argument. If you had a snifter now and then, you'd probably enjoy life a lot more. Buck you up, if you see what I mean."

"I don't," admitted the M.P., but then I never do. Well, I must go and make a final search to satisfy myself that Pauline is not in the house. After that I propose to ring the police."

"Good God, why?"

"Because I feel that my fiancée's disappearance should be

investigated without delay. I regard all this talk of black magic as the purest onion soup – to use your own expression – but I am beginning to think that Pauline has been forcibly abducted. I'm quite certain she didn't leave the house of her own accord."

"True enough. On the other hand I don't see what you want the police to do. Besides, I shouldn't think you want any undue publicity."

"Why not? My conscience is perfectly clear."

"Perhaps, but if I was electing someone to Parliament I'd steer clear of a duck who'd been mixed up in a funny business with walking skeletons, black magic, and bearded doctors who change girls into bats. What ho," he added as Spennie entered. "How's the corpse?"

"If you mean Fredl," said Spennie wearily, "he's gone off to his room, and I hope to goodness he stays there. Terry's the latest casualty. Apparently he tripped over a stair-rod and banged his face on the banister."

Mr. Whittle let out a caw of laughter.

"I don't think it's particularly amusing," Mr. Davenhill said shortly. "His eye looks the devil of a mess. Whisky, please."

Mr. Whittle did the humours, and Mr. Davenhill knocked back a generous peg with obvious relief. "Ratcliffe," he went on, passing back his glass for a refill, "has legged it back to the village to collect his bags. What do you think if him, Roy?"

"I think he reeks. In fact, he strikes me as being a striking argument in favour of birth control."

"So do I,:" Mr. Davenhill admitted frankly. "but if he clears up this infernal mess he;'s welcome to his hundred quid. Incidentally I've noticed that we haven't had so many bells since he came – there's only been one false alarm in the last hour. The thing that worries me most at present is what's happened to Miss Wrightman."

"Me, too. If I find out who's responsible I'll choke him."

"I'm glad to see you taking it so seriously," Mr. Strudwick put in nastily. "Nut since she is to be my wife I feel that I am the person most directly concerned. I have been wondering whether to call the police."

"I thought of that," said Mr. Davenhill, "but I know old

Seargeant Potter. He'll come down to blather about, and make things ten times more awkward than they are already. Ratcliffe seems very certain he can do something about her, so I suppose we'd better hang on for a bit."

"All very well. Suppose Pauline is in danger?"

"I doubt that. In any case old Potter wouldn't know what to do, and he wouldn't consider it important enough to call in Scotland Yard. After all, she's quite likely to turn up – she may have gone for a long walk."

"Starting at three a.m.?"

"Well, people do sometimes go out early in the morning. I do."

"I don't want to be offensive," Mr. Whittle commented, "but of all the inane suggestions I've ever heard that one takes the biscuit. If she felt like a moonlight ramble, she'd have told me. No, she said she was off to bed, and that's where she went."

"You didn't actually see her into her room?"

"No. I was far too occupied with Quinnie. Take it from me, though, she didn't mean to stir until breakfast-time, if then. Inference – someone's got at her, and if it's Weatherill I'll pull his windpipe out. Talk of the devil," he added, looking casually out of French windows, "here he is. What in hell is he up to?"

Something unusual was happening in the middle distance. The view from the dining-room was basically pleasing – several chunks of lawn occupied the foreground, agreeably backed by the tennis-courts and a row of stately-looking trees – but just now it was marred by the lank figure of the aged archaeologist, who was staggering along pushing what seemed gardeners and handymen, all laden with various odds and ends, and finally Aunt Clara, obviously content to do no more than direct operations. The air became polluted by the clamour of voices, topped by the professor's bleating treble and Aunt Clara's strident contralto.

"I should imagine," Mr. Strudwick hazarded, "that they propose to add something to their unsavoury museum. You know, I cannot say that I feel and real regret at the virtual destruction of that statue. I trust I am no vandal, but I'm bound to admit that I found it thoroughly repellent. I think it must have been the horns."

"Horns?"

"Yes. Two of them, one above each ear."

"If they go on like this," Mr. Davenhill observed bitterly, "the house will start to look like a stonemason's yard. My one hope is that Aunt Violet, when she finally gets herself de-mumped, will put her foot down and have a general purge."

"She'll need to be tough." Mr. Whittle stared absently as the procession wound up the path and disappeared round the house in the direction of the servants' entrance. "Once Aunt Clara really gets the bit between her teeth it'll take more than a mere sister – even a well-loved one – to stop her."

"True. Moreover, I don't know about beign well-loved. Aunt Clara says and does things that make Aunt Violet squirm – quite apart from that ghastly salmon business. The only reason they've never actually come to blows is because Aunt Clara's nearly always away tomb-hunting in some remote part of the globe and is satisfactorily out of harm's way. Ouf!" added Spennie convulsively as a deafening crash shattered the noonday peace. "What was that?"

"Glass?" suggested Mr. Strudwick.

Mr. Whittle grunted. "Considering that if they want to get that junk into the museum they'll have to go through the the big conservatory I shouldn't think there's much doubt about it. Well, I suppose we'd better go and view the wreckage."

Sucking his pipe moodily he led the way, and in the fulness of time the three arrived at the scene of the disturbance. They were greeted by three separate volleys of oaths. One of the gardeners was muttering evil things in the corner, and Professor Weatherill was hopping about like a grim canary, clutching his foot and cursing loudly in basic English, while Aunt Clara, mounted upon a packing case, held forth in a strange tongue, waving her arms in the manner of a marionette. Mr. Whittle drew a large chunk atmosphere into his lungs, making them bulge like bagpipes, and unloosed an eldritch shriek that produced a sudden, if temporary, calm. "What the hell's up?" he asked, as the echoes died away.

"Don't ask damn fool questions," Aunt Clara snorted. "Use your eyes."

"I am. Incidentally, why were you gargling? Sore throat?"

"Don't be an addle-pate. I wasn't gargling."

"It sounded like gargling."

"Nonsense. That particular chant was used exclusively by the High Priests of Osiris whenever they wanted to consign some criminal to everlasting fire, and is so exceptionally vile that no translation of it has yet been published. It contains some choice passages, and let me tell you." The old trout paused in order to chuckle obscenely. "There's one stanza about scooping -"

"Please said Mr. Strudwick, in a pained voice."

The aged aunt treated him to a dirty look. "Don't   come near me, you blasted Strudwick. Do you realise that the statue you so clumsily dropped is smashed beyond all hope of repair? You'd make a good subject for that torture," she went on meditatively. "When first formulated – probably by Anhotip, chief adviser to Tutankhamen III in the forty-seventh Dynasty -"

"Hell take Tutankhbodkin – and you too, you scruffy old bastard," Mr. Whittle added unreasonably, as Professor Weatherill stopped his gyrations and came to anchor nearby. "I want a word with you in the near future, and if you want to avoid a really good poke in the snout you'd better start thinking up some snappy answers."

"I really don't see that we have anything to discuss," the professor retorted sullenly. "In any case, I'm far too busy. I haven't finished translating the inscription on this headstone yet, and it'll probably take me the better part of this afternoon."

Aunt Clara stepped down from her packing-case, and the febrile gleam faded from her eyes.

"Well," she said briskly, "we must get to work and take the thing indoors. No use leaving it where it is. A magnificent find, Roy – really superb. Do you realise what it is?"

"Quinnie's girl friend?"

"Fool! His tombstone, complete with all details about his life and death. So far as we can make out – the writing is badly worn – he was mortally wounded by a spear-thrust while leading an attack on a British strong-point, and died two days later in terrible agony. Unfortunately the exact date is not legible, but it must have been either AD 104 or 105."

Despite his mood, Mr. Whittle could not repress a snort of

laughter. "Poor old Quinnie. No wonder he looks so cheerful, if people have been sticking spears up his jacket. By the way, how do you propose to shift that chunk of rock? It looks as though it weighs a ton at least."

"We shall have to use the trolley wheel. It won't be a difficult job." Aunt Clara assured him. "I'd have used it to bring the stone up from the camp, but I wasn't certain whether it would go through the door." She turned to the muttering gardener, was still massaging himself in the background. "Harris, you and Briggs ought to be able to cope with that. The sooner we get it safely inside the sooner we can get on with the excavations, and I believe we're just coming to stuff of great value."

Mr. Davenhill struck a discordant note. "I suppose you don't mine me mentioning that you've done at least ten pounds' worth of damage to the conservatory" he asked tonelessly. "If you will try to bring the thing in this way -"

"All in the cause of science," Aunt Clara assured him. "These things will happen."

"Science my left eyelash." snarled Mr. Davenhill, and made a dignified exit.

The old aunt shrugged, and, producing her pipe, stuffed it to capacity and lit up. Dense clouds of pungent smoke filled the conservatory, and little clouds of sparks rose gaily into the air. Mr. Whittle choked, and turned towards the garden door. He found himself face to face with a short, dark-haired young man of perhaps twenty-two, with dreamy eyes and an amiably vacant expression, carrying a shorthand pad and gazing around him with an air of perplexed interest. Mr. Whittle gave a sharp snort of surprise. He would not have been surprised to see Gregory Tallon, but he had hardly expected Gregory's crony, Nicole Westford of the "Metropolitan Planet".

"Good Lord." Mr. Whittle observed. "Where did you spring from, Nick?"

Mr. Westford extended a vague hand. "What-ho," he murdered "Haven't seen you for an age. How's life?"

"Don't ask! How did you know I was here?"

"Gregory told me. In fact he told me quite a lot." Nichol broke off as Professor Weatherill emerged from the conservatory in the manner of a beetle crawling out from beneath a stone, his face twisted into the ghastly mock of a smile. "Professor Weatherill, I believe?"

"Charmed," the old tomb-hunter assured him, sticking out a grimy paw. "Charmed, Mr. - er -?"

"Westford. I'm a journalist. Special correspondent of the "Planet.""

"Indeed? Most interesting," the professor returned politely. "Are you, too, a lover of the old and the rare?"

"I prefer the young and the common," Mr. Westford admitted frankly.

The aged archaeologist thought this one out and then, with a baffled glance, pushed off. Nichol ruffled his hair thoughtfully. "I've met him before, " he observed. "What do you think of him?"

"I think he's an ideal candidate for the lethal chamber. I'd stake my life he's a phoney, though Aunt Clara seems to accept him at face value."

"Aunt Clara. I take it, is the old trout lying across the rock?" Mr. Westford hazard, gazing through the conservatory window. "I say, old man, is she in love with the thing, or what? She seems to be hugging it for all it's worth."

Roy chuckled. The old aunt had by this time produced her magnifying-glass and become absorbed in the tombstone, holding her snoddle a bare two inches from it and radiating concentration from every pore, and it could not be denied that the general effect was odd in the extreme.

"Not a bit of it. Aunt Clara's not the loving type. Give here a skeleton or two and a bit of Roman pottery, and she'll be happy for hours on end. Do you want a drink?"

"Yes," Mr. Westford admitted without hesitation.

"Come on, then. I've got some whisky in my room."

"Much as the idea appeals to me, I think I'd better have a word with Spennie first. After all, it is his house. Is he seeable?"

"He was here a moment ago. He's probably pottered off to the dining-room."

This suggestion proved to be correct. Mr. Davenhill was run to earth without difficulty, leaning against the sideboard with an empty glass in his hand and a glazed expression in his eyes.

Mr. Whittle clapped him jovially on the shoulder, and produced Nichol rather in a manner of a conjurer taking a rabbit from a hat.

"Brace up, old lad," he urged, when Spennie's initial surprise had subsided and his eyes had returned to their sockets (at least, as far as they ever did). "You look positively sandbagged. Nothing else gone wrong, has there?"

"Yes."

"What?"

"Jules has given notice."

"Mr. Whittle pursed his lips. He could appreciate the seriousness of this bald statement. Monsieur Jules, late of the Azophi Restaurant, was universally admitted to be a peer among chefs, a wizard of the cooking-stove who would not easily be replaced.

"I've just been talking to him," went on Spennie helplessly. "Listening to him, I suppose I ought to say – once he starts there's no point in even trying to get a word in edgeways. What Aunt Violet will say I really don't know."

"She won't be pleased."

"Too true she won't. She'll go right off the deep end."

"I don't blame her. Even for a Frenchie, old Jules doles out some pretty nifty eats. What got under his skin?"

"Bats."

"Eh?"

"Bats. Dead ones. In the refrigerator."

A rather baffling silence followed this observation.

"What the devil were bats doing in the refrigerator?" Mr. Whittle asked at length. "Seems a funny kind of place to keep them. I don't believe even Jules could make a bat taste like anything but a bat. Besides, aren't they covered with a membrane?"

"Fleas," Mr. Westford corrected him.

"That makes it even worse. If we're given stew for dinner, I shall shun it. And the same applies to the sausage rolls."

"Mr. Davenhill let out a hollow groan. "Stop drooling, you two doddle-plates. They weren't Jules' bats. As a matter of fact he seems to have a morbid horror of the wretched creatures."

"Then how did they get in to the refrigerator?" Mr. Whittle

160

inquired closely. "Do you mean they nest there?"

"Fool! From what I can make out Jules decided to get up and see to the lunch, so he went to the fridge. for some ice and found a beastly great bat cluttering the place up. He promptly threw a fit."

"I take it the bat was defunct?"

"Very. Actually I think it must have been dead for some days. I gather that Jules spent some minutes smashing all the crockery he could lay his hands on, and then stormed in to me and dished out his resignation. As if we haven't had enough to cope with," said Mr. Davenhill savagely. "If we have to manage on what the under-housemaid can produce, we shall need iron stomachs. I feel like falling upon the infernal skeleton with some blunt instrument and beating it to jelly."

Mr. Westford ruffled his unruly hair.

"I don't want to harp on the subject, old man," he murmured, "but I don't see even now how this bat could have found its way into the refrigerator. It can hardly have flown in, and it'd be too big to crawl through the keyhole. Are you sure the Frenchie didn't make a mistake? I mean, it isn't just a slab of beef, or something?"

"A slab of beef doesn't usually have wings, claws and a head like a mouse. I've seen this duck, and it's a bat all right – damned awful great brute."

Mr. Westford looked at Mr. Whittle helplessly.

"Well, make up your mind," he said, with infuriating persistence. "Is it a bat or a duck? If it's a duck, I don't see what all the fuss is about."

"Once and for all," snarled Spennie, "the brute's a bat. Not a duck, or an elephant, or a giraffe, or anything of the sort, but just an ordinary, common-or-garden bat. Moreover, it smells."

"If you tried to tell me you'd found an elephant or a giraffe in the refrigerator, "Mr. Westford observed, "I'd call you a liar to your face. But if it didn't get there under it's own steam, who put it there – the bat, I mean?"

Mr. Whittle grunted. "Even I can answer that one. "Stoker."

"Stoker?"

"Naturally. It sticks out a yard."

"It doesn't," Mr. Davenhill informed him. "It was stuffed right inside, with it's claws in the butter and it's wings flopped over the ice."

"I was speaking metaphorically. Since I can't see any reason why Jules should take it into his noddle to go bat-hunting, there's only one solution. Stoker, the botch-eyed old coot, has been messing about with black magic, and he's still firmly convinced that Fredl has turned Pauline into a bat. I don't doubt he caught this specimen and filed it for future experiments. It may even be the one he thinks is Pauline."

Mr. Westford let out a strange croak. "What's all this?"

"Tell him," Mr. Davenhill requested. "It's about time we had someone else's point of view, even if it is only a lunatic like Nick."

Mr. Whittle obligingly gave his friend a brief resume of recent events, frank and accurate except for the omission of one or two minor incidents – such as the episode in the conservatory and the painful scene in Dr Fredl's room. Nichol listened carefully, punctuating the narrative with periodic chortles and snorts.

"Well," he said when Mr. Whittle had finished, "it beats the band. Old Greg didn't tell me the half of it. What beats me so completely is how this Wrightman wrench has disappeared into the blue. You're sure she's on the level?"

"Absolutely," Roy informed him soberly. "Wait till you hear see her, Nick. How she can seriously think of tagging along wit that dehydrated jerk of a small-time politician is a major mystery. She's all set to spend the rest of her like acting as his unpaid secretary."

"Better than spending the rest of her life hanging down from a barn roof," Nichol pointed out.

"Don't be a beetlewit," Mr. Whittle requested shortly.

"Actually," said Nichol, "this black magic business interests me quite a lot. That's how I managed to get time off to come down."

"How come?"

"My Editor wants to run a series on witchcraft. You know – famous witch trials; werewolves; Voodoo – all the usual stuff.

It's not really my line, but as soon as I told him I was on to something he gave me the O.K to hand over my fashion column to Barry Dengeth and see what I could nose out. Mind you, I played it up a bit, by the time I'd finished he was ready to believe that the place was a glorified Borley Rectory. If I don't go back with a decent story, he'll brain me with a printing press."

"Touchy sort of feller?"

"Very. I like the man," said Mr. Westford cautiously, "and I wish him well, but he's extraordinarily inclined to go up in the air on the slightest pretext, and when that happens strong men quake and hide their heads. Moreover, he wears barbed-wire vests and chews broken bottles, and I strongly suspect him of devouring his young."

"All I ask is that you don't give any names." Spennie replaced his glass on the sideboard and lit a cigarette. "Ever since Aunt Clara's last visit to England the whole country has regarded me as a raving lunatic, and anything of this sort would make them send round a deputation armed with chloroform bottles and a straight-waistcoat."

"Don't worry, I won't."

"You know," Mr. Whittle said severely, "I'm disappointed in you, Nick. When you first appeared I thought Gregory had sent you down to lend me moral support."

"He did, you doddle-pate – at least, he put the idea into my head – but I had to have some sort of yarn to pitch old Johnson. Incidentally, Spennie old man, I've put up at the local, so there's no need for you to offer me a bed."

"I wasn't going to."

"Well you needn't."

"In any case," said Mr. Davenhill, "It's only two o'clock. You don't want to go to bed yet, do you?"

"Under the circumstances, I don't. The beds at the local look like ironing boards, but I think I'm better on my own."

"You've certainly got a better chance of a good night's rest," Mr. Whittle assured him. "Spooks or no spooks, this house is like a circus after dark."

"So you said before, but I haven't seen anything funny up to now, apart from that peculiar old coot smelling the rock.

Doesn't anything start up before night?"

"You'd have seen plenty if you'd been here yesterday," grunted Mr. Davenhill. "We had bangs and fires and accidents and explosions going the whole time. Ever since Ratcliffe arrived, though, they do seem to have calmed down. If it's a coincidence it's a damn' funny one."

"I -" began Mr. Whittle, and broke off abruptly. "Spennie, old lad, I rather think you spoke a bit too soon. What the devil's going on? It sounds like a litter of pups."

"No pups could make a noise like that," protested Mr. Westford, cocking his ears and listening hard. "More like rats — no, damn it, bats! Can't you hear them flapping?"

Mr. Davenhill gave a low, bubbling moan, and clutched at his forehead as if afraid it was going to come off. The rushing and squeaking from outside grew in violence, mixed now with human shouts and sounds of heavy articles being hurled about; some solid body collided with the door, and Mr. Whittle, clenching his teeth, armed himself with the nearest available weapon, which happened to be an alabaster Cupid complete with arrow and harp. Next moment two shots rang out from the hall, followed by a deep clang as of some sinister gong presaging the Last Judgement ...

Mr. Whittle, raising the Cupid high above his head and preparing to take a quick swipe at anybody or anything that appeared, flung open the hall door.

Chapter 19

The next few minutes were so crowded with action that even Mr. Whittle felt, for once, that the situation was frankly beyond him. As soon as the hall door opened, the entire dining-room became full of bats – big bats, little bats and medium sized bats – that flapped around in circles, squeaking dismally and beating the walls with their wings. Mr. Whittle swiped at one with the Cupid, missed, cursed, and staggered out into the hall, where still more bats were in evidence; Aunt Clara was also among those present, brandishing her shot-gun and invoking divine intervention at the top of her voice, while Stoker could be seen in full retreat down the passage lumbering along in the manner of a startled hippopotamus.

"What the devil -" bellowed Mr. Whittle, above the din.

"Get them out of here !" wailed Mr. Davenhill piteously. "They're wrecking the house -"

His voice was drowned as Aunt Clara, raising the shot-gun to her shoulder, let rip with both barrels, catching a small light-brown bat cunningly in the seat of the pants and causing it to give a cry of baffled rage before making an emergency landing on the carpet. Filled with the lust for blood, nostrils dilated and flames shooting from her eyes, the old aunt had another go, this time doing irreparable damage to an occasional table and blowing a gaping hole in the dial of one of the old grandfather clocks.

"Put that gun down, you old fool!" Mr. Whittle bellowed, making a lightening leap out of the danger-zone and swinging the Cupid at a particularly peevish-looking bat. "You'll plug one of us-"

"Stand clear, then!" hooted Aunt Clara, unleashing both barrels once more and filling the entire hall with dense black smoke.

"For Gods sake!" panted Nichol, from behind.

Mr. Whittle, knuckling his eyes disparately, became aware of Stoker advancing into action, bearing a small and useless-looking insect spray. Roy, turning to address him, received the full benefit of the aged butler's preliminary squirt. When he managed to bring his streaming eyes to focus once more he saw that the battle was nearly over, with the enemy in full flight; Spennie, with rare presence of mind, had succeeded in getting the front door open, and those bats not lying about in used-up attitudes or writhing frantically on the furniture were making a bee-line for God's clean air.

"Hades!" spluttered Mr. Whittle. "Stoker, you moss-covered old ruin, what the purple blazes do you think you were doing with that squirt?"

"Spraying insecticide, sir. I trust I am not in error in supposing a bat to be an insect?"

"Dolt!" Aunt Clara snorted. "Get some more windows open."

"Very good, madam."

"And hurry up," Mr. Whittle added. "Don't stand there pottering!"

"Just as you say, sir." the butler nodded intelligently. "Might I suggest sir, that somebody waves a newspaper around? This would no doubt help to dissipate the fumes."

"I don't mind what you – oh, shut up!" yelled Mr. Whittle, as Aunt Clara, raising her head, relapsed into torrents of ancient Egyptian. "Collar the servants, for the Lord's sake, and tell them to give a hand in clearing up this mess."

"Dear me," broke in an oily voice, and the tall, stooping figure of Nehemiah Ratcliffe appeared in the doorway. "Honk! Is anything the matter? There seems to have been some sort of disturbance _"

Mr. Whittle gave vent to an animal snarl, and kicked viciously at a small bat squirming feebly on the hat-stand. "Oh no," he said with cold venom. "Just fun and games. Ouf! These fumes make me choke! Stoker, go and open all the windows at the back of the house. Try and get the draught through, or we'll suffocate. Then rally all the servants you can find. And for Pete's sake," he added violently to Aunt Clara, "stop waving that blasted gun at me. You've done quite enough damage for one afternoon."

"Bats, eh?" murdered Mr. Ratcliffe thoughtfully, picking up a nearby specimen and holding it at arm's length. "Most interesting – yes, most interesting. Wherever did they come from,

I wonder?"

"I fear, sir, that I alone am to blame for this latest manifestation," Stoker broke in gloomily, before Mr. Davenhill had time to reply. " I reacted for the best, but the result has indeed been unexpected. I only hope there will be no further disturbances."

"What's that?" barked Mr. Whittle. "Do you mean that you let loose these infernal brutes?"

"I'm afraid so, Mr. Roy," the old butler admitted. "Quite unintentionally, of course."

"Raving," commented Aunt Clara sourly. "Or tight."

"Neither, madam. If I might explain?" Stoker coughed. "As you know, I was recently impressed to make some delicate experiments connected with the supernatural. I am by no means practised in such arts, but I considered it possible that I might be the instrument in counteracting the evil forces at present surrounding us. To assist me in this work I borrowed a book belonging to Dr. Fredl. It is largely concerned with the supernatural aspects of bats and similar insects -"

"Passing over the fact that a bat isn't, and never has been, an insect," said Mr. Whittle wearily, "will you kindly oblige me, you doddering old wreck, by coming to the point?"

"Certainly, Mr. Roy. I am endeavouring to do so. In brief, I have apparently made a mistake in my experiments and reversed the desired effect, thus calling up a swarm of astral or non-natural bats."

"Astral bats! Oh, my God!" Mr. Whittle passed a hand over his brow and sank down on the nearest chair, feeling that the situation was completely out of control and he himself a spent force. "Astral bats ... Talk to him, Nick. I'm speechless."

"What shall we talk about?" Mr. Westford asked diffidently. "I mean to say, astral bats aren't really in my line, you know. I don't believe I've ever seen an astral bat, and I'm not at all sure that I want to. I'd almost rather have a promenading skeleton."

Aunt Clara blew her nose with a noise like a pneumatic drill, and went on the ether. "Astral bats my foot," she snorted. "I've never heard such a load of onion soup. Isch! What I want to know is, who let them loose?"

"Me too," breathed Mr. Davenhill, whose face was still a pale shade of Nile-green. "If they're ordinary bats, someone must have stored 'em up – but who? Ouf! I never want to see one of those brutes as long as I live."

At this point Dr. Fredl tottered down the stairs, attended by Terry and Carole, and the conversation became general, with everybody talking at once and getting nowhere in a very long time. Mr. Whittle seized the opportunity to have a quick check-up. It had seemed to his fevered imagination that the air had been thick with bats, but on a closer inspection he could see only six corpses. A further half-dozen or so had presumably made their escape, though this last might well be an over-estimate.

"What do you think of it?" he asked Mr. Westford moodily.

"I can't think at all," Nichol admitted. "My brain won't work. The only thing that comforts me at all is the thought that I shall be able to face my editor without a qualm. I wish I'd had the sense to bring my camera, but I left it at the local."

Mr. Whittle cursed both editor and camera. "I suppose we'd better do some sleuthing," he said, "though I doubt whether it'll get us anywhere. Yell for silence, will you? My lungs are still full of that beastly muck Stoker squirted at me."

"Why not bong the gong?"

"No reason at all why not," Mr. Whittle did so and produced comparative calm, after which he took the dead bat from Mr. Ratcliffe and held it up for inspection in the manner of an auctioneer trying to dispose of some rare and valuable antique. "Listen. If anyone tries to tell me there's anything ghostly about this thing, I'll call him a liar to his – or her – face. No, some duck's doing his best to pull a fast one over the lot of us. Someone must have let the brutes go, so we'd better have a check on where everyone was."

Eight people spoke at once. Mr. Whittle waved his arms, and restored order by another hefty bang on the gong.

"One at a time! Stoker, where are you?"

The aged retainer cogitated.

"In the kitchen, sir, talking to Harris and Briggs."

"You didn't see where the creatures came from?"

"Everywhere, sir," Stoker informed him in a final tone. "Mainly however, from upstairs. I am of the opinion that most of them materialised on the second floor landing, or possible in the adjoining store-rooms."

"I'm glad I didn't accept your kind invitation, old man," murmured Mr. Westford in an undertone. "I should hate to be woken up by an astral bat materialising under the bed."

"Don't drivel, you beetle-wit," Mr. Whittle requested shortly. "Where were you, Ratty?"

"If you're alluding to me," the ghost specialist retorted huffily, "I was probably in my taxi, coming up the drive. And I have already told you," he added with some heat, "that my name is not Ratty. It is Ratcliffe – Nehemiah Ratcliffe -"

"Stow it! What about you, Aunt Clara?"

"What about me?"

"Where were you when the balloon went up?"

"Never mind."

"I do mind."

"Well, go to hell, then," said Aunt Clara agreeably. "I'm not in the habit of writing down my movements in a diary."

"I'm not asking you to," howled Mr. Whittle, nobly stifling an almost overwhelming desire to clunk his elderly relative on the bean with a dead bat. "All I want to know is just what what you were doing before the shindy began."

"Do you really want to know?" asked Aunt Clara coldly.

A sudden thought struck Mr. Whittle, and he shifted his ground skilfully. "How long did it take you to fetch that gun?"

"About twenty seconds, if that," the old aunt informed him shortly. "I've kept it loaded and ready for the past couple of days. If only you hadn't started leaping about and upsetting my aim, I'd have bagged far more of the brutes than I actually did. Pity about the clock," she added absently, staring at the faceless ruin. "Looks rather like the statue of Memnon."

Mr. Davenhill who had not previously noticed anything amiss with the clock, started violently heavily on the nearest chair. Unfortunately the site was already occupied by yet another defunct bat, and he bounced up as though someone had struck a red-hot knitting-needle up his pants. By the time he had recovered sufficiently to take an active interest in what was going on, Terry was being third-degreed.

"If you want to know," he was saying, "Carole and I were both with Dr. Fredl, and I saw Strudwick go by just before the rumpus started. That lets the lot of us out, bar Weatherill."

"You don't know where he is?"

"No."

"Then we'd better find out." Mr. Whittle raised his voice and let off a high pitched hoot, "Weatherill! Weatherill, you old freak, where are you?"

"Did I hear somebody calling my name?" asked the professor in his customary bleating tones, appearing at the top of the staircase as though he had popped up out of a trap. "I trust that nothing untoward has happened? Dear me, I fancy I can see a number of dead animals lying about -."

"Insects, sir," Stoker corrected him respectfully.

The professor pottered slowly down into the hall, peering through his spectacles and pointing like a retriever. Eventually his eyes fell upon Nehemiah Ratcliffe, and he bowed courteously. "Good afternoon," he said, extending a skinny paw and smiling like a duck. "I don't think we have met. My name is Weatherill – Augustus Weatherill."

"This." Spennie announced tonelessly, "is Mr. Ratcliffe,"

"Blimey!" ejaculated the professor, giving a kangaroo-like leap. "What's that? What did you say?"

Mr. Davenhill looked surprised.

"Mr. Ratcliffe," he repeated. "Why, what .. You expected him, didn't you? I thought he was a friend of yours."

"But one whom I have unfortunately not seen for some years," Nehemiah broke in smoothly. "My dear Augustus, how are you? It is really delightful to see you again. We must have some long chats together during the next few days. Honk!"

The aged tomb-hunter goggled, his eyes bulging and his mouth hanging open like the lid of a hat-box. After a moment or so he made a visible effort to pull himself together.

"My dear Nehemiah! Dear me, how criminally stupid of me. To think I didn't know you – really, your moustache makes the world of difference to your appearance. You're thinner, too."

"Diet." Mr. Ratcliffe seized the professor's hand, and pumped it vigorously as though he expected it to ring a bell. "I was getting far too fat. Rigorous exclusion of the starchy foods worked wonders. I can quite understand how you failed to recognise me."

"On the contrary, it was most dense of me," the old archaeologist admitted. "Partly my eye, I suppose. I have been doing a great deal of hieroglyphic translation lately, and the strain is most severe."

"Naturally, it would be."

Mr. Whittle felt the time had come to put his oar in. "Not so fast, he said softly. Are you buddies, or aren't you? You don't seem to sure about it."

"Buddies?" Mr. Ratcliffe echoed. "Buddies? I'm afraid I don't quite understand, Mr. Whittle. What is a buddy? I seem to connect the term with some sort of a plant," he added thoughtfully. "A rose, possibly – or is it a tulip?"

"Roses my Aunt Fanny – and tulips likewise. By 'buddy' I mean pal – cobber – crony – anything you like. Savvy."

"Ah, of course." the ghost-specialist beamed. But for the fact that he has been abroad thee last few years, we should certainly have met very often."

"And before I went to Egypt," the professor amplified, "you were away yourself, in Alaska if I remember rightly. We have written to each other frequently, of course. By the way Nehemiah, have you heard anything of Sturgess lately?"

"A cablegram only last week. Any news from Professor Sigsbee?"

"In Peru, excavating some Inca monument not far from Lima. Hoffman and Zuttmeister are with him."

"Not Walther Hoffman?"

"Of course. A very clever scientist. I have always considered his ideas on the dynastic evolution of the Ptolemies exceptionally skilful."

"Quite so. I remember that back in 1937, when three of us attended the International Archaeological Conference in Athens -"

"Oh cut it out," Mr. Whittle requested curtly. "You've both done your best to make it clear that you're dear old chums, so let's leave it at that for the moment, shall we?. Personally I'm beginning to find this atmosphere a bit thick."

"There is certainly a marked effluvium," agreed Mr. Strudwick, who had joined the little group and was wrinkling his snoddle in the manner of a piqued rabbit. "I suggest that we continue this discussion in another place."

Nobody raising any objections to this scheme, the council broke up. Dr. Fredl, who for once had been a silent spectator (apart from the inevitable buzzes, snorts and hog-like grunts) trudged back upstairs, still holding the sinister green bottle close in front of his snout; Stoker, sighing heavily, pottered off to organize a repair squad; and Mr. Whittle, followed closely by Nichol and the remainder of the heard, made for the dining-room. Peace descended on the battle-scarred hall.

Chapter 20

"You know," Mr. Whittle remarked presently, filling his pipe and offering Aunt Clara the pouch, "there are certain things we've got to talk over right now. We're all letting ourselves get rattled, and the sooner we snap out of it the better. To begin Weatherill, old lad, where were you when the invasion started?" You seem to be the only one unaccounted for."

The grimy professor rubbed his chin. "I'm really not sure," he admitted. "In any case, I don't see that my exact whereabouts are of any importance."

"Oh yes, they are. I want to make sure you weren't up to any tricks."

"Tricks!" The professor looked pained. "My dear sir! One might almost think you fancied me capable of letting the creatures loose – ha, ha!" He uncorked a rather unconvincing hoot of mirth. "What a laughable idea."

"I wouldn't put it past you," Mr. Whittle admitted frankly, "Well?"

"As a matter of fact, I came out of the museum with Miss Debenham, and then went up to my room to have a wash."

""A wash?" Mr. Whittle echoed incredulously.

"Certainly."

"Anyone see you?"

"I am not in the habit of performing my ablutions in public," the old coot informed him coldly. "There are certain limits to communal life. However, I do remember speaking to Mr. Fane in the bathroom, if that is of any help to you."

"Wrong first time, old horse. Terry was having a cosy little chat with Fredl – weren't you, Terry?"

Terry wriggled uncomfortably, and avoided his cousin's steely eye.

"I did go along the landing once," he said sullenly.

"Why? I mean, why didn't you say so before?"

"Because I hadn't thought of it. Damn it, who do you think you are – Sherlock Holmes?"

"But -" began Miss Czernak, and then stopped.

"Yes?" Mr. Whittle prompted.

"Ah, it is nothing." Carole shrugged. "A thought, that is all."

""In any case," Mr. Westford remarked, "it seems to me that the whole lot of you are going off at a tangent. Bats are all very well, but I seem to remember being told that you'd mislaid a female. Wouldn't it be a sound scheme to find her first, and deal with all this black magic stuff later?"

"I fear that the two are inextricably tangled," Professor Weatherill observed gloomily. "As you know, there is a legend that Quintus Maximus, in common with many other important men of his time, laid a solemn curse on anybody who disturbed his rest – and it would appear that Miss Wrightman has been the innocent victim of his vengeance. Nehemiah, what are your views?"

Everyone hung upon the ghost-specialist's reply. Mr. Ratcliffe massaged his wart carefully, cleared his throat with a couple of preliminary honks, and went on the ether.

"In these cases," he began with the air of a schoolmaster addressing a class of village idiots, "one has to be careful to keep a completely open mind. During my career as a psychical investigator I have come across numerous cases of trickery, so well concealed as to puzzle any but the trained expert." He coughed modestly. "Take the affair at Rusper Abbey, for instance, in 1936. All done by mirrors and hidden microphones. In the present instance, however, there seems to be no doubt that we are faced with genuine psychic phenomena. The evidence is overwhelming."

"You don't mind me saying that I think you're all talking a lot of tinned spaghetti?" asked Mr. Whittle.

"By no means, my dear sir, but consider the facts." Mr. Ratcliffe honked softly. "The skeleton excavated by Miss Debenham is, of course, the crux of the matter. Consider! This Roman – a General, I believe, and therefore probably of an irascible and arrogant nature – has been allowed to sleep in peace for the last two thousand years, and is naturally annoyed at being rudely awoken. Unfortunately he seems to be able to command considerable astral powers. I confess I don't like this latest development. It reminds me of a plague of bats that occurred in the Bavarian village of Sleimhausen just before the 1941 disaster.

"What disaster?"

"Madness and death," the spook-specialist replied casually. "Two hundred of the inhabitants went raving mad and drowned themselves in the lake, and shortly afterwards the entire centre of the village was raised by fire. The trouble was traced to an old woman who had been practising sorcery for years, and is said to have reached the stage of broomstick riding. They burnt her, of course."

Mr. Whittle let out a grunt of disbelief. "First I've heard of it."

"Naturally, my dear sir. Hitler's Government hushed it up very thoroughly – it would have been bad propaganda for their Party – but we experts make it our business to find out these things."

"Oh, by the finger of Harpocrates!" Aunt Clara barked suddenly, sucking her pipe, "this is getting us no where. Onion soup I don't believe a word of it." The old aunt spoke in her usual rasping tones, but Mr. Whittle noticed that she was chewing her lower lip violently as if she liked the taste of it.

"Scoff if you will," Mr. Ratcliffe invited her drily, "but are you inferring that the bats invaded the house, in broad daylight, of their own accord?"

"I'm inferring nothing of the kind. I'm saying someone brought them."

"Who?"

The old aunt thought this one out, revving her brain to full capacity, but was evidently unable to arrive at any solution.

"I think I can answer that," Mr. Whittle murmured. "The same duck who spent the last night dragging Quinnie about the house. I've got my own ideas."

The silence that followed this cryptic remark was broken by a muffled peal from the front door bell. Everybody pricked up their ears, and Mr. Strudwick de-clutched hurriedly, opened his throttle and made for the hall. Roy, steering a zigzag course through the maze of buckets, pails and mops being handled by a labour-gang under the directorship of Stoker, followed, fully expecting to find Pauline Wrightman on the threshold. However, he was disappointed. Not only was Miss Wrightman absent but

175

the front steps were completely deserted, apart from a skinny and moth-eaten cat that made a quick dive into the bushes as soon as the door opened.

"False alarm," the M.P commented wearily. "For a moment I hoped .. well, I suppose there's nothing we can do."

"The bell," said Mr. Whittle, decidedly, "was rung by someone. Moreover, whoever it was had plenty of beef behind him. Look, the thing's still swinging. Stoker, old lad, did you see anyone?"

"No, Mr. Roy."

Mr. Whittle uttered one brief, pithy word and returned to the dining-room. The company as a whole too the news with stoical resignation, but as soon as the hall door was closed Mr. Strudwick collapsed in a chair and unleashed an echoing moan that set Mr. Whittle's teeth on edge.

"Don't do it, you wretched object," Aunt Clara requested curtly. "We've enough to contend with without you're going about mooing like a damned cow. You're sure nobody was lurking in the bushes?"

"Quite sure," the M.P assured her. "The more I think the position the less I like it. I am beginning to have grave fears for my fiancées safety." He polished his spectacles nervously. " I do wish we could get hold of the book."

"Book?"

"The one Stoker stole from Dr. Fredl. It may be dangerous."

"It may be safer with me," agreed Mr. Ratcliffe," "but there is no urgent hurry. Black magic, is seldom effective before dark, which is partly why this bat business worries me so. Meanwhile I should like to see this museum, if I may. The more atmosphere I can assimilate the more chance I shall have of settling this thing quickly."

"Carry right on, old lad," grunted Mr. Whittle nastily. Go on – soak up the atmosphere till your eyes bubble. Much good may it do you."

Mr. Ratcliffe bowed. "I trust so – I trust so. Perhaps somebody will be kind enough to show me where the museum is?"

"Take him along, Terry," Mr. Davenhill requested wearily.

176

"I think I'll come along too, if you don't mind," murmured Mr. Westford. "Haven't had a look at the jolly old morgue yet. Is it anything like Tussaud's?"

"Don't be a doddle-pate," Aunt Clara snorted, in her old manner. "Some of the remains we have excavated are at least three thousand years old. For instance, there's an axe that may have belonged to a soldier in Teutombrochtus' army, and a magnificent collection of early British engravings, done generations before the Romans even thought of coming here. They must have constructed their camp upon an earlier settlement. Quintus' tomb was in a different layer altogether. If you're interested in archaeology," she continued, warming to her theme, "I can show you some material that may alter many of our ideas about prehistoric civilizations. To begin with -"

"I'll love that," Mr. Westford assured her hastily, but hadn't we better keep it until a bit later on? It's bound to take time, you know."

"Just as you like. When we get back to work, you might come down and lend us a hand – the more the merrier."

Mr. Westford, looking rather dubious, followed Terry and Mr. Ratcliffe out, and yet another heavy silence fell, broken only by the sound of the press-gang in the hall. Presently Nichol returned, his expression even vaguer than usual, and running his fingers through his mop of hair.   "I say," he began, "this is dashed funny, don't you know. When did you last have a look at this Quintus duck?"

"Oh, my Lord, don't say it's gone again?" Mr. Davenhill asked. "I can't bear it. We shall have to put a lock and chain on the infernal thing before we're through."

"What do you think? Did you expect it to be playing the trombone?"

Mr. Westford thought this over. "No," he admitted. "I don't even know if it's musical."

"Fool! Whet are you getting at?"

"Merely this, old man – it's giving the V sign at us."

"What?"

"Well, it's got it's arm stuck out in a darned peculiar way. Moreover it looks to me as though it's got a thoroughly dirty leer on its clock."

He was right. Mr. Ratcliffe stood by the museum window making notes in a small book, while Terry sprawled in a chair, roaring with laughter, and Quintus Maximus stood majestically upon his dais gesturing for all to see. The old buster may not have been used to giving the V sign, but he did it extraordinarily well; the effect was the reverse of comic, and Spennie was consious of shivers chasing up and down the knobbles of his spine.

"Damned impertinence," Aunt Clara snorted, seeing the bony arm back to it's normal position. "What addle-pated half-wit is responsible for this?" She knelt down and examined the skeleton critically. "Lucky there's nothing broken. The result of forcing the arm upwards might have been disastrous."

"Always supposing it was forced. Wonder if Quinnie did it himself?" murmured Nichol. "He seems to be a nasty-minded cove. I mean, the whole lot of us were in the hall almost from the time Miss Debenham left the museum. How long would it take to arrange the thing like that?"

"Some minutes," Aunt Clara informed him. "It isn't as though the arms were loose. There certainly wouldn't have been time to do it between my leaving the museum and the start of the bat affair. It must have been done while we were talking in the dining-room."

"Which means," said Mr. Whittle, "that Fredl's the man."

"It doesn't mean anything of the sort. Stoker was in the hall the whole time – nobody could have gone in or out without being seen."

"How about the passage?" Nichol suggested, with a glance at the gaping hole in the wall.

"He'd never get through it. And what," added Aunt Clara grimly, turning to Terry, "do you think you're cawing about?"

Terry did not enlighten her, but caught Carole's eye and went on making noises like a defective soda-siphon. Mr. Ratcliffe looked up from his notebook, and honked importantly.

"Quite evidently this being is able to exert unusual power," he began, as soon as he was sure that he was receiving general attention. "How serious the danger may be I really can't tell you at the moment, but it is fortunate indeed that Augustus had the presence of mind to summon me. I don't think it is boastful to say that I am one of the few men in England capable of handling the situation."

Mr. Whittle made a disproving noise by rattling his tongue against his tonsils, and Terry let out a splutter of mirth, but it was left to Mr. Strudwick to voice the almost universal doubt.

"All very well," he said obstinately, glancing round for support. "We've been talking a great deal, like some beastly Socialist back-bencher, but we don't seem to have decided on any plan of action – and don't forget that my fiancée is still missing. What exactly do you mean to do?"

"Yes," agreed Mr. Westford, who had been making surreptitious shorthand notes on his cuff. "What's the procedure, old man? Do we have to turn out all the lights and join hands, or anything?"

"The lights," Mr. Whittle pointed out gently, "aren't on. They seldom are, at two o'clock in the afternoon."

Mr. Westford pondered.

"All the better," he remarked, brilliantly. "We shan't have to turn them out, shall we."

"Honk." Mr. Ratcliffe protested. "All in good time, gentlemen. That may come later." He removed his spectacles, polished them on his tie, inspected them closely and replaced them on his snoddle. "Before – I – er – get down to business, there are one or two points to be discussed with my kind host."

"Cash down?" Mr. Whittle suggested brutally.

"By no means. Money is a sordid, worthless thing, is it not?" Mr. Ratcliffe blinked. "Of course, if you prefer to get all financial details settled up I am quite agreeable. In fact, it might be as well. I find I am very apt to overlook such material matters."

"Overlook my left eyeball," Mr. Whittle muttered, in an audible undertone.

"Still the same spiritual, absent-minded Nehemiah," bleated Professor Weatherill, showing his fangs in an amiable grin. "Always ready to help others at the expense of yourself."

"Bread-sauce," Mr. Whittle retorted. A hundred quid sounds pretty good gravy to me. It was a hundred quid, Ratty old lad, wasn't it?"

"I believe that was the figure I mentioned." The ghost-specialist waved his hand airily. "Since you insist, my dear Mr. Davenhill, I really don't mind getting it all squared up. Of course, I can't guarantee results at once – these things take time. Moreover, I must have a completely free hand. Anything in the nature of scepticism or non-cooperation would be fatal." He gave Mr. Whittle an evil look. "Mental peace is absolutely essential. Any disrupting influences will play havoc with the vibrations."

"Damn it all," Mr. Davenhill snarled, "We're trying to get rid of the wretched things, not produce them."

"In any case," put in Aunt Clara, "do you think the man carts poltergeists about in his waistcoat pocket? Be reasonable."

"He's not wearing a waistcoat," Mr. Westford remarked helpfully.

"Please, please." Mr. Ratcliffe sighed. "Honk! Used as I am to unbelievers, you must surely realise that it is not an easy matter to produce complete materialisations. It requires a considerable amount of preparation."

"I'll settle for an incomplete one." Mr. Whittle offered cheerfully. "Can't you manage just a head and shoulders, or better still a pair of legs?"

The spook-hunter looked pained. "Really," he said, "I feel you are making no effort to improve the vibrations. Whatever would be the use of materialising a pair of legs?"

Terry unloosed a soft snort, and slipped an arm casually round Miss Czernak's waste.

"I'd prefer them connected up, if you see what I mean," admitted Mr. Whittle, "but they'd be a lot better than nothing. Haven't you any parlour tricks you can pull off?"

This one really seems to get under the ghost-specialist's skin. He drew himself up to his full height, and puffed a small cloud of steam from his nostrils.

"There are certain expressions that we of the astral profession con-not tolerate," he said icily. "Parlour tricks' is one of them. "I feel strongly tempted to abandon the whole case. Your attitude, sir, is intolerable – intolerable, I say!"

"My dear Nehemiah," bleated Professor Weatherill, "Ignore him. Mr. Whittle is -" he hesitated - "Young."

180

"He is also a damned young doddle-pate."

"Inexperienced' might be a kinder term."

"Very well – an inexperienced young doddle-pate."

"Do you two coves want kicking in the teeth?" Mr. Whittle inquired dangerously.

"For God's sake," Mr. Davenhill bawled, "wrap up, Roy. I don't know any more about this sort of thing than you do, but at least my mind's open."

"It is. Wide open."

"Dolt!"

Professor Weatherill coughed, and spoke in his most honeyed tones.

"I also," he admitted, "know little about psychical research, but we have our duty to Miss Wrightman to consider. These angry words may destroy our chances of success. Nehemiah is perfectly right. What we should do is keep calm, and think nothing but clean, beautiful thoughts."

It was so evident that the old buster would not have known a clean, beautiful thought if it had been handed to him on a skewer that nobody had a reply to hand, while Roy spent some seconds in trying to hit on a thought that answered to both adjectives. Mr. Strudwick re-entered the discussion, and brought it back to a practical level.

"Talk- talk – talk!" he said irritably. "What we want is action." He glared malevolently at Quintus Maximus, who glared equally malevolently back. "For the tenth time, Ratcliffe, what do you mean me to do?"

"First of all," Mr. Ratcliffe informed him, "I propose to imbibe in a glass of warm milk - very helpful on these occasions. Then I shall go to my room and spend a couple of hours in meditation. My vibrations are sorely disturbed."

"That'll be a lot of help," Mr. Whittle grunted.

"As soon as darkness falls," continued the ghost-specialist, "I shall turn my attention to the problem of the missing lady."

"Yes, but how?" roared the M.P

"That depends. I shall begin with astral hypnotism. Should she be in the vicinity, this can not fail to bring home the bacon, - to use the common vernacular."

181

"I hardly think the expression a fortunate one, under the circumstances," Mr. Strudwick retorted huffily. "What than?"

"If the result is negative, it may be necessary for me to go in to a trance. This will need certain preparations. By the way, nobody must on any account eat meat for dinner."

"Don't worry," said Mr. Davenhill with a certain grim satisfaction. "You won't get the chance. With a cut-off water supply, an exploded boiler and a temperamental chef, we shall be lucky to get a cup of coffee and a fishcake."

"Fishcakes would be quite suitable." Mr. Ratcliffe assured him. "As soon as I emerge from the trance I shall know a great deal more, and can act accordingly. It's so useful to be able to shed this earthly body for a time."

"I suppose you can't go into a trance and ask who's going to win the three-thirty?" Terry asked.

"Shit up," growled Mr. Davenhill, and Terry subsided.

Mr. Strudwick remained palpably unconvinced. "I don't see that throwing yourself into and out of trances will help. Incidentally, whatever do you mean by astral hypnotism?"

"You want me to give you a brief explanation?"

"I do."

"Very well. In short, it is as follows." Mr. Ratcliffe shifted a couple of skulls and a fossil or two from the nearest chair, and sat down. "You know, of course, that each of us has a particular vibration – wavelength, if you like? A personal vibration, you understand. If one can tune into that, rather in the manner of tuning into a radio, mental communication can be established, and thoughts and commands can be transmitted. That, of course, is the underlying principal behind hypnotism as well as telepathy. The main difficulty lies in making the transmitted thought strong enough to impinge upon the ordinary mental processes of the receiver. You follow me so far?"

"I think so," admitted the M.P slowly. "What you mean is, you're going to try to hit Pauline's wavelength and call her back?"

"Precisely, my dear sir. Should she be alive, well, and near at hand, as seems probable, failure is extremely unlikely."

"Sounds a lot of mint-sauce to me," Mr. Whittle confessed frankly. "Bet you a tenner you can't do it."

"Done."

"Eh?"

"Done," repeated Mr. Ratcliffe, without hesitation. "You made a bet – I accept it." He held out a limp hand, and Roy, feeling distinctly shattered, took it. "I am by no means a betting man, but I feel that on this occasion I can safely depart from my normal custom."

"Well," Aunt Clara remarked, "it's something to know that you've confidence in yourself."

"I know my own powers," said Mr. Ratcliffe modestly, withdrawing his paw from Roy's grip and returning it to store. "Should Miss Wrightman be far off the chances of success will be diminished, but at least there is an excellent prospect of bringing about her return. Astral hypnotism is one of my strongest points. Honk!"

"I've never heard of it, " muttered Mr. Westford. "Can you do ordinary hypnotism as well?"

"Most certainly. Not that I often practice the art."

"Well, now it's time, chum," drawled Mr. Whittle, knocking out his pipe on a casual rib-bone decorating the mantelpiece. "Put the 'fluence on me, Ratty old lad. If you can do that, you can spit in my eye and call me any names you like."

Mr. Ratcliffe looked uncertain.

"I doubt whether I could, under these circumstances," he admitted. "To be candid, my dear sir, your – er – definitive views would set up an astral barrier that even I could not pierce."

Mr. Whittle barked sceptically. "I thought as much. You can't do it?"

"On you, no. On anyone else, probably, yes."

"All right. Hows about Nick? Would he be an unsuitable subject too?"

"On the contrary. I imagine he would be perfectly amenable"

"Hi!" Mr. Westford protested. "Why pick on me? Do you think I look like a guinea-pig, or what?"

"Your personal appearance is totally irrelevant," Mr. Ratcliffe pointed out. "Even if you looked like an African gorilla, it would make little or no difference."

183

"But I don't look like an African gorilla, damn it!"

"I never said you did. Your arms are far too short, for one thing. At least," added the ghost-hunter thoughtfully, "so far as I can tell from the photographs. I don't believe I have ever seen a live African gorilla."

"Not have I," said Nichol viciously, "and I don't want to. What's all this guff about gorillas, anyhow? I'm sick to death of the confounded things."

"If you've quite finished the zoological bulletin," said Mr. Whittle patiently, "we might get back to hypnotism. Do you seriously mean you can tine in to Nick's wavelength, or whatever you call it, and operate him by remote control?"

"Quite easily, moreover, I am prepared to do so at once. I can see that your disbelief will not be banished except by a practical demonstration. Honk! The process is quick and painless, and if Mr. Westford will allow himself to be used as a guinea-pig – or African gorilla, if he prefers the term – I shall be delighted to oblige." He paused,, and handed Roy a curious look. "Since you are prejudiced, perhaps a second trifling bet would not be out of order?.

Mr. Whittle rubbed his chin.

"Not so fast, old lad," he said. "You told us you could black out Nick's mental processes and stick your own on top, didn't you?"

"More or less. Not in those words."

"Well, then you could make Nick go up to old Dr. Fredl and pull his beard, couldn't you?"

"I suppose so, "admitted the ghost-specialist dubiously.

"Right. Another tenner that you can't do it."

"Very well."

"Look here," Mr. Westford protested, "go easy. I don't think for a minute that I shall go under, but suppose I do? I can't go up to a perfect stranger and yank his beard. The blighter will probably try to knife me."

"Almost certainly," agreed Mr. Ratcliffe, "but we shall be at hand to see that no violence occurs. Shall we begin?"

Mr. Whittle glanced at Carole. She was seated in the only comfortable chair, Terry's arms wound around her like the coils of a python, and appeared quite unconcerned at the idea of her revered uncle getting a jerk on the fungus.

"I don't like it, " Nichole confessed. "I don't like it a a bit. How shall I know the old coot, anyhow?"

"You won't know anything. I shall attend to all that. Honk! Mr. Ratcliffe removed his spectacles, and hung them absently on Quintus Maximus' rib.

"Will you sit down, please? Anywhere you like – the floor will do quite well. The great thing is to keep perfectly still and silent during the operation."

There was a pause while the company settled down – Mr. Davenhill and Mr. Strudwick on the table, Mr. Whittle on the window sill and Terry and Carole in the remaining chair, while Aunt Clara lowered herself on to her haunches and crouched comfortably in the fashion of a statue of Buddha, and professor Weatherill perched himself on his desk. Nicol alone remained upright, looking self conscious and slightly foolish. Mr. Ratcliffe drew the curtains, plunging the room into semi-darkness, and honked purposefully.

"Are you ready?"

"I suppose so," Nichol grunted.

"Very well. Concentrate on my eyes, and count up to one hundred. Aloud, please."

"And then take away the number you first thought of," murmured Mr. Whittle.

"Wrap up"! hissed Spennie. "Give the man a chance."

Loudly and clearly Nichol started counting, gazing intently at Mr. Ratcliffe as the ghost-specialist raised his arms and made some mystic passes. Roy repressed an impulse to break into stringent laughter; the scene reminded him of Abanazar's Cave in a second-rate pantomime. Then something in Nicole's voice made him peers sharply. The journalist's voice had dropped, and he was mumbling the figures as though he had a hot tomato in his mouth.

Mr. Ratcliffe was still making signs, and breathing in soft snorts that indicated extreme concentration. At last Nicole, with his score at sixty-two, faltered and stopped, and the spook-expert, nodded with satisfaction, he drew back the main curtains and let a flood of light in to the room.

"He's out," Terry muttered. "Out to the wide."

"Nick!" said Mr. Whittle sharply. "Nick!"

Mr. Westford swayed slightly, but made no reply.

"By the sacred goats of Luxor!" Aunt Clara breathed. "Hi! Wake up, young man!"

"He can't hear you," Mr. Ratcliffe pointed out cheerily." "As I am expected, he proved an easy subject. There's no cause for alarm. Are you convinced yet, or do you wish to continue the experiment?"

Mr. Whittle shook himself like a wet terrier.

"You get your ten quid when Nick pulls Fredl's beard, and not before. I still don't believe he'll do it."

"My dear fellow," bleated professor Weatherill, "you can't deny facts, you know. Of course this sort of thing is child's play to an expert like Nehemiah, but surely even you require no further demonstration?"

"You may have pulled some cheap trick," Roy snarled venomously, well aware that he was being both churlish and obstinate, "but it won't last. Nick, you thundering beetle-wit, wake up!"

Mr. Ratcliffe sighed.

"As you will. Very well, I will carry out the agreement to the letter."

At this point Miss Czernak, who had been a silent spectator, freed herself from Terry's convolvulus-like tentacles and lodged a formal protest.

"But no," she said definitely. "It is too much. Uncle Felix, he is not well. Already this afternoon he has had what you call the crump on the bean. I ask that he should not be fetched."

Mr. Whittle grinned ghoulishly. "Afraid his beard is going to come off?"

"Off?"

"Yes, right off."

"But how? It grows. Always has he had a black beard."

"He must have been a sweet child," remarked Mr. Whittle, "and an even sweeter baby."

"Ah, you make fun. It is not fair!" Miss Czernak stamped her foot. "You are unkind, you. Why is it that Uncle Felix should

186

have his beard pulled?"

"He won't. I only want to see how Ratty'll get out of it."

"Brute!"

"You may have blacked my eye," said Terry suddenly, "but that won't stop me having another crack at you, Roy. You're heading straight for a kick in the guts."

"From you?"

"From me."

"Oh, my Lord!" barked Mr. Davenhill, "this isn't the time or place to start a romp, you dithering addle-heads. Ratcliffe, you'd better bring Nick back to earth. You've shown us you can do it, and I don't like the look of him."

"There's no danger," Mr. Ratcliffe assure him. "Indeed, the experience will do him as much good as a night's sleep."

"I'd rather have the sleep," muttered Mr. Strudwick. You've gone far enough."

He extended a finger, and prodded Mr. Westford tentatively in the stomach. Nichol swayed slightly, and there was a brief pause while everyone thought hard. Suddenly sounds were heard from the hall, followed by a splash and a thud, and raucous voices raised in anger.

"Fredl," breathed Mr. Strudwick.

"None other," Mr. Ratcliffe agreed. "I summoned him mentally. I had already issued full instructions before any objections were raised, and I fear there is no time to countermand them."

Miss Czernak started to say something, but broke off as the door swung open and Dr. Fredl made a dramatic entrance. From the amount of water on his trouser legs it was evident that he had tripped over one of the buckets in the hall, and he was plainly in peevish mood. For a few seconds nothing happened; little sparks of electricity played around the room, and there was a tense silence, broken only by a dull crackling of Aunt Clara puffing at her pipe. Then, with devastating suddenness, the action speeded up. Nichol took two purposeful steps in the direction of the bearded Hun, grabbed a handful of whiskers, and yanked. Dr. Fredl let out a hoot that would have done credit to a steam-siren of the 'Queen-Mary' and swung his fist, catching the luckless journalist a blow on the chin and dropping him as though he had been sandbagged, while Weatherill, Spennie, Terry, Mr. Strudwick and Roy barked simultaneously at Carole, letting off a choking snort, dived at her stricken uncle and grabbed him round the neck.

"I think," Mr. Ratcliffe observed mildly, putting his mouth to Mr. Whittle's ear and shouting fluidly in order to make himself heard above the general racket, "that the demonstration has been an unqualified success, my dear sir. Er – ten pounds was the sum in question, I believe?"

"Blast your eyebrows!" snarled Mr. Whittle discourteously.

"By all means, if you wish," the ghost-specialist conceded amiably. "Of course, I don't care about the financial side of the transaction, but it's always pleasant to justify oneself, isn't it?"

"Instead of drooling on like a duck," Mr. Whittle snorted, "use your loaf and get Nick out of this infernal trance, or whatever it is. We've had quite enough mumbo-jumbo for one day."

Dr. Fredl, who had been expressing himself in vehement German, had now pulled himself together sufficiently to return to his own personal modification of the King's English, and bounded forward, his eyes shooting flame and black smoke pouring from his ears.

"Donner and blitzen! To you a bonk on the snoddle administer I will. The beard to pull you dare, nein? Ver' well. To you also the beezer out by the roots I will drag, your throat down to stuff, ja? I command that to arise you perform at once!"

Mr. Westford opened his eyes dreamily, and yawned.

"Up!" bellowed Dr. Fredl. "Up, I say, prepare the poke on the clock to receive!"

Mr. Westford knuckled his eyes, and gazed glassliy around.

"I say," he said slowly, "I've had the most extraordinary dream – or was it? Did the hypnotism business work?"

"It did," Aunt Clara assured him. "Too well."

"Hypnotism?" Dr. Fredl did a short war-dance, and turned to Mr. Whittle as the one sane member of the party. "Herr Shakespeare, to you I appeal. The explanation I entreat. To me make the insulting! Blitzen, to the police at once I proceed - "

Mr. Whittle revved up his brain frantically, and was

rewarded by an idea of sorts. Signing to the general company to push off and leave him a clear field, he grasped the old buster by the arm and drew him confidentially over to the window.

"Very sad," he whispered. "Pal of mine – badly smashed up in a train accident years ago. Trapped in a burning carriage, and nearly choked to death before he could be rescued. Affected his mind – makes him subject to fits of forgetfulness, you understand."

"A lunatic he is?" queried the doctor, groping.

"Not exactly a lunatic, but he has delusions. He thinks he's a great hypnotist, for one thing, and he always tells people he works for a big daily paper. Actually, of course, he's under constant supervision." Roy pulled persuasively at Dr. Fredl's arm, and saw with relief that the museum – apart from the two of them – naturally was now empty. "He didn't mean any harm. It was just a fit."

"No harm? He to me grab the beard, and you say no harm? Verdammt !" a danger he is. "At once locked up must he be."

Mr. Whittle saw that he would have to do better than this.

"I suppose so," he agreed sadly, "but just think of his poor little wife expecting her third baby. If they put him away in a padded cell, the shock would finish her off, poor soul. A lovely girl too – only seventeen."

"Seventeen?"

"Just."

"With three babies?"

"Two at the moment – No. 3 on the way. Nick's a quick worker. If you complain to the police they'll clamp down on him like a ton of bricks and haul him back to Colney Hatch." Mr. Whittle tried another ponderous sigh. "It'll kill his wife, I'm afraid."

The bearded Teuton thought this over, and snorted emotionally.

"At least I could to him the snout poke," he suggested.

"For heavens sake, don't. The slightest blow on the head might prove fatal." Mr. Whittle, feeling encouraged, tried a new tack. "I know you've every right to feel annoyed, but I'm asking you as a special favour not to do anything about it. Don't forget I did did your niece's life yesterday. If it hadn't been for me she'd have been ironed out flat by a railway engine."

"A railway engine? A lorry was it not?"

"I mean lorry." Mr. Whittle unleashed a careless laugh.

"Ha, ha, stupid of me. Of course it was a lorry – a whacking great Dennis, with six wheels. Well what about it?"

Dr. Fredl cogitated deeply.

"Decided I have," he announced. "Herr Shakespeare, as you request so shall it be. Nevertheless -" he wagged a sausage like finger menacingly -"if again attacked I am, a bop the most fearful to him deliver I will, you comprehend. A man most good humoured I am, but to all things a limit there is, nein?"

"Bully for you." Mr. Whittle patted the old archaeologist on the arm, rather in the fashion of a fond owner caressing a pekingese. "I knew you would see my point. And now, if I were you, I'd help myself to a skinfull of the proper stuff, and then go and have a nice rest."

"Perhaps, but first, Herr Shakespeare, with you a talk the most grave I desire."

"What, now?"

"Completely. Of great urgentness is it."

Mr. Whittle raised his eyebrows.

"What's on your mind?"

"Much," the doctor admitted. "In the garden a walk let us take. Of the air fresh in most dire need I am. You assent, ja?"

Mr. Whittle nodded absently and led the way out through the French windows, wondering what the old coot had got up his sleeve.

Chapter 21

Despite his avowed eagerness to spill the beans, Dr. Fredl was irritatingly slow in getting off the mark. For some time he did no more than prowl up and down making a noise like a heard of hogs wallowing in their trough, and Mr. Whittle was starting to abandon all hope of getting anywhere when he gave a preliminary whirr and went on the air.

"Most difficult it is, " he began. "A position the most false placed myself in I have. A doddle-pate have I been, Herr Shakespeare."

Mr. Whittle bent down to light his pipe. "How come?"

"Of the map I speak," explained Dr. Fredl moodily. "The map which perhaps great riches to lead may."

"You don't mean the thing Aunt Clara dug up from the camp?"

Dr. Fredl gestured. "You miscomprehended. Not from the camp it was dug. By Herr Fane it was found."

This really did shake Mr. Whittle. "Terry found it?"

"Completely."

"But why the devil should he give it to you? It's not as if you we're bosom chums."

"An addle-head he is," asserted the doctor, "of parents most distantly acquainted. To me was not the map given, but to my niece."

Mr. Whittle nodded. This sounded a little more likely, though the whole story simply reeked of decaying fish. "And she passed it on to you?"

"But of course. What else with it have done could she?"

"I know what I'd have done with it, but that's a different matter. And I suppose you passed it on to old Weatherill?"

"Ja. A copy I had made. But to it Herr Weatherill no importance gave, you comprehend? Meinself, not so sure I was. The key to myself I kept."

"Key? You mean a sort of code?"

"Completely. Full instructions gave it did to treasure to discover. Under a board in the hall buried it is."

"Good Lord," muttered Mr. Whittle. "Where is the key? Have you still got it?"

"But no." The doctor aimed a bad-tempered kick at a passing frog, causing it to raise it's eyebrows and hop away in a marked manner. "In a book was it folded, and from my room removed it was. It is of the outrage."

Mr. Whittle had the grace to feel slightly guilty.

"Who swiped it?"

"The man Stoker, possible it seems. To him I intend the liver to extract?"

Mr. Whittle pondered. Mr. Ratcliffe's recent demonstration had shattered much of his self-confidence, but even now he half thought that Dr. Fredl was trying to slip something over him.

"Why the blazes didn't you take it to Spennie?" he asked at length. "It's his pigeon, after all."

"Pigeon? You miscomprehended, Herr Shakespeare. No pigeon it was, but a chart."

Mr. Whittle fought down a desire to say something impolite.

"That's not the point. If there is anything buried under the hall – which I don't believe, mark you – it's Spennie's property."

The doctor looked profoundly uncomfortable, and gnawed his beard as if he had taken a sudden dislike to it. "Completely. Greatly fault at was I. Herr Shakespeare, not a rich man am I. For the monies I care not, but live I must."

"I see," Mr. Whittle said slowly. "So you kept mum, passed a bit of the chart on to Weatherill and started snooping round the hall on your own account – is that it?"

Dr. Fredl whirred.

"Alas, ja. An action most evil it was. Doubtless it is to this due that failed I did the evil forces to destroy. For such spells a mind most pure of a necessity is. Alas, nothing did I find."

"No loose boards?"

"Nein. Unable the search to continue I was, since the key forgotten I have. I am – how you say pricked by the cushions."

Mr. Whittle blinked.

"Come again?"

192

The aged Teuton did so. Mr. Whittle thought it out, and decided that the only way to make sense out of it was to substitute 'conscience' for 'cushion', but the point did not seem important enough to follow up. He was beginning to think that Dr. Fredl was speaking the truth, though his opinion that the chart was fake remained unshaken.

"What do you want to do? I mean, I suppose you've go some reason for telling me all this?"

"Completely. I wish that Herr Davenhill the truth should learn. In this way alone my cushions cleared can be."

"Why the deuce don't you tell him yourself, then?"

Dr. Fredl waved his arms. "Most disgraced I feel. To him I cannot put the face."

"Hmn." Mr. Whittle puffed at this pipe. "Well, I don't in the least mind telling Spennie what you have told me, although I don't expect he'll take the treasure yarn any more seriously than I so. Anything more you want to get off your chest, or is that the lot?"

The old archaeologist shook his head.

"No more to tell there is. Deep thinking must I make."

Mr. Whittle, with a subdued snort, pushed off and left him to it, fully intending to root out Terry from wherever he was and beat the truth out of him. The front door was the nearest means of entrance, but before he reached it the sound of a car engine caught his ear, and the ancient Ford rolled slowly up the drive, burdened with an impressive assortment of trunks and bags. Mr. Whittle peered, and gave vent to a sharp bark.

"My Lord," he said aloud. "Aunt Violet in person! What the devil is she going to say?"

Chapter 22

There is something vaguely humorous about mumps. Why this should be so it is difficult to say, but the fact remains. Pneumonia, angina pectoris, or bubonic plague can be discussed without arousing a flicker of a smile; so also the lesser evils of scarlet fever, influenza or even whooping-cough. But mumps is in a class by itself. Mention that old so-and-so has mumps, and the automatic reaction a coarse of laughter, coupled with some sentiment as "good show! Bet the old devil looks a sight!"

Mrs. Violet Lockfield Fane however, was not noted for her sense of humour, and she signally failed to see anything remotely funny in this situation. As soon as her doctor, an earnest young man named Higson, had summoned up enough courage to tell her what was the matter, she had ordered an ambulance, made arrangements for her immediate reception at an exclusive local hospital, issued a bulletin to the effect that she was suffering from overwork, and withdrawn from circulation. Those who had been at the hall when she departed – that is to say Terry, Spennie, Mr. Strudwick and the domestic staff – had been briefed to hush up the whole affair; no letters were forwarded, and no anxious would-be constituents informed of her whereabouts. From the precautions taken, as one housemaid had remarked to another, "You'd 'ave thought the Mistress 'ad been and gorn and done somethin' like – well, you know." The natural result was that she was totally out of touch with recent events, and not even aware that her loving sister had returned to curse Great Britain with her presence.

If Aunt Violet had found her convalescence trying, the medical staff of Hilltop Hospital had found it even more so. One of the leading resident doctors had retired from the fray as early as the second week from a severe nervous breakdown, and his colleagues were not slow to put two and two together, while the student nurses, one and all, expressed a wish to ram a thermometer down her gullet as far as it would go. However, all things come to an end, and at long last the news filtered through that Mrs. Fane had recovered sufficiently to leave.

"And frankly," Dr. Thornely (X-ray specialist) had

confided to Dr. Barton (senior psychiatrist), "I've never been so glad to see the back of any woman. Not literally, of course," he added hastily, knowing that his colleague, like all psychiatrists, had a mind like a sink. "From the way she went on, you'd think the whole dam' place was being run for her sole benefit."

"A difficult case," agreed Dr. Barton. "Repressed during childhood, without a doubt."

Dr. Thornely snorted.

"Repressed my left nostril. The only way to repress that woman would be with chloroform. If she ever comes here again I'll put her under a strong anaesthetic and keep her in a permanent state of unconsciousness until she's ready to leave. Poker-faced old witch!"

Aunt Violet knew nothing about this conversation, but even if she had known would have dismissed it as unworthy of consideration. At the moment when it took place she was seated by the side of Lt. Gen. Sir Rupert Gore, K.C.B., D.S O., M.C. (ret.)., Conservative agent for the area and a very old friend of the family, driving at full speed towards Wollingham and doing her best to pick up the threads once more. They made a good pair. Aunt Violet was tall and lean and a mass of right angles, with an eye guaranteed to open an oyster at twenty yards range; the General a short, square little buffer, with thinning white hair, a bristling moustache, a brick-red complexion and – rather incongruously – horn-rimmed spectacles. Most of his life during the past forty years had been spent in India, and now that he had come home to roost he was as prepared to take an elephant-gun to any troublesome Socialist as he had always been to pot at an uppish lion or tiger.

"No time to lose," he was saying, in a gruff voice not unlike that of a bull-terrier. "Now that you've got over your - hrrmph! - illness, we must get back to work straight away. Should be a safe seat, of course – old Cotter's held it for the last twenty years – but in these days you never know. Don't know whet the dashed country's coming to."

"Affairs are in a sad state," Aunt Violet agreed. "What we need in Parliament, Rupert, is a grater percentage of women. Where masculine brute force has so signally failed, feminine intuition will succeed."

The General felt distinctly dubious about this, but he was much too wise to say so. Arguing with Aunt Violet about the rights of women was about as safe as tickling the ear of an enraged puma.

"Men," went on Aunt Violet, "that is to say most men, are riddled with selfishness and conceit. So long as they have their beer, their cigarettes and -" her lip,curled - "their football pools, they are content. Drinking, smoking, and above all, gambling – the three courses of modern civilisation. I only hope I may be able to play some small part in introducing some long-overdue reforms."

The General grunted amiably. Silence was golden.

"I understand," Aunt Violet continued, "that Brigadier Cotter wishes to see me as soon as possible. I quite agree. We have much to discuss. I think a meeting should be arranged before the end of the week."

The General grunted.

"I feel that valuable time has been wasted through my unfortunate indisposition," Aunt Violet rattled on. "It is such a relief to have you to lean on, my dear Rupert. Now that you are going to settle down so near, we shall hope to see a great deal of you. I know it is short notice, but are you free to dine with us tonight?"

"Kind of you," he said shortly. "Very kind, dash it. Should like to, only -" He paused. "You're sure it won't be inconvenient, with so many people in the house?"

"So many people? Aunt Violet looked puzzled. "Only Spenser, Terrance and Raymond Strudwick, surely?"

"Then you haven't heard?"

"Heard what?"

The General decided to break the news abruptly, and not waste time trying to soften the blow. He cleared his throat.

"Clara's home" he said briefly.

Aunt Violet let out an animal cry, and slumped forward in her seat as though she had been tapped on the skull with a stuffed eel-skin. "Clara?"

"Yes. Haven't seen her myself – young Strudwick told me

over the 'phone, yesterday. There are several others, too. A Professor Fothergill, I think, a young chap, and some sort of bally foreigner – forget his name; Peddle, I believe it was."

"Clara," Aunt Violet repeated in a dull voice. "How very unfortunate. You say you haven't seen her yourself ?"

"No." The General shook his head, and turned a slightly deeper shade of purple. "Don't know that she'd care to see me. Remember, we haven't met for over thirty years .. not since I first went out to India, dash it. Wonder if she'd recognise me now? When I asked her to marry me I was only a boy – and not a bad-looking one, either – and now I'm a pot-bellied old .." He broke off. "I wasn't worthy of her."

"Don't be absurd, Rupert. It would have been a perfect match. Clara always needed someone to keep her in order. She's very difficult, you know."

"Always was," the General agreed. "Liable to say the most extraordinary things – do 'em, too."

"Extraordinary," Aunt Violet commented bitterly, "is a mild way of putting it. Fond though I am of my sister -" this was a black lie, as both she and the General knew perfectly well - "there are occasions when I could willingly throw heavy objects at her. She's quite impossible. Did you ever hear what she said to the Bishop of Bexhill in 1943?"

"No, what ?"

"I really can't bring my-self to tell you." Aunt Violet shuddered, and the General nobly hid his feelings of disappointment. "There have been other incidents, too."

"Wasn't there something about a salmon?"

"There was. I didn't dare show my face in public for weeks afterwards."

"You don't mean she bashed you with the beastly fish?"

"Of course I don't. I was speaking metaphorically." Aunt Violet let out a ladylike snort, reflecting that thirty years in India seemed to have dulled the General's brain. "If Alistair Heron hadn't been so quick on the uptake we should never have been able to live it down. If Clara means to stay long, I only hope she'll keep to herself. As for Professor Fothergill and this Pebble, I've never heard of them. I expect they're friends of Spencer's and not

Clara's."

There was a short pause while the General negotiated a tricky s-bend. "I've remembered the name of the young feller," he said, straightening out. "Whittle."

"Oh," Aunt Violet said, without any and great show of enthusiasm. "That must be Richard Whittle's son, Roy. He and Spencer have always been very friendly, though personally I don't care much for him. What I call a pipsqueak. Too irresponsible. I thought he was still in the Air Force."

The General growled. "Air Force, eh?" Don't know much about these new services. Most of the young fellers I saw flying about in India could have done with a few months' strict discipline. All hair-cream and dirty buttons. Want smartening up, dash it!"

"I'm sure you must be right." Aunt Violet nodded intelligently. "What was the exact nature of your work in India, Rupert? You know, we've been out of touch for so long that I've really forgotten."

The General coughed.

"Heemph," he said. "Well, as a matter of fact, my own job – well, dash it! Somebody has to do it, but on the whole I think it might be better if we didn't make it known. You know what minds these Socialists fellers have got."

"What was it?"

"You see," the General explained, I was Chief Sanitary Officer for the whole dashed country. Deuce of a lot of work it meant, too – especially with a lot of bally half-wits on my staff – but you know what people say."

Aunt Violet did. Old-fashioned she may have been, but she was no fool, and she saw the danger quite clearly. "Very well, Rupert. In any case, the question is unlikely to arise. You have retired permanently, of course?"

"Most certainly I've retired. As soon as the dashed country split up into dominions, the job became redundant." The General brooded. "Dashed how I can see how becoming a dominion can make any difference to the sanitation, but they don't seem to want any more of it, so as far as I'm concerned they can stew in their own – hrrmpp! - sewage. It's their affair, not mine."

"Quite so." Aunt Violet dismissed the problem of Indian

and Pakistani drainage with a wave of her hand, and returned to more important topics. "Two o'clock already? I feel I should like a cup of tea as soon as we arrive. You will stay, then, Rupert?"

The General grunted with thanks, and the conversation petered out. The gay mood of Hilltop Hospital had evidently communicated itself to the Clerk of the Weather, and the old buster had accordingly dished out a really glorious day; the sun shone down from the azure sky, little fleecy clouds pottered gently to and fro, and altogether the Sussex countryside looked at its best. Even Aunt Violet regarded it with approval, though it would doubtless look even better when Socialism and Male Domination had been weeded out of it. It was not until Wollingham Hall was actually in sight, perched on top of its minor mountain, that she found anything to displease her.

"Rupert," she said suddenly. "This is most peculiar. Is it some trick of the light, or is somebody digging up the lower field?"

The General could answer this one. Raymond Strudwick, in his 'phone call, had been quite eloquent on this point.

"A camp," he explained. "Clara's doing."

"A camp?"

"Yes."

"But my dear Rupert, even Clara would hardly dig up an entire field in order to make a camp. What sort of a camp is it – a Boy Scouts' camp, or - " a horrid thought struck her - "a trippers camp?"

"I suppose you could call it a trippers' camp," conceded the General, with rare humour, "but the trippers have all been dead for two thousand years, m'dear. The Romans built it, Strudwick says."

"You mean, like Pompeii and Hercu -" "Aunt Violet, no archaeologist herself, was not sure whether the word she wanted was Herculean or Herbaceous, and wisely went off at a tangent. "Excavating?"

"That's it."

Aunt Violet compressed her lips into a geometrical line. "Well," she said, "I only hope it keeps her occupied. Any more incidents like the salmon, or that dreadful affair on the tram, would be fatal politically. We must be firm, Rupert – very firm."

"It's not easy to be firm with Clara," the General pointed out. "Never could I do it, myself. Y'know, Violet, I feel dashed queer. Thirty-six years is a deuce of a long time .. wonder if she's altered much?"

"Very little," Aunt Violet assured him grimly. "Very little. I hope and pray we shall find that all is well."

Chapter 23

All was not well, as Aunt Violet began to realise after she had rung the front-door bell impatiently for several minutes without any tangible result. Presently Roy Whittle strolled out of the bushes, and bowed elaborately.

"What ho, there," he began pleasantly, seizing Aunt Violet's paw and wrenching it. "Long time since we met, what?"

Aunt Violet privately thought that it was not long enough, but she mastered her initial feeling of nausea and performed the necessary introductions. Mr. Whittle and the General shook hands and sized each other up. Neither was impressed. Mr. Whittle came to the prompt conclusion that the General was a bullet-headed old bore, while the General found himself in full agreement with Aunt Violet's choice of the word 'pipsqueak', so that the atmosphere was not noticeably chummy from the outset.

"Trying to get in, what?" asked Mr. Whittle, after a short pause.

The General snorted.

"Of course we're trying to get in, dash it. Do you think we enjoy hanging about on a bally step, waiting for some incompetent popinjay to open the door?"

"I shall speak to Stoker most severely," Aunt Violet announced, drawing her coat around her and shivering slightly. "I am far from well, and the draught may easily bring on my rheumatism."

"Really?" Mr. Whittle remarked, without showing any great concern. "Well, it'd be a nice change from the mumps, wouldn't it?"

Aunt Violet breathed hard "Instead of making stupid remarks, will you kindly see about opening the door?"

"Kick it in, you mean?"

"Of course I don't !"

"I could pick the lock," Mr. Whittle mused, stooping down in order to make a quick examination. "A feller in my squadron once showed me how to pick a lock with a hairpin, and once you've got the knack of it it's not nearly so difficult as you'd imagine."

The General, acutely concious of his shining pate, muttered into his moustache, while Aunt Violet drew herself up and uncorked one of her iciest glances "Don't be facetious. Wherever can Stoker be ?"

"In the hall."

"In the hall ?"

"Yes. Clearing up a lot of dead bats."

This really did get under Aunt Violet's guard. She let out a loud squawk.

"Did you say dead bats ?"

"I did. Messy things to leave around, don't you think? Smelly, too."

"But -" Aunt Violet raised her eyes to heaven. "But what were they doing in the hall ?"

"Ah!" Said Mr. Whittle. "That's just what all of us would like to know. Incidentally, it's no good ringing away at that bell. You won't get any answer."

"Why not ?"

"Because Stoker'll only mistake you for another spook."

Aunt Violet passed a hand across here forehead, and turned to the General. "This is beyond me," she admitted helplessly. "Rupert, what does it mean ?"

"I don't know the General bellowed, "but by thunder, I mean to find out. What the purple blazes are you getting at, young man ?"

Mr. Whittle eyed him coldly.

"Under the circumstances, I suggest you go in and find out. And harking back a bit, my name is Whittle – Roy Stanford Alistair St. John Whittle and not 'young man!. Savvy?"

The General's colour advanced a few thousand more angstroms towards the mauve end of the spectrum, and he might easily have had a fit of apoplexy but for a welcome diversion. The front door opened slightly and Stoker thrust his head out, rather in the manner of a tortoise seeing whether the coast is clear before going for a quick early-morning sprint. Aunt Violet spun abruptly on her axis, and fixed him with a withering glare.

"At last," she observed. "What is the meaning of this,

Stoker? We have been waiting here for at least five minutes. Disgraceful!"

The aged retainer, who had shied visibly as soon as Aunt Violet opened turned round, opened the door to it's fullest extent and stood respectfully back, leaving a clear view of all the buckets, mops, pails and general shambles in the hall.

"I beg your pardon, madam," he returned with something like his usual dignity. "Had I known the ringing was of an earthly and not of an astral nature, I should have taken immediate action."

"Astral bunkum," the General roared, marching purposefully indoors and dribbling a casual mop skilfully out of his way. "Looks to me as though there's been a bally riot. Spencer," he added as a harassed young man appeared from the drawing-room, "what the deuce has been going on?"

Mr. Davenhill had had much to contend with during the last half-hour, and the unwelcome sight of his aunt was too much for him. He uttered a hoarse croak, and subsided against the wall, gargling feebly.

"Come on, come on, come on!" The General had no patience with weaklings. "Lost your tongue ?"

"Only his nerve," Mr. Whittle murmured soothingly. "I don't want to alarm you, old lad, hadn't you better be careful of your blood-pressure ?"

"Damn and blast my blood pressure!"

"By all means. I just thought I'd mention it."

The General breathed smoke from his nostrils, trod heavily on a bar of soap, and reeled drunkenly. Mr. Whittle watched his subsequent efforts to maintain equilibrium with interest; bore or no bore, the old buster had an obvious future as a trick dancer if he cared to take it up. At this point Stoker, who had been standing by, cleared his throat mournfully and went on the ether again.

"I fear, madam, that I alone am responsible for the present disturbance," he confessed, sighing heavily and looking Aunt Violet bravely in the eye. "I acted for the best, but in an unguarded I must have released potent forces that have manifested themselves in the form of evil entities."

"What?, what?" Aunt Violet, totally unnerved for once, rounded upon her shrinking nephew. "Spenser, what in the name of sense is the man drooling about? Is he insane?"

"I think we all are," Spennie moaned. "Why didn't you let me know you were coming ?"

"I saw no necessity. I hardly expected the whole house to have been seized with a fit of madness."

"Raving," snorted the General, who had managed to steer himself clear of the soap area. "He ought to be locked up. Astral mint-sauce!"

"It is not mint-sauce, sir. I only wish it were."

"Are you arguing with me, dolt ?"

"Yes, sir. And with all due respect, I am not a dolt."

What seemed to be pointless argument was cut short by the entrance of Aunt Clara, puffing furiously at her pipe and carrying a half-empty glass in her hand. On seeing the group in the doorway she halted, and a sudden silence fell, broken only by the soft crackle of her briar, and the soughing of the General's breath fighting its way through his moustache. The old aunt was first to recover herself, but though she spoke in more or less her usual tone it as obvious that she had been shaken to the marrow.

"Rameses!" she said. "Where did you spring from, Rupert ?"

"Clara!" The General muttered, clenching his hands. "You still recognise me, after thirty-seven years ?"

"Of course I recognise you. "What's thirty-seven years?" I'm used to recognizing objects that have been buried for thousands." Aunt Clara unleashed a harsh caw. "As a matter of fact, Rupert, you haven't changed a bit. You're still the same little fat buffer you always were."

Mr. Whittle was surprised to note that the General took this remarkably well. He even simpered slightly.

"Am I? Well, I suppose I am, m'dear. You don't look much older yourself."

"Liar," retorted the old aunt cordially. "I look sixty at least and you know it as well as I do. Still, I'm good for a few years yet – which is just as well, considering all the work I mean to do."

"Work ?"

"Of course. I've hardly touched the Aztec civilizations so far, and I shall need at least three years to finish with the sixteenth

204

Ptolemaic Dynasty, apart altogether from the new excavations near Luxor. Besides, there's another volume of my book to do, and any amount of research into hieroglyphical records."

"You haven't thought of settling down ?"

"Often - and I've felt sick at the very idea. The twentieth century leaves me cold."

"I insist upon an explanation," hooted Aunt Violet, who had been simmering in the background and had now reached the stage of boiling over. "I leave a well-ordered household, and I return to a positive lunatic asylum. Why ? I take it , Clara, that you are responsible ?"

"I have already placed you in possession of the facts, madam," Stoker informed her sadly.

"Be quiet!" Aunt Violet hissed. "Well, Clara ?"

Aunt Clara tossed off the remains of her drink, and put down the glass upon the nearest surviving table. "I'm damned if I know," she admitted frankly. I'm puzzled. It's quite true that nothing started up until we'd got Quintus into the museum -"

"What museum ?"

"The room that you used to keep the guns in. I've turned it into a store for all the specimens from the camp. I don't believe that even now Quintus has any evil powers, but he's certainly a most interesting skeleton."

"You mean that you've been storing skeletons in the gun-room ?"

"Of course I have. Quintus Maximus has an exceptional background. So far as is known he was born in Rome in or about the year 102 A.D. -"

I don't care when he was born," Aunt Violet shrieked. "For goodness sake, Clara, explain! What has this wretched skeleton to do with this – this chaos ?"

"Mr. Whittle chuckled. "Quite a lot. According to friend Ratcliffe, the old lad's madder than a wet hen at being dug up, and is making his presence felt by scattering assorted curses in all directions."

"Who," Aunt Violet Violet asked helplessly, "is Ratcliffe ?"

"A pal of Weatherill's"

"Who is -" Aunt Violet broke off in order to get a firm grip on herself. "Spencer, I think you had better come into the lounge and tell me exactly what the position is. If I stand here much longer I shall certainly get a chill. Besides, all this ridiculous nonsense about astral quantities, or whatever you call them, is Greek to me."

The General also had a word for it, and said it – but not aloud. In his opinion the whole business simply reeked of decaying fish (or, as he preferred to think of it, inadequate sanitation) He was wondering what to do next when there was a confused noise from the back passage and Mr. Ratcliffe staggered in to view, laden with a large flattish object not unlike the mirror of an astronomical telescope. In his wake trailed Mr. Westford and Mr. Strudwick, manhandling an unwieldy metal stand. Mr. Whittle rubbed his chin.

"A gallows ?" he suggested inanely.

"Honk !" Mr. Ratcliffe, scenting strangers, blinked amiably and extended one limp hand from beneath the mirror. "Sir Rupert Gore, I believe? How do you do. My name is Nehemiah Ratcliffe."

"What the deuce do you think you are doing ?" the General asked feverishly.

"Nothing as yet. Astral contacts are difficult during the hours of daylight," Mr. Ratcliffe informed him. "As soon as darkness falls we can get to work. Will you please put the stand down here, gentlemen? It mustn't be too near the light."

Aunt Violet pawed the ground with her hoof, and wheeled on Mr. Davenhill. "Spencer, who is that man?"

"Mr. Ratcliffe," Spennie told her dully. "He's a ghost-hunter."

"Psychic expert," Mr. Ratcliffe corrected him, setting down the mirror on it's stand and wiping his hands politely an the seat of his trousers. "All supernatural phenomena efficiently investigated – poltergeists a speciality. My card."

"I'd like a note of your address," Mr. Westford put in, scribbling some shorthand notes on his cuff. "Come in useful for my article."

Aunt Violet let out a hoot. "Article ? Did you say article?"

"I did."

"You don't mean that you are a – a journalist?" From the horror in the old trout's voice one would have imagined that being a journalist was a far worse crime than being a leper or a Bolshevik agent.

"Correspondent of the 'Metropolitan Planet'," Mr. Westford informed her. "I do the fashion column, as a matter of fact. Perhaps you've heard of it?"

"I have not! And I absolutely forbid you to publish anything about this – this crazy affair in your scurrilous paper."

"It isn't a scurrilous paper," Nichol retorted, with some heat. "Would you like one of my official cards too? I believe I've got one on me."

"I don't want your card. I don't want any cards. Why, in the name of all that is wonderful, is everyone thrusting cards at me ?"

"You'll soon have a full pack," Mr. Whittle pointed out. "Useful if we want to settle down to a game of bridge. Or perhaps you prefer pontoon ?"

"I do not prefer pontoon!" Aunt Violet snorted. "Oh, Heaven grant me patience! Once and for all, if any hint of this disgraceful episode finds its way into the newspapers, I shall file a lawsuit immediately."

"On what grounds ?"

Aunt Violet paused to think this one out.

"Libel," she said eventually.

"Don't make me laugh. Do you imagine Nick would be idiot enough to print anything that wasn't the sober truth ?"

"He must print nothing!"

"That's a bit harsh," Mr. Westford protested. "Here am I, faced with a whole battery of spooks and perambulating skeletons, and you say I'm not to use it. Who'd be a journalist?" he added sadly.

The General boiled over again. "Walking skeletons my left eyeball," he bellowed, raising his walking-stick and swiping irritably at a passing fly. "Never heard such utter mint-sauce. You may be able to fool some people, but you can't fool me. Anyone who tries to pull the wool over my eyes will find he's up against a fighter – a fighter, dammit! - who'll stand no nonsense!"

"You think I would – er – pull the wool over your eyes?"

Mr. Ratcliffe asked mildly.

"No, I don't. But you might try."

"On the contrary, my dear sir. I am familiar with your great reputation, both as a soldier and a sanitary expert."

The General spluttered as though he had dipped his head in a bucket of water.

"How the purple Hades did you know I was a sanitary expert?"

"By your aura, of course."

"Are you telling me I smell?"

"No, no. The aura is quite odourless," the ghost-specialist assured him, "but most informative, and an infallible key to ones – er – inclinations. Yours, for instance, is brown with yellow flecks. I can see it quite clearly, even without the aid of the ectoplasm condenser." He nodded at the strange-looking machine by the stairs.

"You can, can you?"

"Certainly. I expect my psychic senses have been sharpened by the unusual vibrations."

The General made a noise like a cork being withdrawn from a bottle, and muttered something about vibrations that Mr. Whittle did not catch. At this point Mr. Strudwick, who had been engaged in trying to pacify Aunt Violet, prodded the machine with a tentative finger, as if he half expected it to bite, and put a peevish question.

"I wish you'd tell us what the wretched thing is meant to do," he said. "I've never heard of condensed ectoplasm. Is it anything like condensed milk ?"

"On the contrary. Ectoplasm is the ethereal substance used in the process of astral materialisation. This apparatus helps to concentrate it."

"Astral materialisation!" Aunt Violet echoed. "Rupert, this is too much! Whatever is to be done?"

"I know what I'd like to do," the General admitted. "Ring up the hospital, and have the whole lot of 'em certified and put away in padded cells."

"In which case," said Nichol, I don't see why you're making such a shindy about my article. You couldn't hush up a thing like that."

"You haven't even heard the whole story yet," Mr. Whittle assured them. "Not by a long chalk. "You don't know about Pauline, for instance."

"Who," Aunt Violet asked hopelessly is, "is Pauline? Another skeleton?"

"You couldn't be more wrong." Mr. Whittle leered obscenely. "Praline's skeleton has got some pretty good covering, believe me. Unfortunately Stoker's turned her into a bat."

The aged butler bridled. "Pardon me, Mr. Roy, there is no proof that I did any such thing. I am convinced that if such a transformation has indeed taken place, Dr. Fredl alone must be held responsible".

"Turned into a bat?" bawled the General. "By the cross eyed rhinoceros of Lokanpore, who's been turned into a bat?"

"My fiancée," Mr. Strudwick informed him gloomily. "Not that I believe a word of such nonsense, mind you, but she has certainly disappeared."

"Of course," Mr. Westford commented helpfully, "witchcraft is a dashed funny thing, you know. If you're going to turn a house into a centre for Black Magic, you're bound to run risks."

This really did finish Aunt Violet. She was a strong-minded woman, but there was a limit even to her endurance, and uttering a low bubbling cry she subsided against the General as though her bones had suddenly become jelly.

"Help me," Rupert, she gasped. "I feel faint."

"Pity old Fredl's skunk salts aren't handy," observed Mr. Whittle, seeing that his relative really was on the point of collapse. "What she needs is a stiff whisky."

"And she's not the only one," Aunt Clara said briskly, stepping gingerly forward and grabbing her sister's sagging frame. "Come along, Violet. A quick snort of something strong will soon put you on your feet again."

"I don't want to be put on my feet," Aunt Violet admitted, with unusual weakness. "I want to go back to hospital!"

"Aunt Clara gave a contemptuous grunt and, aided by the General, led the patient firmly off; Mr. Strudwick followed, while

Mr. Ratcliffe busied himself with the ectoplasm condenser and Mr. Westford drifted out through the front door. Mr. Whittle, re lighting his pipe, recollected that his original intention had been to have a heart-to-heart with Terry; so, setting course wearily to leeward of the soap area, he set out in search of him.

Chapter 24

Terry, however, was not to be found. Mr. Whittle ranged through the entire house, even to his own room and (with rather more hope) Carole's, but without success. He then tried the camp, but the only person there was Professor Weatherill, busy examining a twisted piece of pottery. As Mr. Whittle hove in sight, the old coot gave a welcome bark.

"A pleasant afternoon, is it not ?" he observed, removing his snout from the pottery bowl and smiling cheerily. "Far too pleasant to be indoors, so I thought I'd spend a few minutes carrying on down here."

"You haven't seen young Terry about anywhere?"

"Terry, Dear me, no. As a matter of fact I've been absorbed in my work. Every fresh excavation seems to bring to light something new. Would you care to examine this bowl? I believe it's either Augustinian or early Claudian."

"To hell with the bowl. I'm not interested in bowls."

"I am," the aged archaeologist admitted, holding up the battered object as though it had been a rare and beautiful gem. "I find bowls most interesting, and have indeed a large collection of them. Surely you must agree that the workmanship is exquisite."

"Oh, bowls to you," Mr. Whittle snarled churlishly, and went on his way. His next course took him to the rose-garden and the tennis courts, but having drawn blank once more he pottered back to the house, cursing. The museum was deserted (apart from Quintus Maximus), but in the conservatory he came upon Miss Czernak, fooling about with some geraniums. Slightly mollified, he came to anchor beside her.

"Do you know where Terry is ?" he asked abruptly.

"In the village, I believe. Why?"

"Oh, I just wanted a chat with the lad," Mr. Whittle explained vaguely.

"A friendly chat ?"

"I don't know. It all depends."

"There are still some vases nearby," Miss Czernak warned him. "You have a headache, yes ?"

211

"I've got a thick skull," Mr. Whittle assured her.

"You have. Most thick."

"I'm not sure that I like that remark." Mr. Whittle sat down on the bench, and Carole followed suit. "Since Terry's not in view I think a chat with you wouldn't be out of place. You're sure he's gone to the village ?"

"I wish not to - how you say ? Play the tricks," Miss Czernak said reproachfully. "Remember, Terry and I, we are engaged."

"God, what a mind you've got! I've no designs on your maidenly virtue, if that's what you mean. All I want out of you is some information."

"What about ?"

"This phoney map."

"But why should I know anything about it ? I do not comprehend."

"Who're you kidding ? I have it on excellent authority that you and Terry palmed it off Uncle Felix."

Miss Czernak looked annoyed. "Who says so ?"

"Uncle Felix."

Miss Czernak thought this one out.

"It was not my doing," she assured him. "Terry, he found the map in the hidden passage, and said that it should be – what is the word? - followed up."

"The amount of onion soup you talk," Mr. Whittle commented, "would fill a reservoir, let a lone a vase or one of Weatherill's infernal Claudian bowls. In the first place, is Terry is likely to root out a map that all the dead and gone Davenhills have been chasing for at least ten generations at least? Secondly, why shouldn't he have followed it up himself? And thirdly, why the purple hell should he hand it over to that pop-eyed uncle of yours?"

"He is not pop-eyed!"

"Pardon me, he's as pop-eyed as a coot. Lastly, the map and everything about it is faked. It just doesn't wash. I want the truth, please."

"It will go no further?"

"That depends. I doubt it."

"Very well. I will tell you all." Miss Czernak shivered slightly, "It is cold, is it not?"

"Perhaps you'd like me to slip an arm round you?"

"Please. It would help."

"Ha!" said Mr. Whittle nastily. Quite apart from having done your best to murder me a couple of hours ago, you've only just finished reminding me that you're bespoke. I've been made a monkey of too often during the last couple of days to want any more soft soap. Get me?"

"You are unkind, Roy. I like it not."

"Mr. Whittle snorted. "We'll let that pass. I take it that you and Terry are entirely responsible for the map?"

"I drew it," Miss Czernak admitted sullenly, marshalling her thoughts. "Let me explain, please. A week ago, perhaps, I arrived at this house – no, it was two weeks. I met Terry. We – what is it you say? Cleeked?"

"Cleeked."

"Cleeked. But Terry, he was worried. And he feared, too, though I did not know why. It is something to do with that old Weatherill."

"You're sure it wasn't anything to do with Uncle Felix?"

"But of course. How can you be so absurd?" Miss Czernak gave a wan smile. "Uncle Felix is unusual, but he would not hurt a fly."

"I wouldn't trust him too far if I had the misfortune to be a fly. In fact I don't even now. Unusual or not, I don't like the thought of people dabbling in Black Magic."

"Black Magic!" Miss Czernak repeated vehemently. "It is what you call the pure tomato-juice."

"I know that as well as you do, though I'm bound to admit that Ratty knows his onions when it comes to hypnotism. I take it, then, that you and Terry arranged a little treasure-hunt for our pal Weatherill?"

"Yes. We drew this map, and we gave it to Uncle Felix."

"Why not Weatherill direct?"

"He would have suspected. We thought Uncle Felix would take it to Weatherill without thinking more about it. He is so unworldly."

"Instead of which," concluded Mr. Whittle, "the old buster thought he'd slip a fast one over the lot of you, and froze on to it – or, rather, what he thought was the important part of it. I see."

"You knew that?"

"Considering that I've watched him crawling about the hall at 3a.m, pouring over the floorboards, the news didn't surprise me much. It all fits in, apart from one thing."

"One thing?"

"Yes." Mr. Whittle decided to burn his boats. "The fact that your precious uncle's a phoney."

"A phoney?"

"That"s what I said. Whoever he is, and whatever he is, he's no more an archaeologist than I am."

Miss Czernak let out a yip.

"And the obvious conclusion," went on Mr. Whittle, "is that you're playing some deep game. I don't quite know what it is, and I don't know how far you've managed to drag Terry in, but at least I'm on the track."

"Ach! You are as – as barmy as a duck!" Miss Czernak sprang up and waved her arms, upsetting a geranium and sending it spinning crazily to earth. "You say that Uncle Felix is not an archaeologist? But through the world he is known! Many books has he written -"

"The name's genuine enough," admitted Mr. Whittle. "The point I'm making is that this bearded cove who calls himself your uncle and puts on a music-hall accent hasn't any right to it. Damn it all, why don't you come clean? I'm not the police, and I don't care much what the two of you are aiming at, within reason. All I want to do is find Pauline Wrightman and prevent that doddle-pate Spennie being let in for a hundred quid he can't afford. Take a deep breath, and tell Uncle Roy all about it."

"But you miscomprehend. Ach, what can I say? You will not believe me. It is as Terry says – you have the brains of the woodlouse."

"He said that, did he?"

"I also say it."

Mr. Whittle simmered slightly, but before he could think out a reply a loud shriek filtered through the door, followed by a gurgling moan and the sound of running feet. Neither Roy nor Carole reacted violently. Events in the Hall had reached the stage where a shriek more or less made little difference. However it seemed as well to investigate, and Mr. Whittle rose.

"Where do you think that came from? The museum?"

"Might be. I suppose we'd better go and have a look. If Quinnie's on the rampage again," said Mr. Whittle viciously, I'll tie his vertebrae in a knot. And the same applies to that squirming bacillus Ratcliffe."

It was not Quinnie, and it was not Mr. Ratcliffe, but something much more startling – so startling indeed that even Mr. Whittle was shaken to the core. As he reached the open museum door he shied violently and motioned to Miss Czernak to keep back, after which he remained in a state of suspended animation goggling like some weird species of frog.

Chapter 25

In dismissing the General as a bullet-headed old bore, Mr. Whittle had done him rather less than justice. Bore he may have been, and bullet-headed he certainly was, but not even thirty seven years wading about in Indian sanitation had entirely quenched his basic decency and good nature. There had been times when he had felt like consigning all sanitation to the devil, leaving it to stew – figuratively – in it's own juice, and catching the next boat back home; but on the whole he had come through his ordeal remarkably well, and was generally liked. In the mess one night a junior officer, Lieutenant Pottingham, had summed him up briefly but accurately.

"Decent old boy, Gore," he had remarked to his particular crony, Captain Scrubb, "even if he does look like a lobster with indigestion. "Wish he wouldn't snort, though. Wonder if it's adenoids?".

"Love," Scrubb corrected him, adjusting his monocle with an air of profound wisdom and ordering a fresh brandy-and-soda. "I had the story straight from Adj. Old Gore was nuts on some female who went about the place digging things up."

"Gardening, you mean?"

"No, idiot. Arche – archael – what's the word."

"Archway?"

"No, fool. Archaeology. They had some sort of scrap over a brass idol, and Gore told her what she could do with it."

"Did she?"

"Presumably, yes. It's my belief," said Captain Scrubb, who believed he understood human nature, "that when he retires, the old boy'll go back to England, marry the wench, buy a nice little sewage farm on the South Coast, and settle down to a peaceful old age. Here's luck to him."

Scrubb, pin-head though he undoubtedly was, had been on the right track. The General's outspoken remarks about a small idol, dug up near Stonehenge, had been the direct cause of the long rift. A beastly looking thing it had been, with an outsize belly and a dirty leer on its face, but his comments had been far from well received. Even at the age of twenty-five Clara Debenham believed in calling a spade a ruddy shovel, and years later the General could still remember some of the things she had said to him. Wisely, he had left her to cool down and gone off for a fishing holiday in Norfolk, firmly believing that all would be well again on his return. Instead, he had been shattered to learn that his erring ex-fiancée had packed her bags and taken the first boat for Peru. Piqued beyond endurance the General had made tracks to Australia, where he farmed sheep furiously for six months and then came home to investigate the situation. By this time, however, Clara had left Peru and started out for Egypt. Not to be out-done the General had set course for India, accepting a commission in the special services battalion of his family regiment. On his first leave he went so far as to visit Egypt, but to his disgust Clara had left for Mesopotamia the previous month; and this failure so disheartened him that for the next twenty-five years he was content to let things slide, biding his time in true military fashion. Bearing in mind that all this time a great longing was gnawing at his vitals, in much the same way a sewer-rat tucks into a biscuit, we can see that he had every reason to look like a lobster with indigestion.

As he strolled aimlessly into the garden, having handed Aunt Violet over to the tender mercies of Mr. Strudwick, his mood was one of extreme anxiety. Clara had not been displeased at his reappearance – that was something. She had not thrown a fit, sniffed offensively, or shown any signs of wanting to be sick on the carpet. Neither, on the other hand, had she given a glad cry and hurled herself into his arms. The General didn't know what to make of her.

Snorting softly, as was his wont, he pottered across the tennis lawn, down the path and across the camp, not because he particularly wanted to go there but because it seemed pleasingly deserted, and he wanted solitude. He was therefore far from pleased to catch sight of that damned young pipsqueak Whittle, and drew back into the bushes in the hope of escaping unnoticed. Fate was kind, and Mr. Whittle hurried past; the General resumed his potter. He then encountered Professor Weatherill, who wielding a spade with gay abandon and humming snatches of a rather questionable music-hall ditty. Fortunately his back was turned, and the General beat a hasty retreat, musing that what he had taken to be a deserted paradise was turning out to be a metropolis.

It was as he reached the tool-sheds, on his return journey, that he came to a definite decision. Nothing ventured, nothing gained. He'd shown Clara his devotion by going to India and languishing there for nearly forty years – what more could a girl want, in this unromantic world where one-eyed giants no longer flourish and even dragons are at a premium? He'd go to her, put the case simply and clearly, and bung his heart at her feet. Just like that. No need to be scared. She wouldn't bite – at least, he didn't think so.

Yet, Rupert Gore confessed to himself, he was scared – as scared as the devil. He had faced a peevish tiger without wincing, yet now his heart was fluttering like a captive canary, and he felt as though someone had rammed an egg-whisk down his gullet and started churning. Luckily there was an almost infallible remedy nearby. The General laid a course for the dining room, now mercifully free from swooning femails and drooping politicians, and went to work on the whisky. Three generous snifters worked wonders. Filling his glass for the forth time, and knocking it back with a slick efficiency, he brayed like a warhorse, and mentally spat on his hands. He'd show young Clara what he was made of!

It was just then that the first scream came from the museum.

Mr. Whittle, on hearing it, had taken his time before deciding to investigate. Not so the General. Hardly had the initial echo had cannoned off the ceiling and died away before he had revved his engine, let in his clutch with a jerk and burst in to the hall as if he had been shot out of a gun. A second screech had put him on the right track, and he pounded into the museum, panting and breathing fire and smoke like a rather elderly chimaera. Next moment he uttered a startled grunt as Aunt Clara, wild-eyed and white to the lips, gave a long choking moan and launched herself at him, clinging to him frantically and beating her heels on the floor, her whole body shaking like a volcano in violent eruption.

Brains were not the General's strong point, but he had sense enough to recognise a good thing when it was handed to him on a skewer, and it took him almost no time at all to see that this was his big chance. Seizing a moment when the old aunt had to pause in order to supply her lungs with a fresh chunk of atmosphere, he patted her head comfortingly.

"There, there," he said gruffly. "There, there. What is it, then?"

"Rupert, oh Rupert!"

"Yes, m'dear?"

"Don't leave me, Rupert!"

The General assured her he wouldn't. As a matter of fact he was in no position to do so even if he'd wanted to, since Aunt Clara was hanging round his neck grappling with him as though intent upon pulping his Adam's apple.

"You're safe with me, m'dear. What was it – a mouse?"

"No, no!" Fresh sobs shook the old aunt's tank-like frame. "Worse, much worse."

"A rat?" suggested the General, who had a limited imagination.

Aunt Clara shook her head disparately, and made a confused snuffling noise. Reflecting that unless something was done quickly his neck-muscles would infallibly give under the strain, the General waltzed her over to the couch and dumped her on it, rather in the manner of a miller handling a sack of flour.

Aunt Clara hiccoughed, blew her nose, and made a visible attempt to pull herself together. It was the first time in her sixty-three years that she had really lost her nerve, and she didn't like the sensation a bit.

"That thing," she whispered, pointing shakily at the gaunt figure of Quintus Maximus. "That awful thing. Rupert, it – it chattered at me!"

"Chattered? What did it say?"

"It didn't say anything. It just chattered."

The General looked perplexed. "How do you mean, m'dear?"

Aunt Clara shuddered. "I was looking up a reference in my diary, when I happened to glance at it, and – and the jaw started to move. Up and down – with an awful chattering noise. And –

Rupert, it leered at me!" She gulped, and clung to him with such a force that the General felt a couple of ligaments creak protestingly. "Augustus was right. It's powerful it's evil!"

"Evil or not," the |General said belligerently, "I'll smash it's blasted skull if it chatters at you again. I'd – I'd -" He floundered. "That's to say – well, dammit, I'm only a simple soldier but -"

"Yes," Aunt Clara breathed.

The General loosened his collar, and took the plunge.

"You're still all the world to me, m'dear."

Aunt Clara threw off a burning glance.

"Rupert - you mean that?"

"Dammit, I do." The General stretched out his arms, wondering absently whether they would be long enough to go round. "Ever since that beastly idol came between us I've hungered for you, all the same."

"Always? Even when you were in the jungle, surrounded by tigers and snakes?"

"You were always in my thoughts," The General assured her, hoping that he was not going too far. "Every time I shot a tiger or a snake, I felt I was doing it for you."

This went down well. The old aunt positively purred.

"How romantic! Oh, Rupert!"

"It was how I felt. Tell me, Clara, have you ever thought of me?"

"Not often," Aunt Clara confessed. "I've been too dam' busy. But now you've come back at last, Rupert, I know what I've been missing." She sighed softly, like a baby grampus. "All the old life comes back to me. How we used to wonder about the Downs, looking for fossils ... how we went along to the British Museum .. what years ago it seems!"

"It is."

"I know. That's probably why it seems like it."

"There were other things too," the General said boyishly. "Do you remember our golf and bridge, and how we used to off to the races on my tandem? Have you forgotten that?"

Aunt Clara uncorked a wan smile.

"Almost, you know, it's so long since I thought about

anything less than a thousand years old that I've almost lost track of what this modern world is really like. It took you to bring it back to me, Rupert."

A vein in the General's forehead throbbed like a piston of some vast machine. "Then – Clara – dammit, will you marry me?"

"When?"

"Now. Special licence."

"Darling!" said the General, and folded her in his arms.

Time stood still. After what seemed hours the General came to the surface and drew a fresh supply of oxygen, and paused to give Quintus Maximus an affectionate wink. Evil or not, the old buster had certainly done him a good turn that day.

"Ah!" Aunt Clara said at last, breaking away from the clinch and breathing hard. "Rupert, I'm so happy. I feel like – like a ship that has come into harbour at last."

"The comparison was more apt than she realised, but the General made no comment, merely grunting ecstatically and laying his hand upon her arm.

"No more lonely travelling for me," went on Aunt Clara. "To think, Rupert, that I was going to leave for |Egypt next month without a soul to look after me! What a heaven-sent stroke of luck you came back before I left. Why, I might have been bitten by a crocodile, or trampled to death by a camel, or – or anything!"

"Quite easily," agreed the General. "Nasty tempered brutes, camels. "You don't mind about Egypt, then?"

"Of course I don't ." Aunt Clara nestled close to him. "Darling, how could I? I don't mind how many camels and crocodiles I meet, now that you're coming with me!"

Mr. Whittle, who had been shamelessly listening-in by the open door, gave a soft snort of laughter and withdrew.

Chapter 26

Mr. Whittle, as will have been gathered, was a hard-headed young man. He had about as many nerves as one of General Gore's camels, and supreme confidence in himself, but it was idle to deny that his self-possession had been badly shaken by now. Pauline's account he had attributed to the trickery and an overwrought brain, but this latest affair, coming on top of Mr. Ratcliffe's hypnotic demonstration, put a very different complexion on matters. He said as much to Spennie, who nodded glumly.

"We've got to face it. If Aunt Clara says the skeleton chattered, then chatter it did – she's the last person to let her imagination play tricks. I only hope that fool Stoker hasn't let loose anything we can't stop."

"Stoker," Mr. Whittle said patiently, "is a senile old doddle-pate who's done nothing except burn herbs in a pot and howl at the moon, and he's no more responsible for this business than – than Stalin is. Fredl I can't make out, and Weatherill's a slimy duck who wants filtering, but there must be something genuine about Ratcliffe, or he couldn't have put the 'fluence on Nick like that. By the way, where is Nick?"

"I don't know. Probably making a rough copy of his article. He'd better let me vet it, or Aunt Violet will throw a fit."

"Let her. Point is, do we ring the police?"

"We don't. We should have to tell 'em the whole story, and apart from the fact that they wouldn't believe it God only knows what would happen if some flat-footed country coppers stared rooting around here. They might easily get turned into boll-weevils or field-mice," Spennie added, with a pitiful attempt at light relief.

Mr. Whittle shrugged.

"I've no great faith in the Wollingham police force – he's an old dodderer – but we can't go on like this indefinitely. Pauline's got to be found."

"Well I'm hoping Ratcliffe will do something useful."

"Nuts on that. This astral stuff leaves me cold."

"I doubt that," Mr. Whittle remarked dryly. "When I think

of here throwing herself away on that anaemic wet lettuce, I feel positively sick." He rammed some tobacco viciously into his pipe. "By the way I've found out something that might interest you. Remember the phoney map?"

"Yes."

"Well, I've got at the truth behind that, at any rate. Carole drew it."

"What! Why?"

"To make a monkey out of Weatherill – but Fredl walked into it first. At least, that's what she says." Mr. Whittle grinned.

"I take all their statements with several tons of salt. Terry's mixed up in it, of course."

"Terry?"

Mr. Whittle, remembering that his friend was not abreast of the Terry-Carole situation, explained. Mr. Davenhill betrayed little interest.

"Oh well," he said absently, "It's none of my business. I'm good for a fish-slice or a silver-plated toast-rack when the glad event takes place, and after that they can go their own way."

"Don't worry. They will."

"I doubt whether Aunt Violet will go about the place singing 'O Perfect Love' and scattering orange-blossom out of a hat," Spennie added, "but that's not my affair, either. "Is Terry out or in?"

"Out. Apparently he's strolled down to the village."

"I wonder why?"

"I can think of a dozen reasons. Probably he wants to buy something. Aspirins, perhaps, or even cough-lozenges. As soon as he gets home I want to talk to him. The lad's got some explaining to do, and if he doesn't kick in and come clean I'll beat the daylights out of him.

Terry, however, was in no hurry to return, and tea – or rather, a ghastly mockery of it – came and went without him. Mr. Whittle found it a depressing function. Only Spennie, Aunt Violet and Mr. Strudwick were present, and as the last two obviously regarded him as a grade A disease he left them to it and meandered back into the garden, chafing at his helplessness and wondering what to do. All things considered it seemed best to stroll down to the village in the hopes of finding Terry, and he accordingly set course in that direction, passing the time by turning over in his mind just what he would say to Miss Wrightman when he eventually succeeded in running her to ground.

He had not covered more than half the distance to the village when he saw his quarry. Young Mr. Fane was approaching at a brisk trot, tacking slightly to and fro, and wearing a cheery grin on his clock. Roy halted and stared. An old hand himself, he knew all the symptoms.

"Where the deuce have you been?" he demanded, as he cousin came up. "And how did you manage to get into this state? It's only just opening time."

Terry exploded with mirth, and laid his hand affectionately on Mr. Whittles shoulder.

"Want to know?" he asked, pronouncing his words with rather more than ordinary care.

"Not particularly," Mr. Whittle admitted.

"Then why ask? Always think before you speak," Terry advised him with owlish solemnity. "Hic" if you must know, I've been at the races."

"Like hell you have! What races?"

"Horse-races, of course. Do you think I'd go and look at jellyfish races?" Terry laughed uproariously at the idea. "Over at Forthill Park. Had some red-hot tips, ol' man. Simply couldn't lose. Hic."

"Silly young doddle-pate," Mr. Whittle said piously, with bitter remembrance of the dead cert. He had so confidently backed only the previous week. "I suppose you're cleaned right out?"

"Cleaned out? No likely" Terry spluttered. "I told you – red-hot. Won a cool hundred quid during the afternoon."

"A hundred?"

"A hundred and two. Tell you what," said Terry generously, "I'll lend you the extra two, ol' man and you can buy a couple of tips off dear old Ratty."

Mr. Whittle gave a startled yelp.

"Ratty? You don't mean that Ratcliffe gave you these red-hot tips of yours?"

"Of course. Good old Ratty – man in a million." Terry

plucked at Mr. Whittle's arm and led him back in the direction of the hall. "Just throws himself into a trance, and – bing! - up comes a winner. He can do it every time."

"At so much per trance, I take it?"

"Results only – ten per cent. Which means," said Terry seriously, frowning in thought, "I owe him 0 what's ten per cent. Of a hundred and two quid, old man? Damned reasonable, if you ask me."

"The more I think of it, the more it stinks." Mr. Whittle brooded. "He can hypnotise people, he can produce winners merely by chucking himself into a trance .. I wonder what else he can do?"

"He's done enough for me," Terry observed, pausing briefly to do a small jig. "What a feller! Even if he does look like a – what does he look like, old man? Never mind."

"And you haven't actually paid him anything yet?"

"Not yet, but I'm going to. He deserves it – every penny. After that I'll settle with the old basket Weatherill, and I'll still have quids and quids left over." Terry broke into cheerful song. "East is East and West is West, and never the twain shall meet -"

"Can it! What;s this about Weatherill?"

Terry promptly shut up like and oyster.

"Nothing. Sorry I spoke."

"Has Weatherill been trying to get money out of you?"

"Go fly a kite," Terry requested him sulkily. "None of your business. Keep your snout out of it."

"You'd rather I tackled Weatherill in person?"

"You can tackle who the devil you like."

Mr. Whittle's eyes smouldered.

"What I'd like to do to you," he said nastily, "is put you across my knee and get busy with the flat side of a hairbrush. I'll talk to you when you've had time to sober up. Meanwhile, take my advice and steer clear of your mother – I don't think she'd approve either of backing winners or getting sozzled on the proceeds."

"She'd have a fit," Terry admitted with a giggle, "but she's busy having mumps. Good old mumps, jolly old mumps ..."

"Wrong first time. She's home."

"Ouf!" said Terry violently. God, do you mean that?"

"I do. Moreover she's in no amiable mood. What with one thing and another, she's ready to disembowel anybody who has the misfortune to cross her path."

A bucket of water poured over him could hardly have had a more sobering effect. Terry went perceptibly green at the gills.

"What the hell am I to do?"

"I suggest that you come up to my room, via the servants' entrance. I've got some stuff to clear your head, and, incidentally, make your breath smell rather less like a brewery." Mr. Whittle grunted. "I don't know what I am doing this for you, young Terry, but I suppose it's only humane to make you look less like something out of Picasso before Aunt Violet sees you. Come on, and for goodness' sake keep quiet."

Terry nodded, and relapsed into a depressed silence broken only by an occasional hiccough as they passed through the tradesman's gate, along a winding path bounding the kitchen gardens, and into the servant's quarters. Mr. Whittle hoped that they would remain unobserved – to run into Aunt Violet now would be awkward to a degree, though there was always the chance that the shock of seeing her loved child half-seas over the world would startle her into a nervous decline and send her back post-haste to the loony section of Hilltop Hospital. Aunt Violet, however, seemed to be infesting some other portion of the house, and the pair gained the sanctuary of the bedroom without incident. Once there Mr. Whittle, with the efficiency borne of long experience, got busy. Terry was divested of his jacket and shirt, bent over a basin, and soaked with icy pump-water. Next he was pummelled vigorously with a towel, and finally and evil-odoured potion was poured down his throat. The young man submitted to the rough rough treatment without protest. In a case like this, he realised that Roy's was the master hand.

"Better?" enquired Mr. Whittle at last.

Terry managed a grin.

"Ouf ! Yes. Thanks, pal. How do I look ?"

"No more sub-human than usual. I think you'll get by."

Terry stood up and stretched. "Damn decent of you," he admitted. "I was a fool to get like that, but I didn't think there was a chance of Mother popping up out of a trap. What is that stuff

226

you gave me, Roy? It tastes like bad eggs, but it's a miracle-worker."

"I don't know what's in it. A man I know, who's by way of being a chemist, makes it up for me. Harking back a bit what were you saying about owing money to Weatherill?"

Terry hesitated.

"I'd rather not tell you before I've settled with him. I'll do that in the morning."

"Right, I'll hold you to that."

At this moment there was a soft tap on the door, and the saturnine face of Stoker peered in. The butler had aged perceptibly during the past twelve hours; instead of looking a youngish eighty he now looked a somewhat senile ninety, and he breathed with the laboured sound of a defective vacuum cleaner. On seeing Terry he drew back.

"I beg your pardon, Mr. Roy, I had no idea you were occupied."

"Neither am I. Come right in, and put your feet up."

The butler accepted this cordial invitation, and lowered himself wearily into a chair, puffing and blowing as though the effort was almost too much for him. Mr. Whittle, with ready sympathy, poured him a mild tot of whisky, and Stoker downed it gratefully.

"Thank you, Mr. Roy. That was greatly needed."

"What's on your mind."

"Many things, sir. It is not too much to say that I am bowed down with care. I should never be surprised to turn my head and discover that I had assumed the form of a spider, or even a beetle."

"I don't think it's likely," Mr. Whittle assured him. "How are the experiments going?"

"I have discontinued them, sir. I have come to the conclusion that I am not sufficiently practised in the art. In fact, I have already disposed of Dr. Fredl's book."

"Given it back, you mean?"

"No, sir. I would not willingly give Dr. Fredl anything, apart from possibly the measles. I consigned the volume to the fire, and heartily glad I was to see the end of it. I may add that it burned with an intense green flame."

"Hmn. Pity. I'd have liked a look at it."

"The consequences might well have been dire, sir. However, I considered that you should be informed of my actions." Stoker rose heavily to his feet. "Dinner will be late tonight, sir. At eight o'clock Mr. Ratcliffe is holding a meeting in the main hall, and wishes the entire household , excluding the female servants, to be present."

"The devil he does! What's the game?"

"I cannot say, sir, though I have no doubt that his motives are questionable to a degree."

"You've said it, old lad. The more I see of that cove, the less I trust him, hypnotism or no hypnotisim. There's something uncanny about a man who can pick six winners in a single afternoon."

"He did that, Mr. Roy?"

"Seven," Terry corrected him. "On after the other."

"I don't care if it was seventy. I still don't trust him. One false move on his part tonight, and I'll poke him right in the snout."

"A very pleasing prospect, sir. More power to your elbow, if I may say so."

"I shan't need my elbow," Mr. Whittle informed him dryly. "A straight left will do."

Chapter 27

At precisely three minutes to eight, the remaining grandfather clock in the main hall cleared it's throat and started the preliminary chimes of the hour. This was followed by the library clock, the drawing-room clock, the billiard-room clock, the smaller billiard-room clock and various other assorted clocks, all giving tongue until the whole house shuddered and shook with the ghastly uproar. Mr. Whittle, realising that the time for action had come, put the finishing touches to his black tie, knocked back the last remnants of his whisky store, and set course for the main hall.

He was almost the last to arrive. Wollingham had given of his best, and so far as could be seen the entire household – apart of course from Miss Wrightman – was present. Spennie, Nichol and Mr. Strudwick were grouped near the library door, while Terry and Carole lurked nearby, and the General stood with his arm thrown protectingly round Aunt Clara's shoulders; Aunt Violet, radiating disapproval, had appropriated the only arm chair, beating Dr. Fredl to it by a short head, while Stoker and Professor Weatherill hovered in the background like senile vultures. Mr. Ratcliffe leaned nonchalantly against the ectoplasmic condenser, massaging his wart and honking softly to himself.

"All set?" Mr. Whittle asked brightly, resisting a puerile impulse to whoop like a Red Indian and slide down the banisters. "Ready for the big bang, Ratty, old lad?"

"If you mean the demonstration," the ghost-specialist corrected him coldly, "I think I may say that all is prepared. I should like everybody to sit down and join hands. It should help to improve the vibrations. Unless I am personally mistuned," he added nastily, "there are some disturbing influences near at hand."

"Meaning me?"

"Since you ask, yes." Mr. Ratcliffe nodded. "I feel you are not wholly in sympathy with my sincere efforts to restore Miss Wrightman, Honk! I can read you mind like a book, my dear sir."

"You can, can you?"

"Certainly. For instance, at this moment you are thinking how satisfying it would be to seize my ectoplasm condenser and –

well, perhaps there can be no point in emphasising what you are thinking of doing with it, but I am right, am I not?"

"You are," Mr. Whittle conceded grudgingly, "though I am damned if I see how you knew it?"

"Elementary," Mr. Ratcliffe assured him. Honk! Be seated, if you please. The longer we delay, the less chance of success."

"This is quite absurd," Aunt Violet broke in impatiently, "I really don't feel inclined to become a party to this ridiculous nonsense. I trust you agree with me Rupert?"

The General blew his nose with a sound like a mother elephant calling its young, and looked embarrassed.

Well -" He hesitated. "Well, Violet, there's something dashed queer about it all. Clara knows that. I can't help feeling we ought to play the game and see if this mumbo-jumbo business can help. Tricky stuff, 'y know. I remember a case in Lokanpore -"

"He's right," Aunt Clara said with decision. "God knows I'm not the nervous type, but I've had about all I can stand."

Aunt Violet gave in with a ladylike snort, and there was a mild General Post while the company selected chairs and arranged themselves in a rough semi-circle sufficiently close together to hold hands. Mr. Whittle, to his disgust, found himself between Mr. Strudwick and Aunt Violet, and ill-naturedly gripped their paws with as much force as he could. Two bellows rang out, and Mr. Ratcliffe looked pained.

"Really," he began protestingly.

"My hand!" Aunt Violet hooted, withdrawing the mangled remains and massaging them tenderly. "Kindly take more care, Roy. You might have injured me severely."

"Sorry," Mr. Whittle said untruthfully. "Wasn't thinking."

"A common state of affairs," Mr. Strudwick commented sourly, inspecting his flipper for broken bones.

"Was that a dirty crack, old lad?"

"By no means. A simple statement."

"Oh? Well, one more simple statement of a like nature, and I -"

"Shut up!" snarled Davenhill. "Go on, Ratcliffe. What next?"

"The lights." Mr. Ratcliffe bent down and adjusted the

mirror of the ectoplasm condenser. "Not really necessary, of course, but I always find darkness a great help to concentration. Now listen carefully, if you please. As soon as the lights go out, I shall endeavour to contact Miss Wrightman on an astral plane. Complete silence, is of course, essential – the slightest sound would be sufficient to upset the vibrations completely. There must be no shuffling, fidgeting or even throat-clearing. Is that fully understood?"

"Are we allowed do breathe?" asked Mr. Whittle.

"In your case," the ghost-specialist admitted, "I would prefer that you didn't, but you are at liberty to please yourself on that point. Furthermore, I must ask you to cleanse you minds, so far as is possible, of earthly matters. Concentrate only on ethereal and the spiritual." He paused in order to direct a significant look at Terry, who had uttered a subdued snort of mirth. "Are you ready?"

"No," said Mr. Whittle. "I want to scratch my ear."

"I really feel," said Professor Weatherill sourly, "that success is highly doubtful without the willing cooperation of all of us. If Mr. Whittle feels unable to give that cooperation, I suggest that he is asked to withdraw."

"Not on you're life, old lad. I'll cooperate like the devil once we get started." Roy finished scratching his ear, and settled himself in his chair. "Carry on!"

Mr. Ratcliffe made a final adjustment to the mirror, went to the main switch and turned off the lights, plunging the hall into inky blackness. Mr. Whittle strained his eyes. Night-flying had given him vision like a cat's, and after a time he could clearly make out the main details of the hall, even to the dim figure of Mr. Ratcliffe as the spook-hunter settled down by the condenser, put his head in his hands and, to all outward appearances, went to sleep.

Time passed. Mr. Whittle, his eyes now fully used to the darkness, glanced around. The entire company sat like so many statues, and the only sound to be heard was the soft hiss of the General's breath battling through the built-up area of his moustache to the open air beyond. Presently a whirr from the grandfather clock announced that the quarter hour was at hand, and a few seconds later the silence was broken by the thunderous pealing of the Westminster chimes.

Mr. Ratcliffe gave an annoyed grunt, and raised his head.

"Dear me," he said impatiently. "How very irritating. I should have remembered to stop that clock."

Bad for the vibrations?" Terry murmured.

"Be quiet, if you please. Concentrate."

Silence fell once more, broken after perhaps a minute and a half by the chimes of the library clock – an unusually large specimen in the style of Big Ben, with a strident note guaranteed to penetrate even a padded cell. Mr. Ratcliffe sat up, and honked in an overwrought manner.

"Tut," he said feelingly. "These constant interruptions are most disturbing. Moreover I cannot honestly say that I feel myself attuned to any particular entity, human or ethereal. I'm afraid my wavelength must be wrong."

"Try the Third Programme," suggested Mr. Whittle.

Dr. Fredl, who had been unusually silent for an unusually long time, suddenly went on air.

"Forces most potent near at hand are," he said solemnly. "I, Felix Fredl, of them aware am. Mr. Ratcliffe, is it that to make the incarnations permitted I may be? Of a necessity it is with the spirit of Quintus communicate to -"

"Certainly not," Aunt Clara barked. "I thought we were trying to get rid of the spirits, not raise them," commented Aunt Clara. "Let Ratcliffe get on with it, for Rameses' sake."

"A helpfulness I was about to perform," the bearded Hun retorted, in a wounded tone. "Great knowledge have I -"

"Pipe down, you old fool!" Aunt Clara requested curtly.

Rather surprisingly Dr. Fredl subsided, and Mr. Ratcliffe addressed the meeting once more looking – so far as could be seen in the dim light – baffled and ill at ease.

"I am about to make a final effort," he announced. "I fear the conditions are extremely bad, but if all of you concentrate hard we may get results."

"And if we don't?" Mr. Whittle asked keenly. "What then?"

"I shall have to throw myself into a completer trance. A

232

nuisance in many ways, and I hope we shall be able to manage without it. Now, then – concentrate, please."

Everybody obeyed, and froze in their chairs. After some moments Mr. Whittle became uncomfortably aware of the presence of some small insect – a gnat, possibly, or a mosquito – that had settled on his chin and was now strolling gaily up and down, admiring the scenery. His hands being firmly held, Roy made an effort to blow it off, but only succeeded in driving it up his nostril, where it started practising dance-steps – beginning with a gentle waltz, and working it's way up to a hornpipe. Roy stood it for as long as he could, and then gave vent to a thunderous sneeze. Snorts of surprise broke out on all sides.

"Who the devil was that?" Demanded Mr. Davenhill.

"Me. Sorry, old lad. Gnat or something."

"Fool!"

"I consider that the whole demonstration is being wantonly wrecked," Professor Weatherill asserted warmly. "On behalf of the sincere members of the audience, Nehemiah, I apologize. We are not all hair-brained young nitwits."

"Meaning I am?" Mr. Whittle asked softly.

The aged professor was weary enough not to answer that one, and turned away to start up a whispered conversation with Mr. Strudwick. Mr. Ratcliffe sighed and turned on one of those small standard lamps, honking audibly and muttering under his breath.

"Well," he said "there's nothing else for it. In the trance condition I shall be immune to these disturbances, and my wave range will be correspondingly increased." He gave Mr. Whittle a dirty look. "If you particularly wish to sing "Il Bacio", or practice the cornet, do you think you could manage to do it now, before I begin?"

Rightly guessing that this request was not meant to be taken seriously Mr. Whittle said nothing, and watched Mr. Ratcliffe closely as the ghost-specialist completed his preparations. These were, to say the least, odd. First he made some further adjustments to the condenser, then he hung a somewhat grubby handkerchief over the table lamp, spread a rug carefully on the floor and lay down upon it, with his head and shoulders at ground level and his feet propped up against a chair.

"What the blazes ..." breathed the General.

"Devilry," muttered Stoker, from the background.

"He's going to play bears," Terry informed the company, in a strange-whisper. "Who's been eating my porridge? Who's been sleeping in my bed?"

"Quiet!" Mr. Davenhill snarled. "Have we got to keep holding hands, Ratcliffe?"

"If you please." The spook-hunter looked up, and made some mystic signs in the atmosphere. "The vibrations are far from favourable as yet, and we must spare no effort to concentrate the ectoplasm. "A little soft music may be helpful. Have you a gramophone, by any chance?"

"No."

"I can sing a bit," Mr. Westford volunteered diffidently.

"So can I," Terry added. "I know over twenty verses of 'The Quartermaster's Stores' -"

"Vocal music is hardly suitable, I fear," Mr. Ratcliffe informed them regretfully. "Well, well, we shall have to manage without. I don't suppose it will make a great deal of difference. Please keep still and don't move about, whatever happens. Of course, I don't anticipate any major materialisations, but one never knows. If you are ready, I will begin."

"We are," Aunt Clara grunted. "Start away."

The ghost-specialist nodded purposefully, and, laying back on the rug, closed his eyes. Once again silence descended upon the hall, and Mr. Whittle stifled a yawn. In his opinion this farce had gone far enough, and he was about to make some caustic comment when Mr. Ratcliffe uncorked a deep, whistling sigh, threw out his arms and rose slowly to his feet, his mouth slightly open and his eyes bulging giving him a remarkable look of some nightmare fish. Next he clasped his forehead, bowed three times towards the library door, and spoke in deep, ringing tones quite unlike his normal bleat.

"Pauline Wrightman! By the spirits of good and evil, I command you. You are summoned. Hear the call, and return!"

"By Gad," muttered the General. "He's out all right. Look at his face!"

"Out my foot," rasped Mr. Whittle. "He's trying to kid us."

234

"I'm not so sure," Nichol whispered. "My God, what a story!"

"Our fate is sealed," Stoker informed them cheerily. "The forces of evil are unleashed -"

"What was that?" Mr. Davenhill jerked out suddenly.

"What?"

"I thought I heard something – God! Yes, I did! Over by the door – listen!"

Everybody listened. Then, slowly and solemnly, the front door bell pealed out, stabbing the silence like a bayonet. Mr. Whittle, croaking harshly like a frog with laryngitis, bounded to his feet, raced across the hall, and threw the front door wide open. Pauline Wrightman stepped in, blinking owlishly and shaking her head from side to side as though she was just recovering from the effects of being sandbagged.

Chapter 28

"Paul!" barked Mr. Whittle.

"Miss Wrightman!" bleated Professor Weatherill, in much the tone he would have used to announce Napoleon Bonaparte or Nell Gwyn. "Astounding."

"Pauline, darling!" spluttered Mr. Strudwick, hurling himself forward and clasping her in a clam-like embrace. "Good heavens, you look ghastly! Where have you been? What happened to you?"

Miss Wrightman passed a hand across her brow.

"I – I don't know," she said weakly. "My head – it feels all funny. Where am I?"

"Ach, permit me!" Dr. Fredl pushed his way to the front of the teeming mob, and fumbled in his pocket. "Of these a sniff partake, and wonders it to you certainly do will. Gently breath -"

He waved the now-notorious bottle violently, but by ill chance Mr. Strudwick, who was leaning forward to peer anxiously into his fiancée's face, received the full benefit and retired into the background clutching his throat and making unpleasant golluping noises. Mr. Whittle, his eyes watering, gave a grunt of protest and elbowed the bearded Hun firmly back.

"For God's sake," he snarled, "don't crowd round her – and keep those pickled skunks out of harm's way. We don't want to gas her now we've just got her back. Whisky, Stoker – quick."

The old retainer nodded intelligently, and produced a flask apparently out of thin air. "Certainly, sir. I feel sure it is the best remedy."

Miss Wrightman allowed herself to be led to a couch, and tossed off a couple of quick tots in a manner that showed she had definitely given the astral plane the go-by and returned to Mother Earth. She even managed a wan smile.

"Thank you," she whispered. "That's better. Oh, my – my head."

"You certainly look a bit shop-soiled," agreed Aunt Clara, lighting her pipe. "Well, Rupert, what do you make of it all?"

"Nothing," the General admitted frankly. "I just don't

236

know, dammit. Are you all right, Violet?"

"I am not," Aunt Violet informed him weakly, leaning back against the chair and closing here eyes. "I feel faint. Please assist me to my room."

Nobody raising any objections, the gallant Sanitary Officer helped her to her feet and carted her off, creaking in every joint. By this time Pauline was more or less convalescent. Breathing hard, in a manner of a hunted stag, she sat up and leaned against Mr. Whittle's steadying arm, shuddering throughout the entire length of her chassis.

"It's been like a dream," she confessed. "I believe it has been a dream – an awful dream! Have I been away long?"

Mr. Whittle made some rapid calculations. "I last saw you just before three in the morning, and it's 8:30 now, so, you must have been wandering about spare for the best part of twenty hours. Damn it, you told me you were going straight to bed. Didn't you ever get there?"

"Your sure you didn't go and see?" Mr. Strudwick asked keenly.

"Of course I'm sure, you dirty-minded beggar. We said goodnight in the hall."

"I tell you, I've no idea whether I ever got to bed or not." Miss Wrightman gestured. "I remember leaving you in the hall, after we'd seen that awful skeleton, and then – well, something in my head seemed to give way. After that I don't know quite what happened to me. It was ghastly!"

"You're sure you didn't see Whittle again?"

"I don't know!"

"If you keep on harping on that theme," Roy informed him viciously, "I'll hand you out a kick in the teeth you'll remember for one hell of a time. How are you feeling, Paul?"

"Horrible. Can I have some more whisky?"

"The bottle, so far as I am concerned." Mr. Whittle poured out a fresh tot. "You're quite in the dark as to when you went outdoors, then?"

"Of course I am. I saw awful faces – and lights – and skeletons. One skeleton in particular. It seemed to follow me about. Then I – I was called back. I don't know how. Oh, I think

237

I'm going mad!" Miss Wrightman buried her face in her hands. "This house – it's haunted. Take me away

She followed this appeal by a choking hiccup, as though the fine old whisky had struck an air-lock in her gullet, and Mr. Whittle laid his hand comfortingly upon her shoulder. Unfortunately Mr. Strudwick had the same idea, and their paws met. Evil looks passed to and fro, but before anything could be actually said Aunt Clara broke in again.

"Just one moment," she said keenly. "I don't follow just how you got back here. You say you were called?"

"Yes."

"Who by?"

"A voice. I don't really know – but there was a voice inside me saying "Come back!" It's all a muddle. Oh, take me away!"

"Of course I will, Mr. Strudwick promised her gallantly, "as soon as you like. Nothing will hurt you while I'm around."

"That goes for me too," Mr. Whittle grunted, "though I'm bound to admit this astral business is right over my head. Ratty, I take it all back. You've earned your twenty quid, and no mistake."

"Assuredly of great powers possessed you are," agreed Dr. Fredl. "An honour most gratifying to you encounter been has, Herr Ratcliffe. I, Felix Fredl, to you salute with the – how you say - the horse's laugh, is it?"

Terry muttered a semi-audible alternative.

"A remarkable performance, Nehemiah," Professor Weatherill put in gravely. "One might almost say, a classic performance. The forces must be reported in full to the Psychical Research Society,"

"You certainly know your oats," Aunt Clara admitted.

The spook-hunter made no reply to these glowing complements. He was sitting limply in his chair, with one hand upraised and his mouth open as if he was trying to catch insects, obviously not in touch with recent developments. Aunt Clara was the first to notice anything odd about his general attitude.

"Do you know," she said, stepping forward and examining him carefully, "I believe he's still in a trance? Most interesting. He doesn't seem to be even breathing. I should like to take a photograph of him," she went on with marked enthusiasm. "The

238

modern Yogis can, I believe, remain dead to the world for weeks on end, and from what we can tell from the Luxor translations the ancient Priests of Ra were able to do much the same thing during the Sacred Cat festivals, but this is the first time I've ever encountered anything of the sort."

There was a short and rather baffled silence.

"Hadn't we better do something about him?" Mr. Davenhill suggested lamely.

"He certainly clutters the place up," agreed Mr. Whittle. "I should think emptying a bucket of water over him should do the trick."

Stoker coughed apologetically, and took the air "Might I make a suggestion, sir?"

"Well?"

"I think it would be best, sir, to shift him gently into the library, and leave him there until he elects to come to. I understand that it is highly dangerous to disturb a person who has been thrown into a deep astral trance, and should any of the female staff encounter him in his present condition I fear that they would be considerably disturbed. If you will forgive the expression, sir, he looks perfectly bloody."

"Don't be a dolt," Aunt Clara snorted. "Shift him into the library, indeed! He might not come around for a week."

"The fact seems immaterial, madam. I would personally dust him each morning."

"Of trances I have the knowledge. A subject he is much of the study to make done have I." This was Dr. Fredl again, and the old buster hopped forward energetically, his beard waggling and his eyes flashing. "The experiments I may perhaps make?"

Miss Czernak, who had so far been a completely silent spectator, appeared to object to this, and expressed herself in voluble German. It was left to Terry Fane to make the first really practical gesture.

"I heard some duck lecturing on hypnotism once," he said slowly, "and I seem to remember him saying that if anything went wrong the best way to bring anyone round was by a sudden shock. A poke with a pin, or something."

"I've heard that, too," Mr. Strudwick agreed doubtfully.

"It couldn't do any harm."

"Poke away, old lad." Mr. Whittle slipped his arm casually round Pauline. "Got anything sharp enough to poke with?"

"I haven't got a pin," Terry informed him, "but this ought to work the oracle. Stand clear!"

Abruptly he raised his ham-like hand, took a careful swing, and handed Mr. Ratcliffe a full-blooded slap right on the snout. Next moment he gave a yell of sheer horror and leaped back, landing heavily on Mr. Strudwick's feet. Roy, uncoiling himself from Pauline, let out a croak.

Mr. Ratcliffe's nose squashed under Terry's hand. More than that, it bent and twisted, and fell to the floor in a shower of brittle fragments. Mr. Whittle, seized with sudden misgivings, seized a look at the ghost-specialist's lank hair, and yanked. The wig came away in his grip – and with it the side-whiskers, the moustache, the wart, and most of the face. The figure in the chair straightened up, and gave a rueful grin.

"Well, you are a pair of cloth-eared doddle-pates," said Gregory Tallon in an aggrieved tone, massaging his cheek. "What the purple blazes did you do that for?

Chapter 29

Mr. Whittle had had many shocks during the past to days, but this beat the lot with ridiculous ease, and his jaw dropped so violently that it landed on his bow-tie with an audible thud.

"Gregory," he said weakly. "Gregory, my God!" He rounded on Mr. Westford, who had subsided against the clock roaring with laughter. "Nick, you were in on this?"

"Of course, you dope!" Nichol managed to reply between gusts. "Astral hypnotism – oh, my stars"

"Trickery!" This from Mr. Strudwick, who had slipped his arm adroitly round Pauline in place of Mr. Whittle's. "Whittle, you don't mean to say that you know this – this impostor?"

"I understand not," Dr. Fredl admitted blankly, turning to Miss Czernak with a puzzled expression, and tugging at his beard as though to yank it out by the roots. "A hypnotist of great power he is, yet with a false snout he parades. Blitzen! The sense it makes not, nein?"

"Hypnotist my foot!" Mr. Whittle snarled. "Greg, this does more than smell it positively pongs. If Nick was in on the game I take it that Paul must have been too, but why?"

"Oh no, she wasn't," Mr, Tallon finished peeling off his disguise, snorting slightly at a wisp of crepe hair curling up his nostril. "Nick was in on my game, all right, but dear Pauline playing one of her own – or, rather, of her father's."

"What?"

"Fact, old lad. Sorry to break it so brutally."

"Liar!" Mr. Strudwick bounded forward, and brandished his fist menacingly in Gregory's face. "How dare you accuse my fiancée of deceiving us! I am a man of peace, but I wan you I can be driven too far."

Gregory inspected the M.P's paw with mild interest, and pushed it to one side.

"My good doddle-pate," he said gently, "you forget I'm a journalist. I know what I am doing. If I didn't, I wouldn't be here. Once our pal Weatherill accepted me as a bona-fide crook I was right in, and it was childishly easy to ferret out just what was going on."

"Crook ? What's that What's that ?" The aged Professor barked like a seal, and stuck his head forward until he looked like a somewhat unwashen crane. "Nehemiah, have you gone mad? I really fail to see the point in all this. I knew, of course, that you had elected to come here incognito -"

"It was a damn good disguise," Aunt Clara admitted, blowing out a cloud of acrid smoke and sizing up the main differences between the oily, drooping 'Nehemiah Ratcliffe' and the handsome, straight-featured Gregory. "I recognize you now. "You're the boy who wrote a series of articles about my excavations at Uriconium."

"Never mind that. Nehemiah, you owe me an explanation. Unless you are playing some obscure practical joke ..." Professor Weatherill paused and giggled weekly. "Of course! You always had such a remarkable sense of humour, my dear fellow. For a moment I almost took you seriously – ha, ha!".

"Ha ha to you," Mr. Tallon retorted uncompromisingly. "Come off it, old scout. You've lost the trick. Mind you it was a brainy idea, and I think you've been a bit unlucky, but – to put it mildly – you're in the mire."

A babel of voices broke out, topped by the professor's bleating treble. Mr. Whittle resorted to the old expedient of bashing the gong, and though the sudden noise nearly made both Mr. Davenhill and Mr. Strudwick faint from shock he was successful in restoring some sort of order.

"Listen," he yelled, as soon as he could make himself heard. "Let's have some explanations, before we all go ga-ga. Gregory, you dumb-wit, I still don't know what you're up to, but what's all this guff about Paul's father? Who is her father, anyhow?"

"Her father?" Mr. Tallon looked amused. I thought you'd guessed that one. He is, of course."

"Weatherill?"

"Naturally."

"Absurd!" the professor roared at the top of his voice. Nehemiah, you're raving. Miss Wrightman is my valued secretary, but any suggestion of parentage is perfectly preposterous. You know quite well I'm not even married."

"I never said you were. Stick to the point."

Mr. Whittle, feeling as though he had been hit very hard in the solar plexus, wheeled round and grabbed Miss Wrightman by the shoulder.

"Paul, it isn't true, is it? I mean, look at him! You're not going to tell us that that moth-eaten old ruin is your pop?"

Pauline broke free. An angry flush had come in to her cheeks.

"He is not a moth-eaten old ruin!"

"He is a moth-eaten old ruin, and venomous, to boot – but you haven't answered my question. Is he, or isn't he?"

"Yes, if you must know. He is."

"Yuk!," said Mr. Strudwick involuntarily.

"Crikey!" Terry comments. "Beauty and the beast!"

"You two faced bastard," Professor Weatherill breathed, turning his best death-ray glance upon Gregory and puffing smoke from his nostrils. "You treacherous, scheming, viper -"

Mr. Tallon chuckled.

"Naughty, naughty," he said reprovingly. "Not in front of the ladies, old scout. I expect Miss Weatherill is pretty used to it – I assume that her legal name is Weatherill? - but the others aren't. Spennie, do you think I could have another bracer? This trance business is hot work, you know."

Stoker, still looking sandbagged, wandered mechanically round with a tray, and Gregory, selecting two large whiskies, tossed them off with every indication of pleasure. "That's a lot better," he admitted, returning the two empty glasses and taking another full one for luck. "Good stuff this, Spennie. I must come here more often. Got much left?"

"Never mind the whisky!" Mr. Davenhill hooted. "Gregory, for the last time, will you explain?"

"Certainly, old scout. What do you want me to explain?"

"I think, Mr. Strudwick put in helplessly, "you'd better tell us the whole story. Personally, I feel quite unhinges. You'll appreciate that this appalling disclosure comes as a great shock. The idea of having a father-in-law like ...." He paused, and shuddered. "Davenhill, I feel that the time has come to break my lifelong rule. Will you please pass me a glassful of alcoholic stimulant?"

"Take the lot," Gregory offered him generously, passing over the tray. "Well, I'll put the whole thing as clearly as I can. Let me marshal my facts." He turned to Professor Weatherill, who was carrying on a muttered conversation with Pauline. "You don't mind me marshalling my facts, old scout?"

"You can do what you bloody well like with your facts," snarled the professor venomously. "Serpent!"

"Thanks. To put it blandly, then, the whole show was organized by our grubby friend here, aided by his less grubby but equally dirty-minded daughter, specifically to do Spennie out of as much cash as was humanly possible. In other words the spook story, as I'd thought you would have guessed long before now, was pure onion broth from the word go. Quinnie may have a soul of sorts, but it hasn't been around these parts for a couple of thousand years – in fact I don't believe the skeleton you dug up is his at all. More probably it belongs to some tactless rent-collector who was quietly tapped on the dome and liquidated in the middle ages."

Not on your life," Aunt Clara said decisively. "It's genuine Roman, all right, and I'll stake my reputation on it as an archaeologist that it belongs to Quintus. The inscriptions are perfectly legible. Besides," she added, "the thing chattered at me this evening; Rupert can vouch for that."

"Chattered at you?"

"It did."

Mr Tallon shrugged. "That's new on me, but even if it sung 'The Minstrel Boy' it still hasn't anything to do with the general set-up. You've all been having skeletons on the brain."

Professor Weatherill uncorked a harsh, grating laugh.

"Indeed? Then how do you account for the wave of accidents, not to mention the supernatural bell-ringing and the influx of bats?"

"I have already apologized for the bats, sir," Stoker broke in sadly. " fear that my well-meant and, as it would now seem, wholly misguided efforts to assist Miss Wright – er – Weatherill ended in object failure."

"Don't you worry, old scout." Gregory grinned. "The bats

weren't your doing. That was another of Weatherill's little gems. I'm not perfectly sure how it was worked, but I guess it's pretty easy to get hold of a lot of bats, drug 'em, and let 'em go at the psychological moment. That's what he did, or rather what Pauline did".

Stoker let out a deep, whistling sigh.

"You really mean that, sir"

"Of course I mean it."

"Than I was not, after all, to blame for the regrettable incident before tea?"

"No, you doddle-pate."

"Thank you sir. The relief is stupendous." The aged butler threw back his shoulders, much as Atlas must have done when he handed over the sky to his relief. "You cannot imagine what a weight is lifted from my mind, sir. I feel as though I shall like to sing with joy."

"For God's sake don't. Have a drink instead."

"Thank you, sir. Perhaps I might help myself to a small whisky?"

"A large one, if you like. It's not my whisky. Cheerioh!"

"Mud in your eye, sir, if you will pardon the expression."

"Get on with it!" roared Mr. Whittle and Mr. Davenhill, with one voice.

"Where was I?" asked Mr Tallon. "Oh yes, the bells and the bats. They'd rigged up some extra circuits, so they could actually set the bells off from Weatherill's bedroom or from downstairs."

"Which room downstairs?"

"Can't you guess? That was a clever touch," said Gregory dryly. "When you came on Pauline messing about by the front door, Roy, she told you she'd been looking for extra wires. That was a bit of quick thinking on her part – actually, of course, she'd been dismantling them. That trick can't be worked for too long, and even you might have smelt a rat after a day or two."

"I don't like that 'even you', Mr. Whittle muttered darkly.

"Good Lord!" Spennie breathed. "And when Miss Wrightman vanished, where did she go?"

"Nowhere in particular – she merely played hide-and-seek

in the house. As a matter of fact she spent most of her time in my room. Don't look so het up, Struddy old scout. It wasn't my idea."

Mr. Strudwick looked forlornly at his erring fiancée.

"Is this correct?"

Pauline nodded sullenly. Mr. Strudwick gulped.

"Mind you," admitted Gregory airily, "I wasn't altogether averse to the arrangement. We had the deuce of a lot of time on our hands."

"But -" Mr. Davenhill broke in, in a baffled tone. "Damn it, what was the point of all this rigmarole? It doesn't seem to make sense."

Mr Tallon sighed.

"Don't you see even now? Spennie, I always knew you were the last word in doddering mutton-heads, but surely even you must get it? The idea was to convince you, and everybody else, that the place was lousy with spooks."

"Why Why? Why?" Mr. Davenhill hopped about. "What the devil would Weatherill get out of it?"

"One hell of a laugh," commented terry.

"More than that. A hundred quid."

"A .. oh Lord, your fee!" Spennie shook his head. "You don't mean you were in on this too?"

"Dolt! I may be all kinds of things I shouldn't be – in fact, I'm perfectly willing to admit as much -" Mr. Tallon's eyes rested for a fraction of a second on Carole, who was nestling in Terry's arms with her umph paraded for all to see - "but I haven't yet robbed anybody, unless you count bookies and British Railways. No, I cut in as a substitute. As soon as Roy spun me the yarn, and told me that Weatherill had arranged for Nehemiah Ratcliffe to come on the scene, all was clear. You see, I know the gentleman who goes under the pseudonym of Nehemiah Ratcliffe."

"You know everybody, don't you?" the professor growled.

"Most people. Well, I went to see Ratcliffe – or, to give him his proper name, Shorty Johnson – and put the fear of Hades into him. I told him the police were on his track, which is true, and that he was wanted for blackmail – which isn't, though I don't doubt he and his precious friend Peabody make quite a good

246

income out of it, if only I knew?"

Roy bared his teeth. "Aloysius Peabody?"

"Of course. Shorty swallowed the story hook, line and sinker, and you couldn't see him for dust. At the moment I believe he's taking a holiday in one of the less accessible parts of Northern Scotland. To think of him," said Gregory dreamily, "lounging on the heather-strewn moors, stalking deer and munching haggis -"

"Don't start rambling," Aunt Clara requested him coldly. I'm not sure yet what to make of all this, but surely Weatherill must have realised you weren't this – Shorty Johnson, or whoever he was? Unless, of course, you look like his twin brother."

"God forbid." Gregory shivered. "Shorty is an undersized little runt, with no chin and an Adam's apple about the size of the Vimy Memorial. I got round that by the simple method of sending Weatherill a telegram in Shorty's name, saying that he (Shorty) was unavoidably detained, but was sending down a bosom pal to take his place as Nehemiah Ratcliffe. Owing to the vagaries of the nationalised postal service, though, the telegram didn't get here until after I did, with the result that Weatherill was totally unprepared for me. Under the circs., I think he played up pretty well. My congratulations, Augustus old scout."

The professor told him briefly what to do with his congratulations.

"As soon as I got him alone, " continued Mr. Tallon, "I spun him the story, and he swallowed it as well as Shorty had done. Since then all I've had to do is to sit tight and give him enough rope to hang himself, and I'm bound to admit he's made a pretty good job of it."

"How did you work that hypnotism business?" Mr. Whittle asked resentfully.

"Easy as pie. Nick knew what to so, and you were obliging enough to suggest him yourself. Dr. Fredl's appearing when he did was sheer luck, of course. Sorry about the yank, old scout."

Dr. Fredl muttered something unintelligible, but at this point Professor Weatherill pulled himself together and made a gallant, though forlorn, attempt to save the situation.

"I'm bound to admit that I have been deceived," he said weightily. "This man is a rank imposter, but surely it is

247

unnecessary for me to tell you that his preposterous story is a fabrication from start to finish?" He unleashed what was meant to be a carefree laugh. "Absurd! Why, Miss Debenham and I are old acquaintances. My reputation as an archaeologist is world-wide."

Mr. Davenhill rubbed his chin.

"How about it, Aunt Clara? Is this duck an honest-to-God grave-digger, or isn't he?"

"Of course he is." The old aunt snorted. "That's one of the things I can't make out. It's perfectly true that I've known him since I was a girl, and you can forget any stupid ideas about his not being Augustus Weatherill. Nobody else could look like that."

"Thank God," murmured Terry in an undertone.

Mr. Whittle gave a nasty leer, and followed it up with a caw of mirth. "Nuts on that. He's no more an archaeologist than I am. Claudian vases, my left eyeball."

"As a matter of fact," said Gregory, "you're wrong, Roy. Oddly enough he really is a tomb-grubber, and a pretty good one too. He's also a perfectly genuine professor, and he used to be senior lecturer at one of our leading Universities until that little lapse he had some years ago."

"What lapse?"

"Ask him."

Mr. Whittle did so. The professor chewed his lower lip vigorously, but said nothing.

"Tell us, old scout," Gregory invited cheerily. "We're all pals here. Of course, if you'd rather not let us in on the real facts of the case -"

It was obvious that the professor would not. He had turned patchy red under his layer of grime, and was eyeing Gregory as though he would have liked to scoop out his gizzard. At this point Dr. Fredl whirred loudly, and butted in again.

"Of the truth, Herr Ratcliffe," he announced, "of the most grave frightfulness a mistake must there be. Many years Herr Weatherill known have I, and an archaeologist most famous he is. Together we the tombs of Tutankhamen an exploring made -"

"Ha!" Mr. Whittle saw his opportunity, and pounced. "You did, did you?"

"Ja, Herr Shakespeare. Of a certainty."

"Right," said Mr. Whittle briskly. "That puts a new complexion on things, doesn't it? You see, Weatherill or no Weatherill, I can prove that our bearded friend isn't the true-blue Felix Fredl. Fredl, wherever he is, is a tall thin duck with a beaky nose."

"What?"

"Fact."

Miss Czernak gave a bubbling cry.

"What do you say? What is this of a duck with a beaky nose?"

"An outrage this is!" The elderly Hun swung round, his nostrils dilated and his eyes shooting flame. "Never a nose like a beak have I had, and tall and thin certainly not am I. Donner and blitzen! You the onion soup speak, nein? Of a mind am I the bop on the snoddle to administer -"

"Don't forget the lorry," Mr. Whittle requested hastily, recognizing the danger signals and backing away. "If it wasn't for me -"

"Verdammt!" The doctor glared, and swung his fists. "Most grateful I am, but to all things a limit there must be. Herr Shakespeare, the insultings you to me make – I, Felix Fredl -"

"That's all right about Felix Fredl. If you're Felix Fredl I'm Winston Churchill. Care to look at this?" And Mr. Whittle, with the triumphant feeling of a card-player slipping the ace of trumps down his sleeve, produced the book he had removed in his earlier raid. Dr. Fredl eyed it as though it had been a boll-weevil, and snorted.

"Well? The connection do I not see."

"Look at the picture in the front, old lad."

"What the hell is it?" Aunt Clara inquired.

"A police record?" suggested Nichol helpfully.

"Wrong. It's a book written by the original Felix Fredl, complete with authors portrait."

"I still don't get it," Mr. Westford admitted.

"You don't?" Mr. Whittle grinned. "Let me explain it in words of one syllable. "This book has a picture of the real Fredl, and he's a tall thin duck with a beaky nose, as I told you just now. Enough?"

"Nonsense!" Aunt Clara barked. "You're talking like a doddle-head. I've known Felix Fredl for years, as well as Weatherill, and this is him all right. The further we go in this business," she added moodily, "the more it reeks of putrid fish. I shall be damned glad to get back to Egypt."

"You're barking up the wrong tree, Roy," Gregory observed.

"Am I heck! The Felix Fredl in that book isn't the Felix Fredl we've got here, and that's good enough for me. How many Felix Fredls do you think there are?"

"But two, naturally." The bearded Teuton looked up from the book, and peered through his pince-nez. "I and my father."

"What?"

"Completely. My father, the Herr Professor Felix Gottfried Fredl. A man of ability most brilliant, though of temper most evil." The doctor sighed. "In Leipzig he resides. Of him you have perhaps heard?"

"Of course I have." Aunt Clara assured him impatiently. "He's the man who did all that work on the ancient Mexican civilizations, back in the eighteen-nineties. I met him once, in Berlin." She took the photograph, and examined it. "Yes, a pretty good likeness. Incidentally, Roy, this book was written in 1885. I suppose you hadn't noticed that?"

Mr. Whittle gulped, concious of a sinking feeling in his stomach. "oh, Hell!" he said weekly. "Oh! Flaming hell! How could I know he'd got an old man?"

"Most people have, you know," Mr. Westford pointed out brightly. "I have"

"Terry, you were right." This from Miss Czernak, who had been giving Roy the full benefit of her nastiest look. "An oaf – that is the word. An oaf."

It says much for Mr. Whittle's complete demoralisation that he made no immediate reply, but sank down on the nearest chair and heartily wished he could sink through it. Stoker tactfully rallied round with a tray full of bracers, and by the time Roy had recovered sufficiently to take an active interest once more he saw that Gregory again held the floor.

"So that, in a nutshell, was the scheme," he was saying.

"Weatherill and Pauline between them sold you to the spook theory, and then persuaded you to call in Shorty Johnson to de-ghost the place. It's not the first time they've worked this trick, and it might easily have come off again if Roy hadn't had the sense to let me know what was going on. The trump card, of course, was Pauline. All of you might – and did – suspect Weatherill himself, but Pauline's air of efficiency and respectability allows here to get away with a lot, quite apart from being engaged to a member of the house-party."

Pauline looked at Mr. Davenhill, and then at Mr. Whittle. "I - I'm sorry. I hadn't thought -."

"Oh, yes, you had" said Mr Tallon firmly. "I must admit that you did it very well. Any other questions you want to ask, Spennie?.

"Yes," Said Mr. Davenhill flatly. "Several times we heard things when both Weatherill and Pauline were in full view, and anyhow neither of them could have shifted Quinnie when we found him strolling the first time. How do you account for that?"

Mr. Tallon looked vague. "It was done, take it from me. I'll leave you to puzzle that one out for yourself."

"Oh no, you won't," snarled the professor. "Since you're so damned clever, why not tell them the whole truth? You've succeeded in framing me very nicely, I admit, but I don't see why I should be made a scapegoat. Fane helped me all along -"

"What!" Mr. Davenhill hooted. "Terry?"

"It's all a lie!" Terry roared. "The dirty, lousy twister! He found out I'd been loosing money at the races, and he knew that mother would cut off my allowance if she found out, so he blackmailed me into helping him with his tricks -"

"And leant you fifty quid to get straight," Gregory pointed out.

"I meant to keep it under my hat, but I suppose it can't be done. At any rate, you've won enough from my tips to put you in the clear." He chuckled. "I may not be a hypnotist, but I'm pretty sound when it comes to picking winners. Anybody want a hot tip for the two-thirty tomorrow?"

"Yes."

"And it was you who made the groans in the museum and

then locked us in that passage?" Mr. Whittle murmured. "Yes, I thought so. You hauled Quinnie about on his strolls, too, didn't you?"

"Only once, that night you nearly caught me at it. I suppose it was a bit dirty," Terry admitted, " but I was worried stiff, and nobody'd help me to get straight, so I – well, just kicked in. Are you going to tell mother?"

"I don't see why I shouldn't," Mr. Davenhill retorted, with bitterness. "You did your best to let me in for a hundred quid, so why the devil should I spare your feelings? It would do you a lot of good to go short for a bit."

"Please!" Miss Czernak stepped forward, and clasped her hands pleadingly. "Consider. No harm has been done. How can we marry if we are without money?"

"Marry, eh?" Aunt Clara asked keenly. "That's a new one!"

"We love each other," Miss Czernak informed her, making a great effort to produce glistening tears in here eyes." We love each other so much. Oh, it would not be fair of you!"

"I didn't mean any harm," Terry said weakly. "Honestly, Spennie, I wouldn't have let the thing go too far. The slimy old toad had got hold of some of my bookie's letters, and was threatening to send 'em to mother. You know she's got complete control of all my money Dad left, and I sha'n't be able to touch a penny of it until I'm twenty-five. Hell," he added, "that's over six years. Do you expect Carole and me to wait six years?"

"I don't," Mr. Davenhill admitted coldly. "You've got a nerve , young Terry!"

"Please!" Miss Czernak gave him a melting look, and spoke with a skilfully-produced catch in her husky, treacly voice. "We are so sorry."

"All very well."

"Mr. Davenhill!"

"But hang it all -"

"Oh, Spennie!"

Mr. Davenhill capitulated.

"Oh, all right. Mind you," he said with sombre satisfaction, "she's bound to find out sooner or later, and then there'll be merry hell to pay."

A loud snort from the direction of the stairs made everyone spun round sharply, and Aunt Violet made a dignified entrance, looking as though she had rejuvenated herself by a quick dip in Medea's cauldron. The General followed, massaging his moustache thoughtfully. There was a short silence as Aunt Violet allowed here eyes to play like twin steam-jets over the assembled company.

"A vulgar expression, Spencer," she rasped, "but apt – exceedingly apt, if I appreciate its full meaning. Rupert, oblige me by ringing the police-station. I intend to give these – these miscreants in charge without delay, and I shall see that they are prosecuted with the utmost rigour of the law."

Pauline wilted visibly, and took an involuntary step in the direction of Mr. Whittle, but Professor Weatherill was not so easily cowed. Grimy the old coot may have been, and probably - as Mr. Whittle had hinted – verminous, but at least his hat was still in the ring.

"You'll prosecute us, will you?"

"Most certainly. I shall demand a severe sentence."

"Oh no, you won't," said Mr. Strudwick positively. "Mrs. Fane, I appeal to you. I fully appreciate your annoyance, and I am bound to admit that if I found myself in a position to push Professor Weatherill under a train I should feel strongly inclined to do so, but I really can't allow you to send my fiancée to prison. I should hate to spend my honeymoon in Holloway Goal."

"Your honeymoon? What do you mean. Your honeymoon? Aunt Violet barked. "Raymond, are you insane? This woman has been exposed -"

Mr. Tallon uttered a choking sound.

"Exposed or not exposed," said Mr. Strudwick with surprising violence, "I still won't have her sent to Holloway. Imagine the effect it would have on my career! How can a Member of Parliament retain his dignity when his wife is serving a term of imprisonment?"

Aunt Violet drew her hand across here eyes. "This is beyond all reason. You don't seriously mean to tell me that you don't intend to break your engagement?"

"Break the engagement? Of course I'm not going to break my engagement, unless Pauline wishes it." From Miss. Weatherill's expression as the M.P. slipped his arm round her, it was quite obvious that she didn't. "On the contrary, I consider that I have found the perfect life partner."

"What! A woman who's dishonesty has been abundantly proved?"

"Precisely." Mr. Strudwick beamed. "From my point of view, the fact that my fiancée is what is commonly termed a 'crook' is anything but a disadvantage. I have always realised that what every young politician needs to help him in his career is the support of a really well-informed crook. The possibilities are immense. With Pauline behind me, there is no limit to the heights I can reach."

This point of view had not occurred to Aunt Violet, and she spent a moment or two thinking about it.

"Absurd," she snorted at length. "Raymond, I am bitterly disappointed in you. In fact, I shall wash my hands of you. Isch!"

"Personally," observed Aunt Clara, puffing at here pipe, "I consider it a damned good show. Strudwick, I take it all back."

"What?"

"All I've thought about you during the past fortnight – and believe me, that's plenty." The old aunt gave an obscene leer. "You've got some backbone after all. Remind me to send you a wedding present an Egyptian snuff-box, or something of the sort."

"Hear hear," Mr. Whittle felt bound to add. He still felt limp and boneless, but the initial shock had abated slightly by this time. "Struddy, old lad, you're a trump card. I'm even prepared to act as best man."

"You are? Splendid!" The M.P wrung his hands heartily. "We'll shall be delighted, won't we, my dear?"

Pauline swallowed hard, like a cat coping with a fur-ball.

"I'm not worth of you, Raymond!"

"Probably not," Mr. Strudwick admitted, "but I'm prepared to make allowances for that. I really believe everything has worked out for the best."

This appeared to be the general view, and a hum of conversation broke out. It was left to Aunt Violet to strike a jarring note.

"Unfortunately," she said in a voice that sprayed over the hall like a douche of ice water, "I am not prepared to acquiesce in this – this conspiracy of silence. A deliberate attempt has been made to extort money from a member of my family, and justice must be done. As a member of the public it is my duty to take action. You agree, Rupert?"

The General looked uncomfortable.

"Well – hrrmph!" He blew his nose. "Least said soonest mended, don't you think? Don't want to smash up two young lives, dash it. "Why not overlook it just this once?"

"I shall not overlook it."

"Right," said Gregory briskly. You're really determined to raise a stink?"

"If you care to put it in such crude terms, I am."

"Right." Mr. Tallon grinned sadistically. "It's up to you, but I can assure you that when it comes to raising stinks Nick and I are past-masters. Have you roughed out any of your article for the 'Planet' yet, Nick? I've thought out my headlines already 'Sorcery in Sussex'. Dark deeds in country mansion. Special statement by Mrs Violet Fane, prospective Conservative candidate for Chipwood and Whortlebury division -"

Aunt Violet let out a sharp yowl.

"I forbid you to print such nonsense! I – I shall sue you for libel if you dare even to mention this disgraceful affair. Any publicity would be extremely distasteful to all of us"!

"It would," Mr. Tallon agreed blandly. "I wonder what the Socialists would make of it? If I know 'em, they wouldn't let you hear the last of it in a hurry. Why not come down to earth and act like a human being, instead of something out of Anthony Trollope?" Aunt Violet breathed hard. "One squawk out of you, and I'll plaster the whole story bang over the front page – bats, skeletons and all. And phut will go your chances of getting the misguided electorate of Chipwood and Whortlebury to vote you into Parliament. Well?"

Aunt Violet ground her teeth.

"You scoundrel!" Do you realise that this is sheer blackmail?"

"Of course it is. I can't answer for Nick, but those are my terms. After all," said Gregory meditatively, "I'm doing myself out of the scoop of a lifetime. My editor would eat this stuff. Damned decent of me, I think."

"I'll do whatever you do, old man," Mr. Westford murmured.

Aunt Violet looked appealingly at the General.

"Rupert, what am I to do?"

"Nothing," said the General decisively. "Once this gets about, all the electioneering in the world can't help."

"Forget all about it." Aunt Clara advised. "Stop talking about calling the police and prosecuting people, and don't make a pest of yourself. You always did poke your snoddle into other people's affairs, Violet, and one day someone's going to pull it for you. If Spencer doesn't mean to do anything, there's no call for you to."

"Quite so," agreed Professor Weatherill hastily. "A most sensible point of view."

"Then you mean to let these rogues go unpunished?" Aunt Violet was visibly weakening, but her iron courage stood her in good stead.

"Taking the large view," Gregory observed judicially, "I don't see what else you can do, especially as our pal Strudwick's going to marry one of them. Besides, dash it all! This is a festive occasion. We've got no less than three engaged couples -"

"Three?"

"I think it's three." Gregory made a quick count. "Strudwick and Pauline, Miss Debenham and Sir Rupert, Fane and Miss Czernak – yes, three. Not bad going for a week-end."

This revelation was too much even for Aunt Violet. With one long, agonised look at Terry, who put his arms round Carole and glared defiantly back, she swung round and tottered upstairs, a broken woman. Mr. Whittle watched her go, conscious that the end was at hand. It was strange, he reflected, how things worked out. But for his casual telephone call to Gregory ... He became aware of Stoker bearing down and thrusting a glass into his hand.

"Whisky. Mr Roy?"

"Of course." Roy downed it automatically, and led the old

butler into a corner. "Stoker, old cock, do you feel happy?"

"Extremely, sir. I would willingly try my hand at a hornpipe. I Trust that you are also in good spirits? Tum tum tum, ta ra ra ra - are you happy sir."

"Oddly enough," Mr. Whittle confessed, "I am, even though the Whittle heart has been well and truly broken. "Look at 'em," he went on. "Happy as a lot of sandboys .. Why is a sandboy meant to be happy, old lad?"

"I could not say, sir"

"Nor could I. Not that old Weatherill reminds me of a sandboy, or anything else except a slowly mouldering corpse." Roy glared distastefully at the aged archaeologist, who was cheerily clinking glasses with Mr. Davenhill and Dr. Fredl in what was evidently a toast. "Well, I don't think we've left any loose ends laying around, apart possibly from Aunt Clara's chattering skeleton, and I don't take much stock of that. Somehow I don't fancy that my efforts at detecting have been much of a success." He grinned at Gregory and Nichol, as the two journalists wandered over laden with brimming glasses. "Greg, you still have not made it clear how you managed to make yourself up like that. Did you get it done by a professional man, or was it all your own work?"

"Neither. I went down to Milton Waterlow's place, and set him on to me." Roy nodded; He remembered Milton, the erratic and distinctly hair-brined young inventor who was one of Gregory's and Nichol's closest friends "There's not much he can't do if he puts his mind to it, and by the time I'd been finished off my own mother wouldn't have known me. You know, Roy, old scout, I've enjoyed this week-end more than I've enjoyed anything for a long time. Incidentally I've cleared up a mystery that's been on my mind for at least three years.

"What mystery?"

"That incredible business about the salmon."

"Aunt Clara' salmon?"

"Of course, dolt. Haven't you ever heard the full version?"

"No," Mr. Whittle confessed regretfully. "Nobody would ever tell me."

"Well, she's just spilt the beans to me. Do you want to hear about it?"

257

"I do!"

"Right. Here goes. It seems that Miss Debenham and a couple of her archaeologist pals -!

Mr. Whittle listened attentively. He enjoyed what he heard.

Chapter 30

Mr. Whittle crammed the last of his personal belongings into his trunk, slammed the lid, and wrestled with the lock. If he caught the mid-day 'plane from Heathrow he would be in Paris by tea-time, and able to take his place by the ringside to watch MM. Leblocq and Popinot hammering each other's guts out. At the moment he felt more like taking an active rather than a passive part, but doubtless the mood would pass.

A soft tap was heard on the door, and Stoker entered, moving in tog gear with a resilient and springy step, his face radiant. Only a few hours ago he had looked ninety at least, whereas now an unbiased observer might easily have taken him for a mere seventy-five.

"Good-morning, Mr Roy. I came to inquire whether I could be of any assistance to you?"

"All done, old lad." Mr. Whittle inspected the stock of empties in the cupboard. "Jove, there's a noggin or so left in this case. How about polishing it off?"

"A splendid idea, sir"

"Mud in your eye."

"And in yours also, sir. The butler downed his drink with a refined gollup. "Very sorry you are leaving us so soon, Mr. Roy. Your visits are all too rare nowadays."

"Mr. Whittle shrugged. "Apart from the fact that I want to see the fight, I can't say I find the present company altogether exhilarating, especially if Weatherill's staying on as an honoured guest – as apparently he is. How the old buster can have the nerve beats me."

"Quite so, sir. An undesirable character." Stoker sniffed.

"I confess, however, that I was disagreeably surprised at the revelations concerning his daughter."

"I bet you weren't half so disagreeably surprised as I was!"

"No, sir, I appreciate you're feelings."

"Well," said Roy, with stoical resignation,, "It's not the first time the Whittle heart has been broken, and I don't suppose it'll be the last. How's Aunt Violet taking it?"

"I have no idea, sir. Mrs. Fane has retired to bed and is, I believe, making arrangements to depart for a short holiday in Scotland."

"She'll be able to knock ground with Gregory's pal Shorty." Mr. Whittle grinned. "There's absolutely nothing she can do. Weatherill and Co. have got her just where they want her, and so, for that matter, has young Terry. Did you know he and Carole want me to be their best man? That makes two. "I'm even prepared to make it an odd number and officiate for the General, if he wants me to."

"That is very gratifying, sir."

"I wish 'em luck, anyhow." Mr. Whittle paused. "I say, old lad, did you hear anything?"

"Yes, sir."

"What was it?"

"It sounded like a succession of revolver-shots, sir."

"Me, too. Do you think the General has plugged Weatherill in the stomach?"

"I trust so, sir, though I fear that I cannot consider such a contingency likely."

"Right. On your way".

Mr. Whittle set course automatically for the museum, and dead-heated with Aunt Clara, Gregory, Nichol, Mr. Strudwick and Terry, with Stoker and Spennie panting behind. It was at once evident who had caused the disturbance. General Sir Rupert Gore stood in the doorway, his red face and his moustache bristling, and he was brandishing not a revolver, but a double-barrelled shotgun. Aunt Clara applied her brakes, and pulled up in her own length.

"Rameses!" she said. "What in the name of Isis do you think you're up to, Rupert?"

The General breathed hard.

"You were right, Clara," he said hoarsely. "By Gad, you were! It gave me the willies, I don't mind telling you. I'd rather face a charge of a tiger."

"A tiger?" Aunt Clara echoed. "Where?"

"I can't see any tiger," Mr. Whittle confessed. "Are you sure it was a tiger?"

"Of course it wasn't a tiger, you young dolt!"

"I thought it couldn't have been," Mr. Whittle agreed. "They don't breed tigers in England – except in the Zoo, which is rather a different thing."

"Never mind about tigers!" the General bawled. "I'm talking about that damned skeleton."

"What, old Quinnie?"

"Yes – old Quinnie, blast his eyeballs."

"He hasn't got any eyeballs." Gregory pointed out. "Only sockets."

"Not any more he hasn't." The General smiled grimly. "I've seen to that."

"Eh?"

"Look."

The General drew aside, and the others crowded round, peering into the museum with no little interest. A chorus of ejaculations broke out. Quintus Maximus' stand was empty now; a pile of assorted bones littered the floor nearby, and the back wall was liberally peppered with shot.

Aunt Clara let out a despairing cry. "My skeleton! Rupert, what happened?"

"I'll tell you." The General sucked in a bit of his moustache, sucked it for a space, and ejected it again. "I was in the armoury, looking at the shotgun of yours, Clara, when I heard a funny sort of noise. Damned difficult to describe, but I didn't like it, so I loaded the gun – there was some ammo. to fit in the drawer – and came out. I got as far as the museum, and then -"

The General hesitated.

"Well?"

"I looked in, and there the beast was – grinning at me, and chattering, just as you said." The General gave a slight shudder. "Brrrr! I just let him have it with both barrels. There was a sort – of a scream, and a horrid smashing sound, and the thing seemed to – well, dissolve. I've never shot a skeleton before," he added moodily, "and frankly I never want to tackle another. Still, I'm glad it's gone."

"My God!" Gregory breathed. "What a story! The scoop of a lifetime – and I can't use it ... Hell and blazes! Still, nobody would believe it, I suppose."

"I'm not sure I believe it myself," the General admitted, "but it was real enough just now. The brute simply radiated evil."

"Queer," Mr. Davenhill said thoughtfully. "Dashed queer. I don't know – it's probably my imagination – but I feel lighter, somehow, now it's gone." He removed his spectacles and polished them violently. "It's been getting on my nerves. For goodness' sake let's collect the remains and bury them, or burn them, or something.

Mr. Whittle bent down, and examined the depressing heap of bones.

"I still think it was a trick of the light," he said gruffly, "but I'm all in favour of getting rid of what's left. Come on – let's collect a wheelbarrow. We can bring it through the conservatory.

But Quintus Maximus, awkward to the very end, had the last word. When the party returned some minutes later, bringing with them a barrow and spade with the set intention of sweeping up the bones and consigning them to the boiler, the old coot had made himself scarce. The pedestal was still there, also the peppered area of the wall, but of the wreck of Quinnie there was no sign. Mr. Strudwick was the first to find his voice.

"I am inclined to think," he said dryly, "that my – er – future father-in-law has been playing with fire. I take it, Spencer, that there is no possibility of the servants having visited the museum during the past five minutes?"

"None at all. I doubt whether any of the would go near the place. They think it's haunted."

"I don't wonder," Mr Whittle admitted. "I don't wonder!"

Chapter 31

Six months later Roy Whittle, rubbing his hands violently in an attempt to restore some semblance of circulation, and scraping the outer most layer off his boots, pottered up the main steps of Wollingham Hall and yanked lustily at the bell-rope. After a decent interval Stoker appeared and ushered him in, twittering cordially the while. "Delighted to see you again, Mr. Roy, if I may take the liberty. I trust you are in the best of health?"

"Bursting with energy, old lad. "Sorry I didn't let anyone know I was coming, but I didn't know until this morning that I could get the weekend off. Spennie around?"

"No, sir."

"No?"

"No. sir."

"Where is he, then?"

"In America, sir."

"America?"

"Yes, sir, New York, to be precise."

Mr. Whittle rubbed his chin.

"That's damn queer. He rang me the day before yesterday, and he didn't say anything about shooting off into the blue."

"Such was not his intention until the telegram arrived, Mr. Roy. He left the house at an hours notice."

"Good God! You don't mean that the bubonic plague has broken out, or anything of the sort?"

"Worse, Mr. Roy."

"How come?"

"Miss Debenham – I should say Lady Gore – is on her way, sir. She is expected to arrive before nightfall. She and Sir Rupert have announced their intention of spending some weeks here."

"And Spennie didn't feel he could cope, eh?"

"Precisely, sir. Have you ever seen a rabbit emerge from it's hole after an encounter with a ferret?"

"Have you?"

"No, sir, but I can imagine the expression it would wear. Mr. Spencer's was just like that. He has instructed me to cable him as soon as the danger is over."

"Well, well! Then we shan't be seeing him for the next month or so?"

"I consider it most unlikely, sir. As you know Mrs. Fane has removed to London in order to be near the House of Commons. So under the circs., I suppose I may as well be on my way, what?"

The butler's eyes flashed with a beautific gleam.

"Don't do that, sir. Did I mention that there is a plentiful stock of best whisky readily available? Mr. Spencer instructed me to use as much of it as I thought fit."

Mr. Whittle rolled his tongue thoughtfully across his lips.

"He did, did he?" he murmured. Good old Spennie .... What ho, old lad. Lead me to it.

++++++++++++++++++++++++++++++